Cousins of Color

COUSINS OF COLOR

By

WILLIAM SCHRODER

Published in Great Britain by Twenty First Century Publishers Ltd.

A catalogue record of this book is available from the British Library.

ISBN: 1-904433-11-1

This is a work of fiction. Names, characters and incidents are the product of the author's imagination or are used fictitiously, and any resemblance to actual persons, living or dead, is entirely coincidental.

Cover photography be Alexandra Piechoczek.

To order further copies of this work or other books published be Twenty First Century Publishers visit our website:
www.twentyfirstcenturypublishers.com

Acknowledgements

I can't imagine a book written by one person alone. Rather, it is a collaborative effort, the product of the author and many of his friends and loved ones. I owe a great deal of thanks to a number of people, but my never-ending gratitude goes to the love of my life, Elizabeth Jean Jacks, the person who always believed in me.

To the members of my writers critique group - Byron Sacre, Jim Adams, Bob Watters, Dottie Sohl, Bonnie Daybell, Anne Bergsma and Flavius Foster, thank you for your frank and honest criticisms.

Thanks also to the long-suffering individuals who helped me struggle through early drafts and suffered my obsession with David Fagen these last four years - Tom Bishop, Chris Cluett, Kaaren Johnson, Aurora Mancebo, Dennis Ryan, Steve Wald and Dean Welsh.

A special thanks to John Schroder for his insight into all matters philosophical.

Lastly, I would like to acknowledge the contributions of Mr. Fred Piechoczek of Twenty First Century Publishers Ltd. I only brought this work to the table, he did everything else.

This book is dedicated to:

Dr. Willard B. Gatewood
Alumni Distinguished Professor of History (Emeritus)
University of Arkansas

Scholar, Educator, Friend

Preface

I was on the lookout for a good story. You know the kind I mean – big, with all the great themes: love, hate, anger, greed, sacrifice and redemption. Ingredients that properly mixed and baked offered a taste of the pie called the human condition. I was on the lookout and thought I'd found it the day Dr. Willard Gatewood introduced me to Private David Fagen, a black American who, in time of war, traded his future for the chance to help another "colored" people gain freedom. A tremendous story, it contained all the elements, just what I'd been looking for, but it was the wrong war.

"No one knows anything about the Spanish-American War," I complained. There's no sympathy for it, no romance. Where was the sizzle, the sparkle? Easy to envision a good story against the backdrop of World War II and certainly the Civil War, but the Spanish-American War? Dr. Gatewood smiled, regarded me indulgently, and then told me to do my homework. Here's a little of what I discovered:

Influenced by pro-business conservatives eager to take control of Spain's colonies in the Pacific, in 1898 President McKinley asked Congress for a Declaration of War, and then launched America's first adventure in Imperialism. An unprovoked war of conquest and occupation, it was the first time African-American soldiers fought and died overseas.

America destroyed the weakened and spiritless Spanish in six weeks. Later, in the Treaty of Paris, Spain sold her colonies to the United States for twenty million dollars. Under the banner of liberator, America occupied Guam, Puerto Rico and the Philippines and stayed to rule through a system of military governorships for nearly fifty years. To establish and maintain U.S. control, President McKinley implemented a policy of "Benevolent Assimilation" and sent thousands of soldiers to enforce it. Desirous of self-rule, the Filipinos resisted American occupation. A bloody, eight-year campaign ensued against Filipino guerilla forces. Reports vary, but many suggest more than four hundred thousand Filipino men, women and children lost their lives in the fight for independence during this "splendid little war."

Through this work of fiction, I endeavor to explore this extraordinary and highly significant chapter in our nation's past, which I believe echoes other American campaigns for empire in the twentieth century and beyond.

William Schroder, March 2004.

CHAPTER ONE - LUZON, PHILIPPINES
JUNE 1945

"Can you see anything, sir?" Sergeant Rosa shouted over the roar of the fierce monsoon wind.

Captain Nygaard mopped rain from his binoculars with a grimy sleeve, the dense jungle a blur of green and black darkly blanketed by an angry, lowering sky. "I couldn't see a division of Japs marching right past us in this mess."

Rosa studied the captain, saw concern on the patrol leader's face. He said a prayer to the Holy Mother the man's anxiety wouldn't turn to fear. Eight men on a routine reconnaissance patrol, their job to scout the Jap forces in the Mariquina Valley, locate their positions, estimate strength and report back.

Handpicked for the patrol, the men were tough, seasoned veterans of the Pacific campaigns. They'd been on scores of these missions, to Rosa it seemed like hundreds, and this one had begun like all the others, but already things had started to go wrong. Rosa had fought through a dozen Pacific islands, but nothing in his experience had prepared him for the fiendish rain forest jungle of the Luzon highlands. Three days they'd pushed through Satan's back yard, wading in knee-deep mud, *wait-a-minute* vines slashing their faces, tearing skin. During the day, relentless mosquitoes tormented. At night, invisible fanged insects drank their blood. Nature and the terrain important factors in any battle, in this one, Rosa thought, maybe the most important.

He looked hard into the dense foliage. Lobatto and Delaney hunkered in the shelter of a fallen tree. Rosa couldn't see Michaels and Flockheart, but knew they were there somewhere, soaked to the bone, their faces covered with slime. Damn this rain!

Captain Nygaard unfolded a muddy compass, tried to get his bearings. "Who reported their movement?"

Rosa worked at a long thorn imbedded between his fingers, "Wilcox, sir, the scout team NCO over at Baker Company. He said two, maybe three reinforced companies moved behind us sometime today. He thinks we're completely surrounded by now."

"He thinks that, does he? Then why can't our own S-2 confirm?"

"I don't know, Cap, but Wilcox is a good man. We were together at Salamaua. He wouldn't say something like that if it weren't true."

"Damned decent of him to give us a call."

"Yes, sir. That was my opinion too."

Even though bad news, Captain Nygaard was glad to have the information. This man Wilcox was looking out for them, and it really was damned decent of him, but it didn't change anything. They had a mission to accomplish, and that would only change if Tojo surrendered before sundown, and the entire Jap army laid down their arms and went home. Not likely. "Get the men together," he said. "We'll find a place to make camp tonight, but unless we hear otherwise from our own intelligence people, we proceed at dawn according to plan."

Rosa signaled, and Delaney passed it along. The men pushed up under the weight of the monsoon and moved out into the mist. Rosa signaled again. Close it up. Stay together. He knew exhausted men made mistakes. In those conditions, the slightest misstep could be a death sentence. I've been through worse, Rosa thought. So had the rest of the men. Highly trained and disciplined, they were not prone to panic or breakdown.

Captain Nygaard, a ninety-day wonder just over from the States, was younger than Rosa. Someone said he'd graduated from law school just before he was drafted. A lawyer *and* a ninety-day wonder, a walking cliché. Rosa wondered whether the Holy Mother had heard his prayer over the howl of the monsoon.

Flockheart scurried to the top of a low bluff, the terrain level there, good footing on solid ground, free of the dense underbrush they'd maneuvered through all day. He signaled the captain. Rocks and tree trunks for toeholds, one after the other, the men pushed and pulled their way up and deployed a small defensive perimeter, a semi-circle facing the black jungle, their backs to the edge of the bluff. Below them in the distance, the Mariquina River disappeared into a low valley. While the men set up camp, the monsoon swept suddenly past them, the rain stopped as though turned off with a switch and the wind stilled. They would never get dry, but for now at least, the roar of the storm beyond them, for a while their world had returned to "normal."

Captain Nygaard hunched over an oilskin map, a field phone to his ear. "One man for an LP, Sergeant Rosa."

"Right away, Cap. Michaels! Set up a listening post at the one o'clock position, but don't go out more than thirty yards."

"I'm on it, Sarge."

Nygaard tried to make contact, but the radio useless, he pounded the back of it against his knee. Purple veins bulging in his neck betrayed his frustration. He pitched it to Rosa. "See if you can do something with this. I'm sick of it."

No twilight in the jungle, in only a few minutes darkness hung like a mantle over the little squad. Cryder and Lobatto gnawed at the remains of their K rations, while Delaney and Sullivan worked on the radio. Flockheart had replaced Michaels at the listening post. Rosa dug a Dakota hole, started a small fire and watched the captain fold and refold his map, indecision written on his face.

The shriek of the howler monkey, the caw, the growl, the scratching, scraping, yawping noises of the night jungle ceased. The sudden silence sent a shiver up Rosa's spine, and he looked around.

"Captain Nygaard, Sergeant Rosa! We got us a situation here!" Lobatto's shrill cry split the stillness in the camp. Rosa turned to see the rifleman crouched at the edge of the perimeter, his carbine pointed in the direction of the listening post. Then, from the inky blackness beyond the firelight, Flockheart appeared, hands on his head, his face frozen in fear. Four tiny men flanked him. One held a knife at Flockheart's throat. Momentarily stunned by their outlandish appearance, Captain Nygaard thought of the Stone Age tribesmen he'd read about in anthropology class. The intruders wore only loincloths, their bodies elaborately painted and tattooed. Long, rusty-brown hair covered their faces, their noses and ears pierced with shards of bone. One of the men carried Flockheart's rifle in one hand and a long blowgun in the other. Their only other weapons were crossbows and huge curving knives, but the captain shuddered at the damage they'd do at close range.

Tension filled the night as these strange men escorted their captive into the midst of the heavily armed Americans. Despite his battle experience, Flockheart was scared, and he showed it. "I swear, Captain, you got to believe me. I was awake on my post. I never heard a thing. They came out of nowhere and were on me before I knew it."

Captain Nygaard got to his feet slowly, buying time, trying to fully comprehend the strange sight before him. His legal training had taught him to assess a situation before taking action, the calm in his voice masked the fear waxing in his chest. "Steady corporal, take it easy."

The tiny men stood silently among the Americans. Captain Nygaard willed himself to remain calm, only four of them, he had twice that many and the firepower, but he was apprehensive. He knew his men were unnerved by the sudden, startling appearance of these impossible intruders. Their long knives razor-sharp, the stubby little arrows in their crossbows had metal points coated in something black and sticky – poison?

The captain knew the Americans couldn't subdue the men without some of their own blood being spilled. The knife at Flockheart's throat made that a virtual certainty. He steadied himself. The situation outside his range of understanding and certain every passing second increased the odds of this standoff ending in bloodshed, he wished he had more time to think. Nygaard heard the metallic click of safeties moved into the "fire" position and knew he had to do something fast.

He took two steps toward the man he believed their leader and stared into his eyes. Not intimidated by the bigger, heavily armed American soldier, the diminutive warrior returned the captain's gaze. The patrol leader slowly raised his carbine to the center of the headman's chest. The chief responded by raising his crossbow at exactly the same pace, stopping the deadly arrowhead just inches from the captain's heart. Cautiously, without blinking, Nygaard slowly lowered his rifle, and like a primordial mirror image, the man lowered his weapon.

Sergeant Rosa inched to the captain's side. "These are bolomen, sir, mountain people. They haven't hurt anybody yet, maybe they're just hungry."

Captain Nygaard carefully reached for his field pack. "Food? Tobacco? Cigarettes!"

The tribesman responded with silent disdain.

Suddenly, the headman let go a harsh, guttural bark in a strange dialect, but his meaning clear. "Put down your weapons."

Nygaard didn't like it that one of his men had a knife at his throat and held his ground. He hoped their superior numbers and firepower were enough to convince these people to release Flockheart and go about their business. He didn't want to kill when he didn't even know why the men were there or what they wanted.

The tribesman spoke again, louder, an unmistakable command, "Put down your weapons!"

Sergeant Rosa whispered, "Something tells me we should do what he says, Captain."

Nygaard stood a little taller. He wasn't about to surrender so soon to a handful of tribal savages. "I disagree," and he raised his carbine again.

Just then, as if on some unseen signal, more of the bizarre little warriors materialized from the jungle blackness, many more. Dozens emerged side-by-side, their primitive but deadly weapons at the ready. In that one moment, the situation had changed completely, and now the Americans were outnumbered, surrounded and suddenly at the mercy of these strange, silent people.

Nygaard watched helplessly while the mountain men quickly formed a circle three-deep around them. Their leader spoke again, and Flockheart was released. Weak with fear, he sat by the fire, head in his hands and quietly wept. He'd been face-to-face with the Japanese many times, but this situation was too surreal, too extraordinary and too far outside his range of experience. Delaney and Michaels slowly dropped their rifles and put their hands on their heads. Captain Nygaard's eyes darted to his men, then locked on the bolo leader. "You men stand fast!" he ordered, but to no avail. His soldiers realized something he wasn't yet ready to admit, their situation was hopeless.

Slowly, almost imperceptibly, the circle of savage creatures tightened. Sixty crouching mountain tribesmen moved toward them shoulder-to-shoulder, weapons at the ready. The wild, painted faces, feathered headdresses and extravagant, arcane jewelry made from animal parts mesmerized the terrified Americans. The little campfire popped, sparks drifted on the night breeze. Michaels and Delaney squatted by their weapons. Lobatto crossed himself in silent prayer, and Sullivan did the same.

Suddenly, the ever-tightening cordon stopped, and six of the dwarfish tribesmen stepped back, leaving a hole in their circle leading into the jungle. Sergeant Rosa held his breath. What were they doing? Letting them go, offering them a path out? Rosa and the captain exchanged uncertain glances. What was that? A noise outside the perimeter. The Americans strained to listen, to hear anything at all.

Another noise, barely audible. That's when he emerged from the jungle blackness, the ghostly figure of an old black man, a Negro with white hair and mustache. Sergeant Rosa thought the man a retired janitor, or a Pullman porter because he had on some type of uniform. He wore a pressed blue shirt and a red scarf around his neck, brown trousers with leggings and brown leather boots. His freshly brushed campaign hat was square and the brim two fingers above the nose, conforming to military standards. The old man wore a United States Army uniform, but the army of another century! He paused for a moment at the edge of the camp, brown eyes, boots and leather glowing in the fire's light. Stillness reigned in the camp, the Americans afraid to speak, afraid to break the spell. Who was this strange man, this Negro, standing before them looking like a photograph in a history book?

The old man came forward slowly, stopped in front of the captain and saluted. "Private David Fagen, 24th Infantry, sir."

Dumbfounded, Captain Nygaard managed to bring himself to attention and return the salute.

The old man spread his arms to indicate the others. "These fine soldiers around us, my soldiers, are people you might call Igorrotes, mountain people. You see them now dressed for battle, but when they're not fighting Japanese, they're a civilized, peace-loving people. They tell me the enemy has surrounded your patrol, and you're in need of assistance."

Captain Nygaard's fear quickly dissolved into dizzying confusion. He felt lost, spellbound by the man's gentle, but wizened gaze. Was this man real? Was he human? Nygaard reminded himself he was an army officer addressed by an enlisted man, pulled himself together and said, "You and your men may stand at ease, Private…?"

"Fagen, sir. 24th Infantry." Fagen turned to his men and issued a gentle command. The Igorrote soldiers lowered their weapons. He spoke once more, and half of the men disappeared into the jungle, the rest settled into little clusters at the edge of the perimeter. The Americans breathed an audible sigh of relief as their captors dispersed.

Captain Nygaard motioned for the old private to sit. Rosa placed more wood on the small fire. "You have information about the Japanese in this area, Private Fagen?"

"Yes, sir, I do. The information you received on your radio is correct. The 11th and 13th Japanese battalions linked up this morning, and they're on the run. Most of the fight's gone out of them, but they're between you and where you want to go. I can get you out of here and back to your people, but we have to wait until just before dawn."

Suspicious, Nygaard took stock of the man sitting across from him. "How do you know so much about enemy troop movements?"

"I know everything that goes on in the mountains, sir." Fagen nodded to indicate his soldiers. "We've fought the Japanese in these hills for years."

"You say the 11th and the 13th are on the run? Where?"

"To the high ground west of the valley. Most are sick with fever, and they're short on ammunition and other supplies. Two days ago, they

6

disabled their heavy artillery, but they're carrying their mortars and RPGs with them. I expect that's what you came here to find out, isn't it Captain?"

"How many men total?"

"Eight hundred give or take. As I said, they're mostly sick and hungry, but they're still a force to be reckoned with. The Japs fight hard, sick or well."

"If you know where the Japanese are, why are you still here in this stinking place?"

Fagen peered out into the dark river valley for a moment, and then gazed deep into the captain's eyes. "This stinking place is my home, sir."

The patrol leader stood up, paced around the fire, and then turned and faced the old man. "You say you can get us through, back to our line?"

"Yes, sir, I surely can."

"How do I know I can trust you?"

"You can trust me because I'm an American, sir."

"You may be an American, but I don't know anything about you except your name and rank. What did you mean when you said these mountains are your home? Where did you get that old uniform?"

Fagen took a small pipe from his blouse and a black leather pouch, "Do you mind if I smoke, sir?"

A different camp then, crowded with Igorrote tribesmen, Delaney and Sullivan went back to work on the radio, a task that intrigued the Filipino mountain men, but Cryder took center stage with his copy of Life magazine and its war-coverage photos of American victories and dead Japanese soldiers. Sergeant Rosa and the captain sat near the fire with the old man.

Fagen's voice, low but strong, blended with the other night sounds. "My regiment, the 24th Infantry, was the first troop of Negro soldiers to fight in the Philippines, sir."

"When was that?" Nygaard asked.

"In the spring of '99."

"1899? What was a regiment of Negro soldiers doing here in 1899?"

Fagen answered patiently, as though he addressed a child. "We came to fight the war, sir."

"The war? What war?"

Sergeant Rosa spoke up. "The Spanish-American war, sir. After the fight for Cuba, when Spain surrendered to the U.S., we got all her colonies in the Pacific; Guam, Puerto Rico and the Philippines. Guam and Puerto Rico were glad we took over, but here Filipino insurgents had waged war against the Spanish for years. When we showed up, Spain was happy to turn these islands over to us and go home. The trouble was, the Filipinos saw us as just another oppressor. They didn't want foreign masters in their country, Spanish or American."

The old man smiled at Rosa, "You know your history, Sergeant."

"I'm Filipino-American. My grandmother died in that war."

"I'm sorry. How did it happen?"

"Nobody knows. She lived in Santa Cruz, northwest of here. One day, she went out and never came back. My father and mother came to the United States just before I was born, in 1920."

Fagen smiled at Rosa. "Welcome home."

"By the time the Spanish surrendered, the Filipinos had already elected a new President, a man named Aguinaldo."

Fagen gazed deep into the firelight and murmured, "Emilio Aguinaldo."

Rosa continued, "He'd been the leader of the insurrection, and as far as the Filipinos were concerned, the patriot savior of their country. Aguinaldo tried to bargain with Admiral Dewey for U.S. recognition of his Presidency, but America was in an expansionist mood. We wanted these islands, and we weren't willing to turn them over to anybody. Aguinaldo decided to fight. The bloodshed went on for years."

"And took nearly five-hundred-thousand Filipino lives," the old private said.

Rosa nodded, "That too."

Astonished, Captain Nygaard looked sharply at the old man. "Five-hundred-thousand dead? Impossible!"

"I assure you, sir, it was more than possible," Fagen replied.

The captain looked back at Rosa, "What finally happened?"

"Aguinaldo was eventually captured. With him out of the picture, the natives' struggle was hopeless, and the fight for independence petered out. The Americans won. These islands have been under our protection since. I guess that's one reason we're here now."

The old private leaned forward, his black skin tight over his skull, eyes glowing in the firelight. "Those were troubled times, Captain, all throughout this land, but I was young then and proud to wear the uniform of my country."

Out of the jungle blackness a night bird called, and far away the call was answered.

CHAPTER 2 - JUNE 1899

The corporal behind Fagen pointed to the green hills in the distance and called out, "Is that it?" David Fagen, Ellis Fairbanks and several hundred other black American soldiers crowded the port deck to get a look at the inner harbor.

One of the ship's Marines leaned over the rail, looked down the line of black faces and said, "That's it, boys. Manila. The busiest seaport in Asia."

The 24th Infantry sailed in amazed by the magnificent military ships of Dewey's fleet standing guard over a colorful assortment of native outriggers and canoes paddling easily between passenger ferries and pontoon boats. Several large transport steamers like theirs sat stacked against a crumbling row of long wooden piers. Rising above the harbor, Manila itself was a sprawling, overgrown city of sandstone buildings and mud huts crisscrossed by narrow chalky streets. Under clouds of dust, the American soldiers got their first glimpse of the Filipino people, hundreds of them, thousands, little brown men and women in white peasant clothes scurrying about in pursuit of their daily business. In the near distance, surrounded by what looked like a swamp, stood the formidable walls of the *Intramuros*, the fortress the sailors had talked about, an ugly, forbidding reminder to the Filipinos of their centuries under Spanish tyranny.

"A man told me there's a hundred churches in this town," Ellis exclaimed. "You think he told the truth, Davey, or had he added some to the number?"

Ellis Fairbanks looked almost cured from the seasickness that had kept him down since their departure from San Francisco six weeks earlier. Few Negro soldiers had ever been to sea, and at the start of their voyage, many had fallen ill. Fagen had read men stricken with mal-de-mer acquire their sea legs after a while and get over it, but that had not been so with Ellis. Fagen had fed him ginger root and sugar water, tried to make him comfortable, kept the other men away from him, but could do nothing else. A long uncomfortable journey, they were both glad it

9

was behind them. "A hundred churches is as many as I want to count," Fagen replied.

A giant, more than a head taller than most other men, Ellis Fairbanks had the bulk of a young steer, but the wide-eyed, soft-fleshed face of a child, and he was blessed with a gentle, unquestioning spirit. For him, the world was a minstrel show to enjoy now and understand later. Ellis was more likely to tell you how he felt than what he thought. David Fagen and Ellis Fairbanks were cousins, opposites and perfect friends.

Thick brown water surrounded their ship, the *Thomas*, as it bellied up to a long pier and unloaded the 24th Regiment off the gangplanks and yesterday's garbage off the fantail. The 24th was one of the immune regiments, the name applied by American military officers because being of African blood, Negroes were supposed to better resist the tropical diseases that had killed many of the white soldiers the year before in Cuba. The colored soldiers knew this for nonsense, but they'd long ago learned there was no telling what white men would think of next.

Fagen had his own philosophy on racism in the U. S. Army. He believed most black soldiers didn't think themselves superior or better suited than the white to anything, but neither did they think themselves inferior in any way. In his view, Negro soldiers showed what they were made of in Cuba when the brave men of the 9th Cavalry got up San Juan Hill and joined Colonel Teddy Roosevelt in battle when no other soldiers, white or black, could. Fagen had read a poem about the heroism of the Negro soldier that day entitled "Charge of the Nigger Ninth," and while he hadn't particularly liked the title, at least the brave deeds of the colored soldier were put on record, something Colonel Roosevelt himself had not seen fit to do.

The 24th formed up by company on the long wooden dock, each man carrying his own gear, an unaccustomed and unwelcome load after six weeks at sea. White officers hurried up and down shouting orders sergeants did their best to obey. Hot and exhausted from the voyage, the men of the 24th waited alongside hundreds of others, the midday sun a burning copper disk overhead and a constant reminder they were deep in the tropics.

Ellis's blouse encrusted with sweat salt, he showed no other effects of his long struggle with mal-de-mer, and he shivered with excitement. "This is my first time to set foot on foreign soil, Davey," he said grinning.

Fagen gripped his cousin's big shoulder. "It's like a dream for me too, Ellis."

"Aunt Eunice would be proud if she could see you now."

"She'd be proud of both of us." Fagen scanned the hills that ringed the city. "I've waited a long time for this, Ellis. Uncle Sam has given us the call to serve, and we've answered it. We're in Mr. Lincoln's army, and we're here to fight for Old Glory!"

In fact, Fagen's zest for military service had been more recently acquired. Just two days before graduation from Fisk College in Nashville, he'd received a telegram notifying him of his mother's death. She'd been ill for years, but forbade anyone to tell her son of her fainting spells and bloody cough. Not wishing to worry him while in school, she didn't write of the pain she suffered night and day, or of the useless potions and poultices prescribed by the well-meaning, but bewildered local doctor, the best medicine available to her. Those who knew of her deteriorating condition weren't surprised when in late spring, during a midday coughing spell that racked her thin body, her eyes rolled back in her head, and she fell to the floor, never to get up again. By the time David Fagen arrived home, she was already in the ground.

Alone in their little sharecropper's cabin, Ellis had waited with trepidation for his cousin's homecoming. He'd seen so little of him in the past four years. Had he changed? Would he even remember their youth together? Would Davey hold him responsible somehow for his mother's death? Ellis had worshipped his cousin since a child. He'd always assumed one day they'd take over the farm and work it together. Now that day had come, and he despaired that an educated David Fagen had no use for farming and no time for simple, unsophisticated relatives.

Fagen spent his first days at home in his room mourning the death of his mother. He emerged the third morning and sat quietly at the breakfast table studying the latest newspaper while Ellis spent two hours framing his diploma and searching for the perfect place to hang it. Now, he straightened it and wiped the glass with a cloth. "What do you think, Davey?"

Lost in thought, Fagen's eyes drifted from the newspaper to the fields outside the kitchen window. "About what?"

"Your diploma! How's it look right here?"

"It looks fine, Ellis."

Fagen stood up, contemplated their poor cabin and felt the walls press in on him. Ramshackle and in need of repair, the house he grew up in seemed so much smaller than when he'd left for college four years earlier. He knew his mother had sacrificed everything for his education. She'd worked herself to death for the money to keep him in school. A university education for her son had been her dream, no mean feat for a poor family from the rural south. Now he'd done it, she'd not lived to see it, and he wondered whether it had been worth it.

Newspaper under his arm, Fagen leaned against the front door jamb and stared through the tattered screen at the rolling green hills in the distance. "Ellis, I need to ask you something."

"Ask away, Davey."

"You ever give much thought to soldiering?"

"I never did. Why?"

Fagen had been undecided about his future for some time. Well versed in the classics, he'd read history and philosophy and had graduated near the head of his class, but he knew that educated or not, a black man was still just a nigger in most parts of America. Some black folks up north had made names for themselves, Frederick Douglass, Booker T. Washington, Ida B. Wells, and a man whose name was on everybody's lips, W.E.B. DuBois, had just written a book exposing the African slave trade. These people had risen above their station in life and had dedicated themselves to helping the Negro, and their example inspired Fagen. His felt his life had to mean something. He had to right a terrible wrong, or remedy a great injustice, to fulfill himself and justify his mother's sacrifices.

He wanted to do something important, but unlike those popular pillars of northern Negro society, Fagen knew a life of letters would not suit him. Even though educated, he hadn't a scholar's disposition. Fagen thought himself a man of action. Certain he could do something to help the black man, he'd searched until one day he discovered the army and knew he'd found what he'd been looking for. He read everything written on the famous Buffalo Soldiers, black men in service to their country, showing everyone the Negro could serve his country equal to the white man, and they'd fired his imagination. He knew he could fight as hard as the next man, even harder when motivated. Everything considered, the army seemed the perfect path for a serious-minded Negro with something to prove.

Fagen opened the newspaper to the front page and slid it across the table to his cousin. In three-inch letters the headline screamed: *Spain Sinks USS Maine! War Declared!*

"I'm joining up, Ellis. Come with me."

Ellis Fairbanks stared speechless at his cousin. His jaw dropped, and then his eyes darted frantically around the room, as though he looked for a way out. Fagen knew he'd dumped a heavy load on his cousin, the man-child, who'd never been out of Grayson County. Fagen would always remember the horrible night of storms that flooded their tiny fields, turned the road into a quagmire and kept the doctor away until too late. Huddled shivering under his blankets the hours ticked past, his head pounding from his mother's desperate cries for help over the drumming rain as her sister kissed her newborn baby and died. Since that night, they'd always been together, Ellis Fairbanks and David Fagen. Cousins, friends, brothers.

Ellis found his voice. "Join the army?"

"There's nothing here for us anymore, Ellis. No reason to stay. I intend to make a name for myself, get some respect. Isn't that what you want too? Sure it is! Besides, I've spent too much of my life with you for you to stay here while I walk off over the horizon alone."

Ellis swallowed hard. His eyes glistened, and he blinked. "I've never given it much thought, but upon reflection it seems like a worthwhile thing. Do they have mules in the army, Davey? I always wanted to be a teamster."

The afternoon sun burned their hands and wrists as the 24th marched along a wide, dusty road crowded with military traffic. Huge draft horses, bigger than they'd ever seen, and mules with hooves as broad as dinner plates pulled heavy wagons loaded with supplies. Three-ups, four-ups, spike teams and tandems rolled by in an endless procession, kicking up a fine powder that floated over their heads for miles.

All afternoon H Company staggered along in route step under the weight of all their worldly possessions. In good spirits, most of the men were glad to at last be off the boat and once again on solid ground. Companies of white infantrymen passed in tight formation, arrogant, confident, looking like the seasoned veterans they were, and the Negro soldiers tried to stand a little taller when the white soldiers went by.

Just short of a narrow bridge, their column was herded into a ditch to make way for a detachment of soldiers escorting a dozen bedraggled Spanish prisoners. As they passed, the officer, a lieutenant, glared down from his saddle. Ellis, flush with excitement and patriotic zeal, stood outside the rank and saluted, a big grin lighting his face. The lieutenant reined in and looked up and down the length of the column, taken aback at three hundred Negro soldiers marching down a road in Asia. His horse turned circles in the grit in front of Ellis, still standing at attention. The officer returned the salute, touched the brim of his hat with his riding crop. "I heard you smokeys were coming over here, but I didn't believe it."

"Yes, sir. We're surely here."

The officer frowned. His thin hard face displayed the arrogance of a southern aristocrat. "I can see you're here, Nig. Just what do you think you're going to accomplish?"

Ellis hitched up his trousers. "Well, sir, I'd be happy if we can just take up some of the white man's burden."

"You're an insolent bastard," the officer snarled. "You looking for trouble?"

"No, sir. That is, no offense, sir." Wounded, Ellis considered the officer's disdain uncalled for. "I only meant we'd be proud to fight those Spanish devils right alongside you, sir."

"For your information, Nig, those Spanish devils are already whipped. Your best course of action is to get back on the boat and go home to your plantation. There's plenty of fighting left to do, but we don't need any coloreds to do it for us. Besides, I'm told the gugus here prefer dark meat in their stew pots." The lieutenant spurred his horse and rejoined his detachment.

Ellis saluted the officer's back and called after him, "Yes, sir. I thank you very much, sir."

Ellis played easily the part of the shuffling nigger, but Fagen couldn't – refused even to try. He was furious at the officer for his sneering superiority and angry with his cousin for his naiveté. "Why'd you do a stupid thing like that?"

Too much going on, Fagen's question flew over Ellis' head. "Davey, what's a gugu?"

A young soldier next to them spat in the dirt. "It means nigger, you fool."

Ellis winced, didn't like being talked to that way by another private soldier. "Who are you to know so much?"

"I'm Otis Youngblood, and a man don't have to know much to know more than you, cottonback. You can tell by the tone of his voice. He was probably talking about Filipinos, but he meant nigger. They're all the same to him." He spat again. "Looks like Uncle Sam and Jim Crow arrived in the Philippines at the same time."

The column reached Camp McKinley after a three-hour march under a blistering, midday sun. The men were exhausted, but for the most part the local climate did no more damage than Tampa's a year earlier, where they'd waited for weeks for a chance to get to Cuba. At least in Asia they weren't forced to endure the heat and the scorn of the backward Floridians.

The Filipino natives the Americans encountered along their way had been friendly enough, once they got over the initial shock of seeing Negroes in army uniforms marching across their land. To Fagen, they appeared a handsome race. Short, but solidly built and their skin generally lighter, they had open, expressive faces. Ellis smiled at every man and woman they passed, and winked at each of the children. Fagen overheard a young boy whisper to his friend, "They're like us, only bigger." He thought that a high compliment, but wondered whether they really did look upon the Negro as being like them. If first impressions meant anything, Fagen believed the Filipino to be without the mean and narrow-spirited view of the black man held by most whites. Because they were a colored race too, or because they'd come to free them from the tyranny of the Spanish? Fagen made a vow to try to see things from their point of view.

A replacement station, Camp McKinley was a stopover point for troops assigned later out to the war districts. As the 24th was the first colored regiment to arrive, arrangements had been made to accommodate them. Near the parade ground, they'd erected a large mess tent and a colored-only infirmary. These structures provided the necessary separation between the colored and white areas.

On the opposite side of the compound, Fagen saw the officer's quarters, a large U-shaped structure with a tin roof, divided into twelve two-man rooms with windows that opened and real screens. The commanding officer, General Putnam, lived in a neat, newly whitewashed cottage next to the headquarters building. Two hundred yards distant, a supply depot consisted of a long line of warehouses and a heavily guarded armory, behind that the stables and grazing pastures.

H Company pitched tents in straight rows along the south perimeter wall, the rest of the battalion filled in toward the parade field. Some complained about being so far from the assembly area, requiring them to double-time to formations, but most enjoyed being in the last row and having a little of what in the army passed for privacy. Also, just outside the wall, greenish-black water moved in a narrow irrigation trench and made for good bathing during the rainy season.

They settled in quickly after their long boat trip. Everyone in H Company, especially Fagen, was eager to take up arms and get into the fight. A generation had passed since black Americans had basked in the sunshine of emancipation, and since those glory days, the colored man had once again become a victim of the politics of hate in his own country. Theirs was a rare opportunity to show the white man blacks could defend against the enemies of the flag. The Negro soldier had much to prove, and

15

their path to first-class citizenship led them through the battlefield. They were ready, but then learned they'd not get the opportunity. H Company had been placed in reserve.

"Why us?" Youngblood complained bitterly from his cot after lights out. He'd taken the news of their reserve status harder than the rest and became more sullen every day. No one blamed him, the monotony of garrison duty had grown irksome to everyone and tempers flared.

Ellis assumed the role of peacemaker among the men. Apropos, as he had the least emotional investment in their situation. "Somebody has to be held in reserve," he said.

"Why not somebody else? We should be doing the fighting. D Company ought to be in reserve, it's full of damned Mississippians. They're stupid and lazy, and they've got no stomach for a fight. I'm tired of digging ditches and shoveling shit."

Arkansan Otis Youngblood, like many young hill people, was narrow, self-absorbed and lacked the ability to look at life from any perspective but his own. Rumored he'd shown a false birth certificate and bribed a sergeant when he joined the army at age fifteen, the men accused Youngblood of having a chip on his shoulder, always daring somebody to knock it off. Fagen liked the boy, thought he had grit and looked forward to watching him on a skirmish line, under fire, where the true heart of a man was open for everyone to see.

Youngblood's peevishness was eventually shared to one degree or another by almost everyone. Camp life had taken on a familiar monotony dreaded by military men. Their program each day was wake up at 5:10 am, dress and in formation by 5:25, uncover and hear the "Star Spangled Banner." At 5:30 they answered the roll call and fell out for exercises, then the sick reported out and went to the infirmary. At 6:00, breakfast consisted of meat, beans and biscuits with coffee. Roll call for drill sounded at 7:00. Training lasted until 10:00 and included close order drill, combat formations, scaling ladders, bayonet and rifle. Between 10:00 and 12:00 some of the men were detailed to sweep the tents and streets. One good-sized detachment cleaned the officer's billets, one went to kitchen duty and another to ditch digging or road repair outside the camp. At 3:30, the men formed again for drill and trained until evening mess at 5:00. Call for Retreat and Inspection at 6:00, then roll call and dismissal. Nothing more until 9:00. Between 6:00 and 9:00 they were free to bathe, talk, play cards, write home and feel lonely. At 9:00 the company formed once more for roll call, then Taps at 9:30 when the men must be in their bunks and all lights out.

The time between Retreat and lights out passed the slowest. Fighting men entertained themselves during those hours with stories of their victories, villages plundered, the enemy defeated and degraded. The men of H Company had none of that. They talked only of their situation and sometimes of the loved ones they'd left behind. After lights out, in the privacy of his bunk, each man's imagination was free to create whatever reality he chose.

So it went for several weeks. The unrelenting heat and the monotonous, trivial nature of their duties stirred restless agitation. The Spanish had surrendered and turned themselves in by the hundreds, many sick, some starving. The Negro soldiers suspected the Spanish had been beaten before they got there and now just happy to have the protection of Uncle Sam, happier still to be sent home.

H Company became more disillusioned by the day. Would they ever get into the action? Would there be any action? Would there be anyone left to fight? Periodically, they heard reports of hostilities between Filipino guerilla forces and Americans. Rumors abounded about a young Filipino named Aguinaldo who'd declared himself President of all the islands and was willing to spill blood to have it so. Like so many of the other Negro soldiers, Fagen longed for the day when he saw those things with his own eyes.

At last, a break in their program. First platoon had been detailed for a day of work in Manila. Confined to camp for weeks, their first chance to see the capital city put the men in high spirits. Rivers, the company sergeant, warned them the work would be hard, but like young bulls standing at an open gate, they didn't care and shook off the effects of their forced isolation at the mere promise of a day in the city.

After breakfast, they loaded into two large wagons and headed out along the east road into the countryside. A fine, bright morning, along the way they passed an expanse of rice fields, a patchwork of tiny individual plots with no space between them. Each little square was filled with standing water and bermed with earthen dikes that also served as footpaths. Peasants stood ankle deep, bent over their work in long, sweeping rows. A steady, hypnotic rhythm in their movements afforded a slow but continuous, ages-old progression, a pace field laborers set when they know yet another crop follows this. Watching them work their land, a sudden, sharp longing for home reminded Ellis he was half a world away, and he moved on the wagon seat closer to his cousin.

Before long, they passed through a quarter-mile strip of hastily erected bars and brothels on both sides of the road leading from camp. A canvas banner over their heads proclaimed, *Last Chance Village.* Everyone had heard the stories that flew around Camp McKinley about this temporary town, but until then, they'd not had the opportunity to see it first hand. In this shantytown where American service men got anything they paid for, it was rumored black soldiers were catered to equally with whites. At that time of the morning, however, it was a ghost town, the buildings boarded and locked and the lean-tos and kiosks deserted. The Chinese and Mestizos who ran those establishments were night people. For them the world spun in a different direction.

Excited to see Last Chance Village, the Babylon so often whispered about, Ellis, wide-eyed with fascination said, "Sergeant Rivers told me about this place, Davey. The most God-awful things go on here. I just can't remember if he said be sure and *go* here or be sure and *don't* go here."

"We'll come together, Ellis," Fagen assured him. "Safety in numbers." What soldier could not?

They reached their destination while the morning sun still rose, the men astonished by what they saw. The *Intramuros*, the ancient walled city and symbol of Spanish rule, rose above the dusty streets, open-air markets and dry-goods dealers of modern Manila. Constructed by Filipino slaves, the *Intramuros* had been the seat of Spanish colonial government and home to her aristocracy. A fortress surrounded by walls twenty feet high and ten feet across, entrance was gained through seven drawbridges that once had spanned a large moat.

H Company's first platoon marched in formation to the center square, the *Plaza Royal.* The Governor General's palace and the Manila Cathedral lay on their right, in front of them the Chapel of *San Augustin.*

"Do you see that, Davey? That's the oldest church in the Philippines," Ellis exclaimed. "That makes it church number one." Fagen smiled at his cousin's growing fascination for churches, peculiar for him because Fagen had never seen him in one.

Sergeant Rivers led them northwest along broad avenues lined with nipa palms and colorful tropical flowers. There stood the recently abandoned homes of the Spanish ruling elite, once splendorous mansions with large impressive gardens now neglected and overgrown. Fagen passed the dry, weed infested lawns and pictured their handsome, privileged children laughing, playing, so sure of their heritage and completely unaware their world had been built on the backs of a million wretched peasants and like all good things, had to come to an end.

Soon, they fell into the shadow of Fort Santiago, a massive, forbidding stone structure that guarded the mouth of the Pasig River to Manila Bay. An ugly, oppressive place with its parapet walls, gun emplacements and high lookout towers, it had been the headquarters of the Spanish military in the Philippines. Over the drawbridge leading into the fort, a larger-than-life carving portrayed St. James, Slayer of the Moors, his furious rearing stallion ready for bloody battle, a testament to the darkness that dominated men's minds.

They passed beneath the drawbridge and marched to the edge of a vile, stinking swamp, the surface of the water alive with gnats, biting flies and every other floating and crawling insect. Two-dozen Filipino laborers stood under a nearby tree leaning on their shovels. The Americans looked out at the brackish water and shuddered in anticipation of what would come next.

Sergeant Rivers ordered tools passed around. "We've got to get in there and open up this swamp." He pointed to the group of Filipinos. "These men have been recruited to help."

"The hell you say!" Youngblood's fists balled in outrage. In his view, they'd had enough of that kind of work. Everyone felt like speaking out, but Youngblood was the only one young and foolish enough to challenge the company sergeant.

"The army says this backed-up water spreads fever," Rivers said. "We're going to drain this area."

"Sergeant, this is a job I wouldn't give a dumb animal," Youngblood protested.

"The army's got details all over Manila doing this exact thing, Private. You ain't picked on any worse than anybody else."

"Well, it's a hell of a thing!"

Rivers stood over the young Arkansan, a mean look on his face. "If you feel the need to talk about this some more, Private," he growled, "we can walk around that hill over there and settle it. Otherwise, fall out and get to work."

Youngblood wasn't up for a fight. He knew Sergeant Rivers wouldn't permit a challenge to his authority, and he concluded a few hours in a swamp preferable to a month in the infirmary. The incident over, the men stripped to the waist and moved slowly out into the muddy, brackish water. The Filipino laborers moved past the Americans and spread out along a low, wide berm. They toiled steadily, without complaint, grim-faced under their broad-brimmed straw hats. David Fagen and Ellis Fairbanks took a spot on a silt dyke bordering the river. Ellis said he reckoned the air would be moving a little there. The digging was not hard, but the mosquitoes and biting flies murderous. Difficult to find a rhythm, time dragged.

One of the Filipino laborers, a tiny man with a wooden spade much too big for him, moved next to Fagen and Ellis. Not young, well past middle age, his dark face was pockmarked and deeply lined, but he had perfect, straight white teeth. "Do you see the mud more red than black? Rub it on your body. It has an ingredient the mosquitoes don't like."

A local remedy? Native superstition? He might have said, "Tie a horsehair around the middle finger of your left hand," but desperate, the two soldiers tried it, and to their surprise it helped, and they thanked him. Soon the little man told them more, talking while they worked. "Every year the monsoon tides bring silt and a dam is created. The water gets trapped inside and the swamp is formed. Soon, the season will change, and the river will wash this dyke back into the bay."

Ellis put down his shovel, "Are you saying the river's going to wash all this away by itself? When?"

"Yes, very soon, but the Americans have not learned this yet." The man stopped, wiped the inside of his hat with his shirtsleeve and squinted up at the two Americans. "You are the first *Negrito Americanos* I have seen. You're bigger than I thought you would be."

Fagen had never heard that term before, but if Ellis had, he didn't let on. He still wrestled with the news that swamps came and went on their own. He glanced over to make sure Sergeant Rivers was out of earshot, then asked the little Filipino, "You mean to say we don't need to be here doing this?"

"Maybe you don't," the man said, "but I do. These are hard times my friend. Work is where you find it."

The old man rested on his shovel and offered his hand. "My name is Tomas. I am a silversmith. When the Spanish were here I made beautiful jewelry for the soldiers to buy and send home to their sweethearts and mothers. Don't get me wrong, the Spanish were no great lovers of art. They never took my creations seriously or saw their beauty. To them my pieces were only native curiosities, like picking up pretty shells from a beach, but I could very often persuade them to spend a few pesos for an interesting souvenir. Now, no one buys, and if it weren't for the gifts nature brings, this little swamp, for example, there would be no work at all, and many of us would starve."

"The army claims these swamps spread disease," Fagen said. "Didn't the Spanish care about the fever?"

Tomas looked across to the mouth of the Pasig River. "Americans are more concerned than the Spanish with matters of health and sanitation. The Spanish knew where the fevers came from, but as long as enough of us worked their plantations, it mattered nothing to them if the mosquito drank Filipino blood. The Spanish valued the horse and the *carabao* as much as the peasant."

"You don't talk like a peasant. Where did you learn to speak English?"

"For many years, I worked as a deck hand on British trading ships that sailed between Hong Kong and Manila. The English know only their own language, so Asian sailors have to learn it too. I also speak a little Chinese, and of course Spanish and my native Tagalog."

The old man talked casually of his life and the indignities his people had endured under foreign rule. He might have been reporting on the condition of the crops, or the whitewash on his neighbor's house. Caught up in the Filipino's story, Fagen moved closer and pretended to work the sand at his feet.

Tomas continued. "Now, the Spanish are gone, and the peasants have no value at all."

"But Tomas, you're a free man now," Ellis exclaimed. "Everything in your life will change for the better."

Tomas chuckled. "You stand here before the walls of Fort Santiago and tell me my life will get better? I am not so optimistic, *Señor*. Does the prisoner care who his jailer is? The Spanish have ruled our land for ten generations, and now the Americans have replaced them. The peasant's life doesn't change. The average man does not benefit from his masters' struggles for power."

Fagen thought of his own peoples' campaign for freedom at home and understood, but Ellis didn't. Since he'd joined the army, he refused to believe it did any wrong. "But the Americans aren't jailers! We came here to free you from all that."

The old man pointed. "Just there, near the feet of St. James, are the lower dungeons. The Spanish reserved these cells for the most dangerous and subversive of their subjects. Hundreds of Filipino men and women, perhaps thousands, have been imprisoned there, but always their stay was mercifully short. Three times a month, the highest tides in Manila Bay pushed the river back and filled the cells. After a few hours, the guards had only to open the doors and let the falling tide clean up for them. The horned crabs did the rest. The lower dungeons are empty now. Will the Americans fill them up again? Too soon to tell, *amigo*."

"No American would do something like that," Ellis insisted.

The old man picked up his shovel and stabbed at the red mud. "There is a great leader among our people named Aguinaldo. For many years a general in the war against Spanish tyranny, just a few months ago he was elected President of the new, independent Filipino republic. Today, he has been chased from his Presidential Palace by your soldiers and hides in the jungle with the wild animals. So you see, my *Negrito* friend, you speak to me of freedom and a new life, but I think you Americans are not all of the same mind."

That night, in their tent after Taps, Ellis still talked about his encounter with the old man. Like a stalking carnivore, Youngblood smelled Ellis' doubt and confusion and was not about to pass up a chance to work his way under his skin. "Fairbanks, you're a jackass. That old man was right. This man's army will do what it pleases, these Filipino people be damned. Where's it written the American government is so God-Almighty righteous? What's the government ever done for you?" Youngblood threw his canteen cup against the tent canvas, and it bounced to the floor. "Let me tell you something, nigger, Uncle Sam's strong right arm will have plenty of blood on it before we're through in these islands. Mark my words on that."

Ellis glowered at Youngblood. "Why don't you go to sleep?" Ellis' heart was in it, but he wasn't otherwise equipped for long debate. He glanced over to his cousin for support. Fagen smiled, indicated Youngblood not worth the trouble. Ellis ended it the best way he knew how. "Ain't you tired? You're always saying the army drives you like a dog. Just turn over and go to sleep."

Not getting the argument he wanted, in punctuation Youngblood drove his fist into his pillow and grumbled. "You're nothing but a damned fool."

A long, confusing day for Ellis Fairbanks, he sat on the edge of his bunk and folded his hands. Like many recent converts, he'd felt compelled to defend his new religion, but didn't know how. Fagen waited until he heard the sound of regular breathing from Youngblood, and then knelt in the darkness next to his cousin's cot. "Let me tell you something, Ellis. We may be damned fools in that boy's eyes, but at least we believe in something. We believe in our flag and what it stands for. He doesn't, and that's the difference between us. He doesn't hold anything sacred. He's empty on the inside because he doesn't believe in anything."

Ellis sighed deeply and looked out at the rows of dark tents in the moonlight. The sounds of men sleeping carried on the night air. Fagen continued. "We believe in our Uncle Sam and have no doubt he will always do right in the long run. We believe in the army. We think God looks down on us different from other armies. When our men pray before a battle, we know God listens because He knows we're trying not to sin, that we're trying to do good. For us, Uncle Sam is *really* our uncle. He's the rich relative a man always dreams of. And the army is like a wife. We took an oath, and we're joined in the eyes of God, just like in a marriage. Now here's the good part, Ellis. The army is better than a wife. You see, the army can't ever divorce you. You give your life to her, and she can't ever turn her back on you. The way I see it, this man's army is our best chance for happiness and a full life. Let the Youngbloods of the world go their own way."

Ellis sighed again, and then lay back and closed his eyes, but an uneasy stillness dwelt in their tent that night.

Fagen felt justified guiding his cousin's thinking concerning military life. He'd helped Ellis form opinion and make conclusions since childhood. Besides, his own dreams weren't very different. Fagen longed for the day when he'd be called upon to do what he'd trained for. Every particle of his body and mind ready to take on the enemy, he'd not the gift of patience, waiting for his turn in the war was torture. He *knew* he was destined to do great things, to show the world David Fagen was worthy of the duties and responsibilities of a man. But there in the darkness after Taps, Ellis asleep, quietly self-righteous with his faith in Old Glory, Fagen lay awake sharing some of Youngblood's dark feelings. Who knew about them? Who cared? Maybe Tomas had been right. Maybe they were all small, lost souls in a world that didn't change.

CHAPTER 3 - SAN ISIDRO

Colonel Fredrick Funston, seated comfortably at the head of his long dining table, beckoned for a Filipino servant to pour wine. "Gentlemen, allow me to propose a toast." The officers joining him for dinner raised their glasses. "Firstly, I would like to extend a hearty welcome to my old friend, Major William Russell, visiting us once again from the Governor General's office in Manila. Welcome, Bill."

Major Russell acknowledged the colonel's toast with a flash of his large, yellow teeth and chuckled to himself. *My old friend*, that's a good one, he thought. The publicity seeking old buzzard, Fredrick Funston has no friends, least of all me.

The colonel continued around the table. "Secondly, let us officially greet our newest officer, Lieutenant Matthew Alstaetter, just off the boat from San Francisco."

Funston hadn't failed to notice the lieutenant's West Point class ring. Having had no formal military training himself, the colonel was covetous of the young officer's gold college ring and the influence it would one day wield. Damned greenhorn, he growled to himself, another gosling for me to baby sit, but to the others he said, "Lieutenant Alstaetter, gentlemen, is an academy man. We're looking for great things from you, son. I believe you know the other gentlemen here, my executive officer, Captain Baston, and our surgeon, Doctor Forrester."

Matthew Alstaetter flushed at the sudden and unexpected attention. "Thank you, sir. Captain Baston has been very helpful in getting me situated, sir. The doctor and I have only just met."

Small, dark-skinned Filipinos dressed in white carried the officers' meal to the table. The men ate in silence until, according to custom, Colonel Funston opened the conversation. "Tell me, Bill, how is my friend and colleague, General Otis? Still caught between politics and the real world?"

Major Russell put down his fork. "The general sends his regards, Colonel. Indeed, his office grows more difficult each day. I'm certain when he accepted the post of governor, he could not have foreseen the difficulties of a campaign of military occupation here in Asia whose goals are ill defined by an equivocating administration, and then completely obscured by a Machiavellian congress. I don't envy his position."

"It makes my back teeth hurt just to think about it, Bill. I hope he knows we've kept the faith here in San Isidro. You tell him that, by God. Frederick Funston stands with him all the way."

Major Russell recognized the open door and took the opportunity to nurture the colonel's infamous vanity. He smiled. "The general knows that, sir. In point of fact, he relies on your unfailing support. Everyone in Manila speaks of you often and in the most glowing terms. Believe me, General Otis is fully aware and very appreciative of the excellent job you've done here."

Captain Baston's mournful sigh was not quite audible. Listen to those two old frauds, he said to himself. Funston's military career, a foolhardy, grandstanding hoax, and Russell's – Bill's! – a house of cards built on treachery and deceit.

Of the two, Baston knew the major to be far more intelligent than Colonel Funston, and therefore, more dangerous. Every officer in Asia feared Bill Russell. He had spent years assembling an elaborate network of spies and informants, hired guns to feed his rapacious lust for information to use one day against his fellow officers. Bribery and extortion the major's tools, malicious gossip the prize. It didn't matter how obtained or how much really true, only that he had it, and that everyone knew he would use it without hesitation to enhance his career or destroy the career of someone who stood in his way.

As aide to Governor General Otis, Russell was in a unique position of authority. He held power even over those who far outranked him. Captain Baston despised the major. He hated his monthly visits to the districts, loathed the idea of them. To him, Russell was nothing more than the king's favorite knight, scrabbling around the realm peeping through keyholes and eavesdropping on private conversations. Then, his dirty business done, the inevitable bending down to pat the loyal subjects on the head. Baston dreamed of the day when somehow he could topple the great "Bill" Russell. He wished Mr. Thomas Edison would capture the lordly major on his moving-picture camera having sex with a nigger Filipino. That would neuter the arrogant bastard!

Mercifully, Captain Baston endured the major's visits only once a month, and usually then for only an evening before he continued on his rounds. However, his relationship with Colonel Funston was another matter. Funston was the district commander, the captain his executive officer and therefore never completely safe from one of the colonel's many superfluous, bombastic opinion speeches on the state of the world, the state of the war, or the nature and state of just about anything in heaven and earth. Baston had never met a man so completely self-absorbed as Colonel Funston. Soon after he'd arrived in San Isidro, he'd concluded his commander so conceited, so vainglorious and filled with what Carlyle called the "sixth insatiable sense" for so long, he didn't even know what a comic character he'd become.

"Fighting" Fredrick Funston everyone called him. His nickname because the colonel himself insisted on it. Some men, when they put on a uniform, master the revolver or the saber, or if cavalrymen, the horse. Funston had only succeeded in mastering his legend. Simply put, he was a shameless publicity hound, and Captain Baston's chief duty was to nurture and embellish the prestige of "Fighting Freddy." Determined to gain a widespread reputation as a brilliant military strategist and fearless battlefield commander, the colonel wanted it known throughout the army that he, Fredrick Funston, was the man to put the barrel of a cannon between his teeth and swim a river to engage the enemy head-on.

Baston's standing orders from his commander were clear. No exaggeration too great, no fiction too far-fetched, the reality of Colonel Funston's battlefield heroism was not to be denied. Captain Baston took comfort from the certainty that one day his commander's ego would be the driving force behind the termination of his command. He eagerly awaited the day when Funston fell off his horse charging an invisible enemy or accidentally shot himself with his own pistol, and then he, Baston, would jump from the rank of captain directly to colonel, skipping altogether the pesky, supercilious rank of major and take his rightful place as commander of the San Isidro district.

"I'm told the President fell to his knees in the White House and prayed for a solution to the Asian situation when a celestial vision appeared before him, and now the whole matter is settled." Colonel Funston delighted in his own sardonic turn of phrase.

"You are correct, Colonel," Major Russell said. "It seems God has convinced Mr. McKinley that expansionism in Asia is a policy truly heaven sent."

"I wonder whether God and President McKinley have seen fit to inform Congress of their covenant?" Funston asked.

"Officially, not yet," said the Major, "but Mr. Mark Twain and Mr. William Dean Howells of the Anti-Imperialist League got wind of it, and they've stirred up no end of trouble. Twain is furious. He's sent a paper to Congress demanding God be subpoenaed to the floor of the Senate. He said if the devil will debate Daniel Webster, the Lord ought not to be afraid to defend his Asia policy before a batch of humble Congressmen."

Colonel Funston slapped the table with the meaty part of his palm. "Twain's a damned menace! He's nothing but a hack writer out to make a name for himself. If it weren't for this Anti-Imperialism business, nobody would pay any attention to him at all. I predict he'll be forgotten anyway in two years."

Major Russell was circumspect. "In the meantime," he said, "General Otis is concerned about the effect this nonsense will have on our troops here in the islands. A soldier has to believe in a cause to be effective, Colonel. He has to think people back home are fully behind him. The general wishes our men to know all of America supports them in the fight to secure and protect the Filipino people. Too much exposure to the traitorous broadcasts of a radical few unduly harms the morale of our fighting men. He feels it better to focus on the positive, if I am making myself clear on this."

Funston got the message. "Quite clear, Major. The general is a prudent man. Are you clear on this too, Captain?"

"Yes, sir. The entire staff is very sensitive to the situation," Baston replied. "Major Russell, our policy has always been to censor outgoing mail, but for several weeks now we've been censoring incoming mail as well."

"We have?" Funston exclaimed.

"Yes, sir. For several weeks. Pursuant to your order of several weeks ago, sir."

"Quite so," the colonel said.

Major Russell shifted in his chair, tried to keep from smiling. "What's your opinion of this anti-imperialism business, Captain?"

"I despise the whole affair, Major," Baston growled. "By God, I believe Americans have a sacred duty to be loyal to their government. If the Colonel will grant me three months leave, I'll sail back to the states, hunt down Mr. Twain and silence that treasonous cur forever."

Colonel Funston couldn't share the conversational limelight for long. "And if I could spare you, I'd let you go. Hell, I'd even go with you, but I'm afraid that's not in the stars." He turned to Major Russell. "Frankly, Major, I'm more concerned with this pup, Aguinaldo. They say now he's holed up somewhere near Mt. Arayat. God damn it! He's right here in my own district! We've searched, but we haven't been able to find him.

His gang of rebel cutthroats takes potshots at us from behind every rock
and tree, and worse, he keeps the peasants in the barrios all fired up with
his talk of independence."

Major Russell cringed. He saw another of Funston's speeches coming,
and for him this was old news. He interrupted. "Your concern is well
placed, Colonel. General Otis wants this native insurrection, if that's
what you want to call it, nipped in the bud. It wouldn't do for the folks
back home to see us wage a protracted war against the people we came
here to liberate.

"Aguinaldo is a pup, but he's no fool. He's upset because Dewey sailed
into Manila Bay and didn't immediately anoint him king, so he continues
to poison the minds of his countrymen with notions of independence.
President McKinley feels the Filipino people not ready to rule themselves.
He thinks the natives need time to grow under our protectorate. I can tell
you this, gentlemen, he's not about to turn these islands over to Aguinaldo
or anybody else. Not yet, anyway.

"In response to Aguinaldo's troublemaking, all the military districts
will soon go on full alert. More troops arrive from the states every day.
General Otis wants an American influence in every village and barrio.
He desires to pacify the natives, kill them with kindness. *Benevolent
Assimilation* is his phrase. We're to make them see we care only for their
security and well-being. We have to undo what those Spanish bastards
have done over the last three hundred years. Naturally, however, we're
expected to defend ourselves against the insurrectos. No one is safe with
bands of armed fanatics roaming the countryside."

Colonel Funston smelled the diplomatic rhetoric even before he
heard it. He had no gift for it himself, and therefore no patience for it.
"Are you saying, Major, the general wants the countryside cleared of these
rebels?"

"I'm saying, Colonel, General Otis prefers an aggressive defense of
the civilian population in the areas where these hoodlums operate. He
believes this an especially important strategy in the early stages of this
insurrection. You may infer what you wish from his use of the term,
aggressive defense."

Major Russell and Captain Baston exchanged cryptic smiles across
the table. You understand me, don't you my ambitious young captain,
the major thought. Good. Then we understand each other. I know more
about you than you know about yourself. I've seen dozens like you in my
career, domineering with your subordinates, devious with your peers and

obsequious with your superiors. You are the perfect aide to this fool of a colonel.

Captain Baston sat forward in his chair. "Are you enjoying the venison Major Russell?"

Over brandy and cigars, the men discussed more mundane matters. The dinner had gone well, and Funston was pleased with himself. It was important that Bill Russell enjoyed a good meal, and then left the district with a positive opinion of him and his command. This now assured, he turned his attention to the other end of the table. "You've been in the villages for several days, Doctor Forrester. What news?"

"Not good, I'm afraid, Colonel. The peasants have looted and destroyed Spanish garrisons throughout the region leaving the Spanish soldiers with neither food nor shelter. Their command structure, or what little left of it, is ineffectual. The officers exercise control through brute force only, and then only when they think they'll prevail. Spanish soldiers are scattered throughout the barrios sleeping where they can and eating scraps of garbage the peasants throw out for the dogs. It's ugly, sir. There's no attempt at sanitation. I'm worried about disease. We've tried to get them to organize themselves, dig slit trenches, boil their drinking water, but they're just not interested. All they want is to go home. There's nothing more I can do with them, Colonel."

"So it's come full circle," Funston bellowed. "The Filipinos doling out scraps to the Spanish. Now *that's* irony for you!"

Major Russell ignored the colonel's trenchant remark. He turned to the doctor. "It's the same all over Luzon. The Spanish government has deliberately slowed down the repatriation of troops. Their economy at home in shambles, there aren't any jobs for eighty thousand returning soldiers, not even any place to put them. The great Spanish empire is bankrupt. I think the government wishes they'd just disappear so they wouldn't have to deal with them."

Lieutenant Alstaetter spoke up, "When I left San Francisco six weeks ago, Congress had not yet appropriated the twenty million they promised Spain in the Treaty of Paris. Perhaps those funds will help the Spanish get their soldiers home." His first words of the evening, and he immediately regretted them. Suddenly, Colonel Funston fixed him with an icy glare. Unthinkable one of his subordinates spoke in defense of the Spanish at his own dinner table! The officers were silent for a long moment.

Finally, Colonel Funston said, "It is our position, Lieutenant, Congress should never have agreed to any condition, save Spain's total and complete surrender. If Spain's broke, that's her problem. Personally, I wouldn't give them one red cent."

Captain Baston drained his glass then poured another. "The Spanish should have considered this ignominious eventuality before they began their empire building." His speech becoming slurred, Major Russell made a mental note that Baston liked his brandy, maybe a little too well. He raised his own glass. "Let's hope the lesson is not lost on us, Captain."

Colonel Funston stood up, signaling an end to the dinner conversation. "I'll say good night, gentlemen. I have work to do in my quarters. Will I see you in the morning, Major?"

"I leave for Manila at first light," Russell answered.

"Captain Baston, detail a detachment to accompany the major.

"Oh, by the way, Lieutenant Alstaetter, a company of reinforcements arrives from Camp McKinley in two days. I'm assigning you to command them."

"Yes, sir. Thank you, sir."

"Have you ever served with colored soldiers, Lieutenant?"

"Negroes? No, sir."

"Something tells me you're just the right man for the job."

CHAPTER 4 - TANUBA

"Did you hear the news, Davey?" Ellis' eyes shone with excitement.

Fagen smiled at his cousin. "I sure did. I was beginning to think we'd never get out of here."

After the evening meal, Sergeant Rivers assembled the men on the parade field and read the orders. H Company had been taken out of reserve and assigned to the sixth military district garrisoned near San Isidro in the Central Luzon valley; like being born again, the best news they could have received. They were through with camp duty at last.

Rivers said the sixth district was commanded by a colonel everyone called Fighting Fredrick Funston, the name music to the men's ears as fighting was what they wanted most to do. Now their chance had finally come to show the famous colonel and the rest of the U.S. army what a company of determined Negroes could do.

Weeks of daily drills had made them more than proficient at battle formations and marksmanship and as ready for combat as any untested infantry company could be. Sergeant Rivers had kept H Company on track while in reserve. A tower of strength and patience, he never complained about their situation, but he never stopped the men from letting off steam when they needed to. Cold and distant, he was a strange, hard man, but always made sure H Company had the best food and medical attention in the camp, and everyone had grown to respect him.

The march to San Isidro a joy, in high spirits the men easily covered the miles in one long day. To them, the earth and sky were of the same ether, and they moved effortlessly through it. Ellis Fairbanks laughed out loud and waved at every Filipino they passed on the road. Adrenaline flowed like honey through Fagen's veins. He floated on air, his pack and rifle weightless, part of his body. Even the irascible Youngblood, marching in file behind them, wore a smile.

They joined the San Isidro camp near the *Rio Grande De Pampanga*. That night, Lieutenant Alstaetter rode out to their bivouac. He spoke with Sergeant Rivers for a while in private, and then formed ranks and introduced himself. His first field command, he wanted to make a good impression on the Negro soldiers standing before him in tight military formation, so he saluted smartly and kept his remarks brief.

Later, Sergeant Rivers reassembled the company and gave the briefing. "Tomorrow morning we move west to a village called Tanuba, where Filipino insurgents are thought to maintain a cache of arms and ammunition. We destroy anything we find and detain suspected guerilla personnel for interrogation. Any questions? We march at first light."

David Fagen glanced up at a sliver of moon, and then crawled into his pup tent. The excitement of at last facing the enemy had kept him awake long after his usual bedtime. He'd packed and re-packed his field kit and checked his rifle and ammunition. The air around the camp resonated nervous anticipation. Even the older, more experienced men retired to their tents late and didn't sleep.

Not sharing the furor, Ellis sat for a long time leaning against the tent post, his giant hands nervously kneading his bare feet, like a child afraid of the dark. Fagen pulled up a campstool and sat down beside him. "What is it? Tell me."

Not looking up, Ellis said softly, "I heard Sergeant Rivers say guerillas live over there in that village. He said they're normal people during the day, but at night they put on guerilla clothes and pack rifles around. He said you couldn't tell who's the enemy and who's not, and you don't know who to shoot and who not to shoot."

"You got the jim-jams about going out there tomorrow, Ellis? It's okay, I think everybody's a little scared."

"Heck, I'm not scared. I just always thought we'd be battling Spanish men. When did we start fighting with the Filipinos, anyway? None of them ever done anything to me. Why should I fight against a Filipino?"

"You heard what Sergeant Rivers said, these are Filipino outlaws, and they've killed Americans as well as their own kind. We're the only ones who can stop them."

"Are you all fired up about killing like the rest of these men?"

Surprised by the accusation, Fagen chose his words carefully. "I'm not fired up about killing, Ellis. I'm fired up about fighting."

Ellis turned his back on his cousin, so Fagen moved his campstool around until he faced him. "You remember the night we talked about what we believe in…about the army? Well I believe in something more. I believe God's given me this chance to show what I can do for my country. This is my time to prove the black man equal to the white, and Negro blood just as good as a white man's when it's spilled protecting the flag. America is short on opportunities for a colored man to show his worth,

Ellis. I think this war here in these islands is my chance. Spanish, Filipino, it makes no difference. All the enemies of my country look the same to me."

At first, Ellis rejected his cousin's words, but in a moment, his eyes softened, and he lay down for sleep. "I guess I'll be the one looking out for you tomorrow. You'll go out there and get your damned self killed."

"We'll look out for each other."

Morning came and with it a banty-rooster corporal rousting everyone out. The men choked down a hasty breakfast of cold meat, biscuits and coffee, checked their gear one more time and formed ranks. A short time later, Captain Baston arrived riding a huge white mare and circled the column three times. From his place in the second rank, Fagen studied the officer, his horse kicking up dust as he ringed the formation. A big man with a mean look in his eye, he carried a carbine in a red leather scabbard buckled to his saddle, a pistol on each hip and a shiny cavalry officer's saber.

The captain wore spurs with the rowels filed to sharp points and used them constantly. Ellis didn't like the way he bullied his horse. "The man is tormenting that animal, Davey," he whispered to Fagen, "and the day hasn't even started yet." Lieutenant Alstaetter saluted the captain, and the two officers rode together to the head of the formation.

After a two-hour march, H Company arrived at Tanuba, a tiny cluster of nipa palm shacks built on stilts a hundred yards off the main road at the edge of a dense bamboo jungle. The houses looked too poor for human habitation. No rice paddies anywhere near, and with the exception of two large water buffalo in a dung-heaped corral, all the animal pens were empty.

Captain Baston split the company into three battle platoons of twenty men each and kept twenty in reserve to guard the pack animals and call in to fight if needed. One platoon positioned to attack the middle of the village, while the others advanced from either flank to cut off the enemy if he tried to escape into the jungle. Captain Baston commanded the center and ordered Sergeant Rivers to lead the right flank, Lieutenant Alstaetter the left. Grim-faced, Baston huffed and snorted through flared nostrils while he rode his mare in tight circles. To the men, he appeared exceedingly restless, mad at everything.

Everyone waited for the order to commence the attack, when suddenly their company commander threw his daypack and saddle bags onto the road and drew his saber, his big mare skittering at the sight of it. He dug his heels into the horse's flanks, and then galloped the full length of the formation shouting, "Tanuba may look innocent enough, but take my word for it, the enemy is here! Attack with everything you've got, boys!"

To Fagen's eyes, Baston mirrored a caricature of a military leader, a big white man on a big horse bounding up and down the road shouting at the top of his lungs; but he was the captain, and Fagen had never seen combat and didn't know what it was supposed to look like.

David Fagen and Ellis Fairbanks stepped down off the road side-by-side, rifles at the ready, moving on a line through chest-high cogon grass. They advanced quickly, and soon closed to within fifty yards of the village. Fagen's finger light on the trigger of his rifle, his heart raced with exhilaration. The sun shone down from directly overhead and baked his forearms while the sweet-sour odor of humus filled his nostrils. The earth is my mother, he thought. I'm safe in her arms.

Nothing moved in the village, the only sound the chomp of booted feet as the Americans marched through thick grass. Occasionally, Lieutenant Alstaetter whispered encouragement. "That's it, fellows. Stay on line. Eyes up and forward." On they went without incident.

It happened so suddenly, the startled American soldiers barely had the presence of mind to take cover. On some unseen signal, forty rebels opened fire, and in a second the silent field was shattered by the harsh bark of Mauser rifle fire and the air filled with gun smoke. Fagen knew instantly this was the moment he'd waited for. He'd always wondered how he'd feel when he first experienced real combat, and now he'd find out.

His first sensation at being shot at was the unreality of it, the semblance of illusion, as though it happened to someone else, or perhaps to him, but not in that time. Later, he remembered thinking the bullets that zinged past his ear and clipped the grass to his left and right were not really aimed at him and not fired in anger by someone wanting to kill him. He felt in no danger at all. From his perspective, time slowed, almost stopped, and he contemplated the details of the battle raging around him.

He saw the Filipino insurgents rise up from their hiding places and noted how the dark bandoliers around their necks contrasted with their white peasant clothes and broad-billed straw hats. As they shouldered their rifles and let loose a volley, he saw the volumes of smoke from the muzzles, but barely heard the reports and experienced nothing more immediate or compelling than a curious fascination. He saw the men around him, confused and panic-stricken by the sudden ambush, scatter and dive for cover, but he stood there unconcerned, an invisible, incorporeal observer.

He watched Lieutenant Alstaetter run among the men, furiously urging them to return fire. He turned to look for Ellis, to see whether he'd witnessed this spectacle, whether he shared this special point of view. But Ellis not to be found, Fagen stood alone in the grass while those other things took place around him.

The spell was broken suddenly, when he took a hammer blow to the back of his neck and fell to his knees. "Get down fool! You want to get killed?" Ellis pinned his cousin to the ground while the Filipinos fired another volley, and then broke for the safety of the jungle.

Lieutenant Alstaetter came through the grass then, shouting orders. "Advance men! Fire in rushes! Advance!" Sometime during the ambush, he'd lost his hat, and his yellow, sweat-soaked hair made him look younger even than he was. On his order, first platoon rose up and rushed the left flank all the way to the village, Filipino guerillas running away before them.

Second platoon, in the center, had fallen behind leaving a gap in the formation. Seeing this, Captain Baston raced up and down the length of the advancing line, his horse rearing in fright. "To the charge, boys! Come on! We'll whip those gugu bastards!" Third platoon reached the village next, but Sergeant Rivers held the men back and waited for Captain Baston so they all entered at the same time.

Fagen sensed sudden movement to his left. The Filipino rebel had been hiding behind a rotted nipa stump and came out fast swinging a long, curving bolo knife. No time to think, Fagen reacted from instinct, spun left and used the barrel of his rifle to parry the blow. Much smaller than Fagen, the rebel soldier was quick and had the element of surprise. He lunged again, tried to get under the American's defense, and Fagen heard a dull thud as the sharp edge of the big bolo struck his canvas daypack. He felt the force of the blow all the way across his shoulders, and it occurred to him it was only by God's grace he was still alive.

Suddenly, Fagen's subconscious took over again, and he stepped outside himself. Even then, engaged in hand-to-hand combat with an enemy soldier, he couldn't shake the notion it wasn't happening to him. He was witnessing a fight for his life, but wasn't involved in it, not a participant. The Filipino came at him again, this time with an overhead strike, and Fagen saw the determination in the man's eyes suddenly shift to desperation. He'd used both hands on the hilt, and his blade traced a high, sweeping arch and came down fast.

At that moment, that precise instant, Fagen realized for him battle was different than for other men. He'd looked forward to this time, dreamed about it, waited so long, and now life's defining moment had finally arrived, and just then, locked in a death struggle with a man trying desperately to kill him, he suddenly realized God had granted him special power. He'd been endowed with the virtue of great courage. He knew then he was no ordinary man and, armed with God's power, could not die at the hands of another. He felt destined to great and noble deeds, to easily accomplish everything other men never even try. He saw the sun reflect off cold steel, drew a ragged breath and tasted immortality.

The big knife came down gathering speed and momentum. Fagen pivoted ninety degrees on the ball of his right foot and heard the blade swish past, inches from his face. Off balance then, the force of the rebel's attack had pulled him forward on his toes. Fagen pivoted again, this time to his left, used the barrel of his rifle hard, and the man screamed in agony and fell to his knees. The weight of Fagen's weapon shattered the bones in his right shoulder. His arm limp and useless, he was unable even to release the bolo, and it hung there, its tip just inches from the ground. Lieutenant Alstaetter appeared out of nowhere and put his boot on the long blade, pinning the man's hand under it. "Good work, Private."

Alstaetter shouted a command to the men, and the sound of his voice so close to Fagen's ear brought him suddenly out of his trance, and for the first time he looked down and really saw the man whose shoulder he'd shattered, lying at his feet in a paroxysm of pain and fear. He looked around the battlefield and saw it for the first time as it really was - hot, stinking of gunpowder and littered with the torn and bloody bodies of men. He saw Youngblood and some others chase two Filipinos running for the tree line. This time, Lieutenant Alsaetter's voice rang clear in his head. "Let them go, men! They know that jungle. We don't."

H Company now had the village boxed in on three sides. The captain gave orders to move forward, and they cautiously resumed their advance. They'd sustained no casualties in the ambush, but wide-eyed and tight-jawed, they showed their unease. The rebels had caught the Americans off guard, and they'd not liked it. Up and down the line, men cursed the underhanded tactics of the "sneaky" Filipinos. Fagen's prisoner had been moved to the rear and placed under guard. In the distance, Fagen heard his painful cries mixed with the sound of something else — men laughing? It occurred to him then his captive might be in for some rough treatment by the boys in the reserve platoon. They'd watched the advance, seen the ambush unfold, and they too held a low opinion of the cowardly Filipino method of making war.

Nothing moved inside the village. Breakfast fires smoldered, evidence of recent activity, but no signs of life, as though the villagers had simply put down whatever they'd been doing and left. A strange sight, too quiet, certainly not what the Americans had expected after their warm welcome, and the men were spooked by the eerie stillness.

Suddenly, Captain Baston spurred his white mare and charged headlong through the battle cordon into the center of the village, his horse's hooves kicked up dust, sent cook pots and smoldering embers flying as he wheeled to a stop. "Come on you men! Get in here! Take this God damned village! Round up these slope-headed bastards, Lieutenant. Get them out where we can see them."

First platoon split into five-man squads and searched the village. The native lodges built on heavy bamboo stilts six feet above ground, Lieutenant Alstaetter moved from one thatched hut to the next calling into the open doorways. "Come out. No harm will come to you. Come out!"

One by one, the villagers lowered ladders and cautiously emerged from the shadow of their homes. The men came out first, and soldiers quickly surrounded them. Captain Baston ordered them into the corral with the water buffalo where they sat in the dung, hands on their heads. Next the women, many with babies, then the children and old people. The village cleared, sixty frightened Filipinos huddled in the corral, American soldiers in a circle standing guard over them.

The captain gave an order, and the rest of the men ransacked the village. Soldiers charged up ladders into huts, gutted the interiors and threw everything scattered and broken into the street. Bags of rice and baskets of vegetables went into one pile and clothing, shoes, tools and other house wares into another.

While the soldiers went about their business, the women in the corral got to their knees and pleaded with the Americans to spare their possessions. The children heard their mothers' pleas and wailed uncontrollably while the black, uniformed men destroyed their homes. Ellis tried to comfort the children. He walked among the villagers urging them to remain calm. Concerned he'd get too close and attacked by the Filipinos, Sergeant Rivers ordered him back outside the corral.

In a moment, Ellis spotted something behind a rusted, tin watering trough, moved behind his cousin and whispered, "Davey, look at that."

Fagen saw it too, a bare foot in the dust behind the trough. The two men moved closer and saw a torn, bloody sandal. A Filipino.

"Careful," Ellis said.

They split up and approached from opposite directions. He lay face down in the dirt, the back of his peasant shirt soaked with thick, black blood and covered with bluebottle flies. Fagen turned the body over. "He must have been one of the rebels that ambushed us and got hit when he tried to run away."

Ellis knelt, raised the body and removed its straw hat. A child. Ellis cradled the boy's head. "Oh, Davey, he's just a kid. He can't be more than eight or nine years old. He couldn't have been part of any ambush. What's he doing here dead behind this trough? "

Fagen knew Ellis was right, the boy wasn't big enough to carry a rifle. When Ellis moved him, his head rolled and his jaw slackened, his lips parting slightly. The boy clutched a Spanish coin made of silver in his left hand. Someone had drilled a hole in the center and looped a leather thong through it. A very dear keepsake, no doubt, but what had it meant to the child? A magic charm? A lucky piece? He would never tell.

Fagen stood up and looked away. "I'll get Sergeant Rivers." Just then a village woman broke from the corral and ran toward them shrieking and wailing. She threw herself on the boy's lifeless body, and for a long time Ellis sat with them in the dust and held them both in his big arms.

All the huts finally cleared, Captain Baston ordered the villagers to assemble, children and old people in front, women behind them and the men in the rear. The captain dismounted, handed the reins to Lieutenant Alstaetter, and then paced back and forth in front of two large piles of goods belonging to the villagers. The Filipinos quiet now, watched the American captain's every move. The old men squatted in front and smoked homemade cigarettes, no fear on their faces now, only grim resolve. These people had seen conquering armies raid and loot their villages for generations.

Captain Baston raised his voice to the crowd. "Does any of you people speak English?"

One old man stood up. "*Un poco.* A little."

"Listen closely to what I have to say. For some time now, we have suspected this village of providing aid and refuge to insurgent forces. This action today confirms it. I came here on a mission of peace, but now my company has been attacked. I could raze this entire village and place you all under arrest." At that, Captain Baston drew his saber and with one blow, smashed an oil lamp lying among the goods taken from inside the huts. Then he turned his back on the villagers. "Sergeant Rivers!"

"Yes, sir."

"Post yourself!" Rivers ran forward and stood at attention. "Do it."

Sergeant Rivers' face a mask, he bent down and put a match first to one kerosene-soaked pile, then the other. Low flames licked among the fabrics and foodstuff, then rose giving off huge clouds of hot, white smoke. The villagers bawled at the sight of the fire destroying their food and clothing. Some of the young men rushed forward in a desperate attempt to salvage what they could, but the captain gave an order, and the Americans moved in to block their way.

Side-by-side, the men used their rifles as clubs to beat back the frantic villagers. The Filipinos cursed and spat, their eyes wild with anger, but the soldiers held their ground. Fagen learned that day men fought harder for the food that sustains life than for life itself. He understood then when a man fights for food, it's not for just himself, but also for his children. Soon, the women and several of the old ones joined the mêlée. Impressed by the collective strength of the angry villagers, Fagen found himself inching toward Ellis where he knew the line would never break. The crowd surged and pressed again. This time, Fagen wasn't sure they could hold them.

Captain Baston calmly mounted his white horse, drew his pistol, aimed over the heads of the enraged peasants and fired first one shot, then a second. One of the water buffalo grazing in the corral dropped to its knees, rolled over, tried once to get up, and then fell dead. The villagers hushed, and then drew back, their energy suddenly gone. The water buffalo their most valuable possessions, life without them seemed impossible. The act reminded them that, like other conquerors they'd faced in their past, the American captain had limitless power over them and the will to exercise it.

The soldiers finally pushed the villagers back into the dusty corral. A small sea of angry, resentful faces stared back at them. The translator remained standing, but said nothing to his people. The Filipinos didn't need to hear words in their dialect to understand what went on.

The villagers' spirit broken, the captain continued in a casual, conversational tone. "Unlike our predecessors here in the Philippines, Americans take no pleasure in waging war on innocent civilians. Our mission is to rid this district of those who rebel against our protectorate. Your safety, and the safety of your village can only be assured by your cooperation."

The old man removed his hat. "*Con permiso*, Captain. The people of Tanuba are innocent, sir. The guerilla forces come to our village at night. They eat our rice and give speeches to recruit our young men into the fighting. They are Tagalog like us, but not from here. We do not know them. We have told them we will not fight against the Americans, but they say if we do not cooperate, our village will be destroyed and our families broken apart. The boy killed today was not in the fighting. He was only a child, but a bullet struck him down, and now he is dead. You see, *Señor*, our families are already tearing apart."

Captain Baston leaned down, cupped the old man's chin in his palm and gazed into his eyes. "So you say, my friend. I understand. Lieutenant Alstaetter, place this man in custody and one other. That one over there will do. We'll take them to San Isidro with the other prisoner. I'd be interested to know just what kind of liars these people are."

Then he raised his voice to the villagers, "You must not give aid to the insurgent forces. You must not listen to their talk of a peasant uprising. Their claim of fighting for your freedom is a pretense, a guise for outlawry. You must turn them away from your village. The United States Army will protect you. From now on American law prevails in Tanuba, law founded on the principle that all men are created equal. American law! Where every man has certain inalienable rights, and where you, the Filipino people, will enjoy the rights of freedom and independence when you demonstrate you have pulled yourselves up to deserve them."

Lieutenant Alstaetter gave the order, and H Company formed up in the center of the village, the prisoners tethered to the packhorses at the rear of the column. As they moved out, Fagen tried not to look at the silent, sullen faces of the miserable villagers. Two women ran crying beside Captain Baston's big horse, clutched frantically at his saddle with gnarled fingers and begged him not to take their loved ones. After a few yards, he ordered the column to halt and stared coldly down at the desperate, hysterical women, the malevolence in his eyes quickly frightening them away. Then he turned to the lieutenant. "I observed the way you carried out your duties during the ambush today, my young friend. You acquitted yourself well. I'll make sure Colonel Funston hears of it."

"Thank you, sir."

"Now you've tasted a bit of fire, and you've seen how treacherous these natives can be. This has been a good lesson for you and your men."

"The men performed very well, sir," Lieutenant Alstaetter urged.

"They performed well for Negroes, I agree, but isn't there something we've left undone?"

"Sir?"

"That buffalo in the corral back there. I'll wager the insurrectos get as much use out of it as the villagers. I don't think it would be soldierly to leave that resource to the enemy, do you?" Captain Baston didn't wait for an answer. Without a moment's hesitation, he drew his carbine from its red scabbard, aimed and put a bullet through the animal's heart, killing it instantly. "How's that for a good shot, lieutenant?"

The end of a long day. As H Company marched down the main road toward their San Isidro camp, Fagen replayed in his mind the events he'd witnessed at Tanuba and tried to make sense of it. He'd discovered something in himself that day, and he still felt the warm glow of the Almighty's touch, but what they'd done there wasn't like any warfare he'd ever heard of. Certainly not like anything he'd trained for. Had they accomplished what they'd set out to do? Fagen couldn't say. He felt little of the pride due a soldier upon defeating the enemy. Where was the glory, the sanctification? How had he served God or country by squandering His might on defenseless peasants?

Fagen looked around at the faces of the men marching with him and saw no doubt or concern about what they'd done in Tanuba. Was he the only one with an empty feeling in his gut? Had he gone soft in the head? He cursed his faithlessness and asked himself where it was written every private soldier that ever skirmished with the enemy should be raised up, cloaked in the stars and stripes, hailed the conquering hero. Maybe what happened at the village was all there was to war. Maybe he'd been a fool to expect more.

His thoughts drifted to the man whose shoulder he'd injured during the ambush. He knew he'd never forget the terror in the young rebel's eyes the moment he realized he could not defeat his enemy on the battlefield. Fagen considered the man exceedingly brave to stand and face him while his comrades retreated all around him. He felt a pang of remorse for the injuries he'd inflicted upon the man, but glad he didn't have to die. A prisoner now, separated from his people and loved ones, at least he'd sleep under a roof and eat decent food. How bad could that be compared to life in the jungle? He'd certainly made out better than that unfortunate boy in the village who stood up just in time to stop a stray bullet.

David Fagen couldn't deny his first taste of battle had not been what he'd imagined, and he wondered whether war ever lived up to expectation. No matter. He was a Negro soldier in service to his country, and if this was the kind of war he was called to fight, so be it. He turned his attention to the corporal who marched beside him calling cadence. His legs were so bowed Fagen wondered how he kept pace, but he had a beautiful baritone voice, and his songs made the miles melt away. He wore a leather thong around his neck, and just under his collar, Fagen caught the glimmer of a Spanish silver coin.

CHAPTER 5 - CLARITA

Uniforms starched and pressed, Ellis Fairbanks and David Fagen stepped through the front gates onto the road to San Isidro. "I feel like a bird let out of his cage," Ellis said. "We don't have to be back until sundown. What're we going to do, Davey?"

"We're going to eat, Ellis. I can't wait to get some food that's not army and not rice."

H Company had been in San Isidro over a month. The men had worked hard, seen plenty of action and on this Sunday were granted their first leave. To Ellis, liberty on that beautiful morning was just another act of kindness by his Uncle Sam. Looking forward to exploring the town, the two men laughed and made jokes as they headed up the road. As they walked, Fagen couldn't help being touched by his cousin's innocent excitement at what the day might bring, and it struck him that Ellis Fairbanks was the good side of everyone he'd ever known.

San Isidro stretched for a half-mile along the *Rio De La Pampanga* where it made a wide, sweeping turn to the west then back south again. A trading center, the streets were busy, and even on Sunday, most of the merchants and vendors open for business, and shoppers crowded the boardwalks. Compared to the many tiny rice farm villages the Americans had been through on field patrol, San Isidro was a big city.

The two men turned onto a wide, cobblestone thoroughfare, bustling with activity. Two-story buildings lined the street, business offices above and shopkeepers below. On the second floor of one building, a dentist advertised with a three-foot high tooth painted on his window. Next to that was a cartage and trucking business, and at the end an office that dealt in currency exchange. More merchants on the street level offered everything, literally from soup to nuts.

Dogs barked and romped, and children ran everywhere through the crowd playing hoops and stickball, while their parents stood on the boardwalks in little groups and gossiped. Old folks passed the time in the shade of the buildings that lined the street. In the midst of all this, weaving through the pedestrian traffic, a continuous parade of tiny, single-seat, horse-drawn buggies the Filipinos called *caromatas*, painted shiny black or dark green, and some with bright yellow wheels and spokes. The owners of those charming, yet practical buggies showed off for the crowd, sitting tall in their seats, dressed in their Sunday best.

The two Negro soldiers strolled the boardwalk passing countless merchants in makeshift stalls that sold fine looking hand-made knives, ladies hats and more. On one corner, they watched a man roll huge tobacco leaves into tight little cigars. At the end of the block, in the shade of a small palm grove, four young girls sat behind a row of wide, round baskets filled with bananas, mangoes and oranges. Fagen chose a mango and gave the girl a coin. She giggled at the two men and hid her eyes. Since they'd arrived in town, the girls had been the first to notice them. The street so alive, so filled with the energy of people going about their Sunday affairs, two *Negrito Americanos* minding their own business were not enough novelty to draw attention.

They passed by a man with one arm who sat on a wooden campstool holding a gunnysack open between his knees. He tipped it towards them and displayed five tiny brown puppies squirming at the bottom. He took one out and held it in his hand. Fagen said no thanks and gave the man a peso, but then had to drag Ellis away.

At the next intersection, they came to a long building divided into shops with glass display windows under a low tin roof. The signs painted on the windows in Spanish and Tagalog, Fagen couldn't read them, but had only to look through the glass to know what the words said. The shops in that building were devoted entirely to wood products. The first store was occupied by a coopersmith. Inside barrels were of every shape and capacity. Ellis was entranced by the man's system of sorting the staves by size, hung with knotted ropes from the ceiling. A coffin maker was in the next shop, and a furniture maker next to that, but Ellis' favorite, the shop that contained dozens of carved wooden toys and games. There were elaborate chessboards with wild, devilish faces carved on the pieces, sets of brightly painted wooden balls with matching mallets, a family of colorful marionettes on strings and one whole wall of the shop set aside for beautiful dolls in elaborate dresses and real hair.

Farther on, they found what they'd been looking for, a wide-open storefront with a sign overhead. *Restaurant*. The only customers, they entered and sat down on two wooden benches before a small table. Soon, a woman came out followed by a child, a girl of twelve, carrying a pitcher of water and two cups. Fagen smiled and said, "*Buenos Dias.*"

"I speak English, sir," the woman said. She reached deep into her apron pocket and brought out woven place mats and matching napkins. "Here in the islands are many languages, I would guess three or four dozen. Most Filipinos around here are Tagalog, and that is what we speak. Then of course the Chinese have their dialects, not to mention the Thais and the Malays."

Fagen was surprised. In the rural villages, hardly anyone spoke English, but things were different in the city. He thought even the little girl understood everything said.

"Can we buy a meal now?"

The woman nodded. "Yes. We can serve you meat, fried vegetables, rice, beans and beer."

Ellis said, "Everything but the rice, please."

The old woman turned and disappeared into the kitchen while the little girl brought spoons and two sharp kitchen knives. She tried not to, but couldn't help herself and stole sideways glances at the two men while she set their table.

Ellis smiled. "I bet we're the first black people she's ever seen, Davey." He held his big hand out to her. She stopped for a moment, looked at it like it was a museum piece, and then reached out and touched the tips of his fingers with hers. Feeling Ellis' rough skin, much darker than her own, brought a smile, but when the woman barked something from the kitchen, the girl turned and ran, and they never saw her again.

Although spiced more than the Americans were used to, the food was excellent, and they had two helpings of everything but the beer. Sergeant Rivers had warned H Company about the potency of the Filipino brews, and as the men rarely drank spirits, they had only one glass each.

During their meal, several Filipino families came in and carried food away in baskets lined with cloth. Later, two white soldiers sat down at a table across the room and ordered lunch. From the Nebraska volunteers, they didn't like seeing colored men eating in the same restaurant with whites, and they sat and stared menacingly from under their hats. Ellis didn't notice. He liked to talk while he ate, and that day he talked up a storm.

Fagen saw the two Nebraskans come in, but didn't look their way. He knew they'd be offended by Negroes eating at a table near them instead of sweeping floors or cleaning cuspidors. He hoped for no trouble, but in a few minutes one of the men turned his chair, palmed his kitchen knife and flicked pieces of his meal in their direction. Fagen kept his attention on Ellis, encouraged him to keep talking, but little balls of rice and soggy flaps of onion flew through the air and made soft, splattering sounds as they hit the floor around them. Difficult to ignore. The other man, enjoying the show, sat back and laughed, a humorless cackle.

Hate-filled white men had taunted Fagen before, and over the years he'd learned to think before he acted. Bitter experience had taught him, in the army or out, a colored man rarely profited from a confrontation with a white man. He glanced at the two Nebraskans. Not very big and hardly more than adolescents, Fagen guessed they'd intimidate easily, so he interrupted Ellis. "Did you see where the lady put the water pitcher?"

"Sure. You need some? I'll get it."

Ellis pushed back from the table and walked the four steps to the sideboard. Fagen's little maneuver worked. When the white soldiers got a look at Ellis, they realized immediately two of them wouldn't be enough, gulped their beer and left.

Ellis raked the last of his vegetables into his spoon, then tipped his plate and poured off the juice. "Davey, I've been thinking. Filipino people don't seem so bad when we're not fighting them."

"I don't suppose anyone seems so bad when you're not fighting him, Ellis. You generally don't see the best side of a man when he's trying to shoot you or cut your head off."

Ellis pointed his spoon at his cousin. "That's not what I mean, and you know it. If you've looked around today, then you've seen these folks the same as I have. Filipinos are just like regular people! They're polite and they smile. They have jobs and wives, and their kids play the same games as kids in the States. I haven't seen anyone mad at us yet, and a half-day has gone by without anyone calling us nigger. I guess I didn't know what to expect from Asian people, but I sure didn't expect this."

Natural for Ellis to see the sunny side of people and ignore their dark side, but not so for Fagen. He couldn't completely forget they were at war with the Filipinos, at least some of them. Ellis wasn't entirely wrong, nobody had been mad at them all day, nor had anyone called them nigger, but Fagen knew too well they were invaders in that country, foreign soldiers and didn't really belong there. These Filipinos seemed friendly enough, but he'd been in combat against other members of their race and couldn't accept Ellis' notion that a Filipino actually liked an American, no matter how civilized and hospitable the people around them appeared.

When they paid for their food, Fagen left an extra fifty cents on the table, an extravagant gesture, but he wanted to make a favorable impression. He said *adios* to the woman. She pocketed the money, but as they walked out from under the canvas awning into the sunlight, she called to him, "Black solider! It is an insult these days to speak Spanish to a Filipino. Now no loyal Filipino speaks the language of his oppressor." Fagen looked back into the dim interior of the restaurant, couldn't see her, but took her remark to be more than just friendly instruction. He took it to be a warning.

Outside, the sun high overhead, the two men strolled through the crowd until they came to a little gathering of people around a wooden platform covered by a huge umbrella at the top of a long pole. A Filipino man moved among the onlookers playing an accordion and singing a lively tune.

In a moment, two young women climbed the stairs, stepped onto the platform and began dancing to the music. Identically dressed in white blouses and pleated red dresses, each had an arrangement of hibiscus flowers in her hair, wrists and ankles. The man grinned and played his song, but all attention fixed on the dancers as they paraded around the platform in opposite directions, weaving in and out with the music. Then the man played a different melody, and the young ladies took positions at the edge of the floor facing each other. They slowly folded their arms over their heads until the flowers at their wrists joined those in their hair and on the downbeat began the intricate steps of a stately folk dance. Their beauty and grace mesmerized the onlookers as the two girls wound in and out, back and forth. Fagen saw joy on the faces in the crowd. Clearly, the dance had meaning and was symbolic of something important in their culture. The dancers were so expressive, so graceful in their movements, he was sure their performance that day was exceptional.

The spell was broken suddenly when a ruckus broke out a few yards away. Fagen didn't see what started it, but when he looked saw a cavalry officer and a sergeant standing over a young Filipino lying in the street beside an overturned wheelchair. The man had stumps for legs and did his best to protect himself from flying leather while the officer savagely kicked him. The officer, a lieutenant, circled around the man and screamed at the top of his lungs, "You stole my purse! Give it back you thieving gook bastard!"

Immediately, a crowd formed. The old women and children, who just a moment before had been enjoying a peaceful Sunday afternoon, now disappeared. Only men remained in the street and some of their wives, knotted in an angry circle ten deep around the Americans, and by the murderous looks on their faces, it was clear to Fagen the situation could turn ugly fast. The two American soldiers saw it too. The lieutenant halted his attack on the helpless cripple and looked around at the growing mob of outraged Filipinos. Furious, red-faced and sweating, his voice shrill with indignation, he shrieked at the grumbling crowd, "He stole my purse! He stole my purse!"

The sergeant bent down and pulled a small leather bag from inside the cripple's shirt and held it up to the angry mob as proof of the lieutenant's charge, but that made no difference to the Filipinos, who shouted threats and curses while their circle closed ominously.

Fagen didn't know what to do. He and Ellis were unarmed. It was Sunday, the last thing they'd expected to encounter was two Americans in the middle of a Filipino street riot.

They stood just twenty yards away, close enough for Fagen to predict it wouldn't be long before blood was spilled. Neither the lieutenant nor the sergeant had noticed the Negro soldiers standing outside the circle of Filipinos. Fagen worried that if he intruded into the situation then, he might stir the mob into more than just threats, but if he did nothing, he might witness the massacre of two American soldiers. Ellis waited for his cousin to decide.

Just then, Fagen heard a voice at his shoulder. "The man squirming in the dust is Manuel Garcia, the pickpocket. Four years ago, the Spanish caught him taking food from a warehouse. They put him in stocks and left him there until his legs rotted away. Since then, he picks the pocket of every soldier he gets close to. He thinks it's his right."

Fagen turned and beheld the most beautiful woman he'd ever seen standing at his side, shielding her eyes from the sun. Tall, light brown skin, dark eyes and long, dark hair held loosely back by a small mother of pearl comb, she looked very different from the other Filipino women Fagen had seen. She held herself erect, to meet the world face on, and she exuded great confidence. Through all the confusion around them, the girl sensed his indecision, smiled, and Fagen's heart began to melt. "They say if a pickpocket is noticed, his career is at an end," she said with a little wink. "Manuel Garcia must be getting lazy." Again that smile. That smile! How could any woman be so beautiful?

Just then, the lieutenant spotted them. He and the sergeant stood back-to-back facing the mob, their pistols drawn, inching toward their horses tied ten yards away.

"You! You two, over here!" the officer barked. "This God damned town is full of thieves and murderers. Get over here now!"

David Fagen and Ellis Fairbanks moved into the crowd. The girl caught Fagen's sleeve and stopped him for a moment. "Be careful," she smiled, "but don't worry. This is a game we play when Manuel Garcia gets caught."

Ellis took the lead, and they pushed through the angry mob. Not knowing what else to do, they faced the crowd, their arms outstretched in a preposterous, futile attempt to push back the angry Filipinos. The sergeant pulled his hat tighter. "Jesus, Mary and Joseph laddies, where the hell are your weapons?"

"We're on day pass, Sergeant."

Then the lieutenant said, "God damned coons are useless in a uniform."

No choice but to give way by inches as the crowd moved forward, Ellis held his big arms wide, fingers extended, straining against the slow crush. Fagen remembered what the girl had said about this being a game. He hoped she was right and hoped those two white soldiers behind him didn't panic and start shooting.

Soon, the lieutenant and the sergeant saw their chance to make a break and took it. Without a word and without looking back, they jumped on their horses, raced up the street and out of town. At the last moment, for a distraction, the sergeant flung the lieutenant's purse over his shoulder into the crowd, but no one bothered with it. Surrounded by a hundred silent Filipinos, Fagen looked around and observed their faces as they dispersed. He saw no hatred in their eyes; the Filipinos didn't even seem angry any longer. They just walked away as though the two black men were invisible or didn't exist.

It took a moment for Fagen to realize what had happened. They'd come to the aid of fellow Americans, and cowards, the men had turned tail and run. Suddenly, a terrible emptiness swept over him, his head began to spin, and he grew weak as a child. He felt as though he'd been gutted, his insides scraped out and the skin sewn up over the hole. Fagen sat down on the boardwalk and watched Ellis lift Manuel Garcia back into his wheelchair. The little Filipino had a few bruises and a small cut over his right eye, but was otherwise unhurt. Ellis picked up the lieutenant's purse and gave it to him. The cripple snatched it out of his hand as though Ellis were the pickpocket, and then wheeled himself furiously around the corner and out of sight.

"Are you all right?"

Fagen turned, and she was sitting on the boardwalk beside him. When he saw her, his heart skipped a few beats, and in his weakened condition, he thought he might faint. "The Americans say all life is precious, but I think they mean mostly their own."

49

Fagen stammered something in response. Later, when he tried, he couldn't remember what. A full minute passed before he moved from dumbstruck to tongue-tied. The girl sat beside him waiting, smiling all the while. Soon Fagen felt his strength return, and the empty, forsaken feeling fade away.

"I would like to hear the conversation between them when they finally stop to change horses," the girl said.

"Change horses?" Fagen wasn't sure what she meant.

She laughed and pushed a lock of hair over her ear. "They left in such a hurry, the lieutenant rode away on the sergeant's horse."

Clearly, the girl found the whole episode amusing. Fagen wouldn't have thought it possible, but each time he looked at her, she was more beautiful. When she smiled, her mouth turned up at the corners revealing a perfect set of small, white teeth. She had a high, wide brow, prominent cheekbones and a long thin neck. Fagen saw a small jagged scar just in front of her left ear. She leaned toward him and put her cool, dry palm on his arm.

"My name is Clarita Socorro."

"David Fagen. My friend there is Ellis Fairbanks."

"Are you feeling better, David Fagen? What will you and your friend do now?"

"I think we should be getting back to garrison."

A frown crossed her pretty lips. "So soon?"

"We'd better report back. Something tells me we haven't heard the last of this."

"Can you come back next Sunday? I will be here."

"I will if I can."

"Good. I will introduce you to my grandmother."

CHAPTER 6 - SILENT CONFIRMATION

David Fagen didn't go back to San Isidro the following Sunday afternoon, or the Sunday after that. He and Ellis reported to Sergeant Rivers, ate a cold supper and after roll call spent the evening checking their gear and catching up on the latest gossip. On their walk back to camp, they'd agreed it best not to tell anyone about the incident in the village. It had been none of their business. They couldn't fully explain what had happened because they didn't know themselves, and besides, Fagen had always lived by the principle it was best to stay out of the affairs of white men in general and white officers in particular.

Later that night, Ellis stretched out on his cot and fell asleep in only a moment, a gift he had. Events of the day were for the day, the night for sleeping. David Fagen didn't share that gift. He was still bothered by the despicable behavior of his countrymen who ran from the village and left them to face an angry mob alone. Fagen had grown up around blacks. He hadn't much experience dealing with white men, in or out of the army. Either way, what experience he had wasn't good. His mother had told him long ago not to expect much from white folks, and he'd never be disappointed.

He knew most white men didn't care for Negroes. That was a fact of life, but he never imagined American soldiers, black or white, would forsake each other in the face of trouble. One thing was certain, Fagen never again wanted to experience the savage, empty feeling of betrayal that swept over him that day. He felt as though he'd been obscenely, personally violated, that everything he held sacred had been profaned. His foundation had been rocked. He'd learned a bitter lesson, one he knew he'd not soon forget.

As Fagen lay on his cot rehashing events, his head still spun from his encounter with the strange and mysterious young girl who'd called herself Clarita. In the village, she'd appeared out of nowhere, smiling up at him through the chaos and curses and bared teeth of a street riot; and when she spoke, he'd been transported with her into the calm at the eye of the storm, and suddenly, everything around him had become as distant and unreal as a photograph in a stereoscope.

Who was this girl, and why had she spoken to him? He remembered the cool dryness of her fingertips when she touched his arm, and the way she'd remained so calm, almost playful in the midst of the unruliness around them. Never before had he been that close to another human so beautiful, and his heart pounded wildly when he thought of seeing her again. San Isidro was a good-sized town. He wondered how he'd find her. He remembered she wanted him to meet her grandmother. Why? What, he wondered, was in store for him when he next met that strange and wonderful girl?

These thoughts were in David Fagen's mind when an angry roar brought him suddenly out of his reverie. "H COMPANY, FALL IN!"

Sergeant Rivers stood in full uniform in the assembly area with Lieutenant Alstaetter and another officer. "Let's go! Move it! Form up on me!" The Negro soldiers raced from their tents, rubbing sleep from their eyes, buttoning their trousers as they ran. Rivers cast a cold eye on the men as they lined up. Clearly in no mood for complaints, the company sergeant's grim visage radiated trouble.

The men stood at rigid attention in the moonlight. Sergeant Rivers did an about face and saluted the lieutenant. "All present or accounted for, sir."

Lieutenant Alstaetter and the other officer walked down the first rank of soldiers. A corporal followed them carrying a lantern. From the corner of his eye, Fagen saw the man with Lieutenant Alstaetter was the cavalry officer from the village and felt his knees weaken. He wanted to run, but knew he could not. The two officers stopped in front of him, and the corporal lifted the light. "That's him. Now let's find the other one."

Sergeant Rivers stepped forward. "No need to look any further, sir." He turned to the assembled troops. "Fagen and Fairbanks stand fast. All you other men fall out!"

For a moment, the men just stood there and exchanged nervous glances, wondering what had happened, but then Rivers roared again, "I SAID FALL OUT, DAMN YOU!" H Company broke and ran for the tents and left David Fagen and Ellis Fairbanks standing at attention by themselves in the moonlight.

The cavalry officer turned to Lieutenant Alstaetter. "Thank you Lieutenant. I'll take it from here. These men are under arrest. Corporal, place them in the stockade."

As the corporal locked handcuffs and leg chains on the two privates, Sergeant Rivers stepped forward. "Sir, may I know the charges?"

The churlish lieutenant turned toward Rivers and lifted his brow. "If you must know, Sergeant, these men are accused of lewd conduct, brawling, public drunkenness, inciting a riot and any other charges I dream up between now and morning. Now you are dismissed as well. I suggest you leave this matter to me. It appears you have more than a full-time job supervising the men in your charge." The lieutenant turned on his heel and walked away.

The garrison stockade, a walled-off corner of an old paint storage shed, was a temporary holding cell for soldiers who'd committed minor offenses. Those found guilty of more serious crimes were transferred to the stockade at Camp McKinley. David Fagen and Ellis Fairbanks spent that night and two more in confinement. Once a day, a guard opened the heavy wooden door and delivered a pan of biscuits and a pail of water, exchanged the night soil bucket, and then left without a word. The heat of day forced the breathable air from the cell, and fumes from the tins of paint, turpentine and mineral spirits burned their lungs and made their heads pound. Fagen scraped a hole in a corner of the cell's dirt floor for Ellis when the fumes overcame him and he vomited uncontrollably. Heat and poisonous air quickly weakened the two men. To them, each passing hour in the nightmarish room seemed like days.

Late the third night, a sergeant carrying an oil lamp opened the door. Light flooded the cell, temporarily blinding the two prisoners. "Could I have a word with you, laddies?" Immediately, Fagen recognized him. Now, he whistled a merry tune under his breath, and his face showed nothing of the fear of that day in San Isidro when surrounded by the angry Filipino mob. The man's casual, off-hand manner hit Fagen wrong, and a sudden boiling anger surged through his veins. He tried to stand up, but the long days and nights in the cell had taken their toll, and he'd grown weaker than he realized.

He fell back on one knee and glared up at the sergeant. "What do you want?"

"You should take it easy, young fellow. You're not looking so good." The sergeant stopped just inside the doorway and wrinkled his nose. "The smell of paint in here is enough to gag a skunk. I think I'd better set this lamp outside in good air. If these fumes were to touch flame, we could find ourselves blown to smithereens."

Cool night air flooded through the open door into the tiny room. Fagen lifted his head and took in oxygen. Ellis sat up, leaned against the opposite wall, and gazed feebly at the cavalry sergeant. Dried vomit stained his chin, his eyes yellow and bloodshot. "Why are you doing this to us?" he pleaded. "We never did anything to you. I'd rather be horsewhipped than locked up in here."

The sergeant looked around the tiny cell. "I think I'd agree with you on that one, big man, but you'd do well to be careful what you wish for. It's not me keeping you here, you see. I'm Irish, don't you know. The Sons of Erin wouldn't do this to a man. It's not in our nature to be cruel to another. More often than not, we've been on the receiving end of treatment like this. You lads are here because you had the bad luck to get between a cavalry officer from Virginia and his pride."

Fagen needed every ounce of self-restraint to keep from strangling the chatty little sergeant with the pink cheeks and flat round face. "The Irish wouldn't put a man in a hell hole like this, but they'll stay silent while another man does it."

The sergeant squatted, and Fagen smelled whiskey on his breath. "Now there you've done it, haven't you? You've gone straight to the heart of the matter. Silence is what I've come to discuss.

"The truth of the matter, lads, is the story of what happened in San Isidro has already been written. All it needs now is your... What did the lieutenant call it? Oh yes, silent confirmation. It seems you two black fellows, not respecting local custom, tried to have your way with one of the native women. When her family discovered what you were about, they screamed like banshees, and you told them all to go to hell. That's when the real fun started. You lads were in a fine spot. The lieutenant and me happened to be passing by. Seeing the commotion, we stopped to help, and right away half the blessed town was involved. That's when you boys ran and hid yourselves leaving me and the lieutenant at the mercy of the crowd."

"That's a damned lie!" Ellis spat.

The sergeant's tone became conspiratorial. "If I was you, big man, I'd have done with that kind of talk. It won't pay. If I was you, I'd stand before the provost marshal and admit what I'd done. Then I'd be turned loose from this place." The Irishman pulled out his brass pocket watch. "I'd be turned loose and back in me own bunk in less than an hour, slumbering peacefully until bird fart."

"So that's it. All we have to do is admit to a lie and it's over?"

"Repentance and redemption, lad," the sergeant smiled, his eyes wandering to the ceiling. "It's Almighty God's gift to the common man."

"And you could arrange this right now? Tonight?"

"There would be just one other detail, boys. That would be the loss of a month's pay for each of you."

Ellis jumped to his feet, "A month's pay! To hell with that!" He went for him, and the sergeant scrambled for the door. Fagen moved quickly between the two men. The sudden exertion made him nauseous and light-headed.

"That is another matter isn't it?" the Irishman said. "You see, there's the purse that's come up missing. It must have gotten lost or stolen in the struggle to rescue you boys. Who knows what happened to it? The lieutenant said there was eighteen dollars and change in it. Adding that to the cost of the purse itself, he feels it's only right, and a month's pay each is more than fair."

"Fair is what you call it. I call it robbery and a damned lie."

"Take it easy, Ellis. Let this Irish gentleman finish."

The sergeant held up his hands, palms forward. "I've said my piece, boys. You've heard the whole lot. You were caught up in the flow of events, as they say. Truth be told, you probably couldn't have done nothing else. Bad things just happen to common people like us, lads. We don't often have a lot of choices. Hell, in another life I might even believe your side of the story."

The sergeant stepped outside the door and picked up his lantern. He stood for a moment breathing the fresh night air, and then leaned in and whispered to Fagen, "Looks like the big man is a degree more upset than you about the matter of the pay. I can't say I blame him, but whatever you decide, don't let them divide you, son. Stay of one mind. They've been trying to separate my own people for years now, and we've lost everything, but at least we've stayed together. You do the same." He winked, and then turned and disappeared into the darkness.

Fagen paced in circles breathing the poisonous air in the tiny cell. He looked at Ellis' vomit-stained clothes and felt again the painful cramping in his own gut. *Bad things just happen to common people like us.* The Irishman had made a "take it or leave it" offer. Fagen knew what had to be done. He pounded on the door and called out, "Sergeant, you can tell the provost marshal he has our silent confirmation, and apologize to the lieutenant for any inconvenience we may have caused him."

CHAPTER 7 - MT. ARAYAT

Albert Fagen went fishing every day except Sundays or during lightning storms. Each morning after breakfast, Eunice Fagen kissed him on the cheek and sent him out the door and down to the Skunk River with his cane pole and a canvas bag for his catch.

People in Grayson County had known for years Albert Fagen was "touched" in the head. All he ever did was fish, and all he ever talked about was fishing, but he wasn't even particularly good at it. On those rare occasions when he brought home a catfish or a sturgeon, Eunice cleaned it, then rolled it in corn meal and fried it in lard for supper. As a boy, David Fagen listened for hours to his father go over the details of where the fish was caught, what the surface of the river was like when it rose to the bait, and how he played it out just right, and then got it in the bag. Too young then to know his father was "touched," Fagen found out later he'd been stabbed in the neck at a barn dance, the wound hadn't healed right, and he'd never been the same afterward.

On the morning of Fagen's fifth birthday, Eunice finally agreed to let the old man take his son fishing. Breakfast over, he went behind the door for his pole and a smaller one for the boy.

"You keep your wits about you, Bert," Eunice scolded him. "The boy is not accustomed to water, so keep your eye on him and don't let him get turtle-snapped, or worse yet, snake bit."

"Eunice, nothing will happen to the boy only that he catches a fish."

On that clear, late spring morning, man and boy set off down through the fields together. Although not a big man, Albert Fagen walked fast, like he had an appointment to keep, and to stay up little Davey took two strides to his one. The edge of their field dropped off into a dark hollow, overgrown with stands of scrub oak. The ground slippery under their feet, they followed a narrow, winding path and soon made their way to the river.

They traced the shoreline through the shadows until the bank widened, and the sun shone through an open space in the trees. Albert hadn't spoken to the boy since they'd left the cabin. While he walked, he looked down once or twice and smiled like he'd just noticed his son was along. Every now and then he patted the boy on the shoulder, but mostly he just walked, whistling a tune under his breath.

Soon, they reached a spot where the river widened to form a pool, the water black and still. Just behind them, where the bank sloped gently up from the shore, lay a depression in the sand lined with a thick mattress of dry, pressed marsh grass, a nest for a mule deer and her fawns. Albert carried the fishing poles onto the little beach, sat down and carefully pinned a dead grasshopper on each hook and a piece of cork for a float. A quick flick of his wrist, and both lines were cast, the little corks bobbing side-by-side. He handed the smaller pole to Davey, and the boy sat on a rock by the river's edge. Satisfied he had a good set, the old man smiled again, wedged the butt of his cane pole between two logs, and then lay down on his back in the grassy depression. Still whistling that same tune, he carefully covered himself with a thick layer of the dry grass. Soon, completely hidden in the vegetation, only his face showing through, he whistled and sang to himself as he stared up at the blue sky. After a while he said, "A man doesn't like to eat a grasshopper, Davey, but a fish does."

The boy sat for an hour, staring a hole through the cork waiting for a fish to drag it under, but none did. During all that time, his father neither moved nor spoke. He'd talk to himself a while, too low for the boy to hear, laugh a little, sing to himself, and then whistle the whole thing out, *Buck Dancer's Choice*, a common barn dance tune.

David Fagen had never been fishing before, but even as a five-year-old, he guessed his father's behavior out of the ordinary. What he wasn't sure was whether it was not ordinary fishing behavior. Finding no solution to that puzzle, he decided to explore the river around the bend. He discovered the higher ground farther along, where big trees hung over the bank. He walked up and sat for twenty minutes on the edge of a high bluff under an old oak and pitched stones to watch them skitter across the black water.

Davey's midday quiet was abruptly shattered when the earth gave an agonized groan, and the whole bank gave way all at once. Suddenly, the boy was upended and hurled toward the river in a shower of mud, rocks and oak tree. He hit the water hard and was quickly pressed under by the weight of the rotting trunk. At one moment, he'd been a small boy enjoying the pleasures of a sunny afternoon, and the next, a struggling river rat, submerged in rancid, stinking water, fighting desperately to claw his way to the surface. Branches of the tree entwined in his shirt, and try as hard as he might, he was pulled down deeper and deeper. Soon, both the tree and the boy hit bottom. Oily water filled his mouth and nose, and he felt the river flooding in through his eyes and ears. The water was everywhere, devouring him. He knew soon it would take over his body and there would be no more flesh or bone, nothing left of him, only water. He kicked hard against the trunk again and again. He twisted and turned and finally tore out of his shirt. He was free, but now which way to go? Which way was up? Nothing but darkness all around, he kicked hard again and almost blacked out from the shock. Something was wrong with his right leg. He gasped in pain, a good thing, because when he did, he saw the bubbles rise and a dim shaft of light shining on the surface above him. The sun shone through the gap left by the fallen tree, and he fought for it.

Unconscious for a long time, when the boy awoke, the sun had dipped behind the hill, and he felt the mud at the water's edge giving up its heat. He sat up, spat the sour taste of river out of his mouth and checked himself for damage. An ugly gash just above his right knee, but the bleeding had stopped on its own, and he was otherwise unhurt.

When he got back, Albert was busy picking dry marsh grass from his clothes, his fishing pole where he'd left it, wedged between the logs. Smiling, he brought in his line, examined the soggy grasshopper on the hook, and then pitched it into the brush. He looked at the boy and said, "I guess we should have put night crawlers on the bill o' fare, Davey." Five-year-old David Fagen, half-drowned, bruised, bloody and shirtless wanted his father to sweep him up in his big arms and hold him, tell him every thing was all right, that he'd take care of him, but he didn't. Albert Fagen was "touched," and nothing Davey could have done would change that.

Those lingering childhood memories haunted Fagen as H Company worked its way up a creek overflowing its banks under triple canopy in the foothills at the base of Mt. Arayat. The fifth day of their mission to search out and destroy rebel forces, and if lucky, find and capture Aguinaldo himself. So far, all they'd seen was water. In that jungle, sunlight never reached under the canopy. Everything was water. A sticky, spongy slime covered the earth, six feet deep in places, and the trees were covered from trunk to branch in pungent, rotting moss. So much water a man could drown just breathing the air. Their fifth day, and the men were soaked to the bone.

After the second night, before the pack mules turned around, they'd exchanged soggy bedrolls for canvas sleeping tarps lightening their load somewhat, but then Sergeant Rivers ordered them to take on extra ammunition, so no real relief. Since then, they'd carried everything they needed to make war on their backs, and the weight of it cut into their shoulders and raised boils on their hips. Impossible to get dry, some of the men suffered from what they called duck foot, nasty open sores between the toes that oozed blood and pus. Lieutenant Alstaetter showed them how to wring the water out of their extra socks, and then carry them under their hats on the theory that was the driest place to be found, but in those conditions, no one could tell whether any one place was dryer or wetter than another.

Their orders were to link up that afternoon with Captain Baston and a company of Kansas volunteers coming down from the north with fresh supplies: a welcome prospect, H Company had had enough of tinned meat and cold rice. Fagen couldn't fathom how a rebel Filipino lived in that hellish place and kept up the strength and will to fight. Mother Nature's evil, black-hearted twin ruled there. Not a place for men. If they'd pushed the insurrectos into that God-forsaken jungle, then surely they already must have won the war.

No matter, to him anything was better than being locked up in that poisonous tomb back in camp. The Irish sergeant had been as good as his word. Less than an hour after he left that night, someone opened the cell door, and the two jailbirds dragged themselves back to their tent. They slept through the following morning, the first time either of them had missed a formation. Sergeant Rivers didn't speak to them, except to put them on camp detail for the whole of the next week, where they drew every dirty job the army ever invented. Sergeant Rivers knew the truth of what had happened in San Isidro, but it didn't matter the two were blameless. They'd been involved in it and brought unwanted attention to his company. That was enough for him. A sin against H Company was a personal insult to Rivers and unpardonable.

Fagen knew no one ever got close to Sergeant Rivers. The man had no friends. The most distant, standoffish black man Fagen had ever met, he let no one inside him. The men of H Company knew when they were included in his life, under the protection of his umbrella, but when Rivers turned his back on the two hapless privates that week, it hurt them more than all the stable cleaning and latrine duty. Fagen discovered then if you were out of favor with Sergeant Rivers, it was as though you'd never existed. He'd always been a cold man, but when he turned away altogether, it's not like you'd lived once and were now dead, it's as though you'd never lived, never made any difference in his life at all. He so completely shut you out you felt lower than the creatures that scurried about the latrine floor. Incrementally, as the days passed, Sergeant Rivers allowed them to live again, and they prayed the incident was finally behind them. Just then, as Fagen worked his way up that swollen stream, his thoughts were of his father and his childhood baptismal. He heard the echo of the old man's footsteps on the riverbank and wondered how much of Albert Fagen was in him.

On the right flank, clawing through the underbrush, Youngblood spotted it first. Five steps farther, and he wouldn't have seen it at all. Sergeant Rivers sent word, and Lieutenant Alstaetter and the rest of the men came forward. A cave, the mouth hidden by dense foliage that hung from a massive outcropping of solid rock paralleling the stream. It wasn't obvious, but closer inspection revealed it had been recently used.

Lieutenant Alstaetter formed the men into a defensive perimeter around the mouth and sent two reinforced squads to scout the area. Three men climbed the rocks and hacked at the vegetation that concealed the entrance. This done, the lieutenant stripped to the waist, checked his revolver and put a second one in his belt. "I'll need two volunteers to go in with me."

Fagen raised his hand. "I'll go."

"Good. Who else?"

Youngblood had discovered the cave, he wasn't about to let somebody else explore it. "Here, sir. I'll go."

The lieutenant nodded, "Get yourselves ready. Rivers, you're in charge until Captain Baston arrives. If something happens, keep the rest of the men out, but shoot anything that gets past us."

Twenty feet wide and twice that depth, the three men moved slowly into the cave, pressed against the walls and inched their way along. Just inside, Youngblood stopped suddenly and lowered his lamp. Under their feet a thick layer of dark, oozing slime brimmed like blood over the soles of their boots. Lieutenant Alstaetter murmured, "Bat guano. Ignore it."

Instinctively, the two privates glanced overhead, but the lamp light too dim, the ceiling remained hidden by darkness. In a moment, they came to a rock shelf projecting from the wall of the cave. The lieutenant raised his lamp and saw what they'd been looking for.

A thick bamboo door, ordinarily impossible to detect, had been left open slightly, exposing the entrance to a tunnel. The three men passed through, moving slowly into a narrow passage that took them right, then left, then right again, deep into the mountain. Lieutenant Alstaetter whispered, "The rebels build corners into these tunnels to deflect the force of explosive blasts and make shooting in straight lines impossible."

No signs of life, so they moved faster and soon came to a kind of cul-de-sac, a dead end. Fagen and Youngblood searched the area, but found nothing. "The end of the line, sir."

"That's what they want you to think, Private. I'm sure there's more. Give me a leg up." The two men hoisted the lieutenant up, and he searched the tunnel walls high overhead. "Here it is."

There, ten feet above, a trap door. He opened it and pulled a bamboo ladder down revealing a second tunnel on a level above the one they'd just searched. Lieutenant Alstaetter positioned the ladder. "This is where it gets interesting, we take it slow from here. This passage will lead us to the main system of chambers. That's what we're looking for. I'm certain the rebels cleared out hours ago, but be careful. You know about booby traps, and it's possible they've left a few surprises for us."

Alstaetter paced as he spoke, his pale, white skin glistened with sweat, his eyes bright. Fagen had grown to like and respect the young lieutenant. He was smart and had courage. "I'll go first, then you Fagen, then you Youngblood. I'll be in front, so keep your pistols holstered. If anything happens to me, get out fast and report back to Sergeant Rivers."

"Sir, I was in lots of old caves and tunnels like this when I was a boy," Fagen lied. "Let me go first."

"Are you sure you want to do that, Fagen? It's damned dark in there. We don't know what's waiting for us, and if you're the man in front, once you're inside there might not be any turning back."

"I'm the right man for this job, sir."

"All right, you first."

The second, upper tunnel much smaller than the first, the soldiers were just able to squeeze through the entrance. Once inside, they skidded along on their bellies, pulling themselves forward with elbows, knees and toes, their faces pressed against the dirt floor. Fagen pushed the lamp along in front of him, but the tunnel's ceiling was so low, its light extended out only a few inches. In pitch-blackness, they crawled head-first through the narrow passage, one after the other, moving deeper into a dank, claustrophobic nightmare.

Twenty yards, and the air grew heavy with the acrid tang of burning nipa oil. Lieutenant Alstaetter tugged at Fagen's boot. "We're getting close. Keep a sharp eye ahead."

61

Strange, Fagen thought, how another sense takes over when one of the senses is blunted. He couldn't see three feet, but smelled everything. He caught the scent of burning nipa. He knew Filipinos used palm oil for cooking; they must be preparing their supper. He wondered whether he could sniff out what was on the cook fire that afternoon. Certainly rice, and he'd seen a hundred varieties of fruits since he'd marched into that jungle. No doubt the rebels knew the sweetest. His mouth watered as he mentally sliced through a juicy, ripe mango. In base camp, their food was served in a mess tent. In the field, they carried their own provisions, every man his own cook. He wondered about the custom in an underground chamber at the end of a long tunnel. Fagen shook his head and saw stars. *Watch it, you fool,* he told himself. *Pay attention.* Not enough air in there. *Get control of yourself. Keep moving for Christ's sake.* He took a deep breath.

The smell of nipa grew stronger. Fagen neared the end of the tunnel and tried to look ahead for the chamber opening.

It went for his hand, but hit the lantern instead, and lucky for him, because it struck so hard it nearly shattered the glass. He pulled his arm back fast and just in time, because it came at the lamp again with its fangs bared, looking for the kill. Fagen had encountered a bamboo pit viper once before in a ditch alongside the road near San Isidro. Nasty, ill-tempered devils, their venom could bring down a water buffalo.

That one was mad as hell, but Fagen saw something wasn't right. It didn't add up because those snakes don't like people, and unless cornered, they'd rather run than fight. When it struck a third time, he saw the problem, a line knotted around the snake's tail and tied at the other end to a stake driven into the tunnel floor. The rebels had tethered it in their path, and it had probably been there for hours and couldn't escape. That's why it was mad as hell. *It's possible they've left a few surprises for us.* Fagen remembered the lieutenant's words and mopped sweat from his eyes.

Lieutenant Alstaetter wanted to know what had happened, and when Fagen told him, he said they'd have to back out and get a shotgun. To Fagen, that sounded like a good idea, but he wanted to try something first. He'd been face-to-face with the creature long enough to figure out he could get it to back up by pitching handfuls of dirt at its head. It struck like it wanted to stand its ground, but didn't like the grit in its face, and gave way by inches. Fagen kept at it and in a few minutes worked it backward to the end of the tether. The mistake they made was leaving the line too long. Once the snake had backed to the end of it, it was out of striking distance, and Fagen was able to reach out and pull the stake.

When he did, it knew at once it was free and slithered away fast, dragging the tether behind it.

Ten more yards, the tunnel widened, and they came to a large room with a high ceiling crowded with boxes and crates of various shapes and sizes. The damp air smelled of fungus, but the men were relieved to get off their bellies and out of the tunnel. They entered the room, spread out, drew their pistols and searched the area. "Be careful," Alstaetter whispered. "Anything you touch might be booby-trapped." The chamber doubled as a storage area and workshop. More light there than in the tunnel, but still too dark, Youngblood lit a lantern just in time to step around a large bundle of razor-sharp bamboo stakes. The two privates knew their purpose. They'd heard grisly stories about American soldiers falling into camouflaged pits impaling themselves on stakes like those, a horrible death.

Behind tall stacks of baskets filled with rice and onions, the walls of the chamber were covered with political posters. One depicted a squad of Spanish soldiers with whips borne along on the shoulders of Filipino peasants, another pictured brutish Spanish officers raping a child, while the helpless and horrified mother watched.

"Look at this." Lieutenant Alstaetter stood before a long workbench littered with rusted, homemade tools, a vise and several small clamps. He raised his lamp and revealed a line of sardine cans filled with gunpowder and two hand-carved bullet molds. "A typical guerilla work shop. They make everything from sandals to bombs here. Let's keep moving."

The next room had been a field hospital. Long and narrow and smaller than the first, it was crowded with sleeping hammocks suspended three-deep in rows along both walls. It stank of alcohol, sweat and blood. Fagen and Youngblood moved to opposite ends and searched the hammocks. A heavy table occupied the center of the room, its wooden top stained with the dried blood of countless operations. A frightful sight, Fagen wondered what it had been like for wounded guerillas to wait there in that room, watching their comrades suffer under the surgeon's knife, knowing it would be their turn soon.

When Youngblood fired his pistol, the low ceiling deadened the report, and it sounded to Fagen like someone had smashed a bottle. He fired again, called out, and Lieutenant Alstaetter moved fast. Another shot, then he cried, "This one tried to shoot me, sir! He was laying on his rifle, and when I turned him over, he tried to shoot me!"

The lieutenant pulled three more from under a pile of bloody sheets. They'd hoped the Americans wouldn't have the stomach to dig through the gore to find them. Badly wounded and scared, one was hardly more than a child. Lieutenant Alstaetter put his hand on Youngblood's shoulder and said, "You did well, Private. Get them up and check for weapons."

The rebel Youngblood shot had been struck twice in the face and died instantly. No other wounds on his body, Lieutenant Alstaetter speculated he'd volunteered to stay behind and protect his wounded comrades. The others were unarmed and in bad shape. One was very tall, his head completely covered in bloody bandages. He tried to help the man beside him stand up, but couldn't see, so he wasn't doing a very good job of it. The second man short and heavily built, his right leg had been recently amputated below the knee. He was losing blood through the bandages and in a lot of pain, because when the tall man pulled him up, he screamed, went very pale, and then passed out. The third rebel, no more than fifteen years old, sat still, eyes cast down to his feet like a sullen, defiant schoolboy and wouldn't look up. Both his hands were bandaged to the elbows. Lieutenant Alstaetter holstered his pistol. "Fagen, ask Sergeant Rivers to bring first platoon in. We'll have to open up this whole place."

Captain Baston arrived that afternoon with his Kansas volunteers, but they weren't carrying the supplies H Company had hoped for, so excitement over their appearance faded quickly. By then, first platoon had cleared the rebel tunnel complex of weapons, various explosive devices, maps and other documents, which Captain Baston had been unsuccessful in getting the prisoners to translate.

H Company knew they'd hit on something big, and within a few hours, Fagen and Youngblood had achieved celebrity status. All afternoon and into evening, Youngblood told and retold the story of his encounter with the rebel solider. Each retelling strayed a little further from the actual facts, but Fagen didn't find fault. Who was harmed if a young black soldier put a little extra cream on his porridge? A rare enough occasion when a Negro got a flattering remark for anything he did, what did it matter if the praise came mostly from his own people? Besides, the story about the snake had been passed around enough to take on a few embellishments, and the admiring looks Fagen got from the other men meant more to him than an exact recounting of the facts.

Just before sundown, Lieutenant Alstaetter gave the order to detonate a series of small charges sealing the large chambers in the tunnel complex. This was done while Captain Baston and a dozen Kansas boys worked over the three prisoners. Tied back-to-back in the mud at the mouth of the cave, they'd not had an easy afternoon. Convinced they were part of Aguinaldo's rebel cadre and determined to find out what they knew, Captain Baston had not shied away from the rifle butt and billy club. The Filipinos' refusal to talk frustrated him. Not accustomed to being stonewalled, the captain considered their silence a slap in the face.

After a while, he summoned Lieutenant Alstaetter, and together they walked out of hearing range from the prisoners. As they talked, the captain became more and more agitated. Fagen couldn't tell what the two men discussed. The look on the younger officer's face said he didn't like it, but clearly Captain Baston was in no mood for argument.

Abruptly, the captain turned his back on his subordinate and marched to a spot directly in front of the three rebel prisoners. The two that could, glared at him through black, swollen eyes. The tall, blinded man sat up straight, trying to hear rather than see what came next. Captain Baston knelt down, put his arm around the tall man's shoulders and moved him around until the three prisoners faced each other in a tight little knot. Then he spoke to the rebels, his voice calm and reassuring.

"All afternoon I've tried to impress upon you the importance of cooperation. The United States Army was sent here to free you from the tyranny of the Spanish. This we have done. The Filipino people are liberated from the yoke of colonialism, and all across your island nation your brothers and sisters enjoy the benefits of living under the protectorate of the American flag. This is apparent and open for the whole world to see. Surely, you see this too.

"I am a military man. I understand your loyalty to General Aguinaldo."

The amputee glanced sharply up at Captain Baston, surprised to hear him apply the title "general" to Aguinaldo. Until then, the only words he'd ever heard Americans use to describe *El Presidente* were cur, scoundrel, pirate and worse. Captain Baston saw he had the man's attention, but didn't know why. Having seen the flicker of a response from his captive, he went on, his tone more inclusive, even conspiratorial.

"As a military man, I as much as anyone recognize his courage and sacrifice in his long struggle against Spanish oppression. He is a powerful symbol of the determination of the Filipino people. You brave men are testament to his leadership, but now, gentlemen, you must understand and acknowledge that Aguinaldo's great battles are over, and his continued resistance against American forces a sham, a pretense for outlawry. His grand cause has evaporated. The American promise of freedom and protection has been extended to him as well. What is there to fight for now? Can't you see while you remain here, wounded on this field of honor, your great general cowers in hiding, buying time with your blood only to more fully line his pockets with riches that rightfully belong to you? Understand, gentlemen, power is a strong drink, and every Filipino patriot who continues to suffer reveals the truth of Aguinaldo's gluttonous addiction. Won't you consider the facts of this nightmare? With your assistance we can find General Aguinaldo and bring him home so the Filipino people can choose their own destiny."

The captain sat back and waited. The prisoners shifted uncomfortably under his gaze. In a moment, the stocky amputee lifted his head, his words a whistling rush through broken teeth and black, swollen lips. "Your talk of freedom and protection means nothing to us. Aguinaldo does not loot and burn our villages, American soldiers do. Aguinaldo does not torture defenseless women and kill their children. These are the acts of the brave American. Every thing you say is a lie. *El Presidente* will fight until he has defeated you, just as he defeated the godless Spanish. Do with us what you will, Captain, we will not betray our leader."

The speech took every ounce of strength the man had left, but resolve equal to exhaustion, he fastened his eyes full upon Captain Baston's face and did not look away. They held each other a long moment, and then the captain stood up and walked to his tent. "You may light the cook fires, Lieutenant, and put the perimeter guard on night rotation."

In every man's life, two or three events take place so far outside his range of expectation or understanding they are forever imprinted on his brain. No matter how long he lives or where life's journey takes him, he remembers every detail of that moment in time, and no matter how hard he tries, he can never forget. For David Fagen, what happened next was just such an event.

Darkness came quickly, and with it a penetrating, bone-chilling cold. Very little dry wood, the cook fires put out more smoke than heat. H Company ate their rations early and sat in huddled, shivering groups. After a while, Captain Baston emerged from his canvas field tent and ordered his Kansas volunteers to smash several of the wooden crates and pallets taken from the rebel cache, and soon a bright fire warmed the area.

The prisoners sat up as the captain placed a campstool before them and said, "Two hours ago I asked you to consider the facts of your situation, and in my remarks I stressed the importance of your cooperation. At the time, perhaps owing to the strain of the moment, you seemed unable or unwilling to fully appreciate the perilous nature of your position or the gravity of your situation. I ask you now whether you have reconsidered. I think you know where Aguinaldo hides, and I must warn you, it is my duty to ascertain that information by any means I see fit. Do you understand?"

The young boy and the amputee exchanged glances, but said nothing. The tall, blind man sat listening at attention. In a moment he spoke. "Sir, let the boy go. He is an innocent civilian. He knows nothing. Let him go free, and I will tell you what you want to know."

Lieutenant Alstaetter had moved in close, and the firelight reflected the astonishment on his face when Captain Baston suddenly drew his Colt .44 and fired a shot point-blank that blew through the bandages at the blind man's right temple, tore through his skull and out the other side pushing yellow gore, bone shards and black blood before it. The man collapsed like a rag doll and didn't move. Silence reigned in the camp, save for the echo of the report ringing into the jungle. The amputee's jaw dropped as though he himself had been shot. He tried to speak, to say something to the American captain, but strangled on the words.

Lieutenant Alstaetter charged forward, his face contorted with rage. "Why the hell did you shoot that man?"

Captain Baston calmly removed the spent casing from his revolver and reloaded, the barrel just inches from the lieutenant's chest. "At ease, Lieutenant, and stand down."

Just then, for a split second, Lieutenant Alstaetter considered the very real possibility the captain was insane, and he might be the next one shot, but outraged, headstrong and no coward, he continued, "I protest this action!"

"Protest all you like, Lieutenant, but not to me, and not while I'm questioning prisoners."

Baston arose from his stool and circled the fire, scratched under his hat with the barrel of his pistol. "Effective interrogation comes in many forms, my young friend." He spoke as though he lectured a schoolboy. "It's as much art as science. Allow me to instruct you, and you'll do well to pay attention. I'll wager they don't teach this at West Point. For example, you asked me why I shot that man. If I take your question to be why I *shot* that man, it is primarily because the bullet is cleaner than the sword or the axe. After that, of course, one considers the heightened dramatic effect, the roar of the discharge, the flash of the muzzle.

"However, if your question is meant to ascertain why I shot *that* man, then it's a more penetrating one, which I might expect from an Academy graduate, but the answer should be obvious to a man as astute as yourself, Lieutenant Alstaetter." Captain Baston swung the barrel of his revolver around to the corpse at his feet. "Note the man I shot was blind, no doubt the unhappy result of some battlefield injury. The other prisoners, although wounded, have four good eyes between them - stay with me on this one, Lieutenant - four good eyes to witness this method of interrogation. If I had shot one of the others, the blind man could not have seen it, thereby reducing the number of witnesses by half, thus reducing the consequent impact of the method by half. Ergo, when the situation arises, always shoot the blind man." The captain bowed his head slightly, teacher to student.

Not impressed by the captain's little act, Lieutenant Alstaetter said, "I know no method of interrogation that includes murder, Captain Baston."

"Your depth of knowledge relating to the conduct of successful warfare is precisely the subject here, Lieutenant. I want Aguinaldo, I mean to have him, and I do not make deals with insurrectos. Your protest is noted. Now stand down immediately and permit me to continue this interrogation uninterrupted, or by God, I'll have you bound and gagged. Have I made myself understood?"

Fagen had never heard officers speak in that fashion, and it scared him. Having no choice, the lieutenant backed down. Fagen looked around for Sergeant Rivers, but he was nowhere to be seen. Fagen knew for sure he was glad not to be in the middle of it. There was no place safe for a Negro soldier when two white officers squared off, and he now considered Captain Baston a dangerous man.

A sergeant and a corporal dragged the blind man's body into the cave. Captain Baston turned to the two remaining prisoners and shouted, "I know Aguinaldo was here! When he learned of our approach, he fled into the jungle like the yellow dog coward he is and left you poor wretches to fend for yourselves. He has betrayed you and all the Filipino people. Tell me now where he has gone. Tell me the location of his jungle lair, and no harm will come to you."

In shock and speechless, the boy's eyes locked on the black pool of blood and brains where the blind man had fallen, but the amputee surprised everyone. When the captain stepped in front of him, he spat on the officer's boots and cursed him in his native dialect. Captain Baston blinked, shook his head twice, and then grabbed a rifle from a nearby corporal and swung it hard against the butt-end of the amputee's stump. The man screamed in agony and passed out.

"Prepare the water cure!" he shouted, and a sergeant began dragging the amputee toward the mouth of the cave. "Not him, you fool. The boy."

The men of H Company didn't know the water cure, but Captain Baston's Kansas volunteers did. In no time, the camp came alive with activity. Three men carrying ropes scurried up the rock ledge to the edge of the outcropping high over the mouth of the cave. Reaching the top, they dropped the lines down to men waiting below. The soldiers built a sling, placed an empty sixty-gallon barrel in it, and then hoisted the barrel up and positioned it on the highest spot they could find.

The sergeant and two others stripped the boy and staked him out on his back, the barrel twenty feet over his head. The rest of the men formed a chain and passed buckets of water from the nearby stream up the line and fed the barrel until full. This done, a soldier attached a long hose to the spigot at the bottom of the barrel and tossed the other end to the sergeant below.

Captain Baston shook the amputee awake, and then dragged him to the mouth of the cave near where the boy was pegged down. He'd lost a lot of blood from his stump, his face pale and drawn tight with pain. The captain knelt down in front of him while a soldier fisted a handful of hair and raised his head. "I would like to know your name," the captain said.

The man croaked, "Antonio Salud."

"Tell me where Aguinaldo is, Mr. Salud, and you will save this boy's life."

The man looked down at the boy on the ground next to him. "He is my nephew, Captain. I beg you to let him live."

Baston shrugged. "His life is not in my hands, it's in yours. I want Aguinaldo, not you or this boy."

Antonio Salud pleaded through his tears, "I cannot tell you what I do not know, sir."

Captain Baston stood and turned to the sergeant. "Proceed."

The sergeant placed one of his big hands under the boy's neck and lifted his head. Another soldier pried his jaws open, while a third jammed the rubber hose deep into his throat. The young Filipino screamed in horror and struggled desperately against the ropes that held his arms and legs.

"Lay still, you slope-headed gook bastard," the soldier cursed and shoved the hose deeper. The boy wretched and coughed blood, tried to turn away from his tormentors. When the hose would go no farther, the soldier looked up at the captain. "Ready, sir."

Baston gave a signal to the men on the rock outcropping over the cave, and one reached down and opened the spigot.

In the moments that followed, a strange silence settled over the camp. The only sounds were the popping and hissing of the fire, its flames lighting the faces of Captain Baston and the men, as all eyes followed the invisible flow of water through the hose from the barrel high overhead down to the boy on the ground. For a long moment, nothing happened. Fagen wondered whether something had gone wrong; maybe they'd made a mistake somewhere. Even the boy had stopped struggling against the hose, although his eyes still darted in panic from one soldier to the next.

Then it happened. The sergeant saw it first and smiled up at the captain. The rush of flowing water suddenly reached the boy's stomach and forced his mid-section to swell and grow, and then become so grotesquely extended it looked ready to burst. The boy let out a wild, animal scream, his face turned blue, and his eyes bulged as yellow water gushed from his nose. His stomach grew to four times its normal size, and still the water continued to flow.

Fagen was sure the boy would drown in his own bile, but somehow he stayed alive. Another minute passed. Fagen thought then the boy must have been driven insane. He'd stopped struggling against the ropes, but his eyes had rolled up in his head, and his body twitched and flopped like a fish out of water.

Finally, the captain gave a signal, and the sergeant pulled the hose from the young rebel's throat. Baston squatted alongside the boy for a moment, and then turned to the amputee and said, "Mr. Salud, are you willing to let this boy die? By the looks of him, I'd guess you have another ten seconds to decide, and I should warn you, if he dies, you're next."

The amputee looked up at the captain through tears of shock and pain. "Please, no more. I beg you for mercy. I will tell you. Aguinaldo has a jungle camp, like this one, three days northeast of San Isidro near the big waterfalls. I think that is where he has gone."

"Well done, Mr. Salud." Captain Baston smiled, and then with a little flourish said, "Now observe while I bestow the gift of life on this young man."

The captain rocked forward and pressed both knees deep into the boy's bloated stomach. The youth's choked, agonized screams filled the night and echoed through the jungle mountains as a torrent of water gushed from his nose and mouth. The captain pressed harder, bloody vomit pooling around him. Then he let up for a moment and looked around. As the boy choked and struggled for air, the officer stood up and motioned to one of his men, "Finish this," he said. "I've got what I wanted." Then he walked casually into his tent and closed the flap.

Several hours later, Ellis returned from the perimeter. Fagen feigned sleep.

"Davey, the lieutenant wants you out for guard duty."

"Did the lieutenant tell you who I'm supposed to guard against?" Fagen was low. He'd never seen a man tortured before and felt something very dear to him had been stolen, that he'd been diminished in some important way, but he knew it wasn't fair to take it out on Ellis and apologized.

"We already heard about the boy," Ellis said. "Everybody's heard."

"Ellis, listen to me. I want you to stay as far away from that captain as you can."

Ellis shrugged. "Captain Baston has no cause to associate himself with me, Davey."

"I'm telling you! Keep clear of him. He's the devil himself. No man is safe around him."

"The captain's got a dirty job, Davey. He's out here to get his hands on that rebel leader and the sooner he does it, the sooner this killing stops."

Suddenly fearful of Ellis' blind devotion to the army, angry and afraid, Fagen swung around and slapped his cousin hard in the mouth. "That's the trouble with you, Ellis Fairbanks! You can only think of one thing at a time. That Filipino boy was just another nigger to him, and in his mind all niggers are the same. It doesn't matter what uniform they have on! If you ever got between that captain and what he wants, he'd do the same to you, or worse."

Ellis stared dumbly back for a moment, and then blinked tears from his eyes. Fagen had never struck his cousin before, not even in jest, and immediately hated himself for it. He wanted to explain the horror he'd just witnessed, to warn him away from a dangerous animal, but Ellis turned his back and walked away. "I'll take your turn on guard. You need more sleep," he said.

The next morning, H Company moved out in file alongside the high riverbank. David Fagen and Ellis Fairbanks walked rearguard behind the column, and as they passed heard Captain Baston's voice from behind a tree. "Have you set all the charges?"

"All done, sir."

"Give us five minutes and send the whole thing up. The cave too."

"What about those two slopeheads, Captain. They're still in there."

"Are they still alive?"

CHAPTER 8 - ST. ELMO'S FIRE

In less than a week, written accounts of the action around Mt. Arayat reached the Governor General's office in Manila. General Otis, an old school officer, studied the reports and immediately dispatched Major Russell to pay a call on Colonel Funston.

That afternoon, all the troops not on patrol outside the garrison assembled on the parade ground and were called to attention.

Rain threatened. The sun came and went behind low, scudding clouds. Colonel Funston and Captain Baston emerged from the colonel's office wearing dress uniforms complete with sabers and feathered hats, took their place at the head of the formation, did an about-face and stood at attention. Major Russell stepped forward and began reading:

By direction of the President, the Bronze Star Medal is presented to Colonel Fredrick Funston and Captain Lawrence E. Baston, Infantry, United States Army, who distinguished themselves by outstandingly meritorious service in command of military operations against hostile forces in pursuit and capture of enemy cadre from a jungle stronghold on the island of Luzon, Philippines. In the performance of their duties these officers consistently manifested exemplary professionalism and initiative in obtaining outstanding results. Their rapid assessment and solution of numerous problems inherent in a combat environment greatly enhanced the overall effectiveness against a determined and aggressive enemy. Despite many adversities, they performed their duties in a resolute and efficient manner. Energetically applying sound judgment and extensive knowledge, they have contributed greatly to the successful accomplishment of the United States' mission in the Philippines. Their loyalty, diligence and devotion to duty are in keeping with the highest traditions of the military service and reflect great credit upon themselves and the United States Army.

The reading of the citation complete, a sergeant stepped forward holding a silk pillow on which the medals were placed. With great ceremony and solemnity, Major Russell pinned the medals on the two officers, saluted and said, "As representative of Governor-General Otis, it is my privilege to present you with this honor, knowing full well it is poor compensation for the many and continued contributions you gentlemen have made to our cause. Congratulations and well done."

From their place in the ranks, Fagen, Youngblood, Lieutenant Alstaetter and the other men of H Company saw the bronze star twinkle on Captain Baston's chest, while the sun overhead played cat and mouse with the storm clouds building on the horizon.

Sergeant Rivers ignored the impropriety of the award ceremony. He knew his men had done well in their push against Aguinaldo's base camp, no matter that Captain Baston gave them no credit for it. Since their return from the Mt. Arayat operation, Lieutenant Alstaetter had confined himself to his quarters, coming out only for roll calls, and as Rivers had no influence up the chain of command, his was the only praise H Company would get.

Nothing Rivers could do about that, but when they returned to camp, he'd assembled them and congratulated them personally. H Company had grown into a disciplined, effective fighting unit, at least as good as any of the white companies. Sergeant Rivers knew what had taken place between Alstaetter and the crazy captain and thought he understood how the lieutenant felt. The young officer's confrontation with his superior had been a jolting rite of passage, but he'd have to get over it. Rivers liked and respected the lieutenant. He'd done well as H Company's commander, but not a game for the faint-hearted, in war bad things sometimes happen. The best Rivers could do was get his men leave time away from garrison to rest and relax. They couldn't hide in their quarters all day. They needed a break. Rivers knew soon enough they'd be called out for battle duty again.

David Fagen and Ellis Fairbanks set out on the hike to town at midday, but in a few moments hitched a ride with a Filipino rice farmer perched in the seat of a rickety old wagon drawn behind a plodding *carabao*. Only three miles to San Isidro, they could have walked faster, but it was a warm day, the farmer seemed happy to take them, and they were glad to have the ride. Fagen gave the farmer a coin, and as he spoke no English, the two Americans passed the next hour creaking toward town listening to the songs he sang in his strange, duck-quack language.

San Isidro looked much the same as the last time they'd been there. Both sides of the streets were crowded with merchants and tradesmen scurrying between wagons loaded with rice, vegetables and other goods. In their midst, purposeful, well-dressed men, no doubt on some more pressing business, drove up and down the middle of the streets in colorful *caromatas*.

Ellis asked, "Remember when Aunt Eunice took us into Columbus when we were little? This place reminds me of that, with one big difference."

"You've been out in the sun too long," Fagen rejoined. "Nothing here looks like Columbus, Georgia. This place is only half the size, and plenty of other differences too. Those wagons over there are loaded with rice, bamboo and nipa, not cotton, hay or tobacco," he pointed to the *Rio De La Pampanga*, "and that river there sure isn't the Chattahoochee."

"That's not the difference I was thinking of, Davey. Look around. Everywhere you turn, you see people living, raising their kids, working and doing business. There's shops and schools and churches and riverboats, and everybody gets along just fine with their lives, and you know what else? There's not a white man in sight."

Fagen looked at his cousin. He knew what Ellis hinted at, but asked anyway. "What do you mean 'not a white man in sight'?"

"Just what I said. Right here is a place the colored man can live his whole life without a white man telling him how to do it."

"Who have you been talking to?"

"Some of the boys say they'll come back here after the war. Said they might live here, get married to a Filipino woman, maybe start a business."

"Is that what you want to do?"

"No, sir. I already have a wife. She's the U.S. army, and I'm never leaving her." Ellis put his hands in his pockets and looked around. "Though, if I was to start a business, I think I'd get me some horses and a few wagons."

Fagen laughed and slapped his cousin on the back. "You'd make a fine teamster, Ellis."

They reached the end of the block, and Fagen recognized the place where the incident had occurred between the white cavalrymen and the pickpocket. Instantly, all the scenes of that dismal day rushed back to him. Since then, thoughts of the beautiful and mysterious Clarita Socorro had never been far from his mind. Would he see her again? How would he find her, and if he could pick her out of the crowd, would she even remember him?

Just around the corner at the entrance to a narrow alley, they came across a little cluster of street vendors. A crowd had gathered in front of a man and woman selling fried chicken. The man held a live bird over his head displaying it to the crowd. When a customer's hand went up, the cleaver fell, and in seconds the chicken was bled, gutted, plucked and pitched into an iron cauldron filled with blistering hot oil. Immediately, the bird sank to the bottom in a storm of sizzling bubbles. In a few minutes, when done, it floated to the surface, skin cooked to a deep, golden brown. The woman then ladled the chicken out of the oil, wrapped it in newspaper, and the customer walked away carrying his supper under his arm.

Next to them, a young boy and his pet monkey performed a lively, shuffling dance to a tune the boy played on a tin whistle. The dance over, the monkey went among the crowd collecting pennies offered by those sufficiently amused. Ellis laughed out loud as the monkey chattered and did a back flip with each coin pocketed. This continued for some time until Fagen was overwhelmed with the uncomfortable sensation of someone's eyes on him. He looked behind and saw a strange woman staring at him from the alley. She was seated at a table in the shade of a large umbrella, dealing Tarot cards.

Fagen's curiosity took over. When a boy, it had been widely known among the colored people the Widow Moorhead read the Tarot. The children, terrified of her, never spoke her name after sunset. She not only read the cards, but also tea leaves, dry bones, the planets and the path clouds took across the moon on certain nights. He remembered the Widow Moorhead as big as a house and her flesh shiny and black, but the woman who held his gaze now was small and very old. Brown skin drawn tight over her skull and tiny, penetrating eyes, just for a moment Fagen was reminded of the golden brown chicken he'd watched float to the surface of the cooking pot. "Ellis, come on."

"Where to?"

"To get our fortunes told."

Ellis looked into the alley and saw the old woman still staring at them. "Not me, I'm spooked by that stuff. Those old hags give me the shivers. Besides, I already know what my future is."

"Come on, don't be a coward."

"I'm not a coward, I just don't want to. Besides, if she tells my future, how do I know I'm getting the right one? Maybe she can only see Filipino futures."

Fagen insisted, and they took a seat on a low wooden bench in the shade of the old woman's umbrella, her cards already arranged in a pattern on the table. Fagen smiled, "Good day, Missus. My friend would like you to read the cards for him."

Ellis squirmed in his seat, started to say something, but the woman interrupted him, "These cards are not for him, they are for you." She pronounced the words slowly, her voice a low monotone, dry as dust, cracked with age.

Fagen looked at the ten brightly colored cards turned face up before him. He winked at Ellis, and then placed a coin on the corner of the table. "If they're mine and not his, then I'll go first. Tell me what they say."

The woman held her head erect and looked him in the eye. "You think I am a shatter-pated old fool. The arrogance of youth, but there is something you must understand before you give your money. Your destiny is predetermined by the choices you make now and the countless decisions you have made since birth. You may think you have free will, that you can actually choose one course of action over another, but that is an illusion. Your future is compelled by your past and each action you take dictated by a previous action." She fixed them with her glittering eyes. "It is a closed circle, and your opinions and attitudes concerning my ability to see your destiny in these cards do not change that." The woman looked down at the cards and fell silent.

"I meant no disrespect, Missus. Please proceed."

The woman studied the table for a moment, and then looked up and began moving her bony fingers across the cards as she spoke. "You seek ways to resolve the conflict between your inner and outer realities. In this spread – your spread – The Page of Swords, The Fool, The Hangman and The Lovers are dominant.

"The Page of Swords is a messenger bringing you challenges. He bids you not to turn away from difficult situations, but to think of them as trials placed in your path to test your will, and if you prevail, you will grow stronger. You should," she hesitated, "you *must* use the tools of the swords suit to assist you, honesty, integrity and fortitude." The fortuneteller paused again, looked up at Fagen and lifted an eyebrow.

"I understand," he said.

The woman pointed to a second card on which was painted the image of a jester. "In your reading, The Fool signals a change of direction or a new beginning. When you face a difficult decision or period of doubt, The Fool reminds you to keep your faith and follow your heart, no matter how dangerous your impulses may seem. He is reinforced by the Three of Wands, which speaks of expanding into unexplored territory.

"Next is The Lovers." Fagen's eyes followed her finger to a card that pictured a man standing with two women at his feet. "The Lovers shows us the attractive force that draws any two entities into a relationship, whether it be people, ideas or events." She moved her hand to another card. "But the Five of Pentacles in this position influences and is not to be ignored. In this spread, The Lovers shows the classical struggle of a man torn between the virgin and the temptress, a triangle, symbolizing the larger dilemmas men face when at a moral or ethical crossroad and torn between right and wrong. You should know that making a decision to follow your own path can mean going against those who urge you in a direction wrong for you." The old woman stopped and looked up again. "Would you like me to continue? There is one more card."

Ellis pulled at Fagen's elbow. "Let's go now, Davey. I don't understand anything she says, and it still gives me the shivers."

"She's not done yet, Ellis. There's one more card. What are you afraid of? This nice lady doesn't want to hurt you. Do you, Missus?"

The woman fixed her gaze on Ellis, and he froze like a mouse under a serpent's spell. In a moment, she smiled at him, her thin lips parting to reveal a mouthful of black, betel nut-stained teeth. "You must not be in such a hurry, young man. One more card in this spread, then I will read for you." Ellis broke out in a sweat.

The old woman returned to her reading, but paused, looked at Fagen and narrowed her eyes for added emphasis. "The last card in your spread is the Hanged Man. He is the most important." She picked the card up and held it out in front of her. "The lesson of the Hanged Man is we control by letting go, we win by surrendering." She held it higher. "Look at the figure on the card. He has made the ultimate surrender, to die on the cross of his own travails. But look how he shines with the glory of divine understanding. He has sacrificed himself, but he emerges the victor! This, my friend, is your reading."

Fagen watched the woman carefully gather the cards. What a strange person, he thought. Like Ellis, he wasn't sure whether he fully understood everything she'd said, but he knew for certain what he'd just heard was nothing like the unintelligible mumblings, chants and speaking in tongues he remembered from the Widow Moorhead. Glad the reading was over, Ellis tipped his hat to the old woman and quickly escaped to the street to watch the boy with the tin whistle and monkey.

Fagen thanked the old woman, gave her another coin and was about to leave the table when he felt the presence of someone behind him, and then a hand on his shoulder.

"I see you've met my grandmother." He turned to see Clarita Socorro standing over him, her smile brighter than the sun. She bent down and kissed the old woman's wrinkled forehead. "Come with me," she said to Fagen smiling. "I want to show you something."

Fagen drove Clarita's *caromata* north along a dirt path beside the *Rio De La Pampanga* into a wide valley bordered in the distance on both sides by steep hills covered with bamboo and nipa. Clarita had hired a man to take Ellis on a tour of the Cathedral of San Isidro, leaving the two of them with the afternoon to themselves. A warm day, but a cooling breeze came off the river, and while their pony pulled them gently forward, Clarita charmed Fagen with stories of local interest. She stopped the cart on several occasions to point out native trees and colorful wild flowers. For his part, Fagen had no experience with the uninterrupted company of a lady, much less a beautiful young woman who seemed truly interested in him and was content to let her carry the conversation.

After a while, they came to a small village, not much more than a wide spot in the road. At the far end a little park bustled with activity. A celebration of some sort going on, fifty people stood together, all dressed in their finest. Under a grove of nipa, a small platform had been erected, decorated with colored paper and surrounded with bundles of fresh cut flowers hanging from the trees.

Clarita said, "It's a wedding." Fagen parked their little buggy in the shade some distance from the ceremony, but close enough to view the bride and groom kneeling before a priest. Several in the wedding party noticed them watching, and Fagen thought they must wonder about the strangers in their midst. He felt conspicuous in his army blues and, for the first time, not proud to be in uniform. Clarita sensed his thoughts. "Don't worry," she said gently. "To these people, your uniform says invader, but the color of your skin says you do not hate the Filipino."

The priest blessed the bride and groom, and then a pretty young girl in a white dress came forward with the rings.

"In the Philippines," Clarita said, "the priests marry everyone. A civil marriage would not be recognized in the eyes of God."

"Who are all the other people at the altar?"

"The old ones are the *ninongs* and *ninangs* of the bride and groom, you would say Godparents, the rest members of the wedding party. Do you see the woman to the right of the bride? She is the candle bearer. She carries the flame that represents the Light of God. The child beside her, see where she stands? She is the ring bearer. The boy next to her is the coin bearer. He is usually the bride's brother."

"The coin bearer?"

"Yes. He carries the thirteen coins called the *arrhae*. After the exchange of rings, the groom gives the coins to the bride as his pledge of dedication to the welfare of his wife and children."

The priest took the rings from the little girl and blessed them. Next, he administered the vows, and the couple repeated after him. Then the coin bearer came forward, and with great dignity and solemnity, the groom took the money and placed it in the bride's hand. This done, a young woman came out of the crowd with what looked to Fagen like a rope - no, more like a sash, made of silk. She walked to the alter where the bride and groom knelt and placed it carefully around their shoulders.

Clarita said, "The cord sponsor places the silken rope over the wedding couple in the form of a figure eight. This stands for the infinite bond of marriage. In a Filipino wedding, the cord more than anything else represents the one, everlasting life the bride and groom now share.

"See the way the bride's veil is pinned to the groom's shoulder? This symbolizes the union of two people clothed as one. Now the priest will say a nuptial mass, then later there'll be a reception party with music and dancing and lots of homemade beer. Just before the newlyweds retire, they will release a pair of white doves to signify a peaceful and harmonious marital relationship."

"Doves," Fagen mused. "I like that. In America people throw rice at the bride and groom."

Clarita frowned. "Filipinos do not do this. To throw rice dishonors the memory of those times in our history when every grain was precious."

"It's a beautiful ceremony."

Clarita took Fagen's hand and looked deep into his eyes. "Filipino culture is rich in tradition, David. Remember, when you hear Americans call us dinks and gugus, it is they who are ignorant and shallow." Fagen backed the little *caromata* away quietly, and left the villagers to their wedding mass.

They followed a trail off the main road through a small valley between ranges of rocky green hills. Soon, the trail narrowed and darkened, and cliffs to their right and left rose high overhead. At last, they reached a spot under the heavy branches of a huge tree that had managed to take root on a rocky face above them.

"We walk from here."

Fagen was doubtful. Everywhere around them vertical cliffs rose to over a hundred feet. Fagen had read of a goat that traveled on slopes like these, but he thought, certainly a man could not.

Already out of the cart, Clarita called over her shoulder, "There's a path. Come on, I'll show you."

In ten minutes, they'd climbed halfway up. Clarita kept mostly to the rocks and away from the slippery grasses that lined the cliff face. Fagen tried not to show it, but the ascent that had no apparent effect on Clarita, set the muscles in his legs on fire, and his lungs screamed for oxygen. He found a rock and sat down.

Clarita laughed, "Don't worry, the worst is over. It's downhill from here." Fagen looked around, but saw no place downhill unless back the way they'd come. When he turned back, Clarita had disappeared. He looked ahead, and then behind all the way down to their little buggy parked beside the trail at the base of the hill. She was nowhere to be found.

"Here I am! This way. Follow me." She'd stepped through a narrow aperture in the cliff. No more than a small fissure in the rocks, it was completely invisible until right on top of it, the breach just wide enough for a man to squeeze through. Clarita led him into the narrow opening, passing stonewalls that towered over their heads. They wound around inside the meandering passage for a few minutes, but soon the path widened, and they came out the other side.

When they emerged once again into the sunlight, Fagen stopped suddenly and his jaw dropped. Beneath them lay a tiny lake, a pool of indigo water surrounded on all sides by sheer, forbidding cliffs ringed with grasses and huge green trees that seemed to grow out of the water itself. At the near end of the little lake, a beach of pure white sand lay in the shape of a crescent moon. Clarita smiled with amusement as Fagen took in the beauty of the place. "I told you I had something to show you. This is my special place, my *simbahan*. In English you would say temple, or perhaps sanctuary. Grandmother brought me here when I was ten. I come here now when I want to get away from the outside world. This is the one place I always feel safe. Nothing bad can happen here, there is too much beauty."

Moments passed before Fagen found the words. "This is what heaven must be like."

They walked down a gentle switchback trail to the beach. Fagen knelt on the soft white sand, cupped a handful of water and poured it on his arm. Clear and cool, his skin tingled at the touch of it. The white sand continued for several yards into the water then abruptly dropped into inky blackness. "No one knows how deep it is," Clarita said, "but it's perfect for bathing."

When Fagen looked up, Clarita's clothes lay in a pile on the beach, and she was up to her chin in the water. "What's the matter, David Fagen, don't you swim?"

Fagen looked at her moving gently in the pool, so beautiful he had to laugh. "How deep did you say it is?"

"I'll protect you. You can trust me."

They swam together in the cool water. Fagen held Clarita's tight, hard body close and felt the silky smoothness of her skin, the warm glow of her smile. This truly is heaven, he thought.

Later, the afternoon sun high overhead, Fagen lay on the beach and wondered what was wrong with Clarita and her *simbahan*. She was too perfect, too good to be true and her little slice of heaven too peaceful, too pristine to exist in a country ravaged by war. He possessed nothing to attract such a woman in a land so far from home, and he'd seen enough of the world to know every good thing came with a price. He turned to face her. "Clarita, that day in San Isidro during the riot…the day we met. What made you pick me out of the crowd?"

Clarita smiled, kept her eyes closed against the bright sun. "Already searching for compliments? Are you so vain? How does a woman answer a question like that?"

Fagen's skin grew a shade darker, and his cheeks tingled. Foolish to question her like this, he thought, but he couldn't help himself. "I am not vain, and I don't beg compliments from women. You tapped me on the shoulder. You spoke to me first. Why me, I'm nobody special. Why not Ellis, or any other American in San Isidro?"

Clarita rose up on one elbow and put her cool, dry palm on Fagen's shoulder. "I did it because even in the middle of an angry crowd I saw intelligence and sensitivity in your eyes. I saw in you a great capacity for love and no fear or hatred." She smiled and gave a little wink. "I am no longer so sure about the intelligence."

Fagen barely heard the words. He watched her pretty lips move and realized then it made no difference what she said. He only wanted this person to love him. Nothing else mattered.

The sun rested on the cliffs, flashed brilliant shafts of gold and turned Clarita's *simbahan* into a palace for angels. After a while, she told Fagen about her people, how they'd suffered under Spanish rule. Aware of the many atrocities the Spanish had committed during their long reign, Fagen had already heard much of what she said; some from Tomas, the silversmith he met in the swamp, some from the village peasants he'd encountered in the field. No matter, Clarita lay now with her head on his chest, the sound of her low, melodious voice so agreeable to Fagen's ears, he thought he lived a dream. "My grandmother may seem strange to you, but really she's a saint. She told me once she reads futures in the Tarot because she is old and has no future left of her own. I tell her she does it because she enjoys being mysterious. I love her more than my life. She is a god to me. She has been both mother and father since I was a child of ten."

"What happened to your own family?"

Clarita sat up. Her hair still damp, she brushed it back until it hung over her shoulders. "My parents and my brother, Matco, were murdered."

"Murdered!"

"Yes. Ten years ago the Spanish began a campaign to rid the countryside of people they called 'dangerously subversive.' This meant everyone who spoke out against them in any way. They used these words as an excuse to kill thousands of innocent people. My father was a teacher. He and some other men in our barrio had protested against a new tax the Spanish levied on the production of rice. They were not dangerous or subversive men, but one night soldiers came to our village and took dozens of us, whole families, from our beds into the city of San Fernando. There we were held in bamboo cages and tried for treason. We were found guilty, of course, like hundreds of other peasants also brought there for trial. Afterwards, everyone was marched out of town under heavy guard.

"When we reached the place, the men and boys were ordered to dig a long, shallow trench. Then everyone stood at the edge, and the soldiers opened fire." Clarita paused for a moment and cast a glance at the green cliffs towering over them.

"I escaped the death sentence because a Spanish soldier on one of the execution squads had seen me and wanted me for himself. He bargained with my mother. He said if she ordered me to accept him, he would spare Matco and me. If she refused, he would kill us first so she would be forced to watch.

"What choice did she have? My brother was two years older, if he were spared, he at least had a chance at life. I was a girl. How much would I suffer forced to do then what would come naturally in only a few years? The soldier was a pig, too brutish to imagine, but my mother knew he would someday tire of me and turn me out. My youth would have been stolen, but at least my brother and I would live. That is how I escaped the executioner's bullet. The soldier lied about Matco.

"Just before the executions began, the Spaniard dragged me over a low hill and tied me to a tree. All afternoon I struggled against the ropes while I listened to the rifles pop and the agonized screams of my countrymen as they waited their turn while watching their loved ones fall six at a time into the trench.

"Luckily for me, the Spaniard had been careless with his knots. Later, when he came over the hill, I was waiting. I had been free for some time. I could have run away, but didn't. I was determined to avenge the slaughter of my family. The soldier must have been fatigued from his afternoon of killing, and this made him careless, because when he came around the tree looking for me, his rifle was slung, and he was not ready to defend himself. From a low branch I had broken off a small, straight stick, about the size of an arrow and worked for an hour grinding the tip against the bark of the tree until it was needle sharp.

"My heart raced, and I was nearly petrified with fear as his heavy footsteps grew closer. When he came around the tree, he saw at once I was free and lunged at me, but I was too quick. I pushed the stick forward with all my strength and aimed for the center of his chest. He was surprised because he did not expect the attack, and it slowed him down, but my arrow would not penetrate the heavy material of his coat.

"He went into a rage then, and swung at me with his fist, hitting me here." Clarita pointed to the little scar just in front of her left ear. "Then he came at me again. I was dazed from the blow to my head, but I knew then there was no going back for either of us, and my death at the hands of this man would not be so quick as my family's.

"My only hope of survival was to make my next thrust count, but I did not know then if I would get the chance. He picked me up here, by the throat and shook me like a rag doll. I couldn't breath. My head felt ready to explode. My only thoughts were of his hot breath on my face and his curses pounding in my ears. I knew I had to do something, in only a moment I would be dead.

"I realized then I still held the little arrow. With my last ounce of strength, I plunged the sharpened tip deep into the place that was his right eye. It must have penetrated his brain because his knees buckled, he dropped straight down, and just that quickly it was over. I pushed his heavy, stinking body off me and ran as fast as I could. I was ten years old."

Fagen held Clarita in his arms, but it was a long time before she surrendered to his embrace. He felt her heart racing. The horror she'd endured when so young still tormented her.

Clarita wiped a tear from her cheek. "I knew the Spanish would look for me. I had killed one of their soldiers, there was no greater crime. For a month I hid in the alleys of San Fernando. I trusted no one. The Spanish had placed a bounty on traitors and murderers, and I was afraid if anyone knew who I was, they would turn me in for a reward. I lived on scraps and slept under the garbage heaps until my grandmother found me and took me home. I have been with her ever since. As I said, she is a god to me."

For a long while, David Fagen and Clarita Socorro sat on the beach in silence. The pristine beauty of Clarita's *simbahan,* juxtaposed with the horror of her story, invoked powerful emotions in Fagen. He knew he'd never felt this way about any other person. He wanted desperately to protect her, to make everything all right for her, but he was powerless. He was in the army. He'd been sent to the Philippines to kill Spaniards. That was all right, they were the enemy. Hadn't they sunk the battleship *Maine* in Havana harbor? Now it was his duty to kill Filipinos, and for what? All they wanted was to rule themselves.

Fagen thought back over his months in combat. He remembered the young soldier he'd fought with his first day in battle and realized now what he had not then: that soldier wasn't an outlaw, he fought only for his freedom. Did he still live with the pain Fagen inflicted on him? Was he now crippled for life? Then the boy behind the trough in Tanuba, cut down by a stray bullet, a senseless death, and Captain Baston's three prisoners, did they deserve their fate?

Suddenly, remorse swept over him like a dark cloud, hung there a moment, and then settled deep into his gut and burned in his soul. He'd never experienced true shame before, and he felt low and dirty.

As though she read his thoughts, Clarita said, "The Spanish are gone, but Filipinos still struggle for independence. Now the Americans want to rule these islands. Is freedom for our people too much to ask? Isn't that what everyone wants? Isn't that what we all strive for? Filipinos wish only to live free among people we love, to have hope our children can grow up healthy and happy and live better than we did, to experience our own culture, not one handed to us by a foreign power. Tell me, David Fagen, is this too much to ask?"

CHAPTER 9 - THE INFERIOR RACES

P rivate soldiers rarely saw a high-ranking officer so mad he could spit, but Saturday was one of those days, because when H Company formed up for reveille, they found the entire camp strewn with propaganda leaflets. Undetected, rebels had slipped past the guards in the night and scattered hundreds of printed notices, all addressed to "The Colored American Soldier." That one was pasted on Colonel Funston's door was what made him so mad. The men were ordered not to touch them, but there were so many someone got his hands on a few and passed them around.

The leaflet depicted Colonel Funston with the head of an alligator holding a Filipino peasant under each arm, and at the same time kicking a black soldier into battle. It read:

> To the Colored American Soldier: It is without honor that you shed your precious blood. Your masters have thrown you in the most iniquitous fight with double purpose – to make you the instrument of their ambition, and also your hard work will soon make the extinction of your race. Your friends, the Filipinos, give you this good warning. You must consider your situation and your history, and take notice that the blood that is spilled between us is the blood of cousins – Cousins of Color.

The men of H Company had heard about rebel propaganda leaflets, but that was the first anyone had actually seen. A courier from Batangas had come to camp two weeks earlier with stories of notices spread as far north as Manila. They'd been addressed to the Negro soldier and pleaded for them to help the Filipinos resist the yoke of American imperialism by refusing to participate in the war.

The leaflets contained powerful language. Words like oppression, freedom and master had special significance to the Negro. Black soldiers seldom found that level of understanding outside their own ranks. Some of the men said the leaflets proved the Filipino was truly the black man's cousin, and cared more about the Negro than their own countrymen. The white officers told them propaganda lies were designed to divide their loyalty. David Fagen thought he saw truth on both sides, but didn't know the right answer. Either way, the notices reminded the men of the ugliness their race lived with back home. They were in the Philippines to fight a war, to serve their country, yet back in the States the white man still called them nigger and beast, spat at their women and hung their young men, cold facts that left them lonely and isolated.

Nearly time for lights out, as Fagen walked his post between rows of tents, he passed men squatting by their fires, not ready for sleep. They sat by themselves mostly, but sometimes in pairs and cleaned weapons or sharpened bayonets. Some men sat smoking in silence, others told elaborate stories. Fagen heard shouts of laughter from a group of men at one tent. He looked and saw a soldier strut around the fire, his belly and cheeks puffed in perfect mimicry of Colonel Funston just after he'd found the propaganda leaflet on his door. A natural clown, the man's audience was in stitches. Fagen thought he'd better be careful. If the colonel, or perhaps worse, Captain Baston saw that little act, there'd be hell to pay.

Farther on, some men had assembled a prayer meeting. Fagen counted eight sitting in a circle around the leader while he shouted out reverential invocations and the most pious psalms from memory, two lines at a time. He had a strong voice, the kind that could almost reach heaven, and Fagen was surprised he hadn't drawn a larger crowd. That style of preaching always reminded Fagen of home, as it did the other men listening, but then maybe that was the reason.

At the end of the last row of tents, Fagen saw a large fire and heard men laughing. Knotted around the flames, as Fagen approached their laughter mingled first with a flute and then the hollow sound of a homemade drum. They stopped for a moment when they saw Fagen on guard duty, but soon began again. A guitar joined the mix, and some of the men began to sing, their composition a Baptist gospel sung to the tune of an ancient African melody, a song Fagen found familiar, but couldn't quite place because it issued forth in a low moan with the steady beat of an endless chant. As Fagen watched, the music and singing intensified in pitch and tempo. All at once the men stood up and formed a circle, clapped hands and stomped their feet in time to the music. Some of the men did the heel and toe, others began to stoop and rise and whirl and tremble. The circle grew, the beat quickened. Someone shouted, "Call him up, brother," and another cried, "Stand up to him now," and "Hallelujah." The singing grew louder, the endless throbbing of the drum reached a frenzied pace. On it went until Fagen was sure it couldn't go any longer when a sudden crack split the night air, the spell shattered, and the men collapsed in a heap around the fire amid general sighing and laughter.

Fagen stood there a moment, the music ringing in his ears. Suddenly, he realized this had been more than just a put-together barn dance. He'd witnessed doubtful and disconcerted men relieve tension. He'd seen it all around the camp that night. The men tried not to show it, but the propaganda leaflets had had their intended effect. Fagen started to move away, but froze in his tracks at a hand on his shoulder. The grip like iron, when he turned, he faced Ellis Fairbanks. Ellis whispered urgently in his ear, "There's big trouble, Davey. Come quick."

Ellis led them between rows of tents to the west wall where a fight was underway. Several men had gathered in a circle around the scene and pushed and jockeyed for position. "It's Corporal Carter from second platoon," Ellis said. "He's gone out of his head, like he's crazy."

Fagen pushed through the onlookers to the edge of the circle. Two men tried to hold Carter down while another attempted to roll him up in a tent canvas. Smaller than average and not a young man, Carter was in a fit, and summoned strength equal to the men who tried to subdue him. Fagen watched, but didn't know for certain what to do, while a small cloud of dust enveloped the struggling men.

Carter was the kind of man that liked to talk. The men called him "Uncle." He'd been in the army sixteen years, and according to him done every job the army had from mess steward to mounted cavalry. Once, he told how he'd fought Apaches with Black Jack Pershing in Mexico, but not many believed that one. Carter was also a man that liked to drink spirits, and like so many men fond of alcohol, had no real tolerance for it. It was whispered around the camp he'd recently bought quantities of a local brew made from fermented coconut milk and God knows what else. He'd taken too much that night and couldn't handle it. "I think he's poisoned himself, Davey," Ellis said.

Soon, the men with the tent canvas backed off and quit trying. Too wild for them, Carter had bitten, kicked, scratched and gouged, and they didn't think it worth it. "It's like wrestling a pig," one man said, "you get all cut up and bloody and the God damn pig likes it."

Carter had crabbed sideways, his back up against the west wall, and lay there howling like a jungle cat, eyes rolled up in his head, body jerking out of control. White flecks of foam appeared at the corners of his mouth, curled up, and then disappeared into his gray hair. Fagen shivered to look at him, and he had to force himself to stand his ground. He was on guard duty, but unsure of his obligations in that situation. Besides, he carried a loaded weapon and couldn't see adding that to the ruckus.

Just then, Sergeant Rivers shoved past. Wearing only pants and boots, he charged into the circle like a bear smoked out of a cave. "Back off! What's the matter with you? Give this man room to breathe."

Stringfellow, one of the men who'd tried to subdue Carter, stood up, his lower lip bleeding and a finger wrenched out of joint. "Uncle Carter got a letter from home today, Sarge. Some other mule's been kicking in his stall."

Sergeant Rivers surveyed the situation, and then barked, "Minnefee, get the doctor." He turned to Carter. "Stand up, soldier. Get out of that dirt. Where's your self-respect, man?"

Carter's eyes focused, and he lifted his head. Blood trickled from his left ear. "I can't do that, General. There's fish nibbling at my feet and they've taken my toes."

Sergeant Rivers sighed, "Your toes are just fine, and there are no fish hanging on you anywhere."

Carter pressed tighter against the wall. "Stay away from me. You're the general that puts his boots on backwards. You ride that yellow horse. I'm a wounded man, stay away!"

Sergeant Rivers backed up a step and knelt down. "Look at me, I'm Rivers. I ain't no general. You know who I am. Let me get you to the infirmary so the doctor can take those fish off your feet."

A moment of silence. The men held their breath while Carter thought over Sergeant Rivers' offer. The company sergeant didn't notice George Cheeks from third platoon creep along the wall and worm into the circle. Cheeks thought himself a tricky fighter, and he had a scheme to take Carter by surprise. Fagen saw him and thought him foolish and dangerous. Sergeant Rivers had the situation under control. In his state of mind, who knew what Carter might do if rushed by a man with a rifle?

Fagen was about to speak up when the regimental surgeon, Doctor Forrester, flew past dressed only in white linen nightshirt and cap. Stunned by the sudden appearance of a little white man dressed in white, standing among them on skinny white legs, as though a spirit had suddenly materialized before them, the men fell speechless. That's when Cheeks made his move.

Everyone distracted by Doctor Forrester's sudden appearance, Cheeks pushed past the man in front of him and held his rifle at Carter's head. "I've got him covered boys! Take him while you can!"

The only man not bemused by Doctor Forrester was Carter. His head already filled with a host of apparitions, the doctor's strange visage was just one more character in his long list of players. In a flash Carter wrenched the weapon away, swung the butt hard and made contact with the point of Cheek's jaw. Cheeks dropped in a heap, his mouth gushing blood, and then Carter turned the rifle on Sergeant Rivers and the doctor.

If H Company's first sergeant had had a weapon, he would have killed Cheeks on the spot, but just then, he could only stay put. Very slowly, he pulled the doctor down next to him. Carter drew his knees to his chest. Eyes wild, hands trembling, he aimed the rifle at the doctor's heart. "You're the two sons-of-bitches been throwing peanuts at me all night," he growled, drool leaking down his chin. Sergeant Rivers inched between the doctor and the muzzle of Carter's rifle. Responsible for his men, if a bullet were fired, in his mind it was only right that it strike him and not the regimental physician.

"None of us threw peanuts at you, Carter. That was those other guys, but they're gone now."

"Where'd they go? I'd like to kill those sons-a-bitches right now. I want to kill them quick so I can go home."

"I'd like to get them too, Uncle," Sergeant Rivers said, "but no one's throwing any peanuts now. Why don't you give me that weapon, and then we'll get you packed up and ready to leave."

Carter shook his head. "You can't go home with me, General, you wear your boots all wrong."

Exasperated, Sergeant Rivers stood, pushed the doctor behind him, and then moved in a few inches to close the distance. Carter saw it and levered a round into the chamber of the rifle. Everyone backed up a step and held his breath. Afraid of what could happen next, Fagen didn't like it so he cocked his rifle and sighted on the man's forehead. The last thing he wanted was to put a bullet in Uncle Carter, but the situation had gone from bad to worse very quickly, and he didn't see he had a lot of choices.

Just then, Ellis worked his way to the front and walked casually out of the crowd like a man stepping from a streetcar. A smile on his face, he waved at Carter. "Uncle," he said, "how you doing?"

Carter blinked as though he'd just come out of a dream. "Is that you, Ellis? By God, how are you boy?"

"I'm fine, Uncle. Just fine." Ellis closed the distance between them in two long steps, gently lifted the rifle from Carter's hands, helped him up and brushed dust off his clothes. "Let's get you cleaned up, Uncle, and while we're doing that, you can tell me about the time you rode with Black Jack Pershing."

The men let go a long, collective sigh of relief as Ellis and Carter walked away in the direction of the infirmary. Sergeant Rivers helped the doctor to his feet. The incident over, they were about to break up, but everyone snapped to attention when Captain Baston bore into the center of the group. "Just what the hell is going on here? Sergeant Rivers! Post yourself! I want to know just what... Forrester? Is that you?"

"It's me, Captain."

"Take a look at yourself, man! You're in your nightshirt, for God's sake."

"We've had a man taken ill, Captain Baston. That's all."

"Never mind! I don't want to hear it. Look at this mess! Men scuffling in the dark after taps, you in your nightshirt, enemy propaganda all through our camp. Where the hell is Lieutenant Alstaetter?"

Sergeant Rivers answered. "He's on night patrol, sir."

"Night patrol?" Captain Baston sputtered. "What kind of night patrol?"

"I don't know, sir. He didn't inform me."

"To hell with it! I don't want to hear it! I like you, Rivers, but when you people came here, I told Colonel Funston a company of Negroes garrisoned with regular army troopers would lead to no good. Now you see I was right. I've got nothing against you personally, Sergeant, but sooner or later someone has to face fact. The average colored person, man or boy, simply doesn't have the intelligence to make a good soldier, doesn't respond to training and discipline like a white man. This is just another example of what I've said all along. Look at those men standing here! Your men! You leave a colored unsupervised for one hour, and then just look and see what you get."

Fagen saw the muscles tighten in Sergeant Rivers' jaw, and it worried him. He'd heard stories of what happened when Rivers got mad and hoped for his sake he'd control himself and refrain from knocking the arrogant captain down. "We had a trooper sick here, Captain. Nothing more than that."

Fagen rarely spoke up in matters not his concern, but right then couldn't help himself. He raised his voice a little, "That's right, Captain, sir. We had a trooper down sick."

The minute he said it, he wished he hadn't. Captain Baston put his big red face into Fagen's. "What's your name, smoky?"

Fagen felt the man's hatred rush over him, devouring him, and when he said his name, thought he saw a glimmer of recognition in his eyes. "I remember you Fagen, and I know you for a God damned trouble maker. I'm not surprised to find you in the middle of a God damned, stinking mess like this."

The captain glared contemptuously at the men in the little circle. They stood at attention, but were otherwise a sorry bunch. Stringfellow and two or three others were banged up and covered in dirt, Cheeks was out cold, the doctor bent over him, trying to bring him around. Fagen was the only one dressed like a soldier, and only because he'd been on guard duty.

Captain Baston finally turned away and faced the company sergeant. "You don't have a sick trooper, Rivers, because you don't have any troopers." The veins in his temples bulged. "What you've got here is an assemblage, a flock, a gaggle, *a herd.* That's what this is, a herd of men with the minds of children!" The captain spat in the dirt and turned on his heel. Without looking back, he said, "Doctor Forrester, I want a full report on my desk by reveille."

Sergeant Rivers stood watching the captain disappear into the night, and then said, "Couple of you men help the doctor, the rest of you get back to your bunks."

A bad night. The men liked Uncle Carter, and it upset them to see him in a frenzy, but that hadn't been the worst of it. Fagen thought the captain's insults too much to take. There was no reason for him to talk about them the way he did, they weren't a herd of cattle or any other kind of beast and didn't have the minds of children. There wasn't a man among them who hadn't lived every day with some form of racial prejudice. For the black man that was just part of life, but they were soldiers in combat against an enemy of the United States. More than once they'd proved themselves equal to any other fighting men the army had. America was a free country, and under ordinary circumstances, Fagen knew the captain had every right to hate a man because of the color of his skin. But they were Negro soldiers under his command. They served in Mr. Lincoln's army, where the black man fought and died right alongside the white. Fagen despaired of a way to open the man's eyes, some way to really show him the black soldier deserved the same respect and regard as a white soldier. He hoped one day someone would come along who could do this. Until then, the men of H Company would have to eat crow and bite their tongues.

Fagen saw Sergeant Rivers walking towards him. Only fifteen minutes left on guard duty, but plenty of time for more trouble to come his way, Fagen thought he'd better keep some distance between them. A strange night, there'd been something in the air, a darkness of spirit throughout the camp, and Fagen wasn't sure it was gone yet. He would be glad to see morning come and hoped for some truth to the old saying that tomorrow's sun brings a new day. He slung his rifle and headed for his post when Rivers caught up. "Fagen, you and Fairbanks meet me at the main gate at sunup. Bring provisions for one long day."

At dawn, the three men met at the gate. Sergeant Rivers spoke a few words to the corporal of the guard, and in a moment they were outside, headed northwest at a quick pace, keeping to the back roads and covering the miles in silence.

At midday, they came to an abandoned plantation house at the edge of a bamboo forest. Sergeant Rivers led them off the road behind a low wall that took them past the main house to an area of outbuildings surrounding a ramshackle barn and a small corral. Rivers took off his pack and sat down at the base of the wall. "We wait here."

An hour passed. Fagen sat in silence while Ellis nibbled on a biscuit. Sergeant Rivers didn't seem in the mood to offer information, so Ellis finally said, "What are we waiting for, Sarge?"

"We're waiting for something to happen, and when it does, you boys are my witnesses."

That satisfied Ellis, but Fagen didn't like the sound of it. If something demanded that much secrecy, he wasn't sure he wanted any part of it. "Why us, Sergeant Rivers? Why'd you pick us?"

"I picked you two, because I *thought* you boys could keep your mouths shut and not badger me with stupid questions. I guess I was wrong about that."

"No, sir, Sarge," Ellis volunteered, "you weren't wrong. We can keep our mouths shut, can't we, Davey."

Fagen couldn't help himself. More than a little curious about what they were doing out there by themselves, he thought it only fair they know what was expected of them. Consternation written on Fagen's face, when Sergeant Rivers glanced at him, he rolled his eyes and took a deep breath. "All right, listen up. One of the locals, a man named Roberto, a houseboy in the officer's quarters, is up to something. I first noticed it two weeks ago. He hauls firewood into camp every few days in a supply wagon. He stacks some alongside the officer's mess hall and the rest in the shed by the officer's sleeping quarters. There are sideboards on the wagon, and he keeps the bed covered with a canvas tarp so you can't see what's in it, but one day when he left camp, I noticed the wagon springs were compressed, like he still had weight in it. After that, I paid closer attention, and since then I've seen him conduct the same business twice more. Three days ago I followed him here. If he stays on schedule, he'll be back today. I want to find out what's going on."

"Why don't we just put him under arrest or something?" Ellis asked.

"Because what he's doing doesn't make sense. He works in the officer's quarters, the best job a Filipino can get. He wouldn't risk that for a few dollars worth of supplies. I'm guessing he's also selling information to the enemy, and the thefts are only a cover. If the army catches him stealing groceries, he gets fired. If they catch him selling information, it's the gallows."

The three soldiers spread out behind the wall to wait. From concealed positions they had a good view of the barn and other outbuildings. In a while, the sun dropped below the tips of the bamboo, and a light breeze blew. Soon, Ellis fell fast asleep. As the afternoon wore on, Fagen found his own eyelids getting heavy, but he never forgot he might be face-to-face with a Filipino spy in a situation where he had little information, so he forced himself to stay alert.

Later, to Fagen's surprise, Sergeant Rivers moved in next to him, unwrapped some crumbled sugar cookies and offered one. "Fagen, what are you doing in this man's army?"

Fagen had no idea where Rivers was headed, so he said, "I'm doing what I'm told, Sarge."

"That's not what I mean, and you know it."

Fagen had been under the stoic sergeant's command for nearly a year and was no closer to figuring him out than on the first day he saw him. He decided this time as good as any to get things out in the open. "Sergeant Rivers, I don't understand what you want from me. I've been a good soldier. I fight hard and work hard. I had a little trouble once, but you know that wasn't my fault. Why don't you just tell me what you want?"

Rivers leaned back against the wall and lifted his hat. "Fagen, I take pride in knowing every man in my command. H Company's my baby. I'm responsible for everything we do or fail to do. It's my job to know every man's capabilities and limitations. I like to know what makes each of them tick, and I do that by finding out what makes his wheels go around. You take your cousin, Fairbanks there. He's in the army for the rest of his days. Why? Because you've convinced him Uncle Sam's his family, the family he couldn't hold onto in civilian life."

Fagen didn't know where the man came up with that, didn't like it and couldn't help feeling defensive. "Ellis and I had the same family, Sarge. I couldn't hold onto them either."

"Yes, but it's different for you. No two people see the same thing exactly the same way. Fairbanks is satisfied, you're not. He's got what he wants, but you don't. You worry me because you're an educated nigger, and that adds up to trouble every time." Fagen started to object, but Rivers held a hand up, palm forward, and he stopped. "You see, Fagen, a man's motivations are what's important. Take Pettijohn, for example. He's in the infantry, but he'd really like to be a cavalryman. That's all that man wants. It's what he dreams of, and he'll do anything I ask as long as he thinks there's a chance of getting transferred someday to a cavalry unit.

"Youngblood's another one. He's still just a kid, but he'd tear down the gates of hell to make people think he's a grown man. It's the same with all the others. Everybody wants something, Fagen. It's my job to know what that something is, but I haven't got you figured out yet. You're a different breed of cat, and I can't make up my mind about you. I don't know what makes you tick, and that makes you a liability in my company."

"Everybody knows what I want, Sarge. I want to be good soldier, and I want to show the folks back home a black man can fight hard for his country."

Rivers gave a little snort. "Do you know how many times I've heard that old song? That's barracks talk, and it adds up to just so many words. I'll tell you what I think. You've got a picture in your head of how everything should be. You want everyone to behave just the way you call it. If something's not right according to you, you think it's wrong. You've got stars in your eyes, Fagen. You're blind to the world as it is. You only see it as you think it should be."

"If that's what you believe, Sergeant Rivers, then there's nothing I can do about it. I've tried every way I know to make you like me, but if that's not possible, then so be it."

"Hell, man, I never said I didn't like you. You're twice any other soldier in H Company. I like you fine, I just can't figure you out, and so you worry me."

"Then I guess we can't figure each other out."

Another hour passed. Not interested in continuing the conversation, the two men ignored each other until they spotted Roberto driving toward them in his little wagon. He took the right fork past the far side of the main house, but then circled around and tied up at one of the outbuildings, a windowless shed with a solid wooden door. He disappeared inside and remained several minutes.

Roberto had been working in the officer's quarters for months in spite of the fact he was not well liked by most of the officers. Fagen didn't know him well, but thought him a dignified man and naturally serious-minded. Colonel Funston and the others didn't see it that way and usually let it be known to everyone within shouting distance that Roberto was an "uppity God dammed gook" and way too big for his britches.

Sergeant Rivers moved to a vantage point behind a low mound at the edge of the bamboo forest. Fagen nudged Ellis awake and peered out from behind the wall. Roberto came out of the shed, peeled back the canvas from the bed of his wagon, and then carried out three large crates and stacked them over the axel. His little burro sighed in anticipation of the added weight. As he drove away, Sergeant Rivers signaled to spread out and follow.

Apparently unconcerned about the possibility of being followed, Roberto stayed on the trail and rarely looked left or right, much less behind. The Americans stayed close as there was plenty of cover along the way. In those places where they might be seen and were forced to drop back, they easily followed the rough track of the wagon's wheels through the soft ground.

In time, the Filipino turned off the trail and disappeared down a narrow path through cogon grass higher than a man's head. The soldiers spread out and worked their way through, staying close by following the metal-on-wood sounds the wagon made as Roberto drove along. They covered two hundred yards before they came to a glade bordered on the far side by a little creek. In the center of the clearing stood the shell of what had once been a one-room schoolhouse. It reminded Fagen of the school he and Ellis went to except made of limestone blocks, Spanish style. Roberto stopped the wagon by the door, knocked once and went inside.

Sergeant Rivers settled in the tall grass to wait. A strange situation, he didn't like the smell of it. A whole platoon of rebels might be in that schoolhouse, and they could walk into a hornet's nest. Cautious, Rivers thought if this was a trap, it was a damned good one. He saw no indication of guerilla forces in the area. The cart path from the trail showed no signs of heavy use, and the yard around the schoolhouse was free of the typical scarring made by the tents and cook fires of soldiers.

Ellis flicked an ant from his bare forearm. "What are we waiting for, Sarge?"

"I didn't bring us out here to get us killed."

A half-hour went by, and still no movement anywhere around the schoolhouse. Soon a trickle of white smoke arose from the chimney. By then, Sergeant Rivers had run out of patience and made up his mind. "We're going in. You boys cover the windows. I'll take the front door. Move out."

The two privates ran across the yard staying as low as they could. When they reached the schoolhouse, they took positions next to the windows and pressed themselves flat against the outside wall. His men in place, Sergeant Rivers moved in using Roberto's wagon as cover. He stopped a moment, moved again, and then a loud crash, and he was inside. "*Alto!* Nobody move."

Fagen spun to his left, ripped the curtain aside, and put the barrel of his rifle through, ready to fire. When his eyes adjusted to the dim light inside the schoolhouse, he saw Sergeant Rivers framing the doorway, stock-still with a look of utter astonishment on his face. Roberto was seated at a small table in the center of the room, a cup of coffee in front of him, Lieutenant Alstaetter on his left, and on the lieutenant's left, an imposing woman who looked American. In the corner, two small children lay in a crib crying, startled by Rivers' sudden entrance. The woman moved quickly to comfort them. Lieutenant Alstaetter spoke first. "Good afternoon, Sergeant. This is as much a surprise to me as I'm sure it is to you. It appears as though I'm undone. I yield to your advantage."

"Lieutenant Alstaetter, sir," Rivers stammered, "I didn't know *you* were here."

"Quite all right, Sergeant. How could you have known?" The lieutenant looked around and saw the two men covering from the window. "Troopers! Come inside. You men are owed an explanation, and I'd like to give it to you."

The three soldiers stacked their rifles in a corner and took seats around the table while Roberto poured coffee. "Miss Merilee Shaw," the lieutenant said, "allow me to introduce H Company's First Sergeant Rivers, and these gentlemen are Privates Fagen and Fairbanks." Miss Shaw stood up and shook hands. Not a pretty woman even by the standards of her day, she had a large head, oddly too big for her body, and huge dark eyes under a woolly, man-like brow. As they introduced themselves, Rivers discerned what the woman no doubt already knew, her best feature her broad, warm smile. Not the least shy about meeting Negroes, she looked each of them in the eye and said how glad she was to meet American soldiers.

"Miss Shaw and I are related by marriage," Lieutenant Alstaetter said. "She's on a tour of the Philippines and has run into difficulty. I heard of her situation, and naturally, I wanted to help. Roberto has been kind enough to assist me."

Still uncomfortable, Rivers felt the need to apologize further. "We weren't trying to interfere in your business, sir, but I saw Roberto was up to something, and I figured I ought to investigate."

"Absolutely correct, Sergeant. You've done the right thing, and now I'm caught in the act as the saying goes. To purloin army property is a serious offense. Now you've discovered it, it's your duty to arrest me immediately and bind me over to Captain Baston for court martial."

Rivers couldn't believe what he heard. He'd served under the young Lieutenant for months. They'd been in battle together, trusted each other with their lives, and now his commander stood before him, his thin blonde hair neatly combed, telling him it was his duty to send him to jail. Rivers couldn't imagine a more awkward predicament.

Miss Shaw sensed his bewilderment and smiled. "Before you march my Matthew to the gallows, Sergeant, at least permit me to send you off with a good supper under your belt. Roberto will help prepare, and thanks to the army's generosity, we have plenty for everyone."

Sergeant Rivers went silent for a moment, hesitant to accept a dinner invitation under the circumstances. Negro soldiers didn't get asked to break bread with white folks every day, especially in those conditions, but Miss Shaw's smile was so sincere, her voice so cheerful, just then Rivers couldn't come up with a good reason to refuse.

She reached out and took one of his big hands in both of hers. "Please say yes. I know the food is stolen, but by design, aren't army rations intended for soldiers? Then the food you gentlemen eat cannot be considered stolen, and by eating it you're merely putting it to the use the army intended. Besides, we need time to talk."

David Fagen and Ellis Fairbanks unloaded the wagon while Roberto tended to the burro. Sergeant Rivers and the lieutenant gathered and stacked firewood. Miss Shaw put together a pot of meat stew with onions, and while it simmered on the stove, she washed and dressed the babies. Ellis, hardly more than a child himself, was fascinated with the children.

"My little girl's name is Maria," Miss Shaw placed the other child in Ellis' arms, "and that big boy is Carlos."

"Are these your babies, Miss?" Ellis asked. Miss Shaw gave the little girl a bottle and put her in her crib. The babies were adorable, dark skin, black hair and eyes, but clearly not the natural children of a white woman.

Miss Shaw smiled and then turned to face Ellis. "Let's us get on a first name basis too. If you call me Merilee, I'll call you…?"

Surprised, the big soldier stammered, "Ellis, ma'am."

"Fine. That's better isn't it?" she smiled. "No, the children aren't mine. I'm just looking out for them until I find them a home."

"They're orphans?"

Merilee's open, expressive face turned momentarily dark. "In a way, I suppose they are. They're rape babies, Ellis."

"Beg pardon, ma'am?"

"Two years ago, Spanish soldiers attacked their mothers during a raid on a village. With the Spanish gone, the women are afraid for their children's safety. I volunteered to find someone in Manila who'll take them. If I can't, they'll have to go to a government home. Then they *will* be orphans."

Ellis' heart went out to the children. The thought of them facing the world alone saddened him. The same way with puppies and fallen sparrows, if he could, he would take care of all of them. "They're such pretty babies. I hope you find a good home for them Miss Merilee."

The supper stove made the schoolhouse too hot, so after dinner, they moved outside and took in the fresh air. Ellis amused himself crawling around on the grass with the children. After a while, Lieutenant Alstaetter leaned back in his chair, lit a cigar and said, "You've a right to know what's going on, Sergeant Rivers, so here it is. Miss Shaw is from Boston. She is my wife's aunt. I received a letter from Greta a few weeks ago informing me of Miss Shaw's arrival in the Philippines and of her current predicament. She'd had a run of bad luck, and frankly, I wasn't sure she'd survive on her own.

"I went to Colonel Funston to ask for help from the government. There being a lady present, I can't repeat his response, but I was made to understand clearly that whatever her plight, as far as the army was concerned, Miss Merilee Shaw was entirely on her own.

"I had to do something, but felt I couldn't trust anyone in a uniform, so that's when I thought of Roberto. He's highly respected among the locals and a man who knows how to get things done. Needless to say, I was greatly relieved when he said he would assist me.

"Roberto found this place, helped me furnish it and devised a very clever procedure for keeping it supplied. I shudder to think where Miss Shaw would be now were it not for him. We've kept her presence here a secret. Not even the other Filipinos at the camp know of it. You've been the only ones to discover us."

"Pardon me, sir," Rivers said, "but how did the lady come to be in the Philippines?"

"I'll answer that, Sergeant." Miss Shaw interrupted. "Matthew's instructors at West Point failed to teach him it's impolite to speak for someone as though that person were not present. Why does it always fall to a woman to domesticate a man? My niece will have her work cut out for her when this poor specimen is released from the service." Rivers glanced over, certain he saw the lieutenant blush.

Miss Shaw continued, "I arrived in the Philippines with a group of journalists who came to cover the war. I have to tell you, we weren't received with open arms. General Otis hates newspapers and in his words, the 'spies' who write for them. The very idea the conduct of the war here in the islands might be reported back home sends him into a tizzy. He believes reporting the truth about what goes on here an act of treason. Therefore, he keeps a tight rein on everyone, in or out of uniform. Reporters are restricted to Manila, where nothing ever happens, and what little news they do get is spoon-fed to them by his staff. It's almost impossible to get any information that hasn't been strained through the army's sieve. The locals are willing, even eager to talk, but their reports are mostly rumor and gossip, and when you do run across a Filipino in a position to know something, you have to sift through his politics to get anything newsworthy.

"Simply stated, it's military censorship of the press. It's illegal as the dickens and flies in the face of our basic rights as Americans, but we're powerless to do anything about it." She paused, looked at the company sergeant and smiled. "But it doesn't stop with the news. In case you didn't know, mail is censored too, incoming and outgoing. I'm afraid you're being kept in the dark about things happening back home."

Rivers decided Miss Merilee could move from gracious to indignant, and then back again faster than any lady he'd ever met. He still wrestled with the notion that a sergeant and two private soldiers sat down to dinner and chitchat with a white officer and a woman reporter from

Boston, but there they were, and he had to admit, the lady fascinated him. "How did you get so far from Manila?"

"I paid a Filipino merchant an exorbitant sum to smuggle me to San Miguel. He provided me with accommodations and a guide to show me around. I've seen a good bit of this countryside since then, I have to tell you, and a good bit of the war. When I get back home, a lot of people will be very interested in what I've got to say."

Rivers felt himself warming to this over-talkative woman reporter. "The lieutenant said you had trouble, and the army wouldn't help. What kind of trouble?"

Lieutenant Alstaetter interrupted, "Let's don't go into that right now, Merilee."

"Pipe down, Matthew. The gentleman has asked me, and he has a right to know, you said so yourself. You see Sergeant, I'd been touring the small villages in the hills outside of San Miguel trying to make contact with the insurrectos, to learn about the war from their perspective.

"One night, a man came to my room and told me the local guerilla leader, Colonel Vicente Torres, had agreed to an interview. This tickled me no end, I have to tell you. Torres is the most famous man in the district. The locals call him 'Colonel Bloody Shirt' because he's so ferocious in battle. Everyone says he's arranged far more Spanish deaths than any other insurrecto commander. The man told me to have all my possessions packed and ready, he would return after dark.

"Late that night, two men appeared at my door, blindfolded me and took me on a tortuous route through the back streets of San Miguel. When we arrived at our destination, Colonel Bloody Shirt was waiting for me, and I found out then I hadn't been brought there for an interview. Without even a 'hello, how are you,' he ordered his men to confiscate my things, and then he forced me to strip. They stole everything I had, all my money, my jewelry, my dignity, everything. I spent the rest of that night bound and gagged in a chicken coop.

"Later, they returned my clothes and escorted me into his presence. He was a hard looking character, and I would have been more frightened if I hadn't been so angry. I called him every foul name I could think of. 'I came to learn the truth,' I told him, 'to give your struggle greater voice, and you've deceived me.' I was furious, and I wanted to give him a good tongue-lashing.

" 'You are outraged because you thought since you are in opposition to your country's war of aggression, you would be immune to misfortune here in the islands. 'Now you see that is not the case. These are uncertain times, Miss Shaw. You are lucky it is I who relieve you of your valuables and not someone less – how shall I say it – civilized.'

"'If you're trying to scare me, Colonel, it won't work,' I told him. 'Common thugs don't intimidate me. Your actions are a disgrace to yourself and to President Aguinaldo. Ruffians like you give all Filipinos a bad name.'

"He laughed at me, pure evil in his eyes, and I realized then he was a madman. 'You are so very presumptuous,' he said. 'Call me what you wish, but I will tell you General Aguinaldo couldn't care less about the fate of a meddlesome American woman foolish enough to wander alone in a land torn by suffering and war. Go home, Miss Shaw, at least go back to Manila. Here in the country, you're merely a symbol of wealth and privilege and arrogance, virtues our peasants have only seen in their oppressors.'

"One of the colonel's men replaced the blindfold and led me to the door. 'I suppose now that you're freeing me,' I said, 'you expect me to thank you for taking everything I own, leaving me with nothing but the clothes on my back.'

" 'I am leaving you with your life, Miss Shaw,' he said. 'There are those out there who would slit your throat for the buttons on your shoes, let alone the shoes themselves.'

"Well, I have to tell you I was glad to see the last of *Señor* Bloody Shirt. I was alive, but penniless of course and therefore friendless. It was a week before I got word to Matthew and another before he was able to bring me here."

"Where did you find the children?"

"After the incident, I begged a room in the home of an elderly Filipino couple. On the morning I was to leave San Miguel, two young women appeared at the door with the babies. They said Colonel Torres' men had come through their barrio the night before drunk and smashed and burned everything - anything held over from the days of the occupation. Worse, they shot on sight any Filipino who had ever helped or been friendly to any Spaniard.

"The women were afraid for the children because of their Spanish blood. Just two weeks before, I would have thought it inconceivable any Filipino would harm a child, but my experience with Colonel Torres taught me rules are different in time of war. Perhaps these young women's fears were justified. They'd seen far more armed conflict than I, and if frightened enough to give their children to a stranger, who was I to doubt them? If I got the children to Manila, they said they would find them later when the fighting was over."

Miss Merilee stopped and took a deep breath. Then a smile appeared once again on her big, expressive face, and she said, "There you have it, gentlemen. A week ago I was alone with nothing but my pride, and here I am today with a roof over my head, two children who need me and three new friends to chat with and enjoy."

Sergeant Rivers studied her, looked back and forth between her and Lieutenant Alstaetter. He stood up, walked around his chair, and then sat back down. "You told us you worked for a newspaper, ma'am. Is it one I've heard of?"

"I'm sorry, Sergeant, but I didn't say I worked for the press. I said I arrived here with a group of journalists, and I did. We all arrived together just over a month ago on the *Emerald Sea*, and I said I was here to report on the war, but I'm afraid my report isn't for a newspaper, not directly anyway. Do you follow politics, Sergeant?"

Lieutenant Alstaetter interrupted again, "You're determined to tell everything aren't you? For God's sake, Merilee, restrain yourself. There are certain things a soldier in combat doesn't need to know."

"That's your opinion, Matthew. I don't happen to agree. The truth hurts sometimes, but it doesn't kill."

Lieutenant Alstaetter flipped his cigar into the little creek. "My wife's aunt spends as much time making news as writing it, Sergeant. She's what's called a political activist, not elected to any office, but claims to represent the mood of the people. Activists would have you believe they get more done in less time than elected officials and boast they cost the taxpayer a hell of a lot less. There are many who would disagree with that assessment."

Miss Merilee gave the lieutenant a patronizing smile. "Of the many topics on which you are not qualified to speak, Matthew," she said, "politics must be in the very first row." A wounded look crossed the lieutenant's face. Miss Merilee saw it, quickly turned to Sergeant Rivers and added, "Unless you gentlemen think I'm anything but a devoted admirer of my niece's husband, I should tell you I've known him for many years. He and my niece were sweethearts while Matthew was at the Point, and when I behold the professional military man before you now, I still see the towheaded young man who trailed me around the Shaw family home for hours in the desperate hope of catching even a glimpse of his beloved Greta. I need to constantly remind myself he is not that naïve, unsophisticated adolescent now. In truth, I am exceedingly proud of the man he's become.

"But back to the subject at hand. Matthew has branded me an activist. Perhaps that's so, but I have to tell you, gentlemen, there's a movement afoot in America you may not be fully aware of. People at home are quickly losing their appetite for this war. Every day more and more of us become convinced that expansionism, we call it imperialism, is a shameful and dishonorable policy. Several months ago, a group of us gathered in Boston to debate our government's avaricious lust for empire. We discovered then people from all corners of our nation and from all stations in life share our point of view. We call ourselves the Anti-Imperialist League, and anyone opposed to the subjugation of others is welcome in our ranks."

Ellis spoke up, "Does that mean Americans are against us too because we're here fighting this war? There's already enough folks back home who hate us just because we're black men wearing a uniform."

"I tried to tell you," Lieutenant Alstaetter said.

"No one back home is against you, Ellis," Miss Merilee urged. "You mustn't confuse anti-imperialism with anti-militarism. You came here to free the Philippines from the Spanish, not to make war on the Filipino people. Military men such as you only carry out policy. You can't be held responsible for the wrong-headedness of those who misuse you for the sake of shameful purpose."

Sergeant Rivers asked, "Do all anti-imperialists agree on that? Love the soldier, hate the war?"

"Nothing is ever *all* is it, Sergeant? By far, the largest percentage of anti-imperialists rejects the concept of a strong people brutalizing and taking away the liberty of a weak one. We believe it wrong in the eyes of law and the eyes of God, but I can't recall an instance, when in any debate I've attended, the enlisted soldier has been singled out for criticism. When our military is mentioned at all, it's usually by those of us who believe you fine boys are unwitting pawns in a game with rules concocted by power-hungry politicians and profit-hungry industrialists. There is a movement against this Philippine intervention, gentlemen, not against you."

Sergeant Rivers had heard stories from troopers stationed in Manila about war protests back home, but he'd had no hard news to back up the rumors and dismissed them as idle gossip.

Miss Merilee continued, "Several of our league members have appealed to President McKinley not to use our armed forces as a tool of the industrialists. Mark Twain's writing volumes, and last month Mr.

Andrew Carnegie himself paid a personal visit to the White House to register his disapproval, but the President sits squarely in the lap of the eastern manufacturers. It's been said he won't be happy until the entire population of the Philippines is dressed from head to toe in American textiles, and I have to tell you gentlemen, I believe it.

"Our government tells its citizens expansion into the Pacific is our destiny. They say America is no longer just a nation of farmers, but also a nation of industry, and soon a major player on the world's stage. China is the future of business they say, and our doorway into that market is through the Philippines. These islands then, are America's stepping stones to twentieth century commerce. The stakes are high indeed, gentlemen.

"We're asked to believe the Filipino people not capable of self-government, that like children, they must yield to our higher authority. If they surrender their sovereignty to the United States, they'll prosper under our protectorate and in time, when they've shown themselves capable, their independence will be granted. I say horsefeathers! This war is about greed pure and simple.

"But what war isn't these days? The Germans and the Japanese stand shoulder-to-shoulder in Peking right now, mowing down Chinese nationalists in a war for territory they call the Boxer Rebellion. The British are in South Africa killing Boers to get their hands on the Dutch gold mines in the republics of Transvaal and the Orange Free State. Queen Victoria declared she'd not rest until she has Cape to Cairo domination of Africa. These are dark days indeed. We anti-imperialists say let empire building be the path for other nations. Their governments are not founded on the American principles of independence and liberty.

"There is hope, however. If our movement prevails, William Jennings Bryan will defeat President McKinley in the next election, and our government's shameful policy of expansionism will cease." Miss Shaw's big smile suddenly appeared once again. "And now it's the children's bedtime. Ellis, would you like to help me tuck my little darlings in?"

The last of daylight gone, it had begun cooling off. Fagen and the lieutenant moved the chairs back into the schoolhouse while Roberto put a log in the stove. Sergeant Rivers stood alone on the little porch. After a while, the children asleep, everyone sat at the table.

Miss Merilee continued, "So there you have it, gentlemen. I know how difficult this is for you. The last thing a soldier needs to hear is the people of his own nation are opposed to the war he's forced to fight. It's a terrible truth, and it must hurt awfully, but I felt you had to know."

Rivers leaned forward, put his arms on the table. "What happens next for you, Miss Merilee?"

"The *Pacific Star* is scheduled to depart for San Francisco in a week. I intend to be on it. Thanks to Matthew and Roberto, I can return home in one piece to tell my story."

Sergeant Rivers stood up and put on his hat. "With your permission, sir, we'll be heading back to garrison now."

"Without your prisoners?" Miss Merilee asked, a twinkle in her eye. "Does this mean our secret is safe with you, Sergeant?"

"Your secret is safe, Miss Shaw." The men slung their weapons and moved toward the door.

Lieutenant Alstaetter returned River's salute. "Thank you, Sergeant. Roberto tells me the roads are clear tonight. You'll encounter no difficulties on the way back. I'll be returning myself just before sunrise."

Miss Shaw followed them out and shook hands. "Goodbye, Sergeant. I'll be pleased to tell my niece all about the wonderful men her husband serves with here. Thank you."

Sergeant Rivers held her hand for a moment, and then led her away from the others to a spot on the grass near the creek. "Forgive me, Miss," his low voice ghosted on the night air, "but now I want to tell you something." He stopped, took a deep breath, and then continued.

"The army's story is we're not here to take over the Philippines, just to stabilize the situation and knock down a few warlords. They say the anti-war noise back home comes from a handful of radicals, people with too much time on their hands, like you.

"Negroes have black skin, Miss, but we're not stupid. It's a pack of lies, and we know it, but there's nothing we can do about it. Do you want to hear the real story of the war here in the Philippines?"

Merilee Shaw assumed the posture of an attentive schoolgirl, standing erect, her hands locked in his. "Please continue, Sergeant. I want to hear everything."

"Tonight, you said this is a war of subjugation, illegal in the eyes of God and the law. You said it was founded on greed, and our government uses the military for profit, not peace. All this may be true, but the reason this war is so bloody, Miss Shaw, is because it's a race war. The United States is taking over the Philippines, Puerto Rico and Guam because these are all nations of colored people. Their native populations aren't white, and in the eyes of our government, not fully human. They're 'half-devil and half-child.' It's the God given duty, the *burden* of the white man to oversee the lives of the inferior races."

"I'm aware of that horrible sentiment, Sergeant, but I assure you, no thinking person subscribes to it."

"Miss Shaw, you've heard the words nigger and coon and sambo, but have you ever heard dink, gook, slope, bullet-head or gugu? These are some of the names white soldiers call Filipinos, and there's a lot more a lot worse. Where do these names come from? Why do they exist at all? Because without a moral purpose, most soldiers don't have the stomach to brutalize and murder a people; they need to dehumanize them first. If they make themselves believe the enemy is less than human, then it's natural to spit at him, run him down in the streets and kill his children.

"No atrocity's too great here because we've made the Filipino a beast, not a man. This is what it's come to in this war. It's open season on an entire population of dark-skinned people. This is what your Colonel Bloody Shirt tried to tell you when he said there's no law in these islands. Here, if a white man murders a Filipino, he's the envy of his platoon. If he murders enough, he gets a medal. The U.S. Army's training a generation of young men to run roughshod over a nation of colored people.

"All these soldiers will go home someday. How much of what they've been taught here will go with them? What will they teach their children about the value of a colored man's life? The Filipinos tell the Negro if we kill them, we bring down our own race back home. If that turns out to be true, then there's far more at stake than spending-money for a few back-east shirt makers. Take that story home with you, Miss Shaw."

Merilee Shaw, a total stranger, was the first person to ever hear Sergeant Warren Rivers string so many words together. He'd found an audience and felt compelled to voice his growing anxiety over how the war affected men on both sides of the skirmish line.

"I will report this just as you've told it to me, but Sergeant Rivers, I have to ask you, if you know this, how do you keep going? How can you lead men into battle after battle knowing every Filipino insurgent that falls puts your own race in greater peril back home?"

"I can do it, Miss, because I'm a soldier. It's the life I chose for myself. I wouldn't change that even if I could."

"In that case, Sergeant, God bless you and keep you."

A dark, moonless night, they kept to the main roads on their way back to camp. Sergeant Rivers walked in silence two or three paces in front. Fagen had heard his company sergeant's words that night, and they frightened him. When he was growing up, everyone always said a young man wasn't supposed to know or understand a thing, he just thinks he does. Fagen now saw the truth in that. When he arrived in the Philippines, he thought he knew just who he was, just what he wanted out of life. He thought he could read another man as well as anyone, solve a problem better than most. He was pretty sure he could handle just about any situation that came up. Now, he didn't know anything for sure. Every day the war brought him something new to think about, something he'd never had to worry about before.

Life had always been pretty easy for him, now it looked impossible. How was he to know what to do? He couldn't tell right from wrong anymore. It was as though he struggled over a puzzle with too many pieces. He wished then he were more like Ellis. His cousin didn't concern himself with anything out of arm's reach. He had the army - his wife, mother and uncle all rolled into one. He didn't look outside for anything else. Fagen wished he were like that, but knew in his heart it wouldn't be enough.

He thought he could try to be more like Sergeant Rivers. That man walked through the world on his own terms, never faltered, never compromised. He inhaled life, and then carried it around all day in that big chest of his. It worked for him, but Fagen was pretty sure he wasn't man enough for that. He was all turned around, off track and couldn't get his bearings. As they walked silently through the darkness, however, Fagen felt he knew one thing too well. One thing had become clear. He knew he'd never understand why God made inferior races

CHAPTER 10 - THE JUDGMENT OF THE COURT

Colonel Funston had always been self-conscious about his stumpy, elfish legs. Just under average height and fairly well built, even as a youngster, when the situation had presented itself, he could never wear another's clothes because while the jacket might fit properly, the pants were invariably too long. His wife had assured him on many occasions his legs were not too short, he was just "long-waisted" as were many other military figures of renown, ranging from the great Napoleon to their own General Arthur MacArthur. However, the echo of Mrs. Funston's accommodating remarks was little comfort to him now as he and Captain Baston led their column through tall cogon grass to the bank of the river, the captain's horse sixteen hands two, his own a mere fifteen.

Three days of heavy monsoon rains had swollen the river to within inches of its banks. Brown water bubbled and foamed around logs that rolled and tumbled end over end on their way downstream. The *Rio Malimba*, and they had to cross it before sundown.

Captain Baston drew a circle on the map and handed it to the colonel. "General Tagunton was last reported in the area of Rosa Rita, sir, a village just at the head of the small tributary to our left front. If we cross here, we'll have protective cover from the bluff between the village and us. Downstream, closer to the tributary, there's no cover at all, and therefore no chance of concealment. They'd see us coming a mile away. Our scouts spotted a boat tied up on the other side. If we can get it over here, we can cross safely."

Funston studied the opposite bank with his binoculars, tried to ignore his executive officer. This oaf has an opinion on everything but the weather, he thought to himself. He ought to at least pretend he's not lusting after my job. When will the good Lord give me the chance to prosecute this war as I see fit? On the one hand, I've got to deal with that milksop, General Otis, and his henchman, Bill Russell, their noses so far up the nearest politician's arse they wouldn't know a rebel gook if they saw one; and on the other, I've an idiot for an executive officer, two greenhorn company commanders, and an entire detachment of buffalo soldiers whose only real resemblance to a buffalo is their odor. Is this my destiny, the colonel asked himself? What did I do to deserve your wrath, God?

Their spies had informed them that insurrecto General Tagunton, a close confident of Aguinaldo, had been raiding villages just south of the river, securing much needed supplies and fresh recruits from among his countrymen there. The Americans thought Tagunton a heartless barbarian, willing, even eager, to sacrifice Filipino lives without compunction if it furthered the insurrecto cause. Colonel Funston believed defeating Tagunton on the battlefield would demonstrate to the local natives the superiority of American forces and their ability to protect them from other pitiless outlaws.

"Captain Baston, assemble the officers."

Their troop consisted of companies A and C of the 20th Kansas Volunteers commanded by a new man, Lieutenant John Amery, and H Company of the colored 24th led by Lieutenant Alstaetter. As Colonel Funston had decided to accompany the troop into the field, Doctor Forrester was in attendance as well as a small cadre of Filipino servants.

Although he would never admit it in public, Colonel Funston had developed a grudging respect for the colored men of H Company. They'd grown into their uniforms and performed better than he'd expected. He'd been pleased, even impressed on occasion. All the more surprising, he concluded, given their commander, Lieutenant Alstaetter, was a mewling kitten, and worse, a radical. What a shame, he said to himself. An academy man too.

Captain Baston blew three short blasts on his trench whistle, and the two company commanders rode forward at a fast gallop. Funston stowed his field glasses, tried to sit a little taller in the saddle. "Lieutenant Amery, deploy your men on line two hundred yards downstream and prepare to provide covering fire. Alstaetter, I've got a different job for you."

"Sergeant Rivers, we have the privilege of being the first to cross this river. I need nine of our best men." Lieutenant Alstaetter paced in quick, agitated circles. "Only volunteers and strong swimmers. Start the rest of the men cutting bamboo. We need two rafts to float us across. There's some kind of native watercraft tied up over there. The captain says it's big enough to ferry as many as forty men at a time. It's our job to get it over to this side. We'll need to establish a dragline. Send a man to the pack train to round up as much rope as he can find."

H Company went to work and in no time built two small rafts. The lieutenant wanted to save the rope for the ferry line, so Sergeant Rivers ordered the men to lash the rafts together with canteen straps and rifle slings. At the water's edge, Alstaetter and his volunteers stripped to their underwear, loaded personal gear and weapons on the rafts along with extra ammunition, three machetes, a hammer, a saw and a hundred and fifty yards of rope. Alstaetter, first in the water, said, "Fagen, you're in charge of the second raft. Shove off two minutes behind us, but don't get too close, we don't know what's waiting for us on the other side. We'll take the duck course and try not to drift too far downstream. I suggest you do the same. Sergeant Rivers, in case of trouble, you haul them back fast. When we get across, we'll do what we can to cover you. Let's go."

Alstaetter pushed out into the brown water, Corporal Moody and Private Wheelwright on the port, downstream side of the raft, Private Wallace pulling from upstream and Youngblood kicking from the rear. After only a few steps, the bottom fell away, and they started working upstream. As they cleared the shore and moved into the main flow, the water moved faster than they'd expected, and they found themselves losing ground to the current. All eyes were riveted on the swimmers. Lieutenant Alstaetter felt the weight of the raft tear into his shoulder and tasted his own blood in the water around him. He shouted encouragement to the men, "We're nearly through the worst of it men. Keep pushing!"

When the first raft reached midstream, Fagen pushed out into the river. He'd seen the lieutenant struggle with the current, so he put all four men on the downstream side of the raft, Ellis Fairbanks in front, privates Douglas, Normal and McMullen behind him. Fagen positioned himself in the rear to steer and keep an eye on the raft in front. He felt he had the stronger swimmers, and if something were to happen, he had a chance at least, of helping, if help was possible. Sergeant Rivers secured his end of the dragline around a huge boulder and allowed it to flake out behind Fagen's raft as it moved away.

Alstaetter's men struggled through the swiftest flow, but the going got easier as they neared the far shore. Fagen's decision to put all his men on the downstream side paid off, and they pushed through the current with relative ease.

In mid-stream, Fagen heard a shrill, high-pitched call. At first he thought it a bird, but then heard it again, a man's voice. He pulled himself out of the water and scanned the cogon grass on the shore behind them.

What he heard weren't birdcalls but catcalls. Some of the white soldiers from A Company, men detailed to cover them while they crossed the river, were laughing at them. Fagen saw them, hats pushed back, leaning on their rifles, their hard Midwestern accents burning in his ears as the men whistled derisively and shouted rude taunts. "Swim monkey, swim!" someone said.

Another man yelled out, "Hey smoky! Let us know if you see any gooks on the other side of that river. We'll go find somebody to shoot 'em for you!"

A big, red-faced corporal poked the man beside him and shouted, "Look here, John, somebody must have took a crap up-river. You can see the turds floating by right out there!"

The insults more than David Fagen could bear, he seethed with bitter resentment and vowed to find someway to get back at those men. In the middle of a dangerous river, swimming toward perhaps a more dangerous shore, and still the white man showed nothing but contempt for the colored man. Fagen knew why H Company had been given the river crossing, it was a nigger job, and no one else wanted it. He'd grown used to that, but at least those men could sit in the grass and pretend to cover them. He maneuvered to see whether the lieutenant was close enough to hear what went on.

He looked, and what he saw made his blood run suddenly cold. Alsaetter's raft had been pulled into the center of a powerful whirlpool formed by the force of the river rushing around two huge boulders near the far shore. The front end of the raft had been sucked completely under the boiling water, taking Wallace under with it, while the back had been lifted high in the air and spun in dizzying circles. Youngblood, pulled out to his ankles, hung on for all he was worth.

Around and around in a tornado of brown river water, each man tried desperately to hold on, clawing at the air, then the water, and then the air again. Fagen saw flashes of Lieutenant Alstaetter's blond hair near the front of the raft. He shouted something to his men, but Fagen found it impossible to hear anything over the groan of the river and the roar of his own blood pounding in his head.

The young officer had seen Wallace go under, struggled to the front and hooked his arm through one of the straps that held the bamboo poles together. Then he dove, completely disappearing in the foamy water. After what seemed to Fagen an impossibly long time, he surfaced, dragging the exhausted, half-drowned Wallace with him. With his last ounce of strength, Alstaetter lifted the man out of the water to safety on the raft.

Fagen and his men swam as hard as they could, pushed frantically against the current, trying to get close enough to help. The lieutenant had saved Wallace from certain death, but they were still caught in the whirlpool and dangerously close to capsizing. Just as they flew through yet another rotation, the mysterious, unpredictable force of the river changed direction, and the raft shot out of the reeling turbine into a quiet, upstream back-eddy. It happened so suddenly, the men so surprised to at last be free of their spinning nightmare, in unison they turned their faces to the sky as though to reassure themselves it was still there. Youngblood cried out, and Fagen heard him clearly across the small stretch of water between them, "We did it, boys! This old river can't beat us!"

As their raft loitered idly in the back-eddy of the whirlpool, Lieutenant Alstaetter turned his attention to the narrow beach in front of them and assessed their situation. Impossible to see into the thick grass at the water's edge, if the enemy were there waiting, they'd hold fire until the Americans reached shore. Then it would be a turkey shoot, and it wouldn't matter they'd made it safely across the river. When they landed, they'd need to take the first cover they could find.

Later, when he made his report to Captain Baston, Alstaetter recalled those thoughts were on his mind when a huge brown log, eight feet long and the diameter of a fully-grown mule, catapulted out of the maelstrom behind them and crashed into the back of their raft. Hit with the force of a pile driver, Youngblood was impaled against the jagged, butt-ends of the bamboo, his chest a tangled mass of crushed bone and torn flesh.

It happened so fast, no one knew for certain what had hit him. Then just as suddenly, the giant, water-soaked log drifted downstream in lazy circles, Youngblood's broken, lifeless body along with it. The men of H Company, helpless to do anything, watched in horror as the ugly juggernaut careened along its path with Youngblood, now no more than a grotesque rag doll, in its teeth. Fagen looked back to shore. No one moved. His heart sank, and a deep sadness swept over him as he watched the *Rio Malimba* carry the young soldier away.

From his perch on his big horse, Captain Baston lowered his binoculars. "I'll send a detail to retrieve the body."

"Let it go," Colonel Funston answered. "Someone will find it in a month or two when it washes up on a beach in China."

Both rafts finally reached the far shore without further incident. Making use of available cover, Lieutenant Alstaetter posted six men to provide covering fire while he, Fagen and Ellis Fairbanks secured drag lines to each end of the ferry. When ready, he gave the signal and Sergeant Rivers' men hauled the boat across, and the transfer of soldiers and animals began.

H Company made a cheerless camp that night, their backs to the river. Cook fires prohibited, they made do with biscuits and cold meat. Sergeant Rivers set listening posts on two-hour rotation. The campsite quiet, time dragged, no one felt like talking. For the first time since they'd arrived in the Philippines, H Company had lost one of its own.

In all the time he'd been with them, Youngblood hadn't made any real friends among the men. Sergeant Rivers had been right, he was cocky, irritable and always tried to be something he wasn't, a grown-up man. That night, however, everyone agreed Youngblood possessed the courage of a man. Hadn't he always been the first to volunteer for any assignment? Hadn't he been first when the lieutenant asked for men to clean out that insurrecto tunnel? Indeed, he'd volunteered that very day to push a makeshift raft across a swollen and dangerous river, and this time it had cost him his life. But the men had a feeling deep within them that today, if only for an instant, somehow Youngblood knew he'd finally earned the respect he sought.

Night brought cooler temperatures, and a light breeze blew along the river carrying with it the murmur of conversation and occasional laughter from the Kansas volunteers camped upstream.

Colonel Funston planned to move the battalion under the cover of darkness into position just below the crest of a low hill east of Rosa Rita. That, he reasoned, afforded the element of surprise, and they could attack downhill with the rising sun at their backs.

Captain Baston thought the plan unwise. Three companies maneuvering through difficult, unfamiliar terrain in the blackness before sunup was something no commander should risk unless absolutely necessary, and he didn't see the necessity. In this case, the element of surprise just didn't seem worth it. They'd seen no sign of the notorious General Tagunton, and although they'd no hard information about the village of Rosa Rita, nothing indicated it any different from the countless other native villages they'd entered with impunity.

Better to move at daylight in battle formation, he thought, and search out and destroy the enemy throughout the entire valley, but the order had been given, and the captain knew Colonel Funston already pictured himself riding fearlessly through the murky night toward a desperate battle, a column of frightened men following his lead, gaining courage with every step. Baston made a mental note to get that drunken Sergeant Flanagan to do a charcoal sketch of the scene for the old man's vanity wall.

They moved out two hours before sunup, heading north away from the river for a half-mile, then west until in position to encircle the village. A narrow tributary of quiet water led from the river two hundred yards to the village. A good way out, but its banks were barren and flanked the entire length by a low ridge. Insurrectos attempting to escape along this route could be picked off like shooting gallery ducks.

Masters of the battlefield during the day, the Americans' marksmanship and soldiering skills had proved superior in every daylight encounter with the rebels, but the Filipinos owned the night. They trained, transported weapons and supplies, dug trenches and set up traps and ambushes at night. If an American column were caught away from the safety of camp after sunset, the rebels attacked, seemingly out of nowhere, inflicted maximum casualties, and then disappeared under the cover of darkness. Most Americans considered this a cowardly method of making war, unmanly and only underscored the treachery of the sneaky Filipino rebel. In their minds, all the more reason to kill as many insurrectos as they could, whenever they could. Now, in pitch-blackness, groping blindly through a narrow saddle in the hills east of Rosa Rita, the men concentrated on a more immediate concern, keeping up with the man in front.

Terrain permitting, a most effective ambush is in the shape of an "L" with the longer, vertical leg parallel to the long axis of the advancing column. Done properly, the bulk of the enemy force is in the kill zone before the ambush is sprung, and the aggressor force can apply maximum firepower upon the enemy from two entirely different directions, minimizing collateral casualties that often result from friendly crossfire.

For any ambush to succeed, friendly forces must have absolute control of the field. No other friendly units can operate in the area - no snipers on the trail, no night patrols, punji-pits or booby-traps. The opposition must have no hint the friendly force is present. The goal is to maintain the element of surprise until the enemy has moved deep within the ambush zone. Everyone must be cautioned against giving in to "buck-fever" when he sees the enemy walk so close past his position of concealment. Pulling the trigger too soon inevitably reduced the number of opposition casualties.

The most effective defense against the "L" ambush is counter-intuitive to the average soldier. When fired upon, a soldier seeks cover, or at least concealment, returns fire, and then waits for orders from his commander. This is natural, a civilian with no military training would do the same, but in an ambush sure death. The only hope of survival in a properly executed "L" ambush is to turn toward the direction of fire and charge. That this sounds like suicide is why it's counter-intuitive, and it *seems* like suicide to a soldier while he's doing it; but it's the quickest path out of the killing zone and has the potential, at least, of turning a complete massacre into routine hand-to-hand combat, a scenario any commander would choose, given the option.

When Tagunton's rebels sprung their "L" ambush on Colonel's Funston's night column, two things happened that saved the Americans from total annihilation. In his resolve to kill as many invading *Americanos* as possible, Tagunton had decided to augment the power of his men's Mauser rifles with several homemade mines consisting of canisters of nails affixed to quantities of gunpowder wrapped in cotton camphor. He'd planned to detonate the mines along the length of the American column, the explosions the signal for his men to open fire and finish the job.

Under the best circumstances, homemade explosive devices were unreliable, and owing in part to the pre-dawn dampness, two of Tagunton's four bombs didn't explode at all, and the others merely fizzled and spewed black smoke and sparks. Without the detonations that signaled the beginning of their attack, the insurrectos up and down the line weren't sure when to open fire, and the Americans were alerted to their presence.

Lieutenants Alstaetter and Amery rode together near the center of the column. They'd agreed it unwise to conduct a night march across enemy occupied terrain unless absolutely necessary, if for no other reason than the high risk of ambush. Accordingly, when they entered the pass, they alerted the column to return fire and charge at the first sign of trouble. Thus, the Americans were ready when the Filipinos let go their first hesitant volley. One corporal from A Company reported later, "Our blood was up, and we were itching for a fight. We went after those bullet-heads with everything we had. It was like shooting rabbits. We killed everything in sight."

By sunrise, the skirmish was over. The Americans had indeed averted a tragedy, only three from C Company killed, and Lieutenant Alstaetter had received a minor wound to the hand. Colonel Funston sent Doctor

Forrester to attend to the lieutenant's wound and a burial detail to take care of the dead. He also ordered C Company's Gatling gun brought forward.

Sergeants detailed squads to clear the battlefield of enemy weapons and confiscate maps and other documents. Then they used their bayonets on any Filipinos still alive. The final toll taken, the enemy body count totaled thirty-seven, among the dead Tagunton himself, whose bullet-ridden body was placed at Funston's feet. The colonel peered under the dead Filipino's hat brim. "There's one indian that won't go on the warpath again."

At midday, the Americans were in position around Rosa Rita. A cakewalk, Colonel Funston concluded. The rebels now long gone, they could take this village barefoot. A and H Companies entered the village from the north and west while C Company, with their deadly Gatling gun, held the high ground to the east, the terrain providing excellent fields of fire for covering both the village and the tributary leading to the *Rio Malimba*.

The Americans emerged from the nipa groves bewildered by a most unusual sight. A crowd of ragtag peasants stood guard over a little cluster of grim-faced Filipino rebels huddled in a circle near the center of the village. The peasants, armed with bolo knives and long-handled hoes, stood vigilant over a half-dozen tired and dispirited prisoners squatting before them. Captain Baston reined in short of the village. "Lieutenant Alstaetter, I want two of your men at the door of every native hut, and be ready for anything."

Alstaetter gave a signal, and the Negro soldiers quickly dispersed throughout the village. Only the scratch-clucking of chickens under the huts broke the eerie silence. The men in position, Colonel Funston and Captain Baston rode into Rosa Rita.

Two old men in peasant garb met them in the village square and removed their hats as the officers approached on their big horses. One man stepped forward. "*Buenos Dias, Señores*. My name is Gregorio. This is my brother, Rodrigo. We speak for the people of Rosa Rita. On their behalf we bid you welcome, sirs."

For a long moment, Colonel Funston stared down at the two men. Then he turned to Captain Baston. "These two are cheeky bastards."

"Guts like a government mule, I'd say."

The colonel glanced over at the village men guarding the rebel prisoners, and then he turned to the old man. "You've got three seconds to order your gang of murdering thugs to drop their weapons, at which time you will surrender this village."

"But, sir," Gregorio stammered, "we have captured these insurrectos for you."

"Two seconds."

"These men were with Tagunton, sir. We've captured them for you!"

Funston gave a little nod, and the captain drew his revolver and fired, sending a bullet straight through Rodrigo's heart. The man collapsed in a heap amid the sudden barking of dogs and braying of goats. As the report from the pistol echoed through the village, a woman's sudden, shrill, anguished cry issued forth from one of the nearby huts. Gregorio dropped to his knees over the body of his dead brother. Funston leaned down, his voice low and hard. "Now you listen to me, you God damned, slope-headed bastard. You tell those men to disarm at this instant. I've already lost three men today, and one of my officers is wounded. I'm in no mood to be disobeyed by anyone, least of all a villainous scoundrel like you."

The old man gave an order, and the men dropped their crude weapons. Sergeant Rivers barked, and a corporal and four other soldiers moved in quickly and collected them.

Sobbing, Gregorio wiped his eyes and stood up. "Please, sir, no more killing. I beg you. Please believe me. The people of Rosa Rita surrender to you. We are sick of the fighting. We denounce the insurrection. We wish to be under your protectorate, sir. We have captured these prisoners for you. They were with Tagunton, and we captured them this morning as they ran from your guns."

"You're lying to save your own skin," the colonel growled. "Do you believe this cur, Captain Baston?"

"Not for a moment, sir."

"Nor do I. My gut tells me to finish off the whole lot right now and be done with it."

The old man stepped forward wringing his hands. "Sir, I implore you. For years Rosa Rita has been a victim of the insurrection and the lawlessness it has brought to our province.

"Since the fighting began, the river, once a source of life, has become a highway bringing only death to our village. First the Spanish came and killed many of our men and even our women and children. Then rebels like Tagunton and others even bloodier, came at night, kidnapped our young men and stole our rice and animals. They told us it was our duty to provide these things, to support the struggle for independence. Later, roving bands of outlaw Macabebes that live in the south hills plundered what the rebels did not take. They have a blood hatred for Tagalog people and are even more brutal than the Spanish." Gregorio moved another step forward and gazed into Colonel's Funston's eyes. "Please, sir. Rosa Rita is not just another 'amigo' village. There is no treachery in our hearts. We want only to live in peace under the protection of the Americans. I beg you to believe me."

Funston's long held conclusions about the treacherous Filipino were based on hard experience. He knew he couldn't trust the man, but what if he were telling the truth? Wasn't this just what General Otis wanted? Wasn't his mission, after all was said and done, to bring the natives into forbearance of American guardianship? After a long moment, he turned to Captain Baston, "Have Lieutenant Alstaetter clear these huts. You know the routine. Move the villagers to the riverbank where we can watch them, then get Lieutenant Amery up here. I think he should have a talk with those so-called prisoners. In the meantime, we'll have our luncheon."

For the next half-hour, Rosa Rita was alive with activity. Amid cries of *amigo* and *Negrito Americano*, H Company searched the nipa shacks and outbuildings gathering up villagers and crude weapons. The native huts cleared, they herded ninety-four people and an assortment of chickens, geese and goats to the sandy bank of the tiny tributary where they huddled, waiting in the sun while the Americans interrogated the prisoners. As Fagen stood guard over the villagers, he noticed mostly old people and children, no men or women of fighting age among them. There must be some truth to what Gregorio had said, he thought. Rosa Rita's population had been decimated by war.

The insurrecto prisoners knelt in a row, their hands tied behind their backs. Lieutenant Amery strode casually among them whistling softly, wiping sweat from his hatband. He wanted the Filipinos to get a good look at him, to contemplate his absolute authority over them. He knew from experience, in an interrogation fear often produced more information than pain. He noticed two of the prisoner's clothes covered with dried blood, but couldn't tell whether their injuries were from American gunfire or rough treatment by the local villagers. No matter, he knew what had to be done. "Bring Tagunton's body and put it right here in front of their noses, and get that old man over here to translate."

The tools of his interrogation in place, the lieutenant resumed pacing up and down the row of prisoners, pausing every now and then to give Tagunton's lifeless corpse a kick, his boot thudding against pulpous, bloating flesh. He turned to the old man, "Gregorio, tell me how you captured these men."

"They ran away from the battle this morning, sir. In the confusion before daylight, they became separated from the others and demanded we hide them here. As I said, *Señor*, we want no more of this fighting, so we took them prisoner and waited for you to come."

One of the rebel prisoners hurled a guttural curse at the old man. Gregorio cursed back and spat in the dirt before him.

Amused by the exchange, the lieutenant smiled. "Tell them I want to know how many of their number survived the firefight today and where we can find them. Tell them if they help us bring the rebels to justice, the U.S. Government will reward them with a small pension, which they will receive for life." Gregorio raised an eyebrow at this, and then translated, but no response from the rebels.

Lieutenant Amery waited a moment, and then summoned a squad of nearby soldiers. "Let's try that one," he said, pointing to the youngest prisoner. The soldiers wasted no time. They dragged the boy to a tree, threw a line over a limb, and with his hands tied behind his back, hoisted him by his wrists until suspended high in the air. The young rebel screamed at the pain in his shoulders while his legs jerked, and his feet searched for the comfort of the ground.

The rebels averted their eyes. The American couldn't force them to watch their comrade's torture, but they couldn't close their ears to his terrible, agonized pleas for mercy.

"Gregorio, tell these men this boy suffers for no reason. The rebel cause is lost. Their brotherhood is vanquished. Even their own people have turned against them."

The old man translated, but the rebels pretended not to hear him. Lieutenant Amery waited a moment for the prisoners' response. Satisfied they weren't yet ready to cooperate, he gave a signal, and the sergeant holding the rope let out some slack, the boy's arms collapsed, and he plummeted wide-eyed toward the ground. Just before his feet made contact, the sergeant hauled on the rope, and the boy jerked to a sudden, violent stop. This time, the muscles and tendons in his shoulders let go, his arms pulled backwards over his head and made sickening sounds as the bones broke in sequence from his wrists down to his shoulders. The boy hardly had time to cry out before his eyes rolled back in his head, and he passed out.

One of the rebel prisoners jumped to his feet, his face ashen, trembling with fear. "Stop! No more! No more, please. I will talk." Lieutenant Amery smiled to himself. Inevitable, he thought. Sooner or later, someone always talks. A shame about the boy, but that's war.

"I can take you to a very large cache of weapons buried just outside the village," the prisoner choked on his words, "and my brother," he indicated the man next to him, "can show you where important documents are hidden. You can find out everything you want to know."

Lieutenant Amery smiled. "That's more like it, *amigo*. How far outside the village?"

"Not far, sir. My brother and I will guide you."

"Sergeant, detail a squad to accompany us, we're going to take a walk. It seems these two have come to their senses." The lieutenant looked over at the boy lying unconscious under the tree. "You stay here and get someone to clean up this mess."

Lieutenant Amery and six men from A Company's first platoon moved out following the two prisoners north along a jungle path into the foothills behind the village. They'd covered only a few hundred yards when the path narrowed suddenly, and then took a serpentine course through thick, overhanging vegetation. Another hundred yards, and the trail almost completely disappeared. Even as the terrain became more difficult, the Filipinos picked up the pace, and the Americans found themselves struggling to stay close. To lose sight of one another then meant becoming separated, a dangerous gamble none of the soldiers was willing to make. Finally, Lieutenant Amery ordered the men to halt. "How much farther, *amigo*?"

"Just there, sir. Around that corner." The Filipino pointed to a spot ten yards in front of them.

"If you're lying to buy time, you'll pay for it with your life."

"A few more yards, *Señor*. The trail ends, and there is a tunnel."

The lieutenant drew his pistol and cocked it. "Move out then."

When they arrived at the place the Filipino had indicated, the trail ended, and then doubled-back upon itself. Lieutenant Amery looked for any sign of a tunnel entrance but saw nothing. Just then, a low menacing growl came from somewhere in the trees overhead. A jungle leopard, the lieutenant thought, and he scanned the branches around him. Curious, he said to himself, there's no creature like that within fifty miles of here. When he looked down, the Filipinos were gone.

In the fraction of a second that remained of his life, Lieutenant Amery tried to make sense of what happened to him. Maybe, he thought, the cat had taken up residence in the Filipino tunnel. If so, it would only be defending its territory, he would expect that. He'd never actually seen a jungle leopard. He didn't really know what one looked like, but this one in the trees overhead wasn't like anything he'd imagined. Its two-dozen glowing eyes surprised him, and he was confused by the bewildering, repetitive puffs of gray smoke it belched. Its deafening roar sounded like the thunder of gunfire, but more than anything, Lieutenant Amery was amazed at its bestial power as it ripped at his chest and tore at his throat.

The echo of rifle shots rolled quickly down through the village of Rosa Rita. Colonel Funston put down his coffee and pushed away from the luncheon table. "What the devil was that?" Thirty yards away, on the bank of the tributary, the remaining Filipino prisoners jumped to their feet and shouted joyfully at the top of their lungs.

The villagers knew for certain then what had happened. The old men crossed themselves and wept openly, the women frantically reached out for the children and clutched them protectively to their breasts. In a moment all ninety-four villagers grew hysterical, wailed and moaned piteously and pleaded with God to save them. Sergeant Rivers moved in quickly and silenced the prisoners with the butt of his rifle, but too late. The people of Rosa Rita knew they were doomed, as surely as if Tagunton himself had ordered their execution.

"Captain Baston, do something about those savages!" Funston shouted. "Will somebody tell me what the hell's going on here?"

Just then, more shots rang out, closer this time, almost inside the village. The officers saw an American soldier running toward them, firing his rifle into the air. He'd lost his hat and blood gushed from what remained of his left ear.

"Murder!" he cried. "Murder!" and he fired his rifle again. Soldiers rushed in and wrestled the man to the ground. Out of his mind with panic, his eyes darted frantically from one man to the next.

Colonel Funston bent down and slapped him in the face, sending a trail of ear-blood splattering the boots of the men nearby. "Get hold of yourself, trooper! Tell me what's happened."

The man sobbed. "It was those prisoners, sir! They tricked us into a rebel ambush! They killed all of us, sir, Lieutenant Amery too. They're all laying dead up there on that trail." The soldier looked mournfully at his bloody shirt. "I guess they've killed me as well."

Colonel Funston arose in a vehement rage, threw his hat to the ground, and then stomped on it. Red faced, teeth bared, he kicked out hard, nearly striking the men around him. Lieutenant Amery had been a good officer, and the colonel liked him. Moreover, Funston anticipated a career in politics after the war, and he knew every one of his Kansas volunteers had friends and family back home that would hold him accountable in the future for purposeless loss of life.

He turned his back on the stricken soldier and headed straight for the riverbank and the rebel prisoners, moving so fast on his stumpy little legs Captain Baston ran to keep up. Gregorio saw them coming. He stepped forward to intercept the enraged colonel. "Please, sir, I tried to warn the officer. I told him those men could not be trusted!"

Without slowing down, the colonel pushed the old villager off his feet. When the two officers reached the spot where the prisoners knelt, Captain Baston drew his revolver and fired. Two of the prisoners pitched forward face first into the goo that had been their brains. Baston then moved in behind the remaining prisoner. The man turned his head and gazed contemptuously at his executioner. The captain saw no fear or remorse on the man's face, only a bitter, defiant smile on his lips. Colonel Funston screamed at the top of his lungs, "You God damned treacherous savage! You Godless black barbarian! Hell is too good for you!" and Baston pulled the trigger again.

C Company still held its position on the high ground east of the tributary, the men in a foul temper. In just a few hours, they'd lost a number of their comrades, and now their company commander. Sitting idle while events unfolded around them, they felt impotent and ineffectual. Murmurs of reprisal against those "nigger gooks" and "gugu bastards" circulated up and down their ranks. The stories they'd heard about the sneaky, underhanded Filipinos had again proved true. Ambush a cowardly, despicable way to make war, one young Kansas boy remarked to his sergeant, "A damned nigger Filipino won't even stand up and show himself to be shot."

This was the prevailing sentiment among the men in C Company, when before their eyes the unbelievable happened. Captain Baston had just given three of the slopes what they deserved, when suddenly, the rest started running. At one moment, they sat quietly like good little dinks, and then were on their feet fleeing in every direction. Obviously, the villagers were dangerously out of control. A corporal shouted, "They're getting away, Sarge. What do we do?"

"You know the orders, trooper," the sergeant replied as he opened fire. "No one gets down that river."

Twenty villagers were killed with the first volley and three others wounded.

Captain Baston stood on the sand next to Colonel Funston. He knew C Company was aware of the ambush that had taken their company commander, and he knew their standing orders. He wasn't surprised the hot-blooded Kansans were only too ready to exact revenge. Amidst the chaos of flying lead and dying humans, he glanced at the colonel, waited for him to call a cease-fire, but Funston turned his back and walked away.

The villagers in total panic, screamed, ran blindly, searched in vain for a way to escape the storm of bullets raining down upon them.

Another volley. Five more Filipinos dropped.

Villagers dove into the narrow tributary hoping the water would shield them from the gunfire. Others ran along the bank dragging terrified children behind them, attempting to reach the *Rio Malimba*, where they thought the current might carry them to safety.

Captain Baston cringed at the splatter of bullets striking flesh before his eyes. He wished the villagers would just lie down and stop trying to flee, maybe then C Company would end the slaughter. Baston wasn't naïve enough to think these natives innocent. He believed, all Filipinos untrustworthy, and given the opportunity, any of them would murder an American. Still, these people were unarmed and hadn't done anything. For an instant, he considered calling the cease-fire. Four long blasts on his trench whistle, and it would be all over, but he knew doing so would mean the end of his career. At the very least, Fighting Freddie Funston would have him court martialed, and there was a better than even chance he'd be hanged.

Another volley. Eight more dead.

Lieutenant Alstaetter rested under a tree. Doctor Forrester had stitched up his hand and given him a mild sedative. Awakened by the clamorous return of the wounded ambush survivor, when he emerged from the shade, his first view had been of Captain Baston firing his pistol into the head of a rebel prisoner kneeling on the sand before him. Then he saw the villagers, all ninety-four of them, rise up in panic.

H Company's first platoon had been detailed to guard the villagers, a seemingly simple task, but the situation had taken a sudden, tragic turn for the worse. Lieutenant Alstaetter raced to the bank of the little river. When C Company opened fire, it was a wall of lead. He himself had been almost cut down by the withering hail of bullets. His men directly in the line of fire, he shouted for them to get down, to take cover.

Another volley. Ten more Filipinos down.

The Kansans fired indiscriminately into the throng of panicked villagers. Alstaetter wondered how many of his own men would be hit.

When Captain Baston executed the rebel prisoners, David Fagen and Ellis Fairbanks had been standing a few yards away, their rifles loosely trained on the frightened, huddling Filipinos. Fagen had seen enough war by then that to him, the field-expedient dispatch of prisoners was not so shocking as it once had been. He still didn't like it and hoped he'd never get used to it, but it crossed his mind those two had fared better than their comrade who'd been hanged from the tree, and certainly better than those he'd seen endure the water cure.

When the villagers panicked, the H Company guard detail hadn't known what to do. The Filipinos were on their feet, but clearly had nowhere to go. Unarmed women and old men posed no threat. The American commander had just executed three men before their eyes. They were afraid, who could blame them? Fagen saw the muzzles flash, felt the zing-splat of bullets and heard the pop of C Company's rifles. He didn't know who gave the order to shoot or why, but obviously the Kansans weren't too particular who was in their line of fire. To save himself, Fagen dove for cover behind a dune and surprised, found Ellis Fairbanks already there.

"What's going on, Davey?"

"They're shooting wild, Ellis. Are you all right?"

"I'm all right, I guess." Ellis tried to shake the fog from his brain. "One minute I was standing up there and the next thing I knew, I was down here. I don't know what happened."

Fagen checked his cousin for wounds. Finding none, he low-crawled up the dune to look around. At least forty villagers, mostly women and children, lay dead on the sand before him, the rest ran terror-driven toward the river. C Company let go another fusillade, and Fagen scrambled back to safety. That's when he noticed the back of his cousin's blouse torn and soaked with blood.

Fagen cut away Ellis' blood-drenched shirt and exposed a jagged laceration across the middle of his back. "Looks like they nicked you Ellis. I'll go for the doctor when those idiots across the river let up."

"It must not be too bad, Davey. I don't feel anything."

Fagen didn't have to wait long for the shooting to stop. Just then, C Company opened up with its Gatling gun, and in less than one minute of hell on earth, there were no more Filipinos left alive. Within seconds, the deadly machine gun ended the agonized cries of the villagers, and when over, a macabre silence hung along the riverbank, and with it, the saccharin odor of fresh blood.

Ellis lay face down on the surgeon's table while Doctor Forrester attended to his wound. "I've got to put in a few stitches, Private. It may hurt a bit, try to remain still if you can." The doctor closed the wound and pulled the stitches tight. Surprised Ellis didn't flinch as his large, curved needle penetrated raw tissue, he said, "You're as tough as you are big."

"Go ahead, Doc. Start anytime you want."

Doctor Forester glanced up at Fagen, then said to Ellis, "It appears you're numb to the pain of both the wound and the treatment. This is not uncommon. It's the brain's way of defending against the debilitating shock extreme pain induces. It's only temporary, however. Enjoy it while you can."

As he dressed Ellis' wound, the doctor's eyes were drawn to a series of small, purplish spots under one of his arms. Upon closer examination, Forrester discovered three more spots in the center of Ellis' lower back, larger, and their purple color gave way to white in the center. Then he remembered the discoloration around Ellis' bullet wound. He'd noticed it earlier, but thought nothing of it. Curious, the doctor used a magnifying glass to study the larger spots just above his patient's belt. "How have you been feeling lately, Private?"

"I've been fine, thank you, sir."

Doctor Forrester took a probe from his bag and dipped it in a bottle of alcohol. "Tell me when you feel something," he said, and he pressed the instrument into the center of Ellis' back.

"Poke," said Ellis. Then the doctor pressed into the center of the largest purple spot. Ellis gave no response. Next he pricked just below Ellis' right shoulder.

"Poke."

"How about this." He sunk the probe into the center of the freshly stitched bullet wound. Nothing. Then he pressed between his shoulder blades, just above the wound.

"Poke."

Doctor Forrester did his best to hide his growing concern. "I think you have some sort of mild skin rash, Private. I'd like to take some samples. Don't worry, it won't hurt."

"I'm not worried, Doc. Take all you want."

Forrester rinsed a small glass dish in alcohol and put it up to dry. Then he used a scalpel to remove a thin slice of tissue from each of the spots.

When finished, he placed the samples in the dish, sealed it and stowed it in his medical kit. "My diagnosis is you're fine, Private Fairbanks. You're lucky too. If that bullet had come a half-inch closer, you wouldn't be sitting here right now."

"Can I go back to my platoon now, sir?"

"The medical team is returning to camp today with the other wounded and the dead. I'd like you to go with us. No sense risking infection in that wound."

Colonel Funston sat at his field desk in the shade of a nipa palm recording his version of the events just taken place at Rosa Rita. An hour before, he'd ordered the village and all its contents burned, including the livestock. Also, he'd agreed with Captain Baston that the bodies of the villagers be flung into the *Rio Malimba*, a warning to other Filipinos downstream that Americans didn't take kindly to rebel ambushes.

This was the part of any campaign Funston liked least, the tidying up, to him tiresome and devoid of allure, like cleaning up after a party. He knew, however, a civilized army didn't leave its wreckage strewn helter-skelter in its wake; and besides, he thought, the cares of the day behind him, now was the time to reflect on the terrible, but divine attributes of command, a pastime in which he frequently indulged. So his consternation showed when interrupted in his reverie by Doctor Forrester, just up from the field surgery.

"I've been attending to one of the men, sir. One of the Negro soldiers from H Company."

"Go on, doctor. What is it?"

"Sir, I think we have a problem."

CHAPTER 11 - REJECTION

Clarita said she needed to talk to one of her uncles, and it wouldn't take long. Fagen told her she could find him across the street at the *palengke*, the outdoor market. He watched her disappear up the back stairs of an old sandstone office building, and then turned and pushed through the crowd. Saturday in San Isidro, and hundreds of people packed the boardwalks.

Long rows of identical wooden tables side-by-side under a nipa canopy dominated the center of the market. Merchants stood shoulder-to-shoulder behind numbered countertops, each one displaying a variety of goods for the passing shoppers.

The area reserved for butchers was toward the front of the *palengke*, amid a huge cloud of annoying flies. Their hands, arms and aprons covered with stale blood, the meat cutters drew attention to themselves by juggling razor sharp cleavers and bone saws. Again and again they flipped the deadly tools of their trade high into the air, and then magically caught them by the handles until a shopper paused to negotiate for one of the huge ragged cuts of meat on display from rusty metal hooks. Fagen noticed each butcher placed the severed head of the animal on the countertop next to the meat, to declare its source and freshness. Down the row *carabao*, horse, deer, monkey and dog, and twenty yards away, separated from the rest to accommodate the sensibilities of the Muslim shoppers, a few tables bore huge slabs of ham, the pale, grinning hog's head staring blindly over its own flesh.

The center of the market was jammed tight with tables covered with fruits and vegetables. Fagen strolled along one row and counted forty merchants standing next to each other hawking their share of the day's produce. Radishes, washed and tied in bunches stacked on one table, onions on the next, and then yams, carrots and on it went. Lots of delicious-looking fruit, some familiar, apples, bananas and a variety of melons, and some not. An old woman stood behind two low mounds of strange, leathery orange lumps. She offered a sample. Sweet and sour at the same time, Fagen thought it some kind of apricot.

Farther back, the Chinese tradesmen dominated, a hardware man, a book dealer, a confectioner, a tobacconist, several jewelers and a dozen silk merchants. Fagen had come to the market to find something for his cousin, and this looked like the right place.

Ellis had been in quarantine for two weeks under guard, but otherwise alone in a tent the doctor had erected behind the armory. Fagen had been to visit him every day, morning and night, and could talk to him if he shouted, but couldn't really say much because they kept the canvas down, and no one got in but the doctor. Ellis said he felt fine and had no symptoms.

Fagen doubted he'd been placed in quarantine because of the wound he'd received at Rosa Rita. The first rumor they'd heard was he had a skin rash. Everyone thought it must be one hell of a rash, but later Sergeant Rivers said Ellis might have the breakbone fever. That made more sense. There hadn't been any cases of breakbone among the soldiers at San Isidro, but everybody knew it was contagious as hell. Pure misery for Ellis locked up in that tent, and Fagen knew he must hate it, but he'd feel worse if he were the cause of some other soldier coming down with the fever.

Fagen pushed through the crowds to the book dealer and bought the best one he could find, a book about the Berlin Trade Exposition of 1896. Written in German, Ellis couldn't read it, but it had hundreds of pictures and colored drawings, and Fagen thought it would help him pass the time.

Back out on the boardwalk, the sun blazing, Fagen had to watch his step. On the periphery of the main marketplace, scores of peasants had spread their meager offerings along the walks, hoping to catch the eye and the sympathy of some passing shopper. An old woman sat in the dust on a ragged cushion, toothless and wrinkled, her hands and feet twisted by arthritis. Her only goods, three small brown onions, lay in front of her on a page of newsprint. Next to her, a woman with one leg and a little girl sold tiny strips of dried meat in a bowl. Beside the bowl, a cup contained one hen's egg. The little girl had drawn a picture of a butterfly on the shell with colored pencils. This too was for sale.

Farther down, a woman and a boy sat behind an assortment of dried herbs and roots. A potential customer pawed through her goods, but bought nothing because just then the woman's full attention had been diverted to the boy. He shrieked, and then suddenly his body became rigid. He began to shake, his legs kicked uncontrollably, his eyes rolled up, and white foam appeared on his lips. The woman clutched him tightly to her breast and held him until his tremors subsided. The incident over, the boy rested in his mother's embrace while she watched her only customer of the day disappear into the crowd.

Fagen's heart went out to the woman and the other wretched, woeful people. From their faded, tattered clothes and miserable lot in life, it wasn't hard to surmise they belonged to the growing community of refugees - the bedraggled residue of aggression, having fled their native villages to the safety, if not the security, of the city. The dregs of war, they were diseased, disabled, widowed, orphaned, homeless and friendless, stripped of their livelihoods and their dignity. Fagen wondered what would become of them. How would they survive when the season changed and the rains came? Who would be there to take care of them? In a land of so many churches, Fagen questioned so little evidence of a benevolent and protective God.

He turned away from the woman and immediately bumped into a man, nearly knocking him off his feet. "Pardon you, stranger," the man said, "it's a good thing I saw you coming."

Short and round as a barrel, he wore a brown pinstripe suit and white Stetson hat. He stood in front of a large, black box camera mounted on a three-legged stand. "I've learned to keep my eyes open in these native villages. You can't be too careful, I always say." He flashed a big, toothy grin.

Fagen begged his pardon while the man checked the position of his camera, then he looked at Fagen as though he'd just noticed him. "Say, I'll bet you're one of Funston's colored soldiers! I heard the old hawk had a detachment of Negroes under his command." He gave out a little laugh, more a snort. "That's a fact he wouldn't want spread around back home. Fighting Freddie thinks he's too good for most white soldiers, don't even mention a colored. Say, you're somebody I'd like to talk to! You ever had your picture taken? I'm Roland Bettendorf. I work for Mr. William Randolph Hearst. Taking pictures is my trade."

Bettendorf pointed to an old man and his wife sitting on the boardwalk behind a piece of sackcloth and two brown apples. "I'm trying to get this old reprobate to let me take his picture, but so far he's not interested. His woman's trying to talk him into it, at least she's got some sense. You see, I need shots like this to go along with my combat photos. Mr. Hearst wants to show our readers what the Filipino is like when he's not making war on us. We call it human interest." He held a two-peso coin under Fagen's nose. "Look here! I've even offered to pay the old beggar. I guess I'll never understand a Flip."

The poor, draggletailed peasant sat cross-legged with his chin on his chest, his hands covering his face. Clearly the man was starving, but he had his pride and couldn't bring himself to suffer the indignity of participating in the obnoxious American's freak show. His wife stooped over him, tears ran down her face. She whispered in his ear, and Fagen could just make out the words, *Por favor, Antonio. Necesitamos el diñero.* The thought of this man giving up what little self-respect he had left suddenly angered the Negro private. He stepped in front of the camera and said, "The man's mortified, Mr. Bettendorf. Can't you see that? Why don't you leave him alone?"

"Nonsense!" the photographer bellowed. "What's he got to be embarrassed about? Why, millions of people all across America will see his face. He'll be famous!"

At that, he knelt down and pressed the coin into the old man's hand. "*Usted es muy famoso!*"

The old man kissed his wife's forehead and wiped a tear from her cheek. He lifted his head and gazed expressionless into the camera's eye, waiting while the American fumbled with the plates and focused the lens.

In a moment, a metallic sound was followed immediately by Bettendorf's thunderous voice. "There! That wasn't so bad, was it? You're still alive, and I didn't capture your spirit or soul or anything else in my black box, just your image. Put her there, *amigo*. Shake!" He bent down and offered his hand. The old peasant glanced at Fagen, and then quick as lightning, his hand shot out, and his bony fingers clamped around Bettendorf's wrist. Startled, the photographer tried to pull away, but the man held him fast. Fagen watched as he looked into the photographer's eyes, and then deliberately and with great dignity, pressed the two-peso coin into Bettendorf's palm, then reached down and placed one of his two withered, brown apples on top of the coin.

Touched, Fagen witnessed the act of an aristocrat, humble and regal at the same time. An expression of such majesty, Fagen believed that for the first time in his life, Roland Bettendorf was speechless.

The woman sat down with her husband, put her arm around his shoulders and gazed into his eyes. For them, the American photographer no longer existed. In a moment, Bettendorf recovered, pitched the apple into the street and folded the legs of his camera stand. Then he looked at Fagen and said, "I guess I'll never understand a Flip."

Clarita found Fagen at a kiosk that sold nothing but sandals. "Come on," she said, "or we'll be late." She took his arm and pulled him through the crowd.

"Where are we going?"

"Not far, but we'll have to hurry."

They turned left at the next intersection and hurried to the middle of the block to an outdoor theater consisting of a large stage covered with a bright blue canvas awning and surrounded on three sides by rows of benches. Decorated with brightly colored cloth bunting, it supported a wooden backdrop and side wings with doors for the actors to enter and exit. Families of Filipinos scrambled for seats, many carried food and other treats in baskets to eat later, picnic style.

Clarita squeezed into the center of the third row. There didn't appear any place left to sit, but everyone there knew her and made room for them. "Just in time," she said.

The left side of the stage had been covered with blue and white papers laid down to look like water. To augment the illusion, an angled wall in front had been painted blue and bordered with dark green paper cut and folded to represent ferns, marsh grass and mangroves. The overall effect reminded Fagen of the thousands of little inlets and lagoons he'd seen in central Luzon. At the rear of the stage, someone had erected a façade of a village hut with a door, two windows and a covered veranda.

Being at the play, surrounded by so many of her friends, excited Clarita. Fagen watched her from the corner of his eye, and once again his heart pounded in his chest. Other than routine patrols around garrison, H Company hadn't been in the field for weeks. As usual, they'd drawn more than their share of dirty jobs around camp, but Sergeant Rivers had been generous in giving time off, and Fagen spent every spare hour with Clarita.

Fagen felt as though he lived a dream. Finding Clarita had made a new man of him, and his whole outlook had changed. Completely under her spell, he wished he could remain there forever. He'd heard the endless jokes about foolish men in love, but he'd no prior experience and hadn't realized how close to the mark they were. He was in love with Clarita. Head over heels in love, and that she should love him back, that perfect woman with the flashing dark eyes and bright smile, was the greatest miracle of all. Fagen knew he'd do anything for her. Desperate for ways to show her how much he adored her, he'd swim an ocean, slay a dragon, lay riches at her feet, shower her with precious gems, anything, everything she wanted if it convinced her of his devotion. Fagen knew he was just another fool in love like in the jokes, but he didn't care.

The audience applauded as the actors emerged from the door of the hut. The first, an old man, stooped and wrinkled, wore a long golden robe. Two young men dressed as warriors followed and helped him to a chair. The old man started with an angry speech, shook his fist and now and then cast his eyes to heaven. He spoke in Tagalog, but Clarita translated. "The old man is Madia, a nobleman exiled from his native country of Brunei. He has lost everything and lives now in the lowest of circumstances at the edge of this lagoon that connects to the Pasig River. He has been falsely accused of political crimes, and he curses the Sultan and his officers for their treachery. Even the gods were deceived by their lies and have punished him unfairly by taking his beloved wife, Kimay, and his brother, the brave warrior, Tidoy. Now, all that is left of his noble family are his nephews, Kamanchille and Guanar and his beautiful and virtuous daughter, Macapuno. Here she comes now."

The young girl playing Macapuno appeared at the doorway, and the audience murmured with delight. Draped from head to toe in white silk with sky blue plaiting at her neck, wrists and hem, her face was powdered white to represent chastity, her lips an exaggerated red bow. She stood still for a moment, allowing the audience to fully appreciate her beauty, and then walked slowly to the front of the stage and stopped, her head lowered, hands clutching her breast.

The old man resumed his speech and Clarita whispered, "Madia laments their situation. Without their usual regiment of slaves and with no means of obtaining any, his only daughter, a girl of extreme beauty and a princess in her own right, is forced to endure life on the meager offerings the river marsh provides." The old man stood up and raised his arms toward the sky. His nephews, standing beside him, drew their swords and held them high. "Now Madia swears an oath to heaven. His daughter is a princess, a consort to a king, and he commands Kamanchille and Guanar to become great hunters and warriors to support their cousin in a fashion befitting her heritage. Having thus charged his nephews, he dies."

Fagen had never seen a play where the actors wore real costumes and spoke in such highbrow tones. He'd certainly never seen a play done in Tagalog, and maybe that was the problem because the figures on the stage were too extravagant for his tastes, their speeches too long and too loud. Difficult to tell the curses from the prayers, Fagen soon found his thoughts wandering back to Rosa Rita and the terrible massacre he'd witnessed there.

He knew he'd never forget that horrible moment framed by the hammering Gatling gun as it rained hot lead down on the defenseless villagers. Nearly a hundred innocent people had been slaughtered before his eyes, their shrill pleas for mercy burning into his soul. Fagen knew the ruthless face of war. He'd been in combat and seen a hundred craven acts of destruction, but as he lay in the sand that day trying to cover his eyes, to block out the carnage, he realized then Sergeant Rivers had been right, this was a war of extermination, a saturnalia of Filipino blood. Genocide.

Fagen knew many of the other men felt the same way. Daily complaints about the army's cruel and cold-blooded treatment of the natives flew all around their camp. Just a few days before, they'd heard of a general named Jacob Smith who'd recently ordered every Filipino over ten years old shot on site. Their crime, he'd said, was they'd been foolish enough to be born ten years before the Americans occupied the Philippines. Fagen didn't know how much truth was in that story, but he'd learned not to be surprised by anything, and his instincts told him things were just then heating up, and the situation in the Philippines would get worse.

Another actor appeared on stage, a young man dressed in tattered burlap and sandals. He carried a magnificent saber in a leather scabbard, and in spite of his poor clothes, strutted around the stage like a nobleman. Clarita said, "That is Luanbakar. He has heard of the beautiful Macapuno and has come to ask her hand in marriage. Her cousins refuse. They have sworn an oath to protect her from unworthy suitors, and Luanbakar has nothing to offer except his pleasing appearance. Macapuno implores her cousins to permit the marriage. She has fallen madly in love with Luanbakar, and without him, she will die. Reluctantly, Kamanchille and Guanar agree to allow the marriage, but only if Luanbakar follows the custom of the unknown suitor.

"Tradition held the unworthy admirer should labor in service to the family until the elders are satisfied he is an eligible match. Luanbakar readily agrees, and the task appointed him is the construction of a long dike in order to make part of the lagoon into a fishpond. The pond would provide a place for the breeding of desirable fish and become a profitable undertaking for the family."

The actor playing Luanbakar picked up a shovel and rake and waded out into the blue paper that represented the lagoon. Clarita continued.

"The work on the dike progressed for some time, the dredging and building being done by hand alone."

Watching the actor reminded Fagen of the day H Company worked in the little swamp at the foot of the walls of Fort Santiago. He recalled how outraged Youngblood had been, forced once again to perform menial and demeaning labor, how he almost had the courage to take on Sergeant Rivers. That time seemed like a hundred years ago. Now Youngblood was dead, and Fagen still didn't know why. He couldn't have been more than eighteen. Fagen asked himself whether the young man's life had any purpose. Certainly his death had none. Fagen pictured his bones in a glittering white pile at the bottom of the Asian sea, a curiosity for the fishes, and for the first time in his life wondered among which strangers his bones would someday lie.

"Because the fishpond was but a short distance from the house, Macapuno began to carry food and water to Luanbakar while he engaged in his labor of love. They were in the flush of youth and since no love is more consuming, soon found themselves meeting secretly, beyond the watchful eyes of Kamanchille and Guanar. For some time they continued in a state of near perfect happiness. One day, however, the brothers learned of the two lovers. Even though the dike was nearly completed, and even though Luanbakar had in every other way shown himself a loyal and worthy suitor, Macapuno's cousins decided he had betrayed them and plotted his death."

It occurred to Fagen his life was not so different from the once impetuous, now all but forgotten Otis Youngblood's. Like him, Fagen didn't have much of a past, only a half-dozen years older; neither had the time to acquire a history. Fagen had no family to go home to. Ellis was married to the army, and no matter how much Fagen wanted to stay close to his cousin, he no longer saw spending his life in uniform. At one time, he'd believed a black man benefited by serving his country. He'd thought the army like a club in which the members stuck together and looked out for each other, where the color of a man's skin was less important than the color of his uniform, and people didn't hate him without a reason. He knew now that had been a fool's dream. He'd seen just as much bigotry and hatred in the army as in civilian life, even more. He'd found no one who cared about the airy hopes of the artless and unsophisticated Negro, and if having a past meant holding on to a box full of memories and a bright future meant living up to your dreams, then every way Fagen saw it, his past was a blind alley and his future dead-ended.

Clarita's attention was riveted on the actors. She said, "Luanbakar, the suitor, is once again at work on the dike. Kamanchille waits behind the palms with his hunting spear until no one is watching, then he approaches Luanbakar and asks him whether he has seen any game passing that way. Luanbakar says animals rarely take to the river to hide from hunters. When Luanbakar looks away, Kamanchille raises his spear and launches it with such ferocity it penetrates Luanbakar's side, and he falls to the ground. Although mortally wounded, the lover gets to his feet and slays Kamanchille with one thrust of his magnificent saber. Luanbakar then falls beside the body of his enemy. The last words on his dying lips are of his devotion to his beloved Macapuno."

Not much of a fight, Fagen doubted whether either of the actors had ever used a weapon of any kind when not on stage, but he judged them good at dying because when Kamanchille fell down next to the man he'd killed, the audience jumped to their feet and cheered. When the princess came out of the hut and saw what had happened, she knelt sobbing over the bodies of her lover and her cousin. After a while, she gathered enough paper-mache branches to cover the bodies, and then walked to the end of the dike and threw herself into the river. Everything was quiet on the stage for a moment until the other cousin, Guanar, came in.

"Guanar has just returned from a hunting trip. He sees what has happened between his brother and Luanbakar. Frantically, he searches for Macapuno and discovers her body on a sandbar near the mouth of the lagoon. His sorrow is great, but no amount of grief can alter the facts of this tragedy. He buries Kamanchille and Luanbakar and marks their graves with the spear and the saber that were the instruments of their death. Next, he buries his most dear cousin, Macapuno. Having nothing to mark her burial site, he sees a coconut floating in the lagoon. This he retrieves and plants at the head of her grave."

Clarita's apartment, on the second floor of a building just off the main street, was neat and well furnished. Her grandmother lived in two rooms connected by a door in the kitchen. Fagen had taken his boots off, and as he lay on her bed wondered how much she paid for such a place and where she got the money. "I'm sorry you did not like the play," Clarita said.

"I liked it fine. I thought it was a good play, but I'm not much of a judge."

"It is a very old Tagalog legend, but you do not know the end of the story. It goes like this. Guanar planted the coconut on Macapuno's grave, and after many years it grew into a noble palm with graceful fronds that surrounded an abundance of small round nuts. Full of tender meat, they were entirely different from any ordinary variety. Traders from all over Asia took these nuts to propagate, and they were always in high demand. This is the source of the Macapuno coconut, which today is known by everyone and prized for its agreeable qualities."

Clarita lay beside Fagen on the bed. She held a small silver tumbler containing a few drops of a dark liquid. "You are not yourself today, my love. You are troubled. Drink this, it will ease your mind. You can sleep here in my arms."

"I can't sleep. I have to be back in camp by ten."

"Don't worry. I will awaken you." Fagen took the cup and downed the bitter potion in one swallow. "Close your eyes and think about the play. The lesson is that good things can spring from tragedy."

Fagen felt the drink coursing through his veins. Soon, the room began to spin, so he closed his eyes. Just before he dropped into deep sleep he said, "It was only a fairy tale, Clarita."

"Yes my, love, but fairy tales give us hope."

When Fagen awoke, it was dark and night breezes filled the room. He had to get back to camp, but when he tried to get up, found he couldn't move, his arms and legs pinned to the bed. He tried again and felt the sharp edge of cold steel pressed to his throat and saw the man's face very close. "Please, Señor, do not try to move."

He counted five in full uniform, armed with rifles and long, curving bolo knives. One man stood by the open door watching the street below. By their looks, clearly they were out for robbery and murder. Paralyzed with fear and dread, he did not want to die this way, and when his thoughts turned to Clarita he panicked. He knew what this brand of outlaw did to their women captives, and he had to think of something fast. Just then the man pressed the blade a little deeper, and Fagen felt the hilt against his ear. "You must lay still, Señor."

Fagen peered through the shadows and saw the door open from the kitchen. Clarita's grandmother slept in rooms just beyond. He thought she must have heard something and come to investigate. If she walked in on those men, she'd be dead in less than a second. Fagen believed his life over no matter what he did, so he shouted, "Grandmother, no!"

The door opened wider, and to Fagen's astonishment, Clarita stepped into the room dressed in black wearing a leather pistol belt with a heavy, single action revolver in the holster. She was followed by four men, also in uniform, struggling under the weight of dozens of rifles and several crates of ammunition. The men in the room laughed. One of them mocked Fagen's desperate cry, "*Nuno! Nuno, no!*" and then they laughed again. Clarita waited for a signal from the guard watching the street, and then followed the men outside. She stopped at the door, looked back at the American and gave an order to the man who held the bolo to his throat. "Bring him, but make sure his blindfold is tight."

Hog-tied, Fagen bounced helplessly in the back of a wagon wondering what Clarita was up to and why she'd hoodwinked him. They drove fast for a long time, and when they finally stopped, two men untied his feet and put him on a horse. Fagen had no idea where he was or even which direction they'd taken, but as they rode along on horseback, he could tell the way the animal moved beneath him they'd climbed over several steep hills. He tried counting minutes, but without any vision had no way of knowing for certain how long or how far they traveled.

After a while they stopped, soldiers helped Fagen dismount and led him to a chair. Then they untied him and removed the blindfold. Seated at a small table opposite an empty chair, Fagen rubbed his eyes and shook the tingling from his hands. He looked around and saw fifty Filipino soldiers, all in uniform, sitting within easy reach of their weapons. A large fire blazed in the center of the camp and cast an eerie glow off the jungle canopy overhead.

No one spoke. Fagen stared defiantly back at the rebels while they surveyed him in the dim half-light, more than a little curious about the American prisoner in their midst. He felt like a bug under a microscope. He didn't know where he was or why he'd been brought there, but he'd already lived longer that night than he'd expected, so he decided to try something and see how far their curiosity went. Suddenly, he stood up, lifted the chair over his head and snarled, "Come on. I'll take you all on, one at a time!" The unexpected move startled the guerilla soldiers and a half-dozen jumped to their feet. They looked at Fagen then at each other, and then collapsed in a fit of laughter.

That was the second time a Filipino mocked Fagen that night, and he'd had enough. He lifted the chair higher and challenged them again, "Come on over here! Who wants to be first?" Fagen took a step toward them, and suddenly the laughter stopped, and the men snapped to attention. Silence. Fagen stood there a moment, and then heard someone say his name. He spun around ready to attack, the chair held high over his head and came face-to-face with Clarita, a little curl of a smile on her lips. A man was with her, a thin, narrow-shouldered dandy with a boyish face and huge, dark eyes. He wore a clean, white uniform with gold epaulets and gold braid at the collar. Holding his chin high, he looked at the American for a long moment and said, "*Señor* Fagen, I am Emilio Aguinaldo." He took a step forward, pointed to the chair in Fagen's hands. "In the Philippines we sit on those."

Aguinaldo gave a signal, and two soldiers moved in quickly and took the chair. Clarita put a hand on Fagen's shoulder. "*El Presidente* wishes to speak with you."

Dumbfounded and dizzy with confusion, Fagen stared down at the woman he loved. Clarita had spoken to him as though this was just another evening. Couldn't she sense the betrayal burning in his chest? He loved her, trusted her, and she had thrown him to the dogs. Fagen wished she'd killed him in his sleep, or ordered him killed at that moment and gotten it over with, but she only stood there, that enigmatic Clarita smile on her lips.

Aguinaldo stepped forward. "Please, *Señor* Fagen, be seated. You have nothing to fear. Allow me to apologize for the rude manner in which you were brought here. I assure you it was necessary for your safety and mine. The Americans want desperately to get their hands on me, and if they suspected you knew my whereabouts, they'd be extremely persuasive."

Clarita walked to a group of soldiers around a small campfire. The men made room for her, and she sat down among them and warmed her hands.

Watching her, Fagen felt as though he looked at a stranger. How could he have been so taken in by that person with two lives? Since that first day in San Isidro, he'd frequently wondered why that beautiful woman picked him out of the crowd. He'd asked, but she could have said anything in reply, and he'd not listen. Afraid he'd lose her, he hadn't the courage to look past his own self-interests. Now his fears were realized - she'd never really cared. Her interest was a charade, a drama to deliver him into the hands of the enemy. Fagen gave her credit, she'd played her part well, and like a lovesick fool, he'd let her string him along. More than string him along, he'd let her drug and kidnap him in the middle of the night. Disgusted, Fagen shook his head. Usually you have to wait until he's not looking to slip a man a Mickey Finn. He'd taken it from her fingers and drunk it down without a second thought.

Fagen found meager consolation in the realization he was probably not the first, nor the last American she betrayed. He thought maybe next time she'd land a corporal or even a sergeant.

He glanced across the table and saw Aguinaldo studying him, amusement on his face. "Congratulations, *Señor* Fagen. Clarita loves you very much. You are a lucky man."

Fagen didn't feel lucky right then and said so. "She lied to me."

The little Filipino general tossed his head back and laughed out loud. "Oh, the tongue of male vanity, such a magnificent demon! The compelling force behind all our achievements, and the miasma of our ruination. Where would we be without it? No, *Señor* David, Clarita has not deceived you. In point of fact I asked her to bring you here. I wanted to meet you."

"Why me?"

"Clarita told me you are an honest man, a good man, and you have an appreciation for the Filipino people. She said you understand our struggle for independence. Clarita and I have been friends for many years, and I've never known her wrong in her judgment of people. If you are half the man she says, you are very special indeed. I thought if we got to know one another, you could be persuaded to assist us in our pursuit of freedom."

"You've got it all wrong, General. I'm just a private soldier trying to get along. There was a time when I hoped I could make a difference, but I know better now. There's nothing I can do to help you. I can barely help myself."

A soldier brought a pot of tea and two cups to the table. Aguinaldo sat back in his chair. The campfire highlighted the scars on the side of his jaw, the result of a smallpox epidemic that swept the islands twenty years earlier, the only blemishes on his otherwise boyish face. He said, "When you volunteered to come to the Philippines, you came to fight the Spanish. That is natural, the United States was at war with Spain. But the Spanish have surrendered, a peace treaty has been signed. So why do you now kill Filipinos? Did you ever wonder why America changed so suddenly from liberator to oppressor? What have the Filipino people done to cause your country to make an enemy of an ally?"

Those were questions the men of H Company had asked themselves almost since the day they'd arrived. Fagen knew what the U.S. Army thought of General Aguinaldo and also knew what the Filipino people thought of their beloved *Presidente*. "The army says you're an outlaw," Fagen answered, "that you keep the common people stirred up so you can line your pockets with the spoils of war."

Aguinaldo smiled. "Yes, that is the official line, and they repeat it constantly. Outlaw is perhaps the least offensive name the United States army has for me. Certainly your Colonel Funston has worse." Aguinaldo spoke softly, his voice so low Fagen leaned forward to hear. "I would like you to know how the hostilities originated between our two nations, but to fully understand, I have to take you back to the beginning. Please, enjoy a cup of tea." He poured, stirred two spoonfuls of sugar into each, and then passed one to Fagen. The general took a small sip, holding his cup by the handle with just his thumb and index finger

"Three hundred years ago, Spanish warships sailed into Manila bay and declared these islands the property of King Phillip. We were not a true nation then, but a tribal people, our land divided according to ethnic clans constantly at war with each other. We were no match for the most powerful nation on earth.

"The Spanish established a central government in Manila and ruled through a system of provincial governors. Their power over the people was limitless. They controlled even the smallest details of everyday life. They collected taxes, levied fines and imposed draconian penalties upon our countrymen for the most minor offenses. Whole generations of peasants were enslaved on vast estates and worked to death growing sugar, coffee and tobacco. Naturally, a people cannot endure such wretched conditions long, and soon uprisings occurred. Each time the people revolted, the Spanish retaliation was swift and brutal.

"Eventually, a resistance group was formed, the *Katipunan*, and membership spread quickly throughout the provinces. Dedicated to freedom from Spanish rule, it provided fertile ground for our independence movement to flower."

Aguinaldo moved his chair closer. Fagen didn't know whether he was the first to hear that story or how much was true, but the urgent sincerity in Aguinaldo's voice captivated him. Clearly, *El Presidente* had felt the need to tell it to someone. He took a deep breath and continued.

"Four years ago, the *Katipunan* launched a nationwide campaign against the Spanish. We were outnumbered and outgunned, but we believed if we fought together, as a people united, we would prevail. The bloody fighting continued for some time. All across Luzon our rebel forces battled to victory after victory, sometimes using only bolos and nipa sheaves. We taught ourselves the art of guerilla warfare, staying on the move, refusing to confront superior forces head on. During the rainy seasons, the Spanish could not follow us into the jungle mountains, and we used these times to rest and re-provision. Our guerilla tactics worked, but the enemy did not give up without a fight. Thousands of Filipinos at every level of society were executed.

141

"Last Spring, our first real ray of hope appeared when Admiral Dewey asked me to join forces with the United States in a common struggle against the Spanish. He told me both President McKinley and Congress had made a solemn declaration renouncing any desire to occupy the Philippines. The turn of events we'd prayed for, naturally, I agreed to his proposal.

"Upon my arrival in Manila, I was received by Dewey himself and shown all the courtesy due a general officer. The admiral welcomed me to 'the fight' as he called it and promised to send large quantities of arms and ammunition by the next steamer. He said Filipinos and Americans should act as friends and allies toward one another. I asked him then for written assurances of independence for our people, but he said imperialism was contrary to America's founding principles, and his word on the matter was irrevocable. 'Go ashore and start your army,' he told me. 'Drive the Spanish out of the provinces into Manila. When you are ready, we will attack together, from the land and the sea.'

"In less than a month, our forces took control of every province in Luzon. We had taken nine thousand Spanish prisoners, and pushed the remainder of the enemy troops into the walled city, the *Intramuros*. While Admiral Dewey repositioned his fleet for the attack, thousands of our soldiers worked to construct fourteen miles of trenches around Manila, effectively trapping the Spanish inside. Ready to close the net, the entire nation waited, poised to receive the blessings of freedom that for three hundred years had eluded us.

"The battle for Manila was over before we knew it had begun. The Spanish fired a few token shots in the air and then surrendered. Within minutes, American flags went up all over the city. I found out later a deal had been struck. The Spanish made a show of resistance, and then surrendered to the Americans with the proviso the Filipino army be kept out of Manila altogether.

"From that point on, the situation worsened. Governor General Otis issued repeated demands that our forces withdraw from their entrenchments around Manila. Admiral Dewey declared the flag of the Filipino Republic 'unauthorized bunting' and ordered it removed from all Filipino boats. All my attempts at communication with these gentlemen were rebuffed. As far as our American allies were concerned, the new Filipino independent republic had never been born. At the time, we did not know President McKinley had no intention of turning over the sovereignty of these islands to us. American business interests had prevailed in Washington. It was ordained America should fulfill its destiny in the Philippines.

"One night, an American soldier from Nebraska on guard duty encountered two Filipinos walking near the American lines. He ordered them to halt, but the Filipinos had been drinking and paid no attention. The guard fired his rifle at the two men, and quickly other soldiers joined in. Soon, there was firing all up and down the lines. Within two hours, Dewey's battleships began shelling our positions. By noon the next day, our revolutionary army retreated out of the city carrying its wounded with it, but leaving three thousand of our countrymen dead. The next day, I sent a message to General Otis under a flag of truce. I begged him to cease the hostilities between our peoples. His answer was now that it had begun, the war must continue until the 'grim end.'

"Since that day, we have been at war with the Americans. This has been very sad for us. We thought the Filipino struggle for freedom over, but we'd been deceived. Worse, Americans are much better at killing than the Spanish. To them a Filipino is no different than, a troublesome varmint, and this sentiment extends to women and children. You were at Rosa Rita. You know the truth of this. Thousands of our people die every week, and no one can say how many more will be sacrificed before this war is over. It is a terrible, terrible tragedy, but we have hope. There are many people in America against expansionism in Asia. They believe imperialism in any form immoral, especially when pursued by a nation professing to be the land of the free. Filipino nationals living in China and Malaysia are trying to expose the truth of this war to the American people. If we can hold out long enough, outrage at this injustice will grow, and public opinion will force an end to the fighting. Until then, we continue to struggle using the tools we have."

Aguinaldo took another sip of tea. "There you have it, David. An ancient story of the strong imposing their will over the weak and an oppressed people ready to die for freedom. Surely this is a tale you are familiar with. Americans have as much blood on their hands as anyone when it comes to the colored races."

El Presidente stood up and leaned over the little table. "David, you too are oppressed in your own country. White people call you a sulking brute. They burn you on their crosses and kill your children. What future do you have in your own homeland? The doors to fulfillment and prosperity are forever closed to you in America. Is it your destiny to live out your life among people who despise you? Do you think America's attitude toward the colored man will magically change for the better? Look around you, sir. Look at the charred villages of the innocent peasants. Look at the mass graves containing hundreds, no thousands of Filipinos. What kind of war is it when every captain or lieutenant is also a sheriff, judge and executioner? American soldiers enjoy killing colored people, David. Things will not change for the better in America. They will get worse."

Aguinaldo sat down and stared across the table, his glittering eyes burning a hole in the Negro private's heart. Fagen's head pounded from the vitality of the man's eloquent speech. *El Presidente* was certainly not like any other Filipino he'd ever met, or any American for that matter. Consumed by the general's passionate intensity, Fagen's own thoughts were a tangled maze of confusion and indecision.

"General, I'm sorry, but you're scaring the hell out of me. You're a man who eats supper with presidents and admirals. You're a President yourself. You command an entire army. I'm just a private soldier. I can't unscramble this mess we're in. Even if I knew how, nobody would listen. What do you want from me?"

Aguinaldo reached out, refilled the teacups, and then said, "Come with us, David."

"What?"

"That's right, come with us. Right now. Tonight. Join my army. We welcome you with open arms. Come and fight with us."

Fagen couldn't believe his ears. The words burst upon him like a thunderclap. All night he'd expected to be killed, at the very least held for ransom, and now he was invited to join the rebel army. Shocked, he turned away from the Filipino's penetrating gaze. "You're asking me to betray my country? To become a deserter and a traitor?"

"One man's traitor is another man's freedom fighter, David. Think of it this way, you have the opportunity to help a nation achieve its independence. Picture the countless generations of children born into freedom because of your actions. What more lofty pursuit? By helping us, you help your own country too. This war is illegal and immoral. Your great nation betrays you and all its citizens by its involvement here in the Philippines. This will not last. Soon, America will see the error of its ways and make peace. Those responsible for her misguided policies in Asia will be vilified. The patriotic few who stood against the horror of this war will be hailed as heroes. Your joining our fight for freedom will be a signal to other brave men like you that it's possible to love your country and at the same time hate its politics. What is your answer, David?"

Clarita joined them, smiled and then touched Fagen's cheek with her cool, dry palm. He was afraid to look at her, afraid even to move. The only sound the popping of green wood in the campfire. Had a soldier ever been in a more difficult position? Say yes, and his life was changed forever. He would embark on a future he couldn't even imagine. Say no, and his life was changed forever anyway. How could he go on with the sure and certain knowledge Aguinaldo was right? America had betrayed the Filipinos. They had no business enslaving a people ten thousand miles from their shores. As a result, untold thousands of innocent souls had been lost, and it seemed inevitable many more would die before the bloody campaign ended.

Fagen's life had already been permanently altered. He'd seen enough bloodletting to guarantee that. A soldier never really forgets the things he sees in combat. Fagen tried to imagine himself back in the civilian world carrying around the memories of war. He recalled what Sergeant Rivers had said to Miss Merilee Shaw of the Anti-imperialist League. Had he been right? Was the Army training a generation of white men to kill the colored man at home?

What would life be like for a Negro on the streets of America when the war was over? Would every small town police chief become the black man's judge, jury and executioner? Mr. Ben Tillman, Senator from South Carolina, had said just the year before there were already too many niggers living under the American flag. Could a colored man ever achieve the merits of first-class citizenship in a country where his protection under the law was not assured? If Sergeant Rivers and Aguinaldo were right, things could get worse for the Negro, a lot worse.

Fagen's thoughts shifted suddenly to Ellis Fairbanks sitting alone in the dim light of his quarantine tent, and he yearned for his company. He missed his cousin's guileless, trusting outlook on life and realized how much Ellis' naive, simple-hearted acceptance of man's follies influenced the way he perceived the world. He knew the answer to Aguinaldo's question. David Fagen had no choice in the matter.

"I can't do it, General. America has betrayed the Filipino people, but hasn't broken its promise to me. I agree this war is wrong, we shouldn't be here interfering in your lives. I hate what my country does, but it's still my country, and I can't forsake her."

Aguinaldo looked at the man across the table, the flicker of a smile in his eyes. "I would have been surprised if you'd answered any other way," he said. "Men do not renounce their flag for light and transient reasons."

"What happens now?"

"We say goodbye, Private David Fagen, and hope we do not meet again until this contentiousness between our two nations is resolved. We are soldiers. You must do your duty, and I mine. In the meantime, my sincerest wish is something of what we discussed here tonight will remain with you."

At that, Aguinaldo stood at attention and saluted. Caught off guard, Fagen scrambled from his chair to return the courtesy. "Go with God," the general said, and then he turned on his heel and walked away.

Clarita moved closer, her eyes searched Fagen's. "I wanted to tell you. I tried a hundred times, but the words wouldn't come. I fell in love with you the moment we met, but I couldn't tell you because I couldn't risk losing you. Can you find it in your heart to forgive me? I deceived you, my love, but I was never untrue."

Fagen watched her in the firelight wringing a kerchief between her fingers, her brow knotted with foreboding, the first time he'd ever seen her upset. He knew he couldn't ignore the bitter resentment that boiled inside him, and he wondered whether Clarita believed she'd gotten away with it. Would he still be around later for her to work on some more, or would she have to find another piece of meat to throw at her revolution. He knew men were fools and had no shame when it came to love. He'd heard it time and again, but now he resolved it would be different for him. All he really had left in the world was his pride, and he refused to give it up.

Clarita lowered her head and whispered, "I've arranged for Grandmother to take you back to your camp in a *caromata*. She will convince the guards she found you unconscious in the street, that you were the victim of thugs. There should be no trouble."

Frightening hot jets of conflicting emotions burned through Fagen's brain, drained him of energy, but when he lifted her chin and looked into her eyes, he'd never been more serious. "Tell your grandmother no thanks. I can tell my own lies. I just haven't had as much practice as some."

CHAPTER 12 – ACCEPTANCE

Colonel Funston believed good things happened to the deserving, and hard work and attention to duty had rendered him entirely worthy. He leaned back in his chair and scanned his desktop. A week ago he'd unpacked his favorite war trophy and placed it within easy reach, a long, thin dagger with a handle of heavy green jade he'd taken off a dead Cuban revolutionary a little more than a year before. Army regulations prohibited Americans from confiscating equipment belonging to friendly forces. So even though not technically a legal trophy of war, he'd liked the feel of it, and since no one had been around to watch, he'd put it in his saddlebag, and it had been his ever since.

Last week, he'd instructed Captain Baston that henceforth all important documents and dispatches requiring his immediate attention be placed on his desk under the green dagger, all unimportant papers in his inbox in the usual manner. It was up to Baston to make the distinction. Funston believed a collection of eccentricities added layers to a commander's personality and broadened his reputation. To achieve the effect, many of his peers adorned themselves with ribbons and polished buttons. Recently, General Lawton had taken to wearing a bright red sash, but as Funston did not possess the physical stature for such accouterments, he was forced to devise more utilitarian nonconformities.

That day, Baston had finally gotten it right. The colonel smiled to himself as he carefully lifted the dagger and thumbed through his correspondence. On top, a letter from his wife, Eda, posted just before she boarded the ship leaving San Francisco. It would be good to see her, Funston thought. He'd made a good marriage, and he missed having her near. Frequently, he bragged it had been the best decision of his life. Eda Blankart's family had powerful connections in Kansas and influence useful to him when the war ended. Everything considered, she'd been a satisfactory wife, and now she was on the adventure of a lifetime, sailing to the Philippines to visit her husband. Good to see her, he decided, and six weeks just long enough for her to stay.

A gentle tap on his office door, and a corporal entered carrying fresh coffee. Funston took a sip and then said, "Ask Lieutenant Alstaetter to report to my office as soon as possible." The colonel put the cup down and turned his chair around to face the window, idly fingering the papers under the dagger. Nothing official had arrived yet, but it had been whispered for days that Arthur MacArthur would soon replace General Otis as Governor General of the Islands. Funston had been in the army long enough to know rumors like that rarely survived long if there weren't an element of truth in them. That *would* be good news, by God, he said to himself. General MacArthur was a real military man. He'd get these Filipinos under control in no time.

Funston had always admired the General's straight-ahead, man-of-action style of soldiering. If a job needed doing, give it to MacArthur, the popular saying went. General Otis had given his country many excellent years, and he was a good man too, Funston conceded. His nation owed him a lot, but damn it, this Filipino situation was getting out of hand. Time for a younger, more vigorous man to step in and clean up the mess.

If there were a change of command, Funston wondered what would become of the infamous Major Bill Russell. General Otis had needed a strong hand at his side, but MacArthur was a different breed of cat, afraid of no one and didn't need a pirate like Russell to do his talking for him. A few months earlier, Funston had heard the story about a committee of Senators that challenged MacArthur on why the Americans took so few prisoners in the Philippine campaign. "During the Civil War, an average of five soldiers were wounded for every one killed," the committee chairman had said. "In the Philippines, fifteen are killed for every one wounded. Some say there's a 'take no prisoners' policy practiced in the Philippines. How do you account for that, General?"

Funston agreed with his peers, MacArthur's elegant response had been classic. "I give it to the simple fact, Senator, that our boys are better shots than the southern rebels of thirty five years ago; and besides, it's widely known the colored races don't recover from their wounds as readily as the white."

MacArthur was a soldier all right, dedicated, loyal, and mission-oriented. Politics didn't bother him. He knew what was right for the nation, and he went after it. Funston was certain a man like that would quickly recognize those same qualities in others, and if that were the case, it was only a matter of time before the great man called his name and pinned the brigadier's stars on his shoulders.

Another tap on the door, and Lieutenant Alstaetter marched to the colonel's desk and saluted. "You wanted to see me, sir?"

"Yes, Lieutenant. How are you feeling? We haven't seen much of you since Rosa Rita."

"Suffering with a head cold, sir, but I'm fine now."

"Combat will do that to a man. It weakens his immunity, and all sorts of maladies pop up. May I suggest, Lieutenant, the best treatment is prayer and contemplation. Conversation with your Maker will clear your head, and contemplation of your oath of office will invigorate your spirit."

Colonel Funston walked to a map of Sixth District on his office wall. "I want you to take H Company up along the *Pampanga* to this spot here," he pointed to a dotted line that crossed the river, "and set up on both sides of the road leading to this bridge. Our informants tell us the insurrectos smuggle arms and ammunition into the district along this route. Search everyone that crosses, and stop anyone who tries to double-back." Funston caught Lieutenant Alstaetter's look of bewilderment. He regarded the young officer, hooked his thumbs in his suspenders, and then casually added, "Hell, I know it's like sticking your finger in a dyke. There's a thousand other ways they can get in, but we've at least got to make a show of stopping them."

"How long do you want me to stay up there, sir?"

"Two or three days more or less, it depends on what you uncover. Use your own judgment. If you get underway this afternoon, you should be in position by dawn tomorrow."

Lieutenant Alstaetter saluted, did an about face and left the office, closing the door behind him. Funston took a seat behind his big desk and gazed out his office window. Just beyond the armory, he had a view of the quarantine tent Doctor Forrester had set up for that darkey private.

For days now, he'd looked out on the same scene, tent flaps tied securely down, the guards standing at parade rest ten feet away, and then that colored boy, the private who came every day and sat outside the tent. Seemed like he was always there. They must be friends, the colonel thought. Everybody knew coloreds stuck together, nothing new in that, but what in hell could they have to talk about all this time? No matter, he smiled to himself. That was another problem that would be taken care of by tomorrow night.

David Fagen pulled his hat down, leaned forward on his campstool and shielded his eyes from the blazing midday sun. He'd spent so much time talking to Ellis through canvas, it had become almost natural. "How's the jigsaw puzzle coming, Ellis?"

"Pretty good, Davey. I don't think I'll finish it though. The Doc says I'll be out of here soon, maybe tomorrow night."

"That's great news. I'll tell the boys. Everyone's been asking about you, and they'd come see you too, but these guards here don't want a parade of visitors coming around. I guess I'm lucky they let me stay."

"Tell the boys to set me up with a hot bath. Doc's got me rubbing Chaulmoogra oil all over myself, and it stinks like hell."

"What oil?"

"Chaulmoogra oil. Doc says it's good for my skin. I've told him I don't have the itches, but he says put it on anyway, so I'm covered from head to toe. I feel like a greased pig."

"Davey, tell me about Clarita. How's she doing? You haven't talked about her much lately."

"She's fine, Ellis. She asked whether you liked the picture book she got for you. The one about the German fair."

"Tell her I like it fine. I've read it so many times, I've about worn it out."

From the corner of his eye, Fagen saw Sergeant Rivers waving to him, calling him over. "I'll see you later, Ellis. I have to go, looks like something's up."

H Company marched across the bridge spanning the *Rio De La Pampanga* by the light of a full moon. Lieutenant Alstaetter halted the column on the far side. "First platoon, fall out. Sergeant Rivers, take the rest of the company and dig in along both sides of the road. If you see anybody turn around, it means they've seen the checkpoint and probably have something they don't want us to find. Hold onto them and send a man up to get me."

Lieutenant Alstaetter expected no traffic on the road until dawn, so he ordered the men to rest, and then fettered his horse under the bridge for protection later from the hot afternoon sun. Alstaetter knew they were on a fool's errand. In less than two hours every guerilla within range of a fast horse would know of the American checkpoint. He told himself this was the colonel's idea of a joke, and he pictured Funston's delight at the thought of his rummaging through the personal belongings of an endless line of peasants waiting to cross the only bridge within miles.

Alstaetter knew Colonel Funston hadn't liked him since the day he'd joined the command. Major Ryan, his mentor at West Point, had warned him about wildcatters like Funston and their jealousy of his academy pedigree. The young lieutenant knew he could do nothing about that and also knew that since his arrival in the Philippines he'd not helped himself. He could tell from his wife's letters, the strange references to nothing and the out of context remarks, that Captain Baston had been censoring his mail, and he assumed his liberal political sentiments had been reported directly to the colonel; to an old warhorse like Funston, tantamount to having a traitor on the staff.

Then the incident with Merilee Shaw. He'd been an idiot to go to the colonel for help, even though it had been correct procedure. Lieutenant Matthew Alstaetter knew his first field assignment was a disaster, but too late to change that. If later he decided to make a career of the army, he'd have to work a few miracles to get his record cleaned up. In the meantime, he thought, as long as he worked for Fredrick Funston, the best he could do was try to keep as many of his men alive as possible.

The first Filipino merchants and peasants arrived at the river crossing just after dawn. The American blockade consisted of twenty-five men. Twelve searched the natives while the rest stood guard. Local civilians traveling on foot were directed to the left side of the bridge, quickly patted down and allowed to pass on. Searching the merchant wagons was another matter. Ten men were assigned the job of rummaging through every one. Frequently, an entire wagon was unloaded, its contents spread out on the bridge for inspection, while the lieutenant interrogated the driver. A tedious, time consuming job, so Fagen and another soldier purchased hand-mirrors from a Chinese peddler and tied them onto long poles so they could inspect under the wagons without crawling in the dirt. Even with this, the line at the bridge lengthened, the Filipinos grew irritable and tempers flared. Alstaetter sent for another squad, set up a second inspection team and gave up searching peasants traveling on foot unless they carried a particularly heavy load.

This continued throughout the morning and into the afternoon. It grew hot and the Americans soon wearied of raking through wagon after wagon full of fruit, vegetables, firewood and other common supplies. David Fagen felt that nosing through other people's belongings degraded them and dishonored him, and he avoided eye contact whenever possible. Late that afternoon, while he searched a small produce wagon, she spoke to him. "American soldier, you do not remember me?"

Fagen studied her for a moment, and then it came to him, the woman from the restaurant he and Ellis had stopped in on their first visit to San

Isidro. Her little girl sat beside her on the seat. Fagen smiled. "Of course I remember you. How are you and your beautiful daughter?"

"We are fine, but this lazy girl rides in the sun instead of staying where she belongs, in the kitchen preparing food for tomorrow." The girl looked at her mother and said something under her breath. "My daughter wants to know where your friend is. She calls him *oso batahin,* the bear."

"Ellis?" Fagen laughed out loud. "I can see why she calls him bear. He's not here. He caught something, and the doctor put him in a quarantine tent."

The woman crossed herself. "God keep him. Disease spreads quickly in time of war. My own brother suffers from yellow fever. I hope the bear recovers soon."

"He's supposed to be out any day now. The doctor has him rubbing himself with Chaulmoogra oil. I'll tell him we met. We'll stop at your restaurant next time we're in town."

Fagen expected the woman to be pleased and welcome him, but instead she frowned, and then put her arm protectively around her daughter. "May we pass on now?"

The lieutenant nodded, and Fagen tipped his hat. "Good day to you, missus."

The hours passed slowly, and the men on the bridge were glad when, with the setting sun, traffic slowed to a trickle. By nine o'clock, the road was deserted, and when the campfires burned low, Lieutenant Alstaetter posted guards. Some of the men slept where they sat, exhausted from the day and the long march the night before. Others spread their canvas ground covers on the bridge and used their blankets for pillows. Soon, the night air was permeated with the sounds of men sleeping while a giant, chromium moon ghosted up the eastern horizon.

"Halt! Don't come no closer!" the guard said, raising his rifle. The little wagon surprised him because it had come from the far side of the bridge.

She raised a lantern over her head and answered. "Don't shoot. I need to talk to the black soldier."

"In case you haven't noticed, we're all black soldiers, lady."

Lieutenant Alstaetter appeared, pistol in his hand. "What's going on, Minnefee?"

"Sir, there's a woman here says she wants to talk to a Negro soldier. What do I do with her?"

The woman saw Alstaetter and said, "You remember me, Lieutenant. I passed through your roadblock this afternoon with my daughter in the wagon. I spoke to a soldier. I need to speak with him again, sir. It is important."

Fagen had seen the wagon approach, heard the woman's voice and immediately recognized her. Strange, he thought, she'd be out that time of night. Lieutenant Alstaetter checked her wagon and found it empty. Then he ordered Fagen to help her turn it around and move it away from the sleeping men. "Find out what she wants," he said, "and tell her not to come around here at night. She might get shot."

Fagen took the reins and walked the wagon past Minnefee into the darkness at the center of the bridge. The moment they were out of earshot the woman began, "I had to come back and see you," she cried. "God would never forgive me if I did not."

Fagen couldn't see her face in the gray moon-shadow, but heard the alarm in her voice and knew something was very wrong. He reached up and covered her hands with his own. "Tell me, missus. What is it?"

"Your friend Ellis, the bear, you said he was in quarantine."

"Yes."

"You said the doctor had given him Chaulmoogra oil for his skin."

"Yes, I did, but tell me, what's this all about?"

The woman looked around, scanned the area for demons, and then leaned down from her seat, her words an urgent whisper. "Chaulmoogra oil comes from the nut of a tree that grows in Indonesia. I am very sorry to tell you this, *Señor*, but its only use is for the treatment of leprosy."

Her words hit Fagen with the force of a pile driver. Suddenly, his heart stopped, flip-flopped in his chest, and then pounded wildly, the hammering growing in intensity until he was certain it would burst. He couldn't believe what he'd heard. Surely the woman was mistaken. It was not possible she should pronounce the most hideous, the most unspeakable of death sentences upon his cousin, his life-long friend. The pressure in his chest crept upward, strangling him, starving him for air, his head swimming in darkness. He saw the woman's lips moving, but her voice was inaudible over the roar in his brain. "If he leaves his quarantine tent, it is not to return to duty, my young friend, but to be taken to the place of the unclean, where even God cannot help him. The place from which no man returns. God save you both, *Señor!*"

At that, the woman snapped the reins and trotted off into the night. Fagen stood looking after her, his blood turning to ice water. He wanted to cry out, to shower her with odious and loathsome curses, profane her as she had just done to him. If he'd carried his rifle, he'd have shot her on the spot and tossed her remains in the river for the sand crabs, but deep inside he knew what she said must be the truth. Ellis had no fever, and he had no rash. He himself had said many times he didn't have the "itches." The doctor must have known, or at least suspected the truth all along. That's why he'd quarantined Ellis so quickly, why he'd placed armed guards around the tent.

Leprosy! Fagen rolled the awful word around in his mouth, swallowed it, and his bowels turned to water. In his mind's eye, he pictured a rotting shell of a man dressed in a hooded robe, his face too horrifying for words, his fingers and toes lying on the ground all around him. The Biblical picture, the only one he'd ever known, and until now he thought it only happened to people in old books. It was impossible for him to imagine Ellis' face under that hood, impossible even to think about.

David Fagen stumbled dumbly back across the bridge. He pinched himself, knew he was awake, but felt as though he floated through space as if in a dream and saw neither the sky above nor the ground beneath his feet. Suddenly, a blood chilling cold gripped him, and his entire body trembled uncontrollably. At that moment it seemed pain and anguish were the only sensations that kept him in his skin. He walked past the guard station. Out of the white noise in his brain, he heard Minnefee's malevolent cackle. "That your new girlfriend, Fagen? She's too old. I liked the other one better. What was her name…Loretta? Where's she at now? If you're done with her, send her on over to me."

"The place from which no man returns." That's what she'd said. What was she talking about? What kind of place was it a man can't return from? *Where* was it? In the furthest reaches of his imagination, Fagen could picture another man surviving in the land of the unclean, Sergeant Rivers, perhaps, or maybe even himself, but never could he envision gentle, unsuspecting Ellis Fairbanks there.

It couldn't happen. The army wouldn't let it. They'd send him to a hospital, find a doctor to cure him. Ellis had given his soul to the army, they'd not abandon him now. Fagen remembered their conversation that night in their tent at Camp McKinley. "The army's like a wife. She's even better than a wife because she can't divorce you. You give your life to her, and she can't ever turn her back on you." Gradually, Fagen's bone chilling cold turned to fear and then panic. He knew he had to get back to camp, and he had to get back now.

He looked at the men sleeping on the bridge. Minnefee was the only one even half awake, and Fagen knew he'd be no problem. He eased himself over the railing, dropped quietly to the ground, untied Lieutenant Alstaetter's horse and led him up onto the bridge. Minnefee cocked an eyebrow and started to say something, but Fagen spoke first. "Lieutenant saw a snake down there. He wants me to tie his horse up ahead a little way."

The guard yawned. "What are you tellin' me for, lover boy. It ain't none of my business." Fagen walked Alstaetter's Cleveland Bay to the center of the bridge, mounted, and without looking back, dug in his heels and raced away into the night.

The full moon shone high overhead as the horse's hooves pounded a staccato on the dusty road leading to camp. His mind a blur, Fagen had no idea what he would do – what he *could* do to help Ellis. He only knew he must get back to camp that night. Unseen by human eyes, he rode through a dozen sleeping hamlets, and the rhythm of his being fell into time with the steady, metered cadence of the Bay at full gallop, and the miles melted away under him.

Fagen reached the camp two hours before sunup, checked and found the usual complement of guards in the observation towers and at the front gate. He slowed the horse to a walk and waited for the challenge.

Suddenly, without warning, the big gates opened wide, and four horsemen with rifles emerged surrounding a man wearing manacles, his head and shoulders covered by a heavy blanket. Fagen knew immediately these were the men the woman spoke of, the men taking Ellis Fairbanks to the place of the unclean. The land from which no man returns. The sight of his cousin in chains was too much for Fagen. He felt darkness rise in his spine, flood the back of his skull, and then fill all the corners of his brain. Something inside him snapped. Before his eyes a picture of Ellis appeared wearing a hooded robe, his face too horrible to look at. In Fagen's vision, the iron manacles were too heavy, and when the flesh separated at the wrists and the hands fell to the ground, Ellis cried out with joy. He was free at last.

Fagen dug his heels into the horse's flanks and charged the group of riders at full gallop, closing the distance fast. The guards weren't prepared for a collision with a madman just outside their own gates, and the impact sent the two lead riders flying from their saddles as their horses reared wild-eyed, shrieked and then collapsed in a tangle of broken legs. Fagen moved in close, tried to pull Ellis onto his own horse, but it was no good, they'd chained him to the saddle. He had to do something fast, the guards recovered quickly from their surprise, and Fagen heard one of them shout, "Get that crazy nigger!"

155

Ellis shook off the blanket, saw his cousin there to rescue him, and now he wanted desperately to get away. He tried spurring his horse forward, but the guard riding beside him held onto the reins, and together they spun around in dusty circles adding to the confusion of the moment. Ellis didn't want to cry out, but he couldn't control himself. "They're taking me away, Davey! Help me! I don't want to go away!"

Fagen worked frantically to free Ellis' horse, but the reins were hopelessly knotted and the guard fighting him a big man, incredibly strong. If he could just get his friend loose, they had a chance. They could ride away together and figure something out later. He tried to concentrate, to shut out Ellis' painful cries for help. He knew he was running out of time, and he hadn't noticed the other guard move in behind him, but when the butt of the man's rifle struck the base of his skull, Fagen saw a sudden, brilliant flash of light, and then nothing. Ellis' anguished cries for mercy filled the night air, but went unheeded by the soldiers as they tore at Fagen's unconscious body like a pack of wild animals.

"Kick his head off, Jim!"

"Kill that nigger son of a bitch!"

Colonel Funston was in that peaceful, calm place between sleep and consciousness, but heard the angry, insistent pounding on his door and guessed who it was. He lifted the latch and Doctor Forrester pushed into the room. "How dare you come to my quarters like this?" the colonel bristled.

"Sir, I protest! Where the hell are you taking my patient?"

Funston turned his back, walked casually to his table and lit the stub of last night's cigar. He regarded the outraged doctor through swirling clouds of blue smoke. "Your patient? Don't make me laugh. You work for me, Doctor, and you attend to my men as I see fit. When did you forget that?"

"Colonel, I'd planned to move that man to a hospital in Manila where he could receive proper treatment."

"There is no proper treatment for Hansen's bacillus, and you know it."

"I'm sorry Colonel, but I see only one medical man in this room. In point of fact, the latest Surgeon General's report from the States indicates they've made progress in these cases. There's no cure yet, but the new experimental drugs dramatically diminish the symptoms. That man is in the early stages, sir. With care, he has a chance of a relatively normal life, for a few years anyway."

Colonel Funston poured half a glass of brandy from a crystal decanter, sniffed it, and then took a long drink. "That man is a casualty of war, Doctor, the same as if he'd taken a Mauser bullet to the head or been gutted by a dink boloman. There's nothing you or I can do for him. The matter is closed, right here, right now."

"Look here, Colonel, I'm a doctor. I took an oath, and I have a duty…"

Funston exploded. "You impudent bastard! You took an oath to the United States!" "Don't you dare tell me about duty, yours or mine! With everything else facing us, the last thing this army needs is the specter of leprosy hovering over it. Have you considered what that would do to morale? It's bad enough we've got to deal with malaria and God damned yellow fever. What the hell would we do with leprosy? Just the mention of it, and we'd ignite a firestorm of protest back home. The God damned anti-imperialists would have a field day. Everything we've worked for here in Asia would disappear in a puff of political smoke.

"I'll not have it! It'll not happen on my watch." Funston drained the last of his brandy, and then pinned the doctor with his glittering, yellow eyes. "You'd be wise, Forrester, to see this matter from my point of view. That man is gone, vanished, and nothing you can do will bring him back."

Doctor Forrester, confident of his Hippocratic imperative, but nonetheless intimated by his commander's legal authority, lifted his chin and returned Funston's gaze. "Just one question, sir. Would you do the same if the patient were a white man?"

"To safeguard my army," Funston hissed, "I'd do the same to a white doctor."

Fagen awoke in the garrison's makeshift stockade surrounded by the familiar, malodorous stink of turpentine and paint. The inside of his mouth tasted of dirt. He tried to work up enough saliva to spit, but it was no use, the only moisture came from the rivulets of blood that dripped from his broken teeth and pooled in the corner of his mouth. He wanted to sit up, but when he tried, huge purple and yellow fireballs exploded in the blackness behind his eyes, and he lay down again.

Pinned under him, he couldn't feel his left arm, but his right was free, and all his fingers seemed to work. He took stock of his injuries. A piece of his scalp had been torn away and the wound crusted over with dirt. There was no bleeding, but when he touched it the nerve endings caught fire, and he gasped for breath, almost choking on his swollen tongue.

Also, something was wrong with his nose. The cartilage gone, nothing left but a spongy lump of skin shoved to the right side of his face. He pushed up, tried to move his left arm and knew at once it was broken. White-hot, searing pain throughout his left side, the ribs were broken too.

Fagen rolled over on his back and opened his eyes. It was dark in the shed, so it must be night, he thought. He didn't know how long he'd been there and couldn't sort out the events that had led him back to that awful cell. He remembered a long, hot afternoon on the bridge searching wagons. When was that? Yesterday? Last week? In his mind's eye, he pictured hundreds of Filipinos grumbling at him while he ransacked their belongings. Then he remembered the woman driving up with her load of fruit and vegetables, her beautiful daughter beside her on the seat. What was it the little girl had said? What was the word she'd used? *Oso batahin.* That was it, but what did it mean? Horse? No, not that. Church? Not that either. Bear, that was it. Bear.

Then it all came back. Suffocating panic once again gripped his chest. Agonizing, prostrating fear suddenly rushed over him. He told himself he had to get up, had to do something, but when he tried, his head spun, his legs went rubbery underneath him, and he fell to the ground unconscious.

In Fagen's dream, he was a five-year-old boy again submerged in brown river water. He was ensnared and struggled with whatever held him down. Then he saw a shaft of sunlight overhead and kicked hard, fighting to reach it, but it was no use, the water was everywhere, devouring him. He knew soon it would take over his body and there would be no more flesh or bone, nothing left of him, only water. He kicked hard again and looked up into the light. Then he saw it. Someone had come to rescue him. He reached up and took hold of the big, outstretched hand, and his father lifted him effortlessly into his comforting arms.

"Fagen, wake up!" Sergeant Rivers' voice an insistent whisper through the fog in Fagen's brain. Rivers forced water past the private's swollen lips, trying to bring him around. "Get up, man. We've got to get you out of here."

Fagen coughed, and the pressure on his broken ribs sent lightning bolts of pain up his spinal column to the top of his head. "Ellis," he croaked, "I've got to get to him."

"You can't worry about that now. You've got trouble of your own."

Trembling from pain and exhaustion, Fagen pulled himself up on one knee, shook his head and rubbed his swollen eyes. When he focused, he saw the rumpled figure of a soldier lying in the corner of the cell. "Who's that?"

"Your guard. He'll sleep for a while."

"What's going on, Sarge?"

"How much do you remember?"

"Nothing."

"A man died last night. The story is he was trampled under your horse. The colonel wants you tried for murder. You're supposed to be taken to Camp McKinley tomorrow, but the Kansas boys are mad as hell, and they're working themselves up to a necktie party. I don't think you'd ever see a court martial. Lieutenant Alstaetter's arranged for you to hide out a couple days until he can figure a way to get you to Manila in one piece. Let's go. Roberto is waiting outside with his wagon."

Blinded by pain, Fagen crawled in and curled up between stacks of firewood while Rivers drew the cover tight. When clear of the gates, Roberto headed northwest for a few miles, and then stopped to attend to Fagen's injuries. He set the broken bone in Fagen's left arm using two thin sticks of firewood, and then cut a piece of canvas into long strips and bandaged his rib cage. The rest would have to heal on its own.

Fagen willed himself to remain conscious. Everything moved so fast. Too much had happened, and he needed time to sort it out. He knew Sergeant Rivers and Lieutenant Alstaetter had risked a lot to save him from a lynch party, but he also knew if he were court martialed, he'd be just as dead, convicted of a murder he may not have committed. He tried to recall the incidents of the previous night. An ugly, violent scene, a great deal had happened in a short time. He could easily have been the one murdered, or Ellis, kicked to death by hateful white men. He felt remorse for the dead soldier, but who's to say which horse he was trampled under?

Fagen struggled against his injuries and sat up in the wagon. They were passing through the outskirts of San Isidro. He looked around, and even in the darkness recognized the road they traveled. He inhaled the clean night air and welcomed the attending sharp pain under his bandages. The steady clip-clopping of Roberto's little burro through the dusty side streets brought focus to his thinking, and his brain reeled with myriad images that flashed before his eyes in quick succession.

He saw Ellis, bigger even than in real life, marching down the gangplank their first day in Manila, looking back at him with guileless, unsuspecting eyes. Then later, inside their tent after his confrontation with the misanthrope, Otis Youngblood, Fagen heard himself promise his cousin: "The army is like a wife to us. We took an oath, and we're joined in the eyes of God. She's even better than a wife. You see the army can't ever divorce you. You give your life to her, and she can't ever turn her back on you." That hurt Fagen more than all his injuries. If it weren't for him, Ellis would be safe at home on their little sharecropper's farm in Georgia.

Then a thousand more scenes flashed across his mind's eye like a collage of garish pictures painted on a carousel, but the one that came to the forefront over and over was of Ellis in chains, kidnapped in the night, a stinking, vermin-infested blanket screening him from the outside world. "Help me, Davey! I don't want to go away." The image too terrible to contemplate, Fagen banged his head against the wagon sideboard to free himself of it.

Fagen's mind raced over his own time in the Philippines. In the beginning, he'd wanted so desperately to prove himself, to show the world what he was made of. He'd never forget his first day in combat, the exhilaration of discovering himself in battle and the joy he'd experienced believing he was destined for great things. Now, that time seemed like a thousand years ago. Since then, life had handed him harsher realities and darker memories.

Racial hatred among soldiers in the Philippines had been far worse than he could ever have imagined. Youngblood had been right, Jim Crow and Uncle Sam had arrived in the Philippines at the same time. Had they always been traveling companions? The Filipinos were a colored race, and the Americans couldn't kill them fast enough. "Like shootin' rabbits in a field," Fagen had heard one white soldier remark. He recalled the day they marched to Camp McKinley, and he first heard the words "gugu" and "slope." Now, white American soldiers used dink, slope and gugu interchangeably with darkey, nigger and coon.

He saw again the propaganda leaflets the Insurrectos had left in their camp.

Your masters have thrown you in the most iniquitous fight with double purpose – to make you the instrument of their ambition, and also your hard work will soon make the extinction of your race.

Now more than ever, Fagen believed he knew the truth behind that dark prophesy.

He remembered sitting across the table from Emilio Aguinaldo, listening to his earnest appeal. "David, you are oppressed in your own country. White people call you a sulking brute. They burn you on their crosses, kill your children. Is it your destiny to live out your life among people who despise you?" The general's words echoed in Fagen's brain and reminded him that now he'd been charged with murder, perhaps the end of his life was at hand. Was it his destiny to surrender himself to the mercy of a kangaroo court, knowing full well the last thing on earth he'd see was the sneering grin of the hangman as he placed a noose around his neck?

He knew then why Clarita had taken him to see Aguinaldo. Dear, sweet Clarita had tried to save his life, and he'd repaid her with scorn. How could he have been such a fool? Would she ever forgive him? A vision of her appeared before him. She stood smiling alongside *EL Presidente* while he spoke. "Join my army. We welcome you with open arms. You have the opportunity to help an entire nation achieve its independence. Countless generations of children will be born into freedom because of your actions. Your joining our fight will be a signal to other brave men like you that it is possible to love your country and at the same time hate its politics."

Roberto's wagon hit a bump and jolted Fagen out of his brown study. The moon at its zenith in a cloudless sky gave off a steady white luminescence. Fagen was sure he recognized the terrain and when he saw it, knew where he was. Slowly inching his way to the back of the wagon, he hung his legs over the tailgate and when sure Roberto wasn't looking, slipped off and started walking.

He'd seen the trail that led off the main road and followed it through a small valley between ranges of rocky, green hills. Soon, the trail narrowed and darkened, and the cliffs to his right and left became steeper. Ignoring the agony that came with each step, he found the path and started up, keeping to the rocks and away from the slippery grasses that lined the cliff face. Weakened by pain and exhaustion, it was an hour before he reached the narrow opening that led to Clarita's *Simbahan,* her sanctuary. "The one place I always feel safe," she'd said. "Nothing bad can happen here, there is too much beauty."

Fagen made his way down to the beach and collapsed onto the soft white sand. Tormented and tortured, mind and body, he resolved he would no longer let fate have its way. From that day forward he'd be in charge of his own life, and he'd do whatever he needed to remain free. With his last measure of strength, he reached out and put his hand into the cool water. Soon he felt the pain and anguish drain from his body through his fingertips into the pool.

Every inch of him ached, and it hurt wherever she touched him, but her hands were cool and dry, and her nearness gave him great comfort. She lay down beside him and held him close. "I heard what happened," Clarita said.

Fagen rested his head on her shoulder and closed his eyes. "I prayed you'd come."

CHAPTER 13 – DIVORCE

Ellis Fairbanks stood, a forlorn immigrant, before the entranceway while the guards removed the chains from his hands and feet. The big, colorless moon had disappeared below the western horizon, and like it, Ellis's conscious mind had retreated behind a protective barrier in his head. It was still there and still radiated thought, but had taken refuge for a while, and like the moon, when it reappeared, would not be the same shape or shine with the same luminosity as when the night had begun.

The old wooden gates opened, and a woman appeared wearing a long black habit. Ignoring the guards, she smiled at Ellis, and then took him by the arm and led him inside. "Welcome to San Lazaro hospital, *Señor* Fairbanks. I am Sister Adriana."

They walked across a wide courtyard into a long building made of sandstone with a low tin roof. In the candlelight, Ellis saw a desk and two chairs positioned to give a view out a small window. Two walls were lined with bookshelves, on the third, an altar housed a statue of the Virgin Mary.

"Please be seated. It's very late, and I know you must be exhausted from your journey. Tomorrow Doctor Malvar, our chief clinician, will conduct a complete examination, but before I show you to your quarters, may I ask to see your lesions?"

Ellis blinked at the woman and took a deep breath. So much had happened since the guards had taken him from his quarantine tent. He worried about Davey. Was he badly hurt? Was he even alive? The last glimpse he got of his cousin was in front of the gates at their San Isidro camp. He remembered horses shrieking and rearing furiously, their hooves gouging through soft flesh. He'd heard the sound of men's voices, "Kick his head off, Jim!" and "Kill that nigger son of a bitch!" Then he recalled the sound of his own voice, "Help me, Davey! I don't want to go away." He was ashamed he didn't do more to help his cousin and prayed Davey was all right.

He saw the woman's lips moving, but her voice sounded far away. He forced himself back to the present. "What?"

"Your lesions. The places on your body the doctor looks at." Ellis stood and lifted his shirt. Sister Adriana moved the candle closer and examined the purplish spots. "Very good, *Señor,* the diagnosis is correct. I will take you to the dormitory now so you can rest."

"Wait a minute, Sister. What is this place? I can't stay here. I need to get back to camp."

"*Señor* Fairbanks, you can never go back to your camp. You must remain here at San Lazaro hospital with us."

"Why? What's wrong with me?"

"You have Hansen's disease, *Señor,* leprosy."

A black curtain dropped before Ellis' eyes. When he awoke, he was a boy again at home on their tiny sharecropper's farm. He and Davey had returned from school to find the family dog, Rattler, in the barn cowering under a mound of hay and stinking to high heaven. He fetched a bar of lye soap and some vinegar from the kitchen, and together the two cousins led their pet down to the river and spent the rest of the afternoon washing away the stubborn, pungent stink of skunk. The dog whimpered a little when the vinegar invaded the bite wounds on his snout. "This dummy should have known better than to corner a damned polecat," Davey had said.

Later, when the boys and the dog all emanated the same fulsome scent of river, soap, vinegar and varmint, they returned to the house to find Eunice waiting for them on the porch. "Old Rattler got crosswise with a skunk, Auntie, but he's all right now," Ellis had said.

"You boys better give me your clothes so I can put them to soak."

The youngsters put on clean overalls while Eunice heated water in a tub on the stove. "Did you check that dog for bite marks? Skunks carry rabies, you know."

"We checked him, Mama. He's fine." That was the only time Ellis ever heard his cousin David lie to his mother.

Every day for two weeks, Ellis checked on Rattler, looking for anything unusual in his behavior, any sign of the dreaded disease he knew would be his dog's death sentence. He'd never actually seen an animal with rabies. He'd only heard the gruesome stories, and they'd been so frightening to his young ears, he couldn't imagine his lifelong companion with a sickness so horrible.

Davey recognized the first symptoms. For three days, Rattler turned his nose up at the scraps Eunice threw out for him and hardly touched his water. By the fourth afternoon, he'd retreated to a corner of the barn growling at anyone that came near. If he came out at all, it was only to walk in circles for a while and nip angrily at his tail.

Eunice kept the boys indoors until the dog returned to its corner, and then she closed the barn door and forbade them to go near him. That night, Ellis lay awake listening to Rattler's solitary cries. He knew the dog was a danger and needed to be locked away, but his pet hadn't really done anything to deserve the imprisonment, and he agonized over the animal's forced isolation.

Early the following morning, Joseph Tidwell, neighbor from down the road, showed up carrying a long pole with a noose on one end. His brother, Jordan, wore his pistol and carried a shovel. They sat in the kitchen and drank coffee, staring silently at the table top while Eunice got the boys ready for school. When he left, Davey walked out the door and refused to acknowledge the two men. Ellis stopped for a moment, tears brimming. Eunice put her arm around him, but he pulled away, and then shouted at the three grown-ups. "Rattler didn't do anything wrong," he sobbed. "It's not his fault!"

"Are you all right, *Señor?*" Ellis sat up, and Sister Adriana placed a damp towel on his forehead. "Please forgive me, sir. I assumed you knew of your condition. Your doctor did not tell you?"

"He said he didn't know what was wrong with me." Ellis gulped the cup of tea she'd put before him. "How do you know it's…what you said? How can you be so sure?"

"Doctor Malvar received copies of your medical record today. He told me you would arrive here this night. I am not a doctor, *Señor*, but I have been at San Lazaro for many years. I have seen hundreds of victims of Hansen's disease. That's why I asked to look at the affected areas on your body. I make it a point to confirm the diagnosis with my own eyes before I allow a new patient to mix with the general population."

"I thought you said I have leprosy."

"We prefer the term Hansen's, after the doctor who first discovered the bacillus."

"How did I get it? What's going to happen to me? Am I dying?"

"No one knows how the disease is transmitted, or why it strikes some people and not others. It's generally believed the contagion occurs through contact with an infected person. I am not so sure. I have lived among lepers half my life, as has Doctor Malvar, and we are unaffected, but society demands Hansen's victims be separated and live among others with the same illness. It's always been so. According to legend, Moses first required lepers to stay away from other citizens, and if anyone came near, they were to give warning by crying 'unclean – unclean!'

"Old taboos are hard to break, *Señor*. Now, people suffering from Hansen's live in colonies, such as this one here at San Lazaro. In many ways this is better. We've made a world of our own here. What goes on outside these walls is of little concern to us. We are happy to remain among those who understand the illness. No one here recoils in horror and aversion at a patient progressing through the stages of his disease. No one runs away shouting 'fiend' or 'citizen of hell.' No one tries to murder us or clean the streets of our tortured bodies.

"You asked me whether you are dying. I don't think a person can be dying. I think we are either alive or dead. Right now, *Señor*, you are very much alive. Yes, you have Hansen's disease. There is nothing anyone can do about that, but you must not lose hope. The effects are different for every patient. Many people live for years with no apparent symptoms. Some have been known to wake up only to find it has spontaneously disappeared on its own volition. Not a great deal is known about the disease, but hundreds of doctors around the world have dedicated their lives to finding a cure. Until that happy day, *Señor*, you must try to make a life with us here at San Lazaro. Now please, allow me to escort you to the dormitory."

Ellis was too shocked and horrified to think straight. The earnest, well-meaning woman sitting across from him had just rendered the most condemning verdict a man can receive. He wished Davey were there with him, or even Sergeant Rivers. He needed to talk to someone. Maybe he could go back to his quarantine tent and wait there for a cure. He didn't know this Doctor Malvar the Sister spoke of, but certainly the army doctor was equally competent. Why had he been sent here?

"Am I still in the army?"

"I do not know, *Señor*. You can ask Doctor Malvar tomorrow, perhaps he will tell you."

Ellis stood up and looked around the room. He hadn't understood everything that had happened to him that night. It had been too much too fast. He needed time to sort it out. He knew one thing for certain, however. "Well, Sister, if I'm sick and the army sent me here, it must be for my own good." His cousin, Davey, had told him so.

He followed her across the courtyard to a row of identical wooden bungalows. She stopped at the third and climbed two steps onto the front porch. Her candle flickered in the pre-dawn blackness as she held the screen door open and whispered, "There are several unoccupied beds, *Señor*. You may take your choice. We will talk again after you rest." She started to leave, but then turned back and handed Ellis the candle. "Be sure to extinguish the flame before you go to sleep. Fire is the only thing we have left to fear." Ellis had experienced loss in his lifetime, but he'd never before known the sting of such utter abandon, and his whole body trembled as he went inside and closed the screen door behind him.

The dormitory was a long, narrow room with wooden cots side-by-side along the walls. Ellis tiptoed over the rough-sawn plank floor looking for an empty bed. He chose the first one he came to, closest to the door. The other men in the room appeared asleep, so as quietly as he could, he slipped off his boots and lay down on the bare mattress. He must have closed his eyes, because when he felt someone gently tapping the bed frame, he looked up and in the candlelight saw three men standing over him. Draped from head to toe in dull, brown cotton robes, their faces hidden in shadow, when they saw Ellis was awake, they moved in closer and leaned over his bed. One of the men said softly, "Welcome to the San Lazaro leper home, *Señor*."

"Our Sanctuary of Sorrow," whispered the next.

"Welcome to the living death," said the third. Their haunting, disembodied voices sent a chill down Ellis' spine.

"Sister Adriana let you keep the candle. You must be a very important person," the first man said. "I would like to know such a man as you," and he extended his hand out from the folds in his robe. "Shake."

Ellis tried to sit up, but when the man reached out to him, he shuddered in revulsion and fell back on his cot. What appeared before him was not a hand, but a bloated, rotting stump, the fingers gone, and in their place a line of loathsome, putrescent blisters surrounded by glistening infectious ulcers. Ellis tried to breath, but his throat closed against his own vomit as the man waved the offending limb in his face. "Come on, *amigo*, shake hands with me! You are a filthy leper, but I don't mind if you touch me." The man cackled contemptuously, and then returned the hand to its place inside his robe.

The second man bent low over the bed, his face just inches from Ellis' pillow. His breath like a newly opened grave, when he spoke his voice was a harsh, guttural whistle. "I suppose Sister Adriana told you that you are not a leper, but only a victim of Hansen's disease. She probably said your symptoms might not progress and may even go away on their own. God bless her. Such optimism springs from her deep-seated belief in the

Almighty, but there are those of us who do not share her sunny outlook on the future." At that he reached up and removed his hood.

Ellis' body went rigid with repugnance. Wave after jolting wave of nausea swept over him. He cried out and tried to turn away, tried to shut his eyes against the odious specter hovering over him. The man moved in even closer. His face was covered in a mass of hideous, oozing eruptions. His upper lip was gone and his nose a huge, grotesquely distorted, gangrenous strawberry. Something projected from it and moved when he spoke. The man picked up the candle and held it close to his face. "Sister Adriana made these nostril stoppers to keep the blow flies from entering my nose and laying their eggs," he wheezed. "You see, *Señor*, the maggots would feed on my brain, and I would die." The man coughed once, and then to Ellis' horror, he smiled, pulled the wooden pegs out of his nose and held them out for inspection. "Say farewell to the joys of human life, *amigo*."

The third man stood very still at the foot of Ellis' bed. His face hidden in the dark shadows under his hood, he spoke, his voice clear and strong. "Do not be afraid, *Señor*. We mean you no harm. We want only to be your friends. You are here with us now, but you cannot truly be one of us until you abandon all hope. You will understand more fully when, like us, you have suffered the loneliness and helplessness of the living dead. Even though your efforts will be futile and pathetic, you must be diligent in your attempts to come to terms with your situation, because it is only through a desperate struggle with your humanity that you will finally realize you have been forever forsaken and disowned. From this day forward, when you talk to Almighty God, do so in the sure and certain knowledge your prayers will go unanswered. This, my friend, is the path to peace of mind in this Sanctuary of Sorrow."

Ellis turned over and buried his face in his old moth-eaten mattress. He hadn't cried since a young boy, but this horror more than he could bear, now his tears came in a gushing torrent, and his body quaked with each woeful lamentation. Will this nightmare ever stop, he asked himself? He wanted to pray for it to be over, for morning to come, but he was afraid of the unspeakable horrors the light of day would bring. He wanted to pray for himself, to ask God to end this cruel joke, to let him go back to his life. He wanted to pray for death, a quick, merciful death. Whatever lay beyond must surely be better than this world. He wanted to pray, but then he remembered the man's words, *your prayers will go unanswered.*

CHAPTER 14 – ASSIMILATION

"Forgive me, but this will hurt a bit." He rested the heel of his hand against the bridge of Fagen's nose and plucked the stitches out with a pair of tweezers.

"Thank you for everything you've done for me, Miguel."

"It has been an honor to serve you, *Señor.*"

"You're a good doctor."

"My father was a doctor, *Señor.* I am only a *tagapag-alaga,* an enthusiastic amateur, but in war we make do with what we have. You must be careful not to traumatize that nose. Then I think it will be as good as new."

Fagen stood up and moved around, glad to finally get the bandages off his face. Miguel checked his arm, searched for any swelling or unusual pain. Two weeks before, he'd replaced Roberto's makeshift splint with one made from a hollow length of bamboo. An ingenious design, Fagen found he didn't even need a sling.

Everything considered, Fagen felt he was recovering nicely from his injuries. He'd been out of his mind with delirium the first few days after they'd brought him in. He thought he remembered seeing Clarita once during that time and of course Miguel, but he also saw Ellis and Sergeant Rivers and his father too, so he wasn't really sure where reality left off and shock-induced fantasy took over. He recalled someone forcing him to consume large quantities of a bitter green tea, and later, as his strength returned, fresh fruit in the mornings and rice and stewed fish for supper.

As Fagen's condition improved, Sergeant Rivers, Colonel Funston, Ellis and the four guards who took him away all came to visit him, not in some dream world, but in his conscious mind. Some days they were all he thought about. He racked his brain to conjure up another set of circumstances to account for his predicament, but knew he was only fooling himself. He'd done what no Negro soldier before him had even contemplated. He'd deserted, crossed the line, and there was no going back.

Miguel encouraged him to get as much exercise as he could, but when he ventured outside his tent and walked around the Filipino camp everyone ignored him, and he felt invisible. Also, he had no idea where he was. One afternoon, when the clouds lifted, he saw he was in a small valley surrounded by jungle mountains rising two thousand feet. The rebel soldiers in the camp spent the days training or carrying supplies seemingly in all directions, and they went about their duties without looking at him, walking past him as though he wasn't there. A few days before, a boy had taken away his army clothes and replaced them with a guerilla uniform, white shirt and pants, straw hat and sandals. At first, he thought the Filipinos ignored him because he was dressed like them, and they couldn't tell he was the American turncoat, but then common sense took over, and he knew the reason they paid no attention. In spite of his clothes, they recognized a traitor when they saw one.

That morning, with the stitches out, Miguel pronounced him healed and left. Fagen lay on his cot and wondered what he'd do next when the tent flap suddenly opened and a Filipino entered. He wore the same uniform as any other guerilla soldier, but instead of the usual oversized, floppy straw hat, he wore a white pillbox with a narrow, black brim. Fagen thought he looked like a milkman and was about to say so when the man stopped, stood rigid as a plank and shouted at the top of his lungs, "*ATENCIÓN!*"

Fagen had heard that command before and as there was no one else present, assumed it meant for him. He got to his feet and stood at attention facing the little soldier. Nothing happened for a moment, complete silence in the tent, but Fagen had made up his mind he wasn't about to move until the milkman did.

Just then, a tall, middle-aged man entered wearing a splendorous white uniform trimmed in gold, his chest covered in ribbons. He had the regal bearing of a man of great consequence. High cheekbones, long, straight nose and a perfectly manicured goatee accentuated his long face. He gazed at Fagen for a moment, sizing him up, and then said, "Stand at ease, Mister Fagen."

He then turned his back, held the tent flap open, and Clarita came in. Ignoring the officer and the milkman, she ran across, threw her arms around Fagen and showered him with little butterfly kisses. "Oh, David! I heard you were better. Thank God. Are you all right? Let me look at you. Did they tell you I was here to visit you?"

In a moment, the officer made a coughing sound, and Clarita took a half step back and lowered her head slightly. "Forgive me, Teo. David, this is General Teodoro Sandico, a trusted confidant of *El Presidente*, and a great leader of our revolution." The general smiled, gave a little bow, and then extended his hand.

"*Señorita* Socorro is a shameless flatterer, Mister Fagen, but perhaps that's why we treasure her so. In point of fact, I am only a humble teacher serving my country in accordance with my abilities during these unfortunate times. It's an honor to meet you. May I take a moment of your time?"

Fagen knew the expression "blueblood" and thought he understood what it meant, but he'd only heard it applied to earls and dukes and European ladies and gentlemen of high order. General Teodoro Sandico wasn't any of those things, but everything about him whispered thoroughbred. He took Fagen's hand in both of his and held it for a long moment, his eyes darting from head to toe, searching, as though he'd just discovered a gold mine. He gave Fagen the impression he seemed genuinely delighted to be in his presence. In the back of his mind, Fagen wondered whether a school specialized in the general's brand of gentility, and if so, was that where this man taught?

The general cocked his head a little and lifted his chin, waiting for Fagen's answer. Clarita slipped her hand under Fagen's elbow and squeezed. He looked, and she gave him a little nod. "Of course, sir. Take all the time you need."

General Sandico dismissed the aide with the funny hat and took a seat at the small table. Clarita and Fagen sat together on the cot facing him. "*El Presidente* sends his regards and prays for your continued recovery. You've been through quite an ordeal. I myself don't know whether I could have endured the crushing misfortune that has befallen you. There is no crueler fate than to be forsaken by one's own country. I admire your courage, Mister Fagen. When life handed you the ultimate malignancy, you did not surrender. Instead you decided to fight back, to punch the Devil in the nose, so to speak."

Fagen looked away. "You make me sound like a hero instead of a deserter."

"I think you are neither, sir. I think you're a man who chose to follow his heart, to disavow the illegal and immoral actions of his government. Words like hero and deserter are best left with the lawyers and diplomats. It's enough you are here with us now."

The general took a leather wallet from his coat and laid it on the table. "Now, I will come to the point of my visit. *El Presidente* has asked me to propose once again that you join our army and help us in our struggle for an independent Filipino state. In order to help you in your decision, he has authorized me to bestow upon you the rank of *Capitán* and provide you with a company of able-bodied men."

General Sandico picked up the wallet, thumbed through the contents, and then shoved it across the little table. "If you do not choose to do this, please accept this gift. I have prepared letters of transit and enough money to get you safely to the Malay Peninsula. From there, you may go wherever you wish, and your life will be your own." The aristocratic general sat back and smiled at Fagen as though he were his only son whom he'd just asked to choose between two colleges to attend next year.

Fagen knew he had no real choice. He'd never leave the islands without Ellis, and for the first time since they'd met, he saw the very real possibility of a future with the woman he loved. Clarita sat beside him, eyes cast down, hands in her lap kneading her kerchief. He knew going on the run was out of the question. He could tramp all over Asia for years, and the army would never stop looking for him, probably already offered a reward for his head. Even if he found a den of thieves vile enough to accept him, he knew it wouldn't be long before he was murdered in his sleep for the copper in his pockets.

His options limited, finished with false hope, he vowed never again to go into a situation without both eyes open. He looked at the general and said, "I'll ask you the same question I asked General Aguinaldo. Why me? I'm just a private soldier and not a very good one. I've failed at everything I've tried. Hell, I'm a shrine to failure."

"You're too hard on yourself, Mister Fagen. You have much to bring to our cause."

"Begging your pardon, sir, but those are just words. They don't have any real meaning to me."

General Sandico put both hands on the table and leaned forward. "David, you are only a failure if you now choose to be. Fate has brought you to us, and circumstance has made you more than a private soldier, more even than a good man searching for peace of mind. Accept *El Presidente's* offer, and you become a symbol of everything wrong in this world *and* everything right. You become a shining example in your country and mine that truth and moral purpose are more important than anything. We humans are faltering, weak-willed creatures. We rely on the archetypes that rise from among us to show us we can transcend, reach beyond ourselves and overcome life's grim exigencies. Call it God's will, fate or circumstance, it makes no difference. It's only important that you understand you can do more than anyone else to rid these islands of the evil upon us, more even than *El Presidente* himself."

Fagen searched the general's face for signs of dissemblance, but found none, no trace of insincerity or unctuousness in his voice. At first, he scoffed at Sandico's attempt to make him a martyr, or a savior. He knew he was neither, but if there were only a grain of truth in what the general had said, then maybe there was a chance for him actually to do something with his life. If he saw the immorality of this war, maybe others would too, and enough of them would speak up and the awful killing would stop. He looked at Clarita. She sat motionless, her eyes closed, tears streamed down her cheeks. Fagen took a deep breath and said, "I couldn't make war on Negroes, sir."

The General stood up. "Very well. If you'll raise your right hand, I'll administer the oath of allegiance."

"One more thing, sir." Fagen put his arm around Clarita and looked into her shining dark eyes. "I don't think it's wise to take this step alone. I'm not Filipino, I'll need someone to help me with language and local custom."

"*El Presidente* agrees with you. He has authorized me to assign *Señorita* Socorro to that duty, if that is your wish."

Clarita looked at him, a little smile curled her lip. Fagen held her closer. "It is my wish, sir."

The general took a paper from his coat pocket, unfolded it and read in Spanish. The voice of a Roman senator, his words rolled around inside the tent gathering speed until they seemed to overtake themselves. Fagen heard him pronounce his name two or three times, but mostly he concentrated on the woman he loved standing beside him, felt her heart beat clear through his bamboo cast. When the general finished reading, he lowered the paper and looked at Fagen. A long silence until he glanced at Clarita. She nudged him and said, "Say '*Sí*.'"

He did, and the general stepped forward and shook his hand. "Congratulations, *Capitán* Fagen, and may God bless you and the new Philippine Republic. Perhaps now you would like to meet your men." Fagen showed bewilderment, and Sandico smiled. "*El Presidente* anticipated your decision to join us and issued a proclamation last week calling for volunteers to serve with the new American *Capitán*. This way please."

General Sandico held the tent flap open. Clarita led the way, and when they stepped into the sunlight, the milkman shouted "*ATENCIÓN*" at the top of his lungs, and forty young, ragtag Filipinos scrambled to their feet.

Sandico uttered a command, and a tall, thin man wearing a Spanish saber stepped forward, presented arms and said something to Fagen. He held the salute while Clarita translated. "Lieutenant Burgos presents the company for review."

Fagen came to attention and returned the salute. "Ask the Lieutenant to have the men stand at ease." Burgos turned and barked a command. The company went to parade rest, and then another man, shorter than the lieutenant and heavily built, came forward and reported. He carried a Spanish Mauser rifle and wore a black leather pistol belt and shoulder strap. Lieutenant Burgos spoke again, and Fagen caught a name, *Sargento* Canizares.

"The company sergeant," Clarita said. Fagen smiled into the man's hard, no-nonsense face, and a picture of Sergeant Rivers flashed before him. Without thinking, the newly commissioned *Capitán* reached out and shook the bewildered sergeant's hand. Embarrassed by his own inappropriate demonstration of sentiment, Fagen glanced over at the general, unsure what to do next.

Sandico smiled, took him by the arm, and with Clarita, Lieutenant Burgos and the sergeant following, walked to the first row of men. "Surely you've stood review by your company commander on many occasions, *Capitán* Fagen," the general whispered.

"Yes, sir, I have, but it doesn't look the same from this angle."

As the reviewing party passed, each row of men snapped to attention. Fagen noticed many wore ill-fitting uniforms, their gear mix-and-match. Some carried the battle-friendly Mauser rifle, others the older, black powder Springfield .45-70 single shot.

Lieutenant Burgos spoke and Clarita translated. "Most of the men are volunteers, *Capitán,* with no combat experience. They came from all over southern Luzon to serve with the famous *Negrito Americano. Sargento* Canizares and I are from Malolos. We served together in the *Katipunan* and are experienced in war, but we've had little time to get these men ready."

Fagen turned and looked the man in the eye. "Are you and the *Sargento* volunteers as well?"

"*Si, Señor,*" the lieutenant smiled. "Very much so."

They walked down the last row of soldiers, and Fagen's attention was drawn to a short young man in the middle of the rank. He stood at rigid attention, chin up, shoulders back in exaggerated fashion. Fagen stopped in front of him. The boy trembled with excitement. His eyes shone as he tried not even to blink, and he pressed his lips together to keep from smiling. His fingers locked around his old Springfield "trapdoor" rifle, Fagen reached out and coaxed the weapon from the boy's grasp. He opened the breech and looked down the barrel, using his thumbnail to reflect light inside. Pleasantly surprised to find the weapon spotless, he said. "What's your name?"

Clarita translated, and the young man answered. "José, *Señor*."

"Where are you from?"

"I came all the way from Tarlac, *Señor*." The boy's face lit up, and his words came in an impassioned explosion. "A very long way, but I wanted to fight with the *Americano* David Fagen. You are known all over Luzon as a true friend to the Filipino, *Señor* --"

Sergeant Canizares growled, and the boy's mouth slammed shut. Fagen returned the rifle to him. "How old are you?"

"Sixteen, *Señor*."

"Have you ever used that weapon?"

"No, *Señor*."

"What will you do when the Americans charge your position firing their Krags at your head?"

The boy's face lit up again, and he smiled broadly. Clarita listened and then said, "I'll pull the trigger many times, *Señor*. I will shoot every one of them!"

"I think you're too young to fight. Go back to Tarlac and stay with your family."

A pained expression crossed the boy's face, and his shoulders fell. "Oh, no, please *Señor*, I cannot do that."

Fagen looked at Clarita and General Sandico. "Why not?"

"My father said anyone wishing to fight with the famous *Capitán* Fagen should do it now, because the *Americano*s will kill him very soon."

Lieutenant Burgos and Sergeant Canizares turned white with anger, and then red with embarrassment. General Sandico laughed out loud. Fagen smiled at the boy and said, "Then let's pray your father is mistaken and we fight together for a very long time. Lieutenant Burgos, I'll inspect the troops with full field gear tomorrow morning. Please make sure every man's weapon is as clean as José's."

The first three weeks as *Capitán* in charge of his own company were a blur to Fagen. He divided the men into four ten-man squads and appointed a leader for each. They were up every morning before sunrise for exercises, followed by bayonet drills and hand-to-hand combat. Fagen supervised every aspect of the men's training. He still felt the effects of the beating he'd taken at the hands of the white soldiers and pushed himself harder than he should. Still weak, he needed time to build his own strength, but he'd promised himself he'd never ask his men to do anything he couldn't do himself.

Clarita had told him he'd be impressed with Filipino fighters, and she was right. The best soldiers he'd ever seen, they were tireless, performed their duties cheerfully and obeyed their leaders without hesitation. Never a cross word or a dark look among them. Each evening while the campfires burned, after twelve strenuous hours in the field, the men listened attentively into the night to Fagen or Lieutenant Burgos conducting classes in small unit tactics, camouflage, target detection and range finding. Some nights, Sergeant Canizares divided the men according to squads and by the firelight drew out and compared elaborate attack-defend scenarios. Frequently, these battle debates went until well after midnight, and when the chalkboard warriors finally retired, they dropped on their cots and slept like the dead until time to do it all again the next day.

General Sandico never returned, but one day while Miguel conducted a class in battlefield medicine, Fagen received an unannounced visit from a portly little red-faced man walking pigeon-toed across the training ground. A lieutenant accompanied him, and a private followed carrying a valise overflowing with papers.

Until then, Fagen had had no contact with the main body of guerillas garrisoned just over the hill. No particular reason for their separation, but as his raw troops needed more intense training than the seasoned veterans, he liked the idea his men were not distracted by the others.

As the man waddled closer, Fagen saw he was a colonel and thinking he'd need a translator, looked around for Clarita. "*Capitán* Fagen!" the man puffed. "How are you? I am Urbano De Castro, commander of this district. How are you? Forgive me for not coming to see you before now. I've been in the barrios recruiting. How are you?" The little colonel returned Fagen's salute, and then hugged him like a long lost brother and pumped his hand until Fagen thought it would break off.

A breathless, redheaded, sweating runt of a man with a round face, button nose and rubbery, vermilion lips, Colonel De Castro wore the thickest pair of spectacles Fagen had ever seen, and he swabbed them constantly with a large white handkerchief. The heat evidently a problem for the man, he'd cut the sleeves off his uniform blouse and wore it open, exposing his giant, round belly.

The lieutenant placed chairs in the shade of a nipa grove, and Colonel De Castro plopped down. "I'll never get used to this weather. Twenty years I've tried, and it's no use. Too much white blood in me, I suppose. My father was Dutch, you see. Came through here in the sixties, married my mother, and after I was born, we all sailed to California to get in on the gold rush. You ever been to San Francisco?" Fagen opened his mouth to answer, but the colonel wiped his glasses, pinched the bridge of his little nose and plunged on. "Greatest city on the planet. I'll go back some day. Not now, of course, while this damned war's on, but someday.

"Where was I? Oh, yes. The gold thing didn't work out. Those things never do, do they? Anyway, Dad got a job on the waterfront building boats. Logging was big then, and there was a real demand for transport schooners. Plenty of work for a man who knew how to use his hands, but it didn't pay much. Being Filipino, the only work Mother got was cleaning houses. Every penny they earned went to pay for my schooling. We lived like dogs and ate potato soup seven days a week, but by God I went to the best schools in the city. Would you believe I went to the Kingsley Academy? Can you imagine that? The Kingsley Academy! What some people won't do for their kids."

While the colonel talked, the lieutenant took a dozen lemons from the valise and squeezed them into a pitcher of water. Then he poured two glasses and placed them on a tiny folding table. De Castro inhaled his in a few quick gulps, and then held his glass out for more. "Anyway, the folks were both killed in the earthquake of seventy-eight. I was fifteen at the time, old enough to take care of myself, but I learned very quickly American society was no place for an overweight, shortsighted half-caste, no matter how educated, so I caught the first boat back here. Don't get me wrong, Filipinos are not without their prejudices. Urbano Van Lierp is not a name taken seriously, especially in Manila. After a few months, I started using my mother's family name, De Castro, and things got easier.

"I've been the director of public works in Subic for the last fifteen years. Not a very glamorous occupation, I'm afraid and certainly not a fitting background for a military commander, but *El Presidente* thought differently, so here I am."

The colonel used the tails of his shirt to fan his round, red body. Sweat rolled down his fat arms and dripped off his fingertips. He took a gulp of his third lemonade. "Talk about making a name for yourself, you've done that in spades, my boy!" Fagen's ears perked up. He'd no news from the outside world since he'd arrived at the guerilla camp. So much had happened in the past month, he felt as though he lived a new life, and the old David Fagen existed in a far away and nearly forgotten world. He'd wondered whether the army had forgotten him.

"You've upset their apple cart, I can tell you. The whole United States army is looking for David Fagen. Aguinaldo himself doesn't get the attention you've generated. I'm told your Colonel Funston is livid because you're getting more press than he is! Every two-bit officer in Luzon claims to have seen you, or engaged you in a fierce battle from which you just managed to escape. Delightful! Every day a new story emerges of your cunning and audacity. There have even been newspaper articles about you in Boston, New York and San Francisco. You're a legend, my boy!"

"Oh, Jesus, that is not good, Colonel." The first exquisite touch of panic rose in Fagen's spine, reaching for his chest.

"But it is! It's just what *El Presidente* had hoped for. You've thumbed your nose at them good, my boy, and it's made them sit up and pay attention."

Fagen fought for control of his stampeding heart. The sudden reality of his outlaw status turned his blood to water and gnawed at his bowels. He'd let himself believe they weren't looking for him, they'd written him off like a bad debt. He hoped they'd assumed he was dead and closed the books on him. Now he realized that was not the case. No one could hide forever from the United States Government, and Fagen knew sooner or later his day of reckoning would come.

As Colonel De Castro talked, Fagen sat frozen to his chair staring at a portrait of his own annihilation. He wasn't just a dishonored soldier, he was a pariah, a notorious, infamous archfiend. His fate was sealed. No matter which side won the war, no matter how it was resolved, when over, he'd still be a wanted man. Pudgy little Urbano De Castro sitting there beside him, all the other revolutionary officers and all the men, even Aguinaldo himself, would go home, but he could not.

"But now it's time to put you to work. I've got a mission for you, and it's a dinger, as they say."

Fagen sat up in his chair. "A mission! Colonel these men have had only a few weeks training. They're not ready..."

"Nonsense! I've heard nothing but good things about the progress you've made. This is war, my boy. It's time to stir up your stumps! Pull up your socks! Wiggle your boots! It's time to get in the game!"

CHAPTER 15 - REFLECTIONS

Matthew Alstaetter was eight years old when his parents died in a fire that swept the Colorado mining town of Placer, leaving him and his two infant sisters, Hazel and Buena, orphaned and in the care of the shocked and devastated townsfolk. A week later, his father's brother, Les, and his wife, Alice, drove down in their covered wagon to get them. The children bundled in heavy blankets, they set off on a wintry, two-day journey along an icy trail over Berthoud Pass into Grand County.

Lester Alstaetter owned the Sheep's Nose Ranch, a dry, windswept patch eighty-five hundred feet above sea level where the valley met the mountains two miles east of Fraser. Despite its name, Les kept neither sheep nor cattle on the ranch, only a stable of huge, heavy-boned horses to haul thick ties and trestle timber to the railroad crews working on the line through the Rockies.

His whole life, Lester Alstaetter had been a quiet, practical man, always counted on to do the sensible thing. So Alice was more than a little surprised when very much against her wishes, four weeks after they married, Les loaded his bride and their few belongings into a crude wagon and left Springfield, Missouri headed west. Since childhood, Lester had heard about the equable climate and the green valleys of Oregon and felt he could make a life there, away from Alice's hovering, over-protective family.

On several occasions before they married, he'd taken her in his arms and tried to paint a picture. "Haven't you ever wanted to strike out on your own? Think of the places we can go, the sights we can see."

Alice Chapman knew of her fiancé's dream, had known for years. They'd been sweethearts since school, but she'd always considered him too practical-minded, too rational to abandon the familiar bustle and friendly faces of their hometown. Her family had been in Springfield for a generation. Devout Southern Baptists, Alice had grown up in the church. She found it impossible to think about living elsewhere. Les had a good job at the granary and a future in management. Alice was certain after they married, he'd come to terms with his responsibilities and give up the adolescent fantasy of living in what until just a decade earlier had been Indian country. They'd settle down in a little house of their own somewhere on the edge of town, and if things went as planned, in a few years they'd move up to one of the less-grand Victorian houses on Jefferson Street. Alice wanted a quiet, comfortable life under the protective umbrella of church and family.

On the afternoon Lester Alstaetter parked his new, canvas-covered Conestoga wagon in front of his mother-in-law's house, Alice was at the kitchen table addressing thank you cards to their wedding guests. She saw the glow of absolute joy on her husband's face as he stepped down from the seat, and her heart began to race. "Oh, my dear God, no!" she gasped, her cheeks flushed and her head spun in dizzying circles. Les grinned, waved at his bride through the window, and then took the porch steps three at a time. Even before he touched the front door latch, Alice Chapman Alstaetter had fainted dead away.

By the time the Alstaetters reached Wichita, Alice's distress had turned to bitter suffering. She lay nauseated and grieving inside the wagon during the long hot days on the Kansas plain and cried herself to sleep at night. Seeing his wife steeped in misery weighed heavily on Les. He'd no wish to inflict pain upon the woman he loved, but believed they had to get away, start fresh. He hoped the green fields and clear blue skies of Oregon would mend his bride's broken heart.

As they traveled west, Alice became more and more withdrawn. She rarely spoke to her husband and never looked outside at the endless prairie. Day after day, she sat in a corner of the wagon and read the bible, her lips moving silently over the passages. When they stopped in Colorado Springs for supplies, to cheer her up Les rented the bridal suite at the Eureka Hotel and ordered a hot bath. He left her alone in the room while he stabled the horses and commissioned a blacksmith to look over the wagon. Then he went to the general store and bought a book of poetry by Elizabeth Browning and a box of chocolates. When he returned to the hotel, Alice was gone.

He checked the hotel dining room first, and then as he crossed the street to the dress shop, he saw the commotion at the train depot. A crowd had formed. Men laughed derisively, while the women hustled their children away. Les elbowed through and found Alice on her knees desperately clutching her bible to her breast, pleading with the embarrassed ticket clerk. Her face flushed, tears streamed down her cheeks. "Please! If you have a spark of humanity in you, please!" She ripped a cameo brooch from her lapel and offered it to the clerk. "This is all I have, but I can send you money when I get home. I'll send you whatever amount you want, just put me on that train before my husband finds me."

Les put his arm around her, tried to lead her away, but Alice's dark eyes glazed over, she bared her teeth and shrieked gibberish. "She's speaking in tongues!" someone shouted, and the crowd backed away. Les cradled her head, hoping to get out of there with a scrap of dignity, but at the last moment, Alice reached out, seized the ticket clerk's collar, and they all fell in a heap on the depot floor.

Amid cries of "Show her who's boss, kid!" and "Tame that tiger, boy!" Lester Alstaetter threw his struggling bride over his shoulder and carried her up the street and into the hotel.

Alice slept fitfully through the night and awoke the following morning to find Lester, fully dressed, sitting at the foot of her bed. She started to speak, but he put a finger against her lips and then placed a roll of bills in her hand. "It's nearly everything we've got. I kept a little out for myself, just enough to get me where I'm going. The rest is yours. A train headed east leaves in two hours. You can be in Springfield day after tomorrow." He looked down and saw a distant coldness in her eyes. "I shouldn't have insisted. Maybe after I'm settled…"

Alice sat up in bed, pulled the covers to her chin and threw the wad of bills on the floor. "Don't be silly. I'm your wife. It's my duty to go where you go. The bible is clear on that."

Alice had always made the big decisions by way of scripture. She'd been brought up with the New Testament and was a pious believer. If the answer was in the Good Book, and it always was, the debate was over and the subject closed. Les sat on the edge of the bed. "It's not fair that you should be so unhappy."

"Nonsense," she spat, her voice hollow and dry. She turned her head and spoke to the wall, would not look at her husband. "You speak for this family, but God speaks for himself. Seraphim came last night and watched over while God spoke to me of my duty. In my selfishness, I'd forgotten His word as quoted in Matthew 19:29: 'And everyone who has left houses, brothers or sisters, fathers or mothers, children, or fields because of my name will receive one hundred times more and will inherit eternal life.' She stood up, turned her back and wrapped herself tightly in the bedclothes. "Now get out of here so I can pray. I'll be ready to leave in an hour."

Lester Alstaetter planned to get over the mountains before the season changed, but winter came early, and they only got as far as the Fraser Valley before the snow drifted as high as their wagon and the temperature plummeted. Nothing had gone right since they'd left Colorado Springs. They broke a wheel on the trail and camped four days on the high plateau north of Pike's Peak waiting for a replacement. When they reached Denver, they found themselves in the middle of a war over beef prices, and everywhere they turned, bands of hard, rough men roamed the streets between saloons armed with blackjacks and clubs, looking for trouble.

Halfway up Market Street, they tried to drive clear of a riot blocking their way, but there were too many men, and the liquor had taken over. When the rival gangs collided, the Alstaetters were suddenly swallowed up in a violent, cursing, head-splitting mêlée. Les dragged Alice into the back of the wagon and covered her body with his own. It seemed as though the fighting went on for hours. All at once, a volley of shots rang out, Les felt the wagon lurch and heard the mob disperse as everyone ran for cover. In a moment the street was empty, save for scattered bits of broken glass and a few battered hats. He checked on Alice and found her unhurt, praying with dry-eyed, thin-lipped determination. When he sat up, he saw his lead horse, Bonnie, on her side, the harness twisting her head at an odd angle, blood squirting from the bullet hole in her throat.

Ten days later, when they finally crossed the continental divide near Berthoud Pass and drove into the valley, Alice announced flatly, "Stop the wagon, Lester. I'll not go another mile." The first words she'd spoken to her husband in two weeks. Startled by the sound of her voice, Les hauled on the reins and looked around. The tiny, cheerless settlement of Fraser lay a mile in front of them, so remote, so forlorn, it might as well have been on the surface of the moon. Jagged, snow-clad peaks towered over them in every direction. He turned and tried to hold Alice's mittened hand, but she pulled away.

"We can wait here until the weather breaks, we're past the worst of it. It's easy going now, all the way to Oregon."

"I'm not going another mile, mister. You can do what you please."

"But I thought we'd agreed... You even quoted scripture."

Alice pointed to the eastern hills. "I saw the hand of God, back there, beckoning me. It was a sign, a message directly from the Holy Spirit. I have to obey." She saw the confusion on her husband's face turn to astonishment. "Don't look at me that way, Lester Alstaetter! It was a sign, I tell you. The wind blew away the snow clouds and there it was, the hand of God."

Lester had heard of the strange rock formation that stands above the peaks near the divide. The Indians thought it had mystical powers, even had a name for it. He'd been concentrating on the icy trail and missed it, but Alice had not. "You saw the Devil's Thumb. It's a well-known geological monument. The Indians think it's sacred."

Alice's dark eyes flashed, and her fists balled inside her woolen mittens. She looked her husband full in the face and hissed through quivering lips, "Don't you blaspheme around me, mister! I won't listen to your pagan fantasies. Here's where I saw God's hand, and here's where I stay." Resolute, she sat straight-backed on the seat and folded her arms across her breast, her chin held high and defiant into the wind. Les' heart sank, and he slumped in the wagon seat. He couldn't leave her and couldn't go on. He knew his young wife was lost in melancholy, and he felt partially to blame. He wanted to help, but she wore the New Testament like a suit of armor, and he couldn't find a way through to her. He hoped she'd come to her senses on her own. In the meantime, he'd just have to make do.

Early afternoon, and as the sun fell behind the peaks, an eerie, pinkish-brown shadow fell over the little town before them. Lester flicked the reins, and his team started forward. He gave the horses their head and closed his eyes, listened to the crusty sounds of iron on snow and gave in to resignation and despair, while the cold, winter wind scattered his dreams across the high valley floor.

Les listened grim-faced while the county sheriff told him about the fire that killed his brother, James and sister-in-law. It had started in the Chinese laundry and spread quickly up the street, gaining in blistering intensity as it swept through City Hall and Rosie's Steak House. The hotel had gone up like a tinderbox. Barely time to get the children out, thirteen people had died in the flames, and several more had been injured. The Alstaetters had been passing through. They'd stopped to rest a night in Placer before continuing to Utah, where James had secured a position with the Bureau of Indian Affairs. Of the two brothers, James had been the handsome one with the quick smile and bright future. The family had expected great things from him. Now he was dead, and Les and Alice were the parents of three children they'd never met.

Les had often thought about the capriciousness of fate, and he'd concluded most of life was the sum of countless trivial decisions a man made every day. Choices as light and seemingly inconsequential as whether to eat the meat first or the potatoes, sharpen the axe now or wait one more day, had dramatic, life-altering effect. Worse, a man didn't really need to do anything at all. Sometimes, destiny just took over completely, put the handwriting on the wall for him, and all he could do was hunker down and go with it. Les could never share these thoughts with his wife. She had no uncertainty about destiny. She didn't believe in random chance. Her faith taught her everything was pre-ordained by God. "If a man's destiny is in his own hands," she'd said, "and he finds salvation, then he was his own benefactor. Where's God's will in that?"

Certainly, Les thought, fate had slapped him in the face three years earlier when Alice looked up through a hole in the fog and saw the Devil's Thumb monument silhouetted over Indian Range. If their wagon had hit a bump, a rabbit had hopped out of its hole, if he'd spoken to his wife, just one word on any subject, her attention would have been diverted, the Devil's Thumb would have disappeared behind the clouds, and they would have continued on their journey. Fate had not been kind. Alice's attention had not been diverted, she'd seen the hand of God, and at that exact moment, Les knew he'd never see the green rolling hills of Oregon.

For Les, the children were a welcome addition to the family. He hoped they'd bring joy to their dreary household, but since their arrival, Alice became even more obsessed with religion, now lost in a reasonless, impenetrable dementia.

They had no friends. Les maintained contact with the outside world through his business dealings, but Alice had no interest in others. He'd encouraged her to meet people, join the ladies at their coffee socials, but she wouldn't hear of it. In her opinion outsiders were not true believers. Les pointed out that many of the ladies in Fraser were Baptist like herself, but Alice was not persuaded. A Southern Baptist, for her it was a sin to join with her co-religionists from the north. Determined to remain faithful to the south and its standards and vision, she shook her finger in her husband's face. "You leave me be on this subject, mister. The Bible says, 'Have no fellowship with the unfruitful works of darkness, but rather reprove them.' Ephesians 5:11."

Despite her determination to remain true to her beliefs, Alice wasn't happy in her isolation. The sting of expulsion, of ostracism took its toll on her. She'd only to look in the mirror to see the hopeful young girl just a few years before had transformed into a stern, humorless, willful woman compelled grimly to play the hand God dealt her.

Alice couldn't help it God had given her a sign. Not a volunteer in His army, He'd commanded her service. She didn't know why He'd called, or what He wanted, but she was resolute in her intention to await His orders. In the meantime, she found strength, if not comfort in Southern Purity. She'd made up her mind to live in exile as a committed Southern Baptist Christian practitioner. If Lottie Moon could serve the Lord in the wilds of China, she could endure the Rocky Mountains.

For a while, Alice thought her calling evangelical in nature. She sent away for Sunday school materials and offered classes, but no one attended. She'd made it clear to the townsfolk she didn't believe in the baptism of a child. "Infants are incapable of believing," she'd said. "Children are protected by the grace of God until they reach the age of accountability." To the Lutheran and Methodist mothers of Fraser, a shocking, misguided belief, and they kept their freshly baptized infants far from her.

Although she lived in the Rocky Mountains, Alice remained anti-Yankee and anti-modern. Liquor was evil as was dancing, most forms of music and any over-exuberant, ostentatious display of emotion. She believed Negroes inferior, and while a strict segregationist, she allowed that colored people had a special need for personal services, which compassionate white people should provide. Later in life, she would memorize the works of Thomas Dixon and go to her grave believing the Ku Klux Klan an heroic army fighting to preserve the Southern way of life.

She had a deep and abiding disdain for anyone whose views differed from hers, convinced they were condemned to the infernal region, including that dim-witted husband of hers, who every day became more and more blinded to the True Way. This was the household that eight-year-old Matthew Alstaetter and his sisters entered.

The boy enrolled in the little one-room schoolhouse in Fraser, but received his religious education at home. Uncle Les had signed a contract with the government and traveled much of the time delivering timber as far away as Ft. Collins. Night after night, all through the long, dark Rocky Mountain winters, Matthew sat in a straight-backed chair by the fire, Hazel and Buena asleep in his arms, and read scripture with his Aunt Alice. Early in his instruction, she made it clear this was serious work and demanded his full attention and countenance.

She drilled him on the verses of the New Testament until he could recite from memory. "I am the way, the truth and the life. No one comes to the Father except through me," Matthew repeated.

"Draw me not away with the wicked, and with the workers of iniquity which speak peace to their neighbors, but mischief is in their hearts," she prompted, and Matthew responded. During those cold, cheerless nights, Matthew developed exceptional reading skills, and his ability to memorize long passages far surpassed the other children in his school.

After a while, Matthew learned to enjoy some of the lessons. He discovered the New Testament brimming with fantastic stories of revenge, lust and greed. He taught himself to think of the men and women in the stories as living in the modern day. He stripped them of their beards and rough cloaks and put them in corduroys and cotton. In his mind, they wore boots instead of sandals and carried Winchesters instead of staffs. Seen from a secular point of view, the stories were entertaining, almost fun.

In time, Matthew realized he'd never be like his Aunt Alice. He'd never believe every word of the Bible literally true, and once when he questioned a certain passage, he witnessed firsthand his Aunt's shift from dour, unsparing guardian to venomous, outraged defender of the faith. He'd only pointed out a minor inconsistency in a particular verse, and she'd exploded in a fit of angry reproof. She locked him in his room and fed him nothing but bread and water for three days. After that, Matthew learned to be two people, always careful to show his Aunt only the side she wanted to see. In time, he taught himself to have many faces and discovered he didn't ever need to reveal the man inside.

When Matthew turned fifteen, Alice lectured him on the Abstract of Principles, the fundamental Laws of the Southern Baptist Church, a subject she was fervent about. During a particularly long, impassioned session, Matthew discovered something else about himself, he had a mind of his own and the will to use it. "The Abstract says," Alice droned, "all humans inherit a corrupt nature at birth, wholly opposed to God and incapable of moral action. Salvation lay in a person's acknowledgement of his manifold evil, and then through his humble self-abhorrence and detestation of it. Do you understand, Matthew?"

Matthew understood, but flatly rejected this. He'd heard enough. He refused to believe self-abhorrence led to anything good or holy. He'd observed that in his aunt for years and knew self-loathing only led to unhappiness and bitter distrust of others. Had the Law brought joy or peace of mind to her or Uncle Les? What kind of Law bids us find comfort in the proclamation that we are craven, corrupt creatures worthy only of self-abhorrence?

Matthew told himself his Aunt Alice was not just misguided, but wrong, and if she were in error, so was the Baptist dogma she espoused, and so too the millions of people around the world who believed it. If the Baptists were wrong, why not Lutherans, Catholics, Jews? Bitter experience had taught Matthew never to reveal his inner thoughts, to keep his opinions to himself, but he wanted to shout out loud, "What if it's not true? What if you're all wrong? Who gave you exclusive moral authority?" But he could not. Agnosticism was a maverick notion even in the most liberal circles, unspeakable at home. No choice but to live with his aunt's smothering articles of faith, he soon found it difficult to ignore the new person developing inside him, the determined, challenging skeptic.

That spring, Matthew graduated first in his class. He looked forward to working with his Uncle Les in the business, getting away from Aunt Alice for a while, so he was as shocked as his aunt horrified when Lester Alstaetter barged in the cabin one evening, a big grin on his face, waving a telegram in circles over his head. "Matthew, they've accepted you! I met Governor Waite a few months ago at Ft. Collins. He's a Populist, you know. I told him about you and he's done it! You're accepted at West Point!" Matthew Alstaetter later recalled that was the first time he'd ever seen his uncle smile.

"How's it coming, Lieutenant Alstaetter?" The hawk-faced young supply officer checked lines and columns in his book as soldiers scurried about moving small mountains of freight into the boxcars. Alstaetter recognized the man's pinched New England accent, and then saw the shoulder patch of the 15th Maine Volunteers. "Mind if I take a look at what you've done?"

The two men walked up the line stepping between ties until they reached the day coach, directly behind the coal car. Sergeant Rivers saluted. "About two more hours, sir. We're doing the best we can with the tools we've got."

The officers went on board and squinted through clouds of sawdust at two squads of H Company's first platoon at work on the car's interior. The soldiers had removed seats and installed wooden platforms on each side the entire length of the car. They'd removed the window glass and boarded the openings, leaving six-inch square holes every three feet.

Lieutenant Alstaetter said, "There's fifteen firing ports on each side." He pointed to two rows of straight-backed benches facing each other with a center aisle in between. "Twenty men can ride here and spell the men at the ports. We've built ammunition storage under the seats. In case of real trouble, these men can re-load for the shooters. Ration and water storage is in the back."

The young officer, his notebook under his arm, surveyed the job. "Your Negroes do good work."

Alstaetter ignored the remark. He didn't need dissembling compliments about his men from a rookie supply officer. He was in no mood. For several weeks, H Company had been on garrison detail, drawing every servile job the army handed out. Alstaetter knew why, and he knew what to do about it. He clumped the floor of the car with the heel of his boot. "We've cut emergency escape hatches here and overhead. The upper one is hinged for light and ventilation."

"Looks like you've thought of everything."

"There's no sleeping arrangement, but none was requested."

"For the time being, our longest run is twenty hours. They can stay awake that long." The officer stepped outside and looked up and down the car. "They make the first trek into indian country tomorrow. Colonel Funston says the rebels are sure to try something. I say let 'em. The insurrectos that attack this supply train will have a surprise in store for them."

CHAPTER 16 - ENTERPRISE

A little man, Cecelio Segismundo staggered under the weight of the firewood he carried on his back. Blistering hot, he wished he could find a stream to bathe his aching feet. One of Emilio Aguinaldo's most experienced couriers, Segismundo was exempt from the demanding and dangerous duties of the front line soldier, but when carrying documents, he found it prudent to disguise himself as a peasant to moderate the suspicions of any American patrols he encountered on his way.

Segismundo carried *El Presidente's* important dispatches in a concealed pouch sewn inside the waistband of his exceedingly ragged and filthy peasant garb and if challenged, hoped no American would actually search him. So far, the Americans he'd met had only made degrading comments and stole some of his firewood for their own campfires.

For many months, the little Filipino had conveyed his precious cargo through the province of Nueva Vizcaya, to a shopkeeper in the village of Dupax. Segismundo was a primary thread in the delicate web of communication Aguinaldo had spun across Central Luzon.

Often during his deliveries, when sure no one watched, Segismundo peeked at the documents he risked his life for. He was Ilocano, and each time he scanned the pages, he found most of the messages in Tagalog, written in elaborate code and without the key, meaningless. No matter. They were really none of his business, and he was content to get paid regularly and help the revolution without actually having to fight the Americans. Only a few more miles, and he would complete this delivery and get paid again.

"You there! *Alto!*" Segismundo looked up from the dusty path and beheld a burly cavalry sergeant and three privates on horseback blocking his way. "Haven't I seen you on this road before?"

"Maybe, *Señor.* I do not know." The sergeant dismounted and looked him up and down. As the American neared, Segismundo's mouth went suddenly dry, and he swallowed hard. The cavalry sergeant *had* seen him before, but not on the road. They'd bumped into each other on the boardwalk in Dupax one day when Segismundo came out of the barbershop having just had a shave and haircut. Dressed in his finest black pants, white linen shirt and new straw hat, he'd been on his way to see Maria, his new lady friend.

When they collided, the sergeant pushed him into the street and said, "Hey you! Open them slant eyes!" Segismundo apologized and grinned stupidly. Americans considered Filipinos halfwits, better to play the role. "Ain't you the fancy-britches? It ain't Sunday, you must be the mayor!" A losing situation, Segismundo muttered gibberish, bowed and backed away quickly.

Now, the Americans stood in a circle around him. The sergeant pointed to the bundle of wood. "What are you doing with them sticks?"

"Firewood, *Sargento*. For old people who cannot go out and get their own."

The sergeant drew his pistol and placed the muzzle over Segismundo's heart. "I seen you someplace before. Suppose you drop that load, and we have us a little talk."

Brigadier General Funston stood before the full-length mirror in his office admiring the shining new stars on his shoulders. The rumors had been right after all. MacArthur had succeeded Ewell Otis as Governor General, and with a little help from his friend, General Wheaton, Funston had received the promotion he'd coveted for so long. He lifted his chin, and then turned his head left and right, searching for the most flattering profile. By God, he'd deserved the promotion, he told himself. He'd rawhided that cold-blooded, murdering Aguinaldo clear out of Central Luzon, and he was well on his way to teaching the rest of those bullet-headed Asians to stay out of the way of the bandwagon of Anglo-Saxon progress and decency. Now that he commanded First Brigade, he'd finish this mess and get back home to his wife, Eda, and his future on the Kansas - perhaps national - political stage.

Duty had obliged him to send Eda home two weeks early. Good to see her, but there'd been just too much to do, and besides, Funston noticed shortly after she arrived that perhaps the war had hardened him a bit. He felt he'd changed to some degree, and his military-oriented temperament and calloused ways had rendered him unaccustomed to and impatient with the hovering ministrations of a wife.

He blamed that on the pressures of command. The war itself had changed in the past months, no question in his mind about that. The whole Filipino army had gone underground, and his commanders no longer reported the high body counts they'd enjoyed for so long. The insurrectos couldn't face American boys in a stand-up fight, so they'd gone to guerilla tactics. He could rarely send a patrol into the countryside that wasn't ambushed by a gang of peasants who'd pop up, fire a few shots, and then slip away into the jungle. Cowardly beyond belief, he thought, and took its toll on everyone.

Funston lit the remnant of his second morning cigar and stared out the window. At least he'd been able to contain that leprosy business. That would have blown the lid off everything. Too bad about that Negro private, but what else could he have done? Ever since his days in Cuba, he'd subscribed to the popular belief that coloreds were generally immune to the tropical diseases, but now he wasn't so sure. He was just thankful he'd caught it in time. He'd had to knock some sense into that commiserating Samaritan of a doctor, but now, the incident over, he too had fallen into step like a good little soldier.

The most irritating grain of sand in the general's oyster was that bastard, Fagen. Nothing made a commander look worse than mutiny in the ranks. Funston vowed that if it were the last thing he ever did, he'd get that traitorous scoundrel.

Baston had done a good job engineering the murder charge against him. A white man had died that night, Fagen started it, and he had a record as a hothead and troublemaker. The guards testified he'd come out of nowhere, like a "mad dog," and he'd been "out for blood." Baston had found several witnesses to corroborate their statements. Funston figured he'd dodged a bullet on that one. His report to the Governor General's office had been carefully constructed, and so far, he'd heard nothing back. The only lasting effect of the incident was the heightened tension between his Kansas Volunteers and the Negroes of H Company. His boys were plenty mad and looked for revenge. No real problem. Any more trouble, and he'd lay it in Lieutenant Alstaetter's lap. The newly appointed brigadier took one last look in the mirror, and then made a mental note to bump the price on Fagen's head to three hundred dollars.

Funston took the framed photograph of Eda from the corner of his desk and put it in a drawer. She was a woman, of course, and could never understand the subtleties of command, but everything else considered, she'd been a good wife. As for himself, the general allowed he'd have some polishing up to do after the war.

A gentle tap on Funston's door, and Major Baston entered with two guards escorting a skin-and-bones Filipino peasant dressed in rags. "Who's this gugu, Major?"

"His name's Segismundo, sir. He's a courier from Dupax captured three days ago carrying this." The newly promoted major placed a leather pouch on Funston's desk. "I thought you'd want to look into the matter personally."

The general sat down at his desk, removed a stack of papers from the pouch and thumbed through the pages. In a moment, he growled at the exhausted prisoner. "Start talking, you."

The dreaded day had arrived for Segismundo. He'd known sooner or later he'd be caught and long ago devised a strategy to save his own skin. As he traveled his courier route, he'd rehearsed it over and over in his mind, but now, the critical moment at hand, he knew his lies would take him only so far. In the end, he was at the mercy of the American general with the cold blue eyes who sat across the desk before him.

"*Señor* General, look at me, I beg you, sir. I am no fighter. I am a sickly man. All the men in my village laugh at me for my lack of vigor. This poor specimen cannot be your enemy, sir. I carried these papers because the insurrectos forced me to. They gave them to me to take along the road until someone presented himself and relieved me of them. That is all, *Señor*. I did not even look at the documents. I cannot even read them, they are written in Tagalog, and I am Ilocano. We are of different tribes. I spit on the Tagalog war against our American friends."

Funston's glare froze the little Filipino. "How do you know they're in Tagalog?"

"*Por favor, Señor?*"

"If you didn't look at them, how do you know what language they're written in?"

"I do not know, *Señor*, I am such a pitiful man. I..."

Funston slammed the desk with his fist, and then picked up the jade-handled dagger and lunged at the courier. "Get him out of here! Get him the hell out of my sight! I want the whole story from this Malay bandit, Goddam it, and I want the truth! Don't bring him back here until he's ready to talk." The guards snapped to attention and shoved Segismundo, begging for mercy, out the door.

"Just a minute, Major, I want you to see something." General Funston had sorted the captured papers into two stacks, one containing ordinary dispatches, the other personal letters. He handed the letters to Baston. "Look there man. Recognize any of those names?"

Amazed, Baston scanned the signatures on the documents. In his hands he held personal correspondence from Aguinaldo's inner circle: Pablo and Simon Tecson, brothers and brilliant tacticians; the urbane school teacher, Teodoro Sandico; José Alejandrino, *El Presidente's* friend since childhood; but the most astonishing name was Colon de Magdalo, a code name for Aguinaldo himself. Baston trembled at the thought of it. If real, he held an original letter from Emilio Aguinaldo signed in his own hand. He glanced up at Funston, who had a broad smile on his face. "First, we have to determine these documents are genuine and not some Filipino trick. To do that, we need to cure that courier of his perfidious ways. I'll leave that job to you. By the looks of him, it won't take much. Then get that Spanish turncoat, Segovia, in here. He's always trying to get in my good graces. We'll give him a chance to earn his stripes."

The three men met in Funston's office after supper, their task formidable. Written in Tagalog, Segovia could easily translate Aguinaldo's personal letters, but the other papers were official documents, written in Spanish and coded using an alphanumeric matrix. If they could discover the key and decode the text, they'd then need only to translate the information from Spanish to English. Funston was satisfied with their authenticity. Major Baston reported there'd been no need to insert the hose, only to roll the water wagon near Segismundo's head, and the little messenger blurted out the whole story. He'd received the dispatches from Aguinaldo, and he was sure of the general's exact whereabouts. The rest of his information had checked out, and Baston was certain he'd told the truth. Segismundo had ended his confession by swearing allegiance to the Americans and promising to be of service.

Funston lit the lamps and contemplated the Spaniard at his table. Lazaro Segovia had never before been invited to serve the general directly. For him, a very special occasion, and to make a good impression, he'd bathed, worn his best clothes and sat listening attentively, hands folded in his lap. Funston didn't trust the man, but right then he needed him.

Originally from Madrid, Segovia had served for years with the Spanish army in the Philippines. When Spain surrendered, he chose to remain in the Islands with his Filipino wife and eventually joined the Filipino insurrection. Soon, however, Segovia saw which way the war was going and decided to get on the winning team. One afternoon, he presented himself to a sentry outside the 20th Kansas Volunteer garrison. He declared himself an adventurer, a man of high intelligence and many talents. He wished to throw himself on the mercy of the famous fighting general and prayed the great man would accept his offer of loyal service.

Precisely the kind of man Funston was drawn to, Segovia was tall, handsome in the classic tradition and well educated. His devotion to

Funston bordered on chauvinistic. Whenever he had the chance, he lavished praise on the general in three languages. Funston had been so taken with the man, he himself administered the oath of allegiance and arranged quarters for Segovia inside the garrison. How often, Funston had asked himself, do you come across a non-native who can mingle freely with the Filipinos and is at the same time intelligent and totally unscrupulous?

Funston immediately put Segovia to work translating the letters, starting with the big prize, the one from Aguinaldo. "Read this one aloud now," he said, "copy it later." Addressed to Baldomero, Aguinaldo's cousin, the two officers listened breathlessly while Segovia's rich baritone voice filled the room:

After many and risky adventures we were able to reach the Cagayan Valley, where we are at present. I have not sufficient people of my confidence to garrison this province. I want in the first place, that you take charge of the command of Central Luzon, residing wherever you deem best. Send me about 400 men at the first opportunity with a good commander. If you cannot send them all at once, send them in parties. The bearer can serve as a guide to them until their arrival here; he is a person to be trusted. We are preparing a large arsenal in this camp, which can furnish Central and even Southern Luzon with ammunition. Some of the commercial houses of Cagayan and Isabela have promised us machinery and tools.
    Colon De Magdalo

Funston couldn't believe his ears. He'd just confirmed the location of Aguinaldo's command headquarters and heard the little monkey ask for more men. For a long moment, he gazed into the middle distance imagining the possibilities. For months, he'd tried everything to crack Aguinaldo's intelligence network, and now, here it was, handed to him by one of *El Presidente's* own people. He looked hard at Segovia. "Are you sure that's what it says - that you got it right?"

"Oh, yes, General, very sure."

"Then continue the translations and write them out exactly, word for word."

Funston leaned back in his chair, his heart racing. Little beads of perspiration grew on his forehead. He wanted to act immediately, but knew he couldn't trust the contents of the letters unless the information in them supported the coded documents. He snapped up a handful of papers and pitched them to Baston. "Our work is right here in front of us, Major. Let's start with the little words first; I, a, at, of, he. Look for repetitions in the letters."

"*Yo, un, en, de* and *el*," Segovia offered.

The two officers began at the top, scanning the rows and columns. The hours passed slowly as the men labored, bent like vultures over their work. For a long while, the code seemed impenetrable. Numbers and letters jumped around their brains like popping corn. Bad enough they were written on rough, water-stained paper, the ink was such poor quality, many of the documents would have been illegible in English. The men struggled like schoolboys, the general's pendulum clock striking the night away.

Major Baston figured it out first. In several of the coded supply lists, he'd found a two-word series of numbers frequently repeated. On a hunch, he substituted the words, "Mauser rifle," and as both words are spelled the same in Spanish and English, in only a few moments he hit on it. That done, he found it a fairly simple cipher. Numbers had been used in place of letters in the Spanish alphabet starting from front to back, and then back to front, reversing every twenty-nine characters. The code broken, Baston spent the rest of the night copying the documents while Funston underlined dates, locations and the names of key personnel.

By noon the following day, all the data were translated, decoded and organized. Exhausted, the men's heads throbbed, and their stomachs burned from too much coffee. Funston opened his office window. Drafts of hot, midday air stirred the stink of stale cigar smoke. Baston and Segovia slumped in their chairs while the general paced around his desk in agitated circles, pausing only occasionally to smile at himself in the mirror. At last he stopped and faced his comrades. "Major, send an immediate dispatch to MacArthur. Brigadier General Funston has a plan to end this war!"

CHAPTER 17 – CHANGELINGS

Amerloan patrols everywhere, they traveled by night, kept off the trails and clear of the main roads. Fagen had never seen such tireless men. For two nights, they hacked through nipa and bamboo under the cover of darkness, and then dug in and slept when they could during the day. If discovered, they'd have to abandon their plan, and no one wanted that. Lieutenant Burgos said the American army had control of the central valley, and that's why they'd decided to send a supply train along this route.

When little Colonel De Castro came to Fagen's training camp and gave him the mission, the American thought it an impossible, hare-brained scheme, but Lieutenant Burgos and Sergeant Canizares immediately made a plan and got the men ready. Burgos withheld the details from Fagen until they arrived at their destination. For everyone's safety, Clarita had assured him. The most wanted man in the Islands, if captured, the Americans would know everything Fagen knew within hours.

Fagen despaired of failure on his first mission. He knew the Americans better than Colonel De Castro and realized they'd expect an attack on their train, especially on its maiden run. During their march, Fagen had witnessed the selfless, vigilant nature of his men and their devotion to leaders. He'd seen them perform well in training and admired their spirit, but this was the real thing. The Americans would be looking for trouble and loaded for bear.

The raiding party halted in a canyon at the base of a little cluster of foothills where the track made a bend, and then leveled out and paralleled a narrow river. Sergeant Canizares said the train would be vulnerable there. It would pick up speed coming down the hill, and its center of gravity shift when it entered the curve. The men set up camouflaged positions in the trees on the opposite side of the river, well away from the track. They knew the Americans had guards and track inspectors walking every mile of the line looking for signs of someone tampering with the rails.

Clarita conferred with Sergeant Canizares under a nipa frond shelter. She wore black peasant clothes, her hair pushed up under a green, leafy hat she'd woven out of cogon grass the day before and had strapped a huge bolo knife on her hip just under her pistol belt. Fagen wondered whether she'd ever used it. Even after everything she'd told him and all that had happened between them, Fagen couldn't grow accustomed to the notion his dear, sweet Clarita was a guerilla soldier, ready and fully capable of taking human life.

Clarita sensed his thoughts, smiled and beckoned him to join them. "Lieutenant Burgos will launch the diversionary attack here," she pointed to a spot on the map, "in one hour." As if to confirm this, Sergeant Canizares displayed the face of his big pocket watch. "The blast will be loud enough for the guards in this sector to hear, but will not damage the tracks. When the smoke clears, the Americans will believe it just another bungled job by the stupid Filipino. *Sargento* Canizares has posted lookouts up and down the line. When the coast is clear, he'll take a squad of men to the curve in the tracks. They'll have these." She handed Fagen a burlap bag. He looked inside and saw two-dozen individual pieces of iron, each two inches long. "Railroad spikes," Clarita said. "At least they used to be before the *Sargento* cut the tails off." Fagen looked again at the rusty lump of metal and noticed each was indeed a stubby, railroad spike head, the top end smashed flat by the sledgehammer and the other, just underneath, bearing the signs of fresh cutting.

"I don't get it."

"We'll pry out the existing spikes along two sections of track and replace them with these. We expect the guards to patrol this section at least once before the train comes through. If we're lucky, they won't notice the difference. When the train runs over the loose rails, that big old engine will grind to a stop right in front of us." Clarita took the bag and shook it, the metal pieces inside clinked musically. She smiled. "What do you think?"

"I think you're insane. They'll have guards - with guns."

Clarita folded the map and handed it to the *Sargento*. "We have guns too, my love."

"Clarita, this train's too important. The Americans aren't going to let you just walk up and take it without a fight. This plan is crazy." She translated for Sergeant Canizares. He laughed, shrugged his shoulders, and then winked and said something in Tagalog.

"The *Sargento* wants me to tell you the story of the panther and the field mouse."

Fagen already felt like an orphan at a family reunion, he didn't need to hear a Filipino parable. Somebody else's wisdom wouldn't do anything to raise his confidence in this mission. He held his hands up, palms forward. "Clarita…"

"A panther spent two hours in the heat of the day trying to catch a field mouse he'd found outside the protection of its hole. No matter how fast he ran, the mouse stayed one step in front. Finally, when the panther could run no more, he lay down in the shade and called to the mouse. 'How can you run so hard? I am the fastest animal in the jungle, and I cannot catch you.' The mouse responded, 'You are running for a tidbit – I am running for my life.' You see, my love, the supplies on that train are luxuries to the Americans. To us they mean the difference between life and death."

Later, Sergeant Canizares and *Capitán* Fagen walked out and checked the troops. Concealed in ten, three-man firing positions, they'd dug in ten yards apart along the slope. Canizares checked weapons and ammunition while Fagen tried to explain how to establish overlapping fields of fire. Spread thin, it was important they exercise fire discipline. If the Americans saw holes in their skirmish line, they'd know why and come up after them. Mission over.

Fagen had picked up a little Spanish, but not enough to talk military procedure. No use trying to tell it, he'd have to demonstrate. Fagen remembered what Sergeant Rivers once taught him during a night exercise. He climbed into a foxhole and stuck bamboo stakes in the dirt left and right in front of each Filipino soldier. Then he grabbed a Mauser and squinted through the sights, pretending to shoot. He swung the rifle right until the barrel made contact with the bamboo, then left with the same result.

Sergeant Canizares understood at once. His face lit up and he smiled. "Ah! *Kaayaaya!*" He passed instructions up and down the line, and in no time bamboo stakes were driven in front of each foxhole and overlapping fields of fire established.

Satisfied, the two men returned to the command post to wait. Clarita was there searching the hill on the far side of the tracks with a pair of rusted binoculars. She'd removed her hat, and Fagen watched her delicate fingers move on the casing, bringing the glasses into focus. A stranger would have thought her completely calm, but Fagen saw the little scar pulsing on her right temple, and knew her heart raced as fast as his. "Do you see the rocks on the hill just above the nipa grove? Lieutenant Burgos will move his platoon into position there after he detonates the diversionary charge. When the train stops, he'll attack with us, and the Americans will be in a crossfire."

"Clarita, when this train stops...*if* it stops, I want you to keep your head down. We don't know what will happen. All hell could break lose. It's better if you stay covered." She put her hat on, pulled it down over her eyes and smiling, looked up at Fagen from under the leafy brim.

"*Si, Mon Capitán.*"

"Clarita, I'm serious. I don't want you getting hurt."

"*Si, Mon Capitán.*"

"Are you mocking me?

"*No, Mon Capitán.*"

"Clarita, I will not have you mocking me..."

Then they heard it. *Karumph!* The blast echoed ominously up the little canyon in waves like the chanting beat of a war drum. "Time to go to work," Clarita said.

Two minutes after the blast, Clarita gave a signal. Sergeant Canizares and one man from each foxhole raced down the slope, splashed across the shallow river to the tracks. Eight men carried crowbars, two held hammers, Canizares the bag of phony spikes. "I figure they've got ten or fifteen minutes," Clarita said. "Those guards know we're around here and will be double-timing up and down this track looking for something to shoot."

The Filipino guerillas deployed into two-man teams, proceeded to the apex of the curve and with the crowbars, began pulling spikes. They worked furiously, prying at the stubborn iron nails. Canizares scurried between them urging them on. In a matter of moments, they'd loosened several, and the *sargento* collected them in a burlap bag while another soldier followed behind and placed the cut-down imposters in the empty holes. They'd rehearsed this aspect of their mission dozens of times during the past week, and now they moved like a well-oiled machine.

Clarita raised the glasses, and then pointed to the opposite hill. Flashes of white moved through the trees and sunlight glinted off a rifle barrel, "Lieutenant Burgos," she said. "Right on time. So far, so good."

Another minute, and the men on the track finished. Sergeant Canizares hustled them back up the slope to their foxholes, leaving behind two Filipinos with huge green nipa fronds to sweep away their footprints and tidy the area. Clarita had said they'd have ten to fifteen minutes to sabotage the rails, they'd needed only five. The *Sargento* dropped into the command post and emptied the bag of rusty railroad spikes in the dirt. Like a cat that had just eaten his neighbor's pesky canary, he winked at

Clarita, smiled broadly at Fagen, and then said something in Tagalog. "He wants to know if you would like a souvenir of your first action on behalf of the new Filipino Republic."

"Tell *Sargento* Canizares today we will carry away very much more than just a few rusty nails. Today we take the Americans' weapons, ammunition and their pride."

Clarita translated, and Canizares lifted his eyes towards heaven and crossed himself. "*Capitán* David Fagen *es muy magnifico!*"

Fagen wished he felt the confidence he showed his company sergeant. He knew how the Americans operated and was sure they'd not let this train be taken easily. Some high-ranking officer, maybe even Funston himself, had responsibility for the successful completion of this, its maiden run, and Fagen was inwardly afraid they'd bitten off more than they could chew. Crouched in the hole beside him, Clarita read his thoughts, looked at the pocket watch and said, "If they're on schedule, one more hour, and we'll find out."

The afternoon sun drifted in little circles high overhead, and in spite of his anxiety over their situation, Fagen found his mind wandering. His classmates at Fisk College would be in the world of business, art or science now. Only little more than a year since he'd left there and entered the Army, it seemed like a lifetime. He wondered whether like him, any joined up, volunteered to fight for their country, to show the folks back home what the black man can do given the chance.

Such a lofty, jawbreaker of a goal, Fagen thought. He couldn't reach it, hadn't even come close and probably did more harm to his race than good. Maybe one of his classmates would be more successful. Fagen remembered what Aguinaldo had said the night they talked in his secret base camp. "The war is illegal and immoral, and soon the Americans will see the error of their ways. The patriotic few who stand against these horrors will be hailed as heroes one day. Your joining our fight will be a signal to others that it's possible to love your country and at the same time hate its politics."

Fagen still hoped Aguinaldo was right, that in the end he would find vindication. He didn't need to be hailed a hero, had never wanted that, but he needed to know he'd done the right thing, that his actions weren't dictated solely by his self-interests. Clarita put her hand on his. "Be still," she said. "Keep down."

Just then, a corporal and two privates rounded the corner walking the ties, their rifles at port arms. They moved slowly, taking their time, checking the track and searching for signs of guerilla activity. They neared the loose rails. The *sargento* and his men had done a good job. Visually, there was no way to tell the track had been tampered with. If the Americans stayed on the ties, they'd never know, but if one even touched the loose rails, the insurrecto mission was over. Clarita smiled, lines of concern on her brow. "Cross your fingers," she said.

The Americans moved to the center of the bend in the tracks and stopped. Clarita's breath caught in her throat as the corporal took a little cigar from his blouse and lit it, striking the match on one of the sabotaged rails. Then one of the privates rummaged in the gravel between the ties, selected a flat rock and skipped it across the river. The Filipinos held their breath. *Sargento* Canizares glanced at Clarita, then Fagen, defeat in his eyes. Just then, two more Americans rounded the corner, spotted the patrol and called out, "Lieutenant wants us down the line. Move out!" The corporal spat, snubbed out his cigar, took one last look around, and then hurried down the roadbed until out of sight.

Clarita pushed her hat back and smiled, still confident. "According to plan," she said.

Fagen knew the really dangerous part of their mission lay ahead of them. The train would be along soon, and then all hell would break loose. In spite of the anxiety he felt at coming face-to-face with American troops for the first time, he wanted it to be over. On pins and needles, time began to drag. After a while Lieutenant Burgos sent a man down to the tracks. He put an ear to the rails, but came up shaking his head.

Another half-hour passed. Clarita scanned the peaks above the canyon walls looking for smoke. "It's coming!" Sergeant Canizares sprang from his hole and jackrabbited down the line passing the word. The guerilla soldiers braced themselves and hefted their Mausers, Krags and Springfields into position. Movement on the opposite slope, Lieutenant Burgos getting his men ready.

They saw the engine coming down the hill just before they heard it. It moved faster than they'd expected, the roar of the furnace reaching them at the same time as the clanking and rattling of iron on iron. Black smoke trailed over the coal car partially obscuring the rest of the train. Clarita handed the field glasses to Fagen. "Look at the third car back."

He saw it through the smoke and flying cinders, and his heart skipped a beat. He'd warned Clarita and the *sargento* the Americans wouldn't let the train be taken easily, now he saw they wouldn't let it be taken at all. The third car in line had been a passenger coach, but they'd modified it, turned it into an armored car. Fagen counted the rifle barrels. If an equal number were on the other side, there were as many as thirty riflemen inside. "What do you think it is?" Clarita asked.

"Suicide."

Not a long train, just ten cars, the last seven apparently normal freight haulers, it picked up speed coming down the hill. That, at least, was in their favor, Fagen thought. When it hit the loose rails, those guards would be in for a rough ride before the whole thing ground to a stop. Who was he kidding? Rough ride or not, that guard car was a fortress. No one was getting close to that train. It was no go, mission over. If they turned tail and ran now, they'd be lucky to make it over the hill before the Americans started picking them off.

Clarita rose up and waved at Canizares, tried to get his attention. "We'll have to split up and attack from three directions!"

"What?" Fagen couldn't believe his ears. "Clarita, if we attacked from *all* directions, it'd be no use. There could be thirty or forty men in that car, and we can't touch them. They could hold off an entire army for a week. Face it, we're finished."

"No we're not! It's not over. We have to think of something…" The rest of her words were lost in the clamor and clatter as the supply train barreled down the hill, nearing the bend in the tracks. It moved faster now, the roar of the engine temporarily muffled by three long blasts on the whistle as it neared the blind curve. Clarita crawled out of the foxhole and waved her arms, trying desperately to send a signal to Burgos and Canizares. Fagen saw three short puffs of white smoke appear from the armored car firing ports, and then the bullets snapped and thudded in the dirt at Clarita's feet. Fagen stood up, hooked her pistol belt and pulled her backward into the hole. They hit the floor hard, with her on top fighting like a tiger, clawing, kicking and climbing until she'd made it over the protective parapet once again, dragging Fagen behind her.

That's when it happened. The drive wheels hit the loose rails propelling them backward under the coal car. In the middle of the curve, the engine's momentum carried it in a straight line toward the river. The coal car bucked once, dragged the mangled rails through soft gravel, and then the weight of the heavy cars behind pushed everything over the riverbank. The engineer hit the brakes, and the big iron wheels locked up, and then spun backwards, sending sparks and burning rocks in front of it, but it was no use. The engine went over the bank and crashed nose first into the river, the coal car riding high over it, pushed up and held in place by the armored car. When the engine hit the water, the boiler exploded, the ground shook, and the force of the blast split the sky, sending twisted metal, scraps of wood and chunks of coal high overhead. Huge balls of orange flame arose surrounded by giant, rolling clouds of black smoke and raging geysers of steam. The heat came up in waves. Fagen covered Clarita, shielding her from the blast until the worst of it passed.

When it was over, the coal car lay on its side suspended high in the air locked between the rear of the engine and the front of the armored car, like toys, stacked up by a mischievous child. It happened so fast, the Filipinos sat stunned, unable to react. An eerie stillness gripped the canyon for a moment, and then they heard the groan of twisting metal and watched the whole thing teeter then collapse, hissing and belching fire, into the riverbed like a mortally wounded dragon. The guerillas leapt from their holes and cheered. Clarita turned, teeth bared, face flushed, black eyes glowing. "God is on our side today, my love."

The Filipinos moved down the hill, cautiously at first, but like the train, gained speed and momentum as they progressed. Clarita and Fagen followed. Three of the freight cars had remained upright on the track, the rest flipped onto one side or the other. Burgos reached the wreckage first, and his men sifted through the debris for survivors. When Fagen began crossing the river, he noticed movement from the armored car. They'd built large escape hatches into the roof and belly of the car and suddenly, like ants out of a hole, Americans in blue uniforms spilled out, injured, dazed and shooting in every direction. Fagen shouted a warning, but too late. Three Filipinos fell in the first five seconds. In the middle of the river without cover and nowhere to hide, they did the only thing they could. They charged.

The Filipinos were quick and closed the distance fast, returning fire at maximum rate. Two more guerillas went down, then another. The riverbed rose as they neared midstream, the water only a few inches deep, and they picked up speed. Fagen ran, fell, got up again and made it to the nose of the engine. He peered cautiously around the cowcatcher and came face-to-face with an American corporal. The man's arm broken, a jagged end of bone protruded through the sleeve just below his elbow. He was dazed and walked in circles, his face covered in blood. He saw Fagen and stopped, a flicker of recognition in his eyes. Fagen's pistol was in his hand, but he froze, couldn't move. Abruptly, the American turned his back and splashed unsteadily in the opposite direction. A shot rang out next to Fagen's ear, he blinked once and watched the corporal fall face first into the water. Fagen turned and saw Canizares behind him, the muzzle of his Mauser still smoking. The *sargento* tipped his hat, smiled and said something, but the discharge so close to Fagen's ear had temporarily deafened him, and all he caught was *Capitán* Fagen.

No two people see a battle exactly the same way. It starts out a concentrated effort by groups of men trained to fight as a unit, but in the fever pitch of it, each man fights his own war, finds his own courage, and the battle is won or lost on the separate, individual acts of the many. Men fought and died all around now. The Americans took cover where they could find it, on the defensive, but returned fire with deadly accuracy. The Filipino guerillas seemed everywhere, fearlessly charging straight ahead, scampering over railroad cars, shooting from the hip. The bittersweet smell of gunpowder and fresh blood filled the little canyon.

Gradually, the pop of rifle fire and the screams of wounded and dying men supplanted the ringing in Fagen's ears, and once again he experienced the strange phenomenon that overtook him on the battlefield. He saw the bloody fighting, heard the crack-splat of flying lead, but like a moving picture reel, time slowed, and he saw things from an outsider's perspective.

The American kneeling behind the charred wreckage of a supply car wore no boots and hadn't buttoned his pants. He must have been napping when the train hit the water. Fagen raised his pistol and squeezed off a round. The man's body jerked once, he looked down, felt his chest for the wound, then slumped backward into the river. Fagen saw Lieutenant Burgos on top of the guard car firing into one of the ports. He noticed the Filipino's empty cartridge belt. When he'd spent his last round, an American sergeant stood up behind him and fired a bullet that struck Burgos' groin and shattered his hip. He fell onto the car, screamed at the sight of his own ruptured intestines and died. Fagen thought this an ignominious death for the tall, urbane lieutenant, and fired his pistol again, sending a round through the sergeant's back.

"*Capitán* Fagen!" He heard it through the din inside his head. "*Capitán* Fagen." Twenty yards behind, *Sargento* Canizares pointed to his left. Two Americans had backed Clarita and another Filipino, a young man named Baltazar, against the belly of a supply car. They shot Baltazar immediately, but intrigued to find a woman on the battlefield, didn't fire on Clarita. She'd lost her pistol, and now faced the American soldiers with her bolo knife brandished before her. The men stopped in their tracks.

Cowards, but not willing to admit they were intimidated by the fiery Filipino woman slashing the air with her long, razor-sharp knife, the two men hesitated for a moment, exchanged nervous glances, tried to make a joke of the situation. All the time he needed, Fagen covered the distance fast, shoulder-blocked the first man and delivered a hard elbow smash to the throat. The soldier was dead before he hit the ground. Clarita lunged at the other American, but he spun away in time and countered with a rifle butt to the small of her back. She went to her knees, slumped against the train car, and just before her eyes rolled up in her head, managed to toss her bolo knife to Fagen.

The American lunged at Fagen. All he had to do was shoot, and it was over, but instead, he stepped over the body of his friend and moved Fagen in circles until they were behind the car. Determined not to go without a fight, Fagen slashed at the dagger-like bayonet on the barrel of the American's Krag.

The man sneered, and then laughed out loud, brown tobacco juice leaking down his chin. "You're Fagen, that turncoat nigger everybody's talking about. You're not near as big as they said you were. I take your ears back in a bag, I'm the most important man in the U.S. Army." He stopped, pointed the rifle at Fagen's chest and pulled the trigger.

They say if you're close enough, you can hear the discharge before you die. Fagen didn't think he'd feel the bullet rip through his heart, not enough time for that, but he'd expected to see the muzzle jump, maybe see the flash then hear the bang. Like most men, Fagen had wondered occasionally about his thoughts at the exact moment of his death. He always assumed they'd be of his loved ones - his mother, Ellis, now Clarita. Strangely, in the instant he had left, his mind flashed on the warm, sunny afternoon in San Isidro when among the crowd he first saw Clarita's grandmother, and she read the Tarot. No time to reflect on the entire reading, of course. The American had pulled the trigger, the hammer was falling, but Fagen remembered the lesson of The Hanged Man. "We win by surrendering," the old woman had said. "We control by letting go." It had seemed absurd at the time, now it made more sense.

But something was wrong, something left out, not right, and Fagen suddenly realized what it was. Where was his divine understanding? Grandmother had said it was his reward for letting go. He didn't mind dying on the cross of his own travails, that was in the cards, but he couldn't abide not getting what was promised him. It wasn't right, and he wouldn't stand for it.

Click. The hammer fell on an empty chamber. Out of ammunition, the soldier's jaw dropped, and he stared down at his rifle in disbelief. He could have used his bayonet, it was only inches from Fagen's chest, but he really had no chance. Fagen knew something the man didn't. Fagen knew it wasn't his time to die.

In one quick motion, he stepped to his left and brought the big bolo up in a sweeping outward arc, striking at the base of the skull. The knife passed effortlessly through, and the man's head hit the riverbed and tumbled ten yards with the current before his knees buckled, and he dropped, spraying black blood all over.

Clarita had a nasty bruise on her hip, but was alive and otherwise unhurt. Fagen sat with her in the cool water and held her until she caught her breath. Maybe she'd been right, maybe God was on their side that day. Fagen looked up and noticed the shooting had stopped. *Sargento* Canizares had slung his weapon, climbed on a railroad car and shouted orders. A squad of Filipinos with bolos moved among the Americans making sure none was left alive. A man scampered up the hillside and returned with four mules. The others quickly tied on bundles of rifles and crates of ammunition.

Clarita stirred, tried to get up. "We have to get out of here." She was right, but Fagen had come so close to losing her, he needed to hold her for another moment, to make sure she was all right. An ugly picture formed in Fagen's mind. They say you can only kill a man once, but if that filthy, tobacco-chewing soldier had injured Clarita, Fagen knew he would have killed him, and then himself and followed him to hell so he could do it again.

A little breeze came and cleared the canyon of gunpowder and coal smoke. The sun shone on the river, and in the quiet backwater where they sat, Fagen looked down and saw the reflection of a guerilla soldier. His white peasant shirt torn and spattered with blood, he stared back with angry, wild animal eyes. His jaw set, teeth clenched, his face a ghastly, open wound that shouted to the world, *Beware! I'm a man with something to kill for!* Suddenly terrified, Fagen tried to close his eyes against the terrible visage. Too horrible to look at and too compelling to turn away from, Fagen forced himself, looked in the water again and realized the hideous, forbidding creature was he.

They climbed out of the canyon and headed west into the jungle mountains, confident no one could follow. They'd bagged nearly two hundred rifles, several thousand rounds of ammunition and killed forty-one Americans. For the Filipinos, the biggest one-day body count of the war. Fagen's head screamed what he did was horribly wrong, but his heart said otherwise. The generals couldn't cover this one up. It would be called a massacre, of course, and Fagen saw his name in the history books alongside Judas Iscariot and Benedict Arnold. No matter. It was grist for the anti-imperialist's mill. They'd make sure the American people learned of the senseless taking of life. Outrage could force an early end to the war, Fagen thought, and then his part in it would have been justified.

The little band of insurrectos moved west under triple canopy until dark, and then made a joyless camp. They'd scored a huge victory, but lost eight men including Lieutenant Burgos, and that saddened them most. They settled in, ate bananas and rice, and Fagen told Clarita something he knew she wouldn't want to hear.

"You can't," she said. "It's too risky. You'll be captured by sunup."

Fagen told her it was no use trying to stop him. He had to see Ellis. He reminded her of her own foolish bravado that day in the canyon. "You're in no position to talk to me about taking risks." He knew he could make it to the leper colony before dawn. He'd have to lay low during daylight, but with a map could find his way back the following night.

Clarita begged him not to go, to put it off for a week. "Wait until things calm down. After what happened today, American patrols will be everywhere."

"The Americans will be in the hills looking for you, and besides, I don't intend to let anyone see me."

Clarita realized she'd not talk him out of it, called him *obstinado Capitán* Fagen and came back in a few minutes with one of the men. "This is Panteleon. He grew up near San Lazaro and has friends there. He has agreed to be your guide."

The young guerilla stood at attention smiling from ear to ear. Fagen smiled back and indicated he could stand at ease. "Is he aware of the risk?"

"He knows the dangers, but doesn't care. He is another one who thinks *Capitán* Fagen is *muy magnifico.*"

Fagen kissed Clarita on the cheek and followed Panteleon south into the night.

San Lazaro hospital stood by itself in the flatlands near the Pasig River. A leper home for many years, the locals avoided it. A high wooden fence surrounded the entire compound. Fagen and his guide worked around back, concealed themselves under a fetid compost heap and waited for sunup. Fagen dozed until Panteleon nudged him and whispered something under his breath. He opened his eyes and saw the sun shining through river fog and people moving on the other side of the wall. Instinctively, he looked around for cover. Panteleon said, "Don't worry, *Capitán*, few people come this close to San Lazaro, and no one comes to this back wall."

The two men moved low along the fence to a small gate. Panteleon looked through. "The lepers use this exit in the evenings to tend their fish traps." He worked the latch and pushed it open a few inches. Fagen saw them clearly then, dressed in long, brown robes, some carried water from the well, others waited in line for the latrines. The sun hadn't topped the high perimeter wall yet, and they moved in silent shadow like aged and diseased monks in an ancient monastery.

Panteleon gave a low whistle to a figure walking near. "*Pssst, Señor! Señor!*" The man walked on without looking up. "The sickness has affected his ears. He is probably deaf."

Moments later, a one-legged boy on crutches hobbled their way. "I can hear you, *amigo*. How may I serve you?"

"We wish to speak to one of your tortured brothers."

"Which one, *Señor?*"

"The *Negrito Americano*."

The boy's face lit up, and he smiled. "*Señor* Fairbanks. He is a friend of mine!" Then he got a look at the visitors' clothes, filthy and covered in slime from the compost heap, and his eyes narrowed. Suspicious now, he asked, "What do you want with him?"

"We want no backtalk from an insolent boy! A great man is here to see the *Americano*." Fagen raised his hat, and the boy saw his face and understood.

"*Si, Señor*, I will get him for you."

"Hurry!"

The two men sat down against the wall and waited. After the battle for the train, Fagen had felt compelled to see Ellis, to re-connect, find out whether any of the old David Fagen was still inside him. The night they'd taken Ellis away seemed like another lifetime, another world. So much had happened since. Fagen worried about his cousin. Was he still the same man-child he'd known nearly all his life? Had his tragic circumstances transformed him into another person? As he sat waiting for Ellis, the morning sun washing over him, Fagen realized he didn't have the slightest idea what he'd say to him.

"It was a mistake to come here, Davey." Fagen looked up and there he was, a voluminous, hooded robe exaggerating his height and bulk. He'd opened the gate and stood an inch or two inside the threshold, head down, arms crossed, his hands hidden in the folds of his garment. Fagen heard the sound of Ellis' voice, and at that exact instant everything was the way it should be, the way it had been for so many years. Ellis was there. Ellis had always been there. Seeing him gave hope, maybe they hadn't traveled too far.

Fagen's heart filled with joy. He jumped to his feet and reached out to his cousin. "Ellis! Thank heaven you're all right."

Ellis pulled back quickly and turned his face away. "I'm all right if you don't look too close."

Fagen moved toward him again, wanted to be near him, feel his wide-eyed, little boy energy. "Ellis…"

Ellis backed up two quick steps and extended his arms. "Davey don't… Don't come any closer."

That's when Fagen saw the purplish welts on his hands, the abscessing skin between his fingers. Ellis quickly crossed his arms and pulled the folds of his robe tighter. "If you don't keep your distance, I'm going back inside. That's the way it's got to be."

Panteleon had been curious and stayed by the gate, but now moved away and hunkered under a low bush, pretended to sleep. Fagen hadn't seen his cousin's face, but the sadness in his voice and the finality of tone told Fagen his foolish fantasies about recapturing the past were just that – fantasies. The pathetic delusions of a coward, too afraid to face life the way it was. Ellis had always been the one to look past the cruelties of life. Now, Fagen craved the child's flight from reality.

Fagen backed off and sat down. Ellis sat just inside the gate, his body deep inside his leper robe, would not let his cousin see his face. Fagen turned his eyes north, across the Pasig River where the mangrove trees rose, and then disappeared into the bamboo jungle. Peasants rowed their outrigger canoes up and down the opposite shore, careful not to get too close to San Lazaro. They sat in silence for a long while, David Fagen and Ellis Fairbanks. Then Fagen heard his cousin's voice, a dry, creaking, whispering sound, filled with dread and despair, like closing a cellar door, and it was as though someone had driven a stake through his heart.

"Things change, Davey."

CHAPTER 18 - DECEPTION

Get a grip man! General Funston scolded himself. He'd tried, but just then he was too excited. The last few days had been a dizzying whirlwind of checking and re-checking the details of his plan. When he'd gone to Manila and presented it to MacArthur, the Governor General had been skeptical at first, but after a while, when he recognized the immensity of the proposition, he'd been all for it. The Great Man had even walked from behind his desk and pumped his subordinate's hand. "Nothing you come up with surprises me anymore, Freddie." *Damn, that was good.* He called me Freddie! Funston inwardly smiled. To hell with the risks, he said to himself. God will provide, and when I bring that cur Aguinaldo in by the scruff of his neck, I'll be the biggest man in the nation.

Captain Harry Newton stood at attention for several moments before the general's big desk. He stole a glance at the young officer beside him, Lieutenant Burton Mitchell. Neither man was told why he'd been summoned to the commander's office, only that it was urgent and to say nothing to anyone. They waited for some time while the general shuffled papers under an odd looking dagger with a jade handle. To Newton, Funston seemed agitated, out of sorts. He thought he'd never seen the general so preoccupied. He'd sensed the tension the moment he came in and didn't like it. The unexpected presence of Segovia, the turncoat Spaniard sitting at the foot of the conference table, made him even more doubtful. Well aware of the spy's treacherous nature, he'd immediately concluded whatever his commanding officer was up to, if it involved Segovia, was at the least foolhardy and at worst, dangerous.

At last, the general looked up and acknowledged their presence. "Good morning, gentlemen. Please be seated. I presume you know Lazaro Segovia." The Spaniard didn't move, said nothing in the way of a greeting, only a slight flicker of the eyelids at the sound of his own name. Funston walked to a large wall map and drew back the canvas cover. "I am in possession of certain documents that reveal the whereabouts of Emilio

Aguinaldo. In less than two weeks, I intend to launch an expedition to find the insurrecto bandit and bring him back to face the gallows. I've chosen you two men to assist me."

Newton felt the perspiration build under his shirt and trickle down his spine. He looked across the table at Mitchell. Suddenly pale, the boy's thin lips quivered, and his eyes darted first toward the door, then the window. Burton, my young friend, Newton thought to himself, we've gotten ourselves into something now.

The general continued, "How I obtained these documents is unimportant. What matters is that both *Señor* Segovia and I are convinced of their authenticity." Funston used his jade handled dagger as a pointer. "Aguinaldo is holed up in a mountain village called Palanan, here, on the northeast coast. He's requested reinforcements. I intend to honor that request."

Burton Mitchell gulped a quick breath and squeaked, "Beg your pardon, sir?"

"You heard me, Lieutenant. Segovia here's been busy recruiting a gang of Macabebes... How many so far?"

The Spaniard sat at attention, lifted his head. "Eighty, sir. All good men."

"Fine. Cutthroat bastards, those Macs. You can't turn your back on them, but they'll do just about anything to kill a Tagalog." The general turned to his map. "Anyway, in a nutshell, the plan is to outfit them to look like insurrectos and sail up past Corregidor Island to the village of Casigurian. From there, we take shank's pony the last ninety miles to Palanan. Aguinaldo will think his reinforcements have arrived, but what he'll get instead is a lethal dose of Yankee-By-God ingenuity."

Lieutenant Mitchell wheezed, lifted a finger to indicate himself and Captain Newton. "Where do we fit into all this, sir?"

Momentarily taken aback, Funston cocked an eyebrow, then put his arm around the young officer's shoulder and bellowed, "You're going along! Hell yes, we're all going! That's the beauty of the plan. We'll send word the reinforcements are arriving with American prisoners, a survey party they came across in the mountains. We're the icing on the cake. Aguinaldo will be busting at the seams to get a look at us. Then just when that little monkey thinks he's won the big door prize, we get the drop on him, and this war's over. I tell you men, it's utter genius. We'll all be in the God damned history books!" Pleased with himself, Funston sat down heavily at the head of the table.

Captain Newton's grim forebodings had been justified. All the officers in the Kansas volunteers were aware of their ursine commander's self-approbation, and they'd learned to live with it. This time, Newton thought, he's gone over the edge. Funston was on a suicide mission, and he hated the idea of going with him but knew he had no choice in the matter. The general didn't take opinion surveys. The plan was set, and he'd have to put on the best face he could. "It's brilliant, sir," Newton said. "The Trojan Horse in the Philippines."

Funston's eyes lit up. "By God, that's a good one, Newton. Ha! Trojan Horse indeed!" The general slapped the table exultantly, and then leaned forward and whispered. "I've asked you to join me on this mission because you're men who can get things done and keep your mouths shut while you're about it. Lazaro is making lists of everything we'll need. Mitchell, I want you to handle the victuals. Captain Newton, you'll look after the weapons and uniforms. Everything is to be on board the steamship, *Vicksburg*, in Manila Bay in one week. Report only to me. I'll inform your superiors you're on special liaison for the rest of the month. Any questions?"

General Funston dismissed the officers and turned to Segovia. "Have you done what I asked?"

The Spaniard bowed his head. "Of course, sir."

"Show me."

Segovia picked up pen and paper and wrote the name, *Urbano Lacuna*, several times. Lacuna was one of Aguinaldo's most trusted generals. Ten days before, Funston had ordered Segovia to practice his signature until he could make a perfect forgery. "Good," he said. "Very good."

He then went to his desk and retrieved several sheets of official stationery from the new Philippine Republic his men had captured some months earlier and laid it before Segovia. "Take this down exactly as I present it to you."

Funston paced the office floor while Segovia took dictation.

The Honorable President of the Philippines:

Having received orders from the Commanding General of Central Luzon to send your Honor one of my best companies, I do so. I must state that the men the company is composed of are to be trusted entirely.

The Commander, Major Hilario Talplacido, is the best officer I have. He was taken prisoner by the enemy, but when released, returned and joined me. I recommend him to your Honor to be raised to lieutenant colonel as he has worked hard. The same I say of the valiant and energetic Capitán Segovia, who being a Spaniard has joined us working for our cause. I pray you may raise him to major.

The Commanding General of Central Luzon directs me to state to your Honor that he is in receipt of all your correspondence and he will comply with your orders. He directs me to advise you that he has forwarded to you correspondence by sea, as it is safer than by land. I have provisioned the troops the best I could. All the guns are in good condition.

May God guard you many years,
General Urbano Lacuna

Segovia finished, taking great pains with the signature. Then he said, "It is a magnificent letter, General."

Silent for a moment, Funston wiped perspiration from his throat and regarded his handiwork. "I think I'll sweeten the pot a little. Write this."

The Honorable President of the Philippines:
I tender to you my most sincere thank you for your kindness confirming in me the rank of Brigadier General. I shall work until death overtakes me fighting the enemy, and I will sacrifice if necessary even my life for my unfortunate country. In this Province, myself on the one hand, and General Sandico on the other engage the enemy every day and inflict upon him great loss. I have forwarded your correspondence to General Sandico, but he has not yet answered. The bearer of this correspondence, your own Cecelio Segismundo, goes as guide to the company I sent you. Without anything further, I remain yours that you will never mistrust your servant.
U. Lacuna

Segovia put down his pen, looked at the general and smiled. "A personal note to accompany the official correspondence. Very clever. You have conceived a wonderful plan, sir"

Funston scowled, leaned in and put his big face inches from Segovia's. "It's not lost on me, *Señor Spaniard*, that most of the actors in this little show are one kind of cutthroat traitor or another, and they're all on your side of the table. If I even get a whiff of treachery, you'll be dead the same instant."

Hilario Talplacido fought in the revolution because his father-in-law was second in command of the local *Katipunan* and expected the husband of his daughter to serve his country. The truth was Talplacido hated war and fighting. No part of military life suited his nature or person. Well past the age of most fighting men, he was soft in body and spirit. Although no doctor could identify it, Talplacido was sure he suffered from a condition that weakened his bones, causing him to tire easily and resulted in his need for frequent periods of rest and rejuvenation.

Before the war, he'd been a dealer in herbs, specializing in the therapeutic cocoa leaf, which he obtained from Malay tradesmen, and then resold to certain high-ranking Spanish officers in the *Intramuros*. It was there he'd met Lazaro Segovia. Early on, he'd recognized the man for a venal, double-dealing mercenary, but the Spaniard was well connected, Talplacido's path in, and he'd needed someone then to open doors for him.

Now, his wife and father-in-law were dead, killed in the battle for Manila. He himself had been wounded slightly, but fortunate to surrender at the onset of hostilities to a compassionate American lieutenant, and after swearing an oath of allegiance, returned to the herb trade. Since then, life had been good. He lamented the loss of his wife, of course, but he'd quickly learned to appreciate the quiet, contemplative life of the widower and thrived, even picked up a few extra pounds, necessary he thought to cushion his fragile skeleton.

Thursday last, when the Spaniard showed up at his door, had been the worst day of Talplacido's life. He'd been enjoying a morning cup of palm wine when the sanctity of his home was violated, and Lazaro Segovia had pressed him into service. With typical Spanish arrogance, the man gave no details, only that the job would require a minimum of three weeks. Talplacido had tried to object, but Segovia assured him it was for a worthy cause, and then reminded him Americans hang narcotics dealers. Talplacido knew then he'd been caught in the web of his own deceit, and his heart sank. He'd wondered when Segovia's petty extortions would grow to blackmail, and now the day was upon him.

Since then, he'd been quartered in a musty warehouse inside a fenced compound on the outskirts of Manila. The reluctant conscript despaired the lack of food and only water to drink. Worse, a small army of silent, sullen Macabebes had trickled in over the past few days. They'd strung their hammocks everywhere and paid no attention to civilized sanitation practices. Like most Tagalogs, Talplacido had little use for the Macabebe race. A vicious, unscrupulous people - not as bad as the savage Igorrote tribesmen that lived in the northern mountains - but bad enough, and even though Talplacido had in the past dealt successfully with the Macs, he didn't trust them and was shocked when Segovia told him his job was to train them in insurrecto tactics. "It'll never work! I can't teach these people to fight like soldiers of the New Republic. They're incapable of learning."

Segovia placed a heavy hand on Talplacido's shoulder. "*Amigo*, you do not have to teach them to fight like insurrectos, only to look like them. You say it is impossible. I remind you your life depends on your success."

"Why? To what end?" the Filipino pleaded.

"All will be revealed in due time, *Señor*. Until then, remember, if you try to leave here, I will have you killed. If you speak to anyone outside these walls, I will have you killed, and if you fail in your assignment…"

CHAPTER 19 - HARVEST

Lieutenant Alstaetter galloped to the head to the column and saluted Major Baston. "H Company is deployed on the right flank, sir." "Very well, Lieutenant." Baston lifted his chin, looked around and surveyed 7th Battalion, all his now, marching behind him. A fine morning, the dry season was nearly over, but the oppressive humidity of the monsoon not yet upon them. Alstaetter touched his hat and turned his horse to rejoin his unit. "Matthew," the major called, "ride with me."

The two officers rode together in silence for a while, and then Major Baston spoke. "I know how difficult it was for you to come to my quarters last week. It's never easy for a man to admit he's wrong, but you did, and it showed me what you're made of."

Not searching for compliments, Alstaetter stared straight ahead, acknowledged the major's remarks with a nod. He'd gone to Baston to apologize, prostrate himself, beg forgiveness, whatever necessary to get back in the major's good graces. He did it because H Company was being punished for his behavior. They'd endured weeks of low and subsidiary duty because their company commander had proven not a team player. "Sometimes you have to go along to get along," Major Ryan had told him at West Point. He hadn't understood then what his mentor had meant by that curious phrase, but it was crystal clear now.

On his own, Alstaetter wouldn't have minded the ostracism. He sought neither the company nor the friendship of his fellow officers and wanted nothing from them. The men of H Company had wants, however. They hadn't joined the army to dig ditches and shovel manure. They'd come to the Philippines in search of respect, and no matter how much crow he had to eat, Alstaetter was determined not to let his personal sensibilities stand in their way.

Baston continued, his tone conversational. "This may surprise you, Matt, but we're very much alike, you and I." Alstaetter glanced sharply at his superior officer. The major smiled, "Hell, man, I was young once too, sure of my opinions, quick to judge, dominated by righteous indignation. We all go through that. At least the good ones do.

"Are you married, Matt, have any children?"

"A wife, sir. We're planning to start a family when my tour of duty here in the Islands is over."

"I am a widower, myself. Two boys, ages eleven and thirteen. They're staying with their grandparents on a farm just outside Topeka."

The road took them through a wide valley past vast rubber tree plantations. As they rode in silence, it suddenly occurred to Alstaetter they'd seen no locals for several miles. When marching on the main roads, it was unusual not to pass peasant laborers on their way to the rice paddies or the copra groves. It wasn't Sunday, where were all the people? Perhaps celebrating a Filipino holiday, they seemed to have so many. Alstaetter let his mind drift to his beloved Greta. It was night where she was. She'd be reading a book or getting ready for sleep. Alstaetter wondered whether right then she thought of him too.

"You know, Matt, with the general gone down to Manila, I've been given extra responsibility." The major removed a flask from his coat, opened it and took two long swallows. "Everything's on my shoulders until he gets back, and I'm going to need the full support of every officer in my command."

Alstaetter looked Major Baston in the eye. "You can count on me, sir. You have my full support."

"That's good to know, Matt. Remember back a ways when I said you're a lot like me?"

"Yes, sir. You said we are like each other."

"Well, I meant it." Baston spread his arms to indicate the countryside around them. "Hell man, I'm sensible to the mess we're into here. I don't like this killing anymore than you do. Sure, it isn't a fair fight, our heavy artillery against their knives and rocks. Where's a soldier's pride in that?"

The major looped his reins and used both hands for emphasis. "Matt, I want you to look at it from a different angle for a minute, if you can. I used to be just like you. When I was young, I knew only one kind of truth. A thing was right or wrong, good or bad, black or white, and I didn't scratch around long for moral equivalence. I found answers to life's questions in *right action*. It was simple, just do the right thing. Do good, tell the truth, eschew deceit and perfidy, a good foundation for a young man.

"Trouble was, it didn't work. I soon found life rarely handed me easy questions. The older I got, the harder to be sure of my conclusions. What at first seemed like right action, very often got turned upside down when I looked a little closer. Eventually, I had to come to terms with the notion there may be no right answers, that a man can only do what he thinks is right at the time. History, Matthew, is the means by which right and wrong are determined."

Alstaetter flashed back to his Aunt Alice and her warehouse of convoluted, self-serving panaceas and felt his mind close. He pulled himself up short. Hear the man out, he told himself. You've made the decision to go along to get along, at least listen to what he has to say.

"I know what you think of the general and me, the other officers here. You think we're no better than murderers, we've no regard for innocent life, that we pursue this conflict with just a little too much zeal. I ask you, how can you fight a war any other way? Think about it for a moment, man. How do you engage an enemy halfway? How many Americans would die in a contest we weren't committed to win, where all our punches were pulled, our holds barred? That would be the worst kind of insanity. We may as well line up the troops and shoot them ourselves. Believe me, Matt, if you're going to lift your hand against another, you can't ask yourself in the process who's right or wrong, only who's left."

Alstaetter felt the muscles in his jaw tighten. He didn't want to say anything now. He'd swallowed his pride and eaten plenty of humble pie to get back this far with Major Baston. He tried to go along, but just couldn't. "Permission to speak freely, sir?"

"Of course."

"I agree with your thinking about fighting the war, sir. Better one hundred Asians die than a single American boy, but should we be here in the first place? What's right about traveling half a world away to depose a tyrannical government, and then step into their shoes? There's no moral or legal imperative for America to possess colonies. Just a hundred and twenty years ago, we fought to free ourselves from foreign domination, and we've enjoyed the blessings of liberty ever since. Surely the Filipino people deserve no less."

"Good points all. If I understand you correctly, you're speaking about *right action*. What's right about forcibly imposing our will on another people? What's right about installing a white, capitalist American government in a land of war-weary Asian peasants?

"Consider the matter first from the Filipino point of view. No one knows for sure, but let's say Aguinaldo has an army of forty thousand men ready to die for freedom. Forty thousand in a land of four million. How do the other ninety-nine percent feel about his bloody experiment with independence? How do the tens of thousands of educators, merchants and bureaucrats in Manila feel about their loved ones conscripted into his band of renegade outlaws and in most cases never seen again? How does the starving peasant feel about paying a 'freedom tax' on pain of death to every petty warlord that happens through his village? Certainly Aguinaldo's vision of *right action* can be held up for critical examination.

"Remember, Aguinaldo represents only a small percentage of the population, almost all Tagalog. Who speaks for the Ilokanos, the Ilongos, the Bikolanos, and the Waray-Waray? Who speaks for the Filipino Muslim, the Chinese Buddhist, the pagan Igorrote? Were they asked whether *El Presidente's* reckless, presumptive campaign for power is in their best interests?

"This land has a long history of poverty, ignorance, disease and endless struggles for clan domination. I'd wager a year's pay outside of Aguinaldo's band of fanatics, there's not a Filipino man, woman or child who wouldn't welcome a little American prosperity. Think of it, Matt. We can bring schools with good teachers, hospitals with doctors that really cure, farm machinery and new ways to grow and harvest crops. With our help, they can live better than they ever dreamed. At home, we teach our children to thank God every day for His blessings. What could be wrong with sharing those blessings? What could be right about a delusional monomaniac denying all that to his countrymen?"

Major Baston gave a signal and his new executive officer, Captain Welsh, rode forward. "Have the men break for midday meal. Post security patrols from A and H Companies." The captain saluted smartly, turned and passed the orders along. "Luncheon with me, Lieutenant, and we'll pursue this further."

The two men sat at a field table in the shade of a collapsible umbrella. A cook poured coffee, the major topped his with a splash of whiskey from his flask. Lieutenant Alstaetter ignored this, smiled at the major. "I was on the debate team at the Academy, sir, and I concede your argument well conceived, eloquently and persuasively delivered. However, isn't the argument itself flawed?"

Baston bit into an apple. "How so?"

"I mentioned the overthrow of an oppressive government, and you countered with the elusiveness of *right action* and the reliance on moral equivalence. If equivalence is the determining factor, then can't Aguinaldo's pursuit of freedom be compared with the American adventure? Who's to say his struggle won't yield the same fortunate results?"

Major Baston picked a little green flap of apple skin from his teeth, examined it, and then flicked it into the weeds beside his chair. "You'll remember I said history is the means by which right and wrong is determined. For example, to this day, England enslaves every race they encounter, but we live free. History has determined Thomas Jefferson, George Washington and an unlikely band of citizen soldiers were right. Not so for Aguinaldo, because history has not made the determination."

"Sir, that's precisely my point. How can we be sure now whether it's we or Aguinaldo who does the right thing?"

"We can't. Precisely *my* point. As officers and gentlemen it's up to us to take a broad view and use our best judgment, the only tools we have. President McKinley has a vision of America far different from what she is today. What if he's right? What if taking these Islands means our nation will grow and prosper into the next century? What if it's our destiny to rule the world? Don't we have the right to look out for our best interests? Aren't we obligated to make a better, more prosperous world for our children and grandchildren? Who's to say building a strong, proud America is not *right action*?" Warming to his subject, Baston drained his cup and signaled for more. "What if, as Shakespeare said, a divinity shapes our ends, rough-hew them as we will with our meddlesome *right action*?"

"What you describe, sir, is chaos. If the end justifies the means, then there's no standard for moral or ethical behavior. Men are free to pursue any course of action whatsoever once they manufacture a potential or perceived greater good. It's anarchy."

Major Baston sat forward in his chair and closed one eye, better to focus on the young officer while he made his point. "What I describe is both chaos and anarchy, Lieutenant. It's war!"

Suddenly, a volley of high-pitched gunfire broke the midday silence. Mausers. Lieutenant Alstaetter then heard the deeper, throaty sound of Krags in an answering salvo. The shots came from just over a low hill on their right flank. H Company had found the enemy. The two officers jumped to their feet, Baston knocking his chair backward into the weeds. Alstaetter caught the major by the elbow. "Permission to go to my men, sir."

"Hell yes, man! This is why we're out here. Give those dink bastards what for!"

Alstaetter crested the hill and surveyed the action below. The enemy was well dug in along a line spanning a narrow valley. The men of H Company had taken cover and furiously returned fire. Through thick clouds of gun smoke, Alstaetter saw Sergeant Rivers lead a platoon around the insurrecto's left flank, firing in rushes. Rivers knew the book as well as anyone, he thought.

He spurred his horse, galloped through the zip-crack of bullets and dismounted when he reached the men. "Corporal Minnefee, take ten men around the right flank and establish a crossfire." Staying low, Alstaetter crawled through the thick, dry grass encouraging his troops. "Hold your ground, boys! Help is on the way."

A hole in the firing line, somebody was missing. Alstaetter inched forward, staying just under the click, click of Mauser bullets overhead. He pushed the grass apart to catch a glimpse of the enemy, but the onslaught was too intense. These insurrectos were better marksmen than they'd encountered before. He wondered what guerilla commander had taught them to shoot.

Private James, on his back, arms and legs askew, stared toward heaven. His jaw blown away, black blood pooled around his head and crusted in the sun. Next to him, Metcalf had a single bullet hole in his forehead. Just a few feet away, Private George lay in a crumpled heap, his body still jerked as the insurrectos put round after round into his lifeless corpse. Alstaetter felt his gorge rise, fought for control. He wondered how many had fallen victim to this deadly assault. He heard another soldier scream, rise up, and then fall. Who was it? Hicks, he thought. Maybe Johnson, he couldn't be sure.

More shooting, right, then left. Krags. Rivers and Minnefee attacking from the flanks. Suddenly, the enemy ceased fire, and quiet fell along the flanks. He pushed up, tried again to get a view of the guerilla trenches. Something wasn't right. The Filipinos had them pinned down, did some real damage. Why would they stop? Then he saw it, A and C Companies coming over the hill in formation.

The guerillas sprang from their trenches and retreated, seemingly headed for the forested foothills behind them. Alstaetter noticed Major Baston and Captain Welsh on horseback watching from atop a little hill. A and C Companies saw the rebels flee and quick-marched to close the distance, their sergeants out front, pistols drawn. Still, something wasn't right. Alstaetter watched the retreating guerillas disappear from view first singly, then in pairs and threes. It appeared they retreated, but then they vanished well short of the tree line. Suddenly, it dawned on the young officer what the rebels were doing. They weren't running for cover, they'd dug a second trench line behind the first and with the arrival of the American reinforcements, fell back to the new position.

Alstaetter looked up and saw Sergeant Rivers standing atop a low mound frantically waving. "They're moving into defilade, Lieutenant!" Alstaetter saw it too. The Filipinos had dug trenches perpendicular to the first to defend against frontal assault. To make matters worse, Alstaetter saw fresh troops in the secondary battlements. The guerillas had reinforcements of their own. Alstaetter knew he had to attack the secondary trench, divert some of the guerilla gunfire away from the advancing Americans.

He shouted to his troops. "Give them every thing you've got, men!" H Company rose up and moved forward. They sent a hail of bullets into the guerilla trenches, but to little effect, the Filipinos had cover and concealment. The attacking Negro soldiers didn't faze them.

When the guerillas opened fire on the Kansans advancing down the hill, a wall of lead penetrated the first and second ranks. Then the third and fourth. Soldiers stumbled over the bodies of their comrades as their momentum carried them into the iron jaws of the trap. Another broadside, more Americans fell.

By now, the Kansans realized what was happening and panicked. Some threw their weapons aside and fled, some dived for cover, others dropped and returned fire. Not enough of them, and low on ammunition, H Company had the enfilade, and with the Filipinos firing in the other direction, they had a chance of doing some damage, taking some pressure off the frightened and confused Kansans. Alstaetter gave the signal, and Sergeant Rivers urged the men forward. "Pick your targets, boys. Make every shot count."

Alstaetter stayed behind the line, tried to keep the battle in perspective. The Filipino guerillas saw the advancing black soldiers and turned weapons their way. Dimly conscious of a shrill sound over the pop of rifles and the screams of wounded and dying men, Alstaetter glanced up and saw Captain Welsh blowing retreat. He knew the command was not intended for him, but for A and C Companies. On instinct, he looked again, making sure he followed orders.

Astonished, he stopped in his tracks. Taking advantage of the carnage and confusion on the battlefield, a small party of guerillas had moved unseen to the top of the hill and as Alstaetter watched, dragged Major Baston and Captain Welsh roughly from their horses. The other Americans, an aide to the major and the battalion clerk, put up a fight, but it all happened too fast, and they were quickly overwhelmed. Alstaetter shouted, but his cry was lost in the noise of battle. He considered firing into the struggling men, but knew they were outside the range of his Colt .45.

In a matter of seconds, the Filipinos disarmed their captives and lay them on the ground. In three blinks of an eye, the blade of the big bolo fell three times, and Captain Welsh and the two enlisted men were dead. Horrified, unmindful of the bullets flying past his own head, Alstaetter looked around for help, and then spotted Sergeant Rivers. He too had seen the assault, took careful aim and fired his Krag until the magazine was empty. Alstaetter saw one guerilla stumble, reach for his leg. One of Rivers' rounds had found its mark, but too late. Both men watched helplessly as the insurrectos threw Major Baston facedown over his saddle. Another mounted Captain Welsh's horse, dug his heels in and raced away at full gallop.

The guerillas on the hill raised their weapons and shouted. It sounded at first like a victory yell, but Alstaetter knew at once it was a signal, because the Filipinos in the trenches immediately lighted torches and set the dry grass around them on fire. Huge clouds of gray smoke enveloped the battlefield. "Keep firing, men!" Sergeant Rivers cried. "Keep firing." H Company stood and fired until they'd exhausted their ammunition, but with no result. In moments, the Filipinos escaped into the foothills, concealed by smoke and the confusion of spreading flames.

The Americans were now alone in the little valley. Sergeants shouted orders to re-group, distribute ammunition, tend to the wounded. Like most of the men, Alstaetter was in a state of mild shock. He walked among the disoriented, battle-weary soldiers and realized they'd faced a well-armed and highly trained Filipino fighting force. The guerillas had conceived an elaborate plan, executed it perfectly, and now Major Baston was a prisoner. Too terrible to contemplate, Alstaetter thought. He wondered whether they'd demand ransom or an exchange of captives. Through the smoky haze in his brain, he heard Sergeant Rivers' voice, and then felt a hand on his shoulder. "You're in charge of the battalion now, sir."

Still in a daze, Alstaetter looked around him, contemplated the monsoon clouds building on the eastern horizon. The dry season is almost over, he thought to himself. In a moment, he turned and stared dumbly at the big company sergeant. "What now? Go after them and try to find the major?"

"The major's gone, sir. I say we go home and lick our wounds."

CHAPTER 20 - ACHERON

A t the start of the monsoon season, it rarely rained before noon. The clouds needed time and the warming rays of the sun to draw all the water up, purify it and send it back to earth. That was why they scheduled the wedding for 11 a.m. Fagen hadn't seen Clarita more than a minute at a stretch in two days, yet she seemed everywhere. A dozen people followed her around night and day. Her childhood priest, Father Antonio, had agreed to perform the ceremony and had come all the way from San Fernando. Her dressmaker, a woman named Alicia, was at her constantly for fittings, adjustments and more fittings. Ramundo Del Rosario, a portly sergeant from Cavite and renowned acquisitions specialist, had volunteered to supply and oversee the wedding feast. Baskets of flowers were brought in and stacked in the infirmary. A covered platform was constructed for the actual wedding ceremony, and twenty kegs of a drink the Filipinos called *alak* were placed in the shade of a cluster of nipa palms. Of course, one keg was immediately sacrificed, some of the men feeling obligated to sample the brew and testify to its suitability for such a grand occasion. A small army of Clarita's friends carried out the rest of the preparations.

Only ten days since their raid on the American supply train, Fagen's troops, now considered combat veterans, had joined the main body of the guerilla base camp. In a very short time, Fagen's reputation had grown from *true friend to the Filipino* to *hero of the people*. When they'd returned from the raid on the train, a messenger from General Sandico awaited with a letter congratulating Fagen and conveying his most heartfelt thanks for the *Capitán's* service. A party of local village chiefs called a few days later to pay their respects. One of them told Fagen his cousin in Manila had read an article about him written by an American reporter in San Francisco.

Fagen wasn't comfortable in the spotlight. He felt he hadn't really done anything. Clarita and *Sargento* Canizares made the whole thing a success, and Lieutenant Burgos had given his life for it. All he'd done was the best he could, and in his view, it hadn't added up to much. Clarita told him to let it go. She said the publicity, however exaggerated, was good for their cause. The Filipinos were proud of their *Capitán* Fagen, and guerilla soldiers everywhere exhibited new confidence. An American soldier joining their fight proved their cause just. As for America, Clarita said Fagen's actions were pure joy to the anti-imperialists. Nothing could more eloquently express their arguments about the immorality of expansionism than the deeds of a Negro private, a man with little to gain and no one to impress. Fagen thought Clarita probably right, but he knew a big reputation did little but fan the flames burning his bridges, and the day would come when he'd feel the heat.

In spite of everything, Fagen was a happy man. Clarita's love made his life worth living. He felt he must have done something right for God to send her to him. Without her he had no future. If anything happened to Clarita, Fagen's life was over. *Finis.*

"A courier brought this for you." Clarita entered the command tent holding a letter. "It's from Ellis." Dated three days earlier, the envelope was hand-made from rough paper, wrinkled and water stained. Fagen opened it and immediately recognized Ellis' crude, boyish scrawl. "Would you like to be alone?"

"No, please stay. May I read it to you?"

"If you like."

They sat down at Fagen's small table. Clarita saw his hand tremble and put her cool palm on his arm.

Davey,

The man who brings you this letter is loyal to the revolution. I don't know how long it will take him to find you, but he has promised not to rest until he completes the mission. As we have no money here in San Lazaro, and I cannot pay him, will you please reward him for me?

Sister Adriana helped me make this letter, but I am writing it out myself. I think by the time it reaches you I will be gone. There is a new leper colony being built on an island called Culion, and they have asked for able-bodied volunteers to help with construction. They've told me I can drive a team carrying logs and other supplies to the site.

The Filipinos believe Culion is the entrance to hell. They say the Devil keeps a special bunch of demons there to kidnap stray souls and send them into the underworld. There are stories about fishermen kidnapped by hobgoblins that patrol the beaches. They say only a few have lived to tell about it. The survivors told of suffering the hell-fire and witnesses say when they were rescued, their bodies were covered in blisters.

I don't think there's much to these stories, Davey. Sister Adriana says the Filipino has an overactive imagination, and I've been around them long enough now to agree with her. But so what if Culion is an island for lost souls? That's what lepers are anyway. Maybe it's the best place for us. Besides, you know I always wanted to be a teamster.

Every day of these last months, I've tried to fool myself into believing I would get better, that God would hear my prayers and make a miracle. Every night I dream of returning to San Isidro, to H Company, and you are there too. Every morning I lie in my bunk and imagine none of this has happened to me, and when I open my eyes everything will be the way it used to be. Day after day I hold on to the stupid, desperate dream that I will get better, that I will see home again, that people will not turn away from me in horror.

Davey, it's time for me to stop living a lie. I look forward to Culion and whatever terrors or pleasures await me. I only pray my stay there will be short. I have been betrayed by this life, and I am ready now for the next. Somewhere out there is the land of milk and honey, where all souls are pure of heart and spirit. We'll meet there again one day and start over. I have to stop now. It's raining and my paper is wet. My love to Clarita.
Ellis.
P.S. The price on your head has gone up to $600. Be careful.

Fagen dropped the letter. Clarita stood, wiped tears from her cheeks and left the tent. In a moment, she returned accompanied by the courier Ellis had sent. "This is Gracio." Exhausted but determined, the stocky little Filipino stood hat in hand before the American *Capitán.* "He says the lepers will be boarding a cutter at Sampaloc for the journey to Culion. He's agreed to take you there, but you'll have to leave now. I've arranged for two Igorrote scouts to guide you on a shortcut through the mountains. If you hurry, you can make it before the ship sails."

"Clarita, the wedding... Everything is arranged."

The Filipino girl put her arms around Fagen's neck, kissed him tenderly and whispered, "I can arrange another wedding. Go, find your cousin and tell him we will all meet in the land of milk and honey."

The two Igorrote tribesmen stood in the shade silently waiting. Dangerous looking, lean and muscular, their skin shaded a rusty brown, the mountain men were naked save for bands of tattered, faded cloth tied around their loins. One man carried a hand-made bow a foot taller than himself and a bundle of long, dart-like arrows on his back, the other, a razor-sharp bolo. Shaved heads, tiny, penetrating eyes and broad, flat noses added to their menacing appearance.

Clarita introduced them, said their names, but to Fagen unpronounceable, and after a few awkward attempts, he gave up trying. The best he could do was Atias and Marthee, but good enough, because they smiled at the American and rubbed the skin on the back of his hand.

Filipinos grew up hearing fantastic stories about the savages that lived in the remotest hills of Luzon, people so ferocious not even the Spanish dared invade their territory. Gracio's childhood nightmares were of demons in the form of fierce, primitive men who feasted on human flesh and drank nothing but blood. Now, he stood two steps behind Fagen, not wanting to get too close. "You can trust them," Clarita said. "Like us, they'd rather die than live with a foreign invader in their midst."

Ten minutes after the four men left camp, the jungle closed in around them, and they began to climb. The Igorrotes blazed a trail, hacking their way through dense undergrowth. After some time, they reached a high forested plateau, and the going got easier. Fagen thought they traveled south, but surrounded by giant trees and with no horizon, he couldn't be sure. Overhead, the double and triple canopy parted only occasionally to reveal a thick, rolling fog scudding through the upper branches.

The little mountain men picked up the pace. Puffing and gasping for air, Gracio strained to keep up. "*Capitán* Fagen," he choked, "who will know if these men intend only to run the fat off our bones, and then serve us for their dinner? Everyone says they are headhunters, *Señor*, and cannibals."

"You will be safe, my friend. I'm told these men only like dark meat in their stew pots."

They marched all night, stopping to rest only once. Fagen wondered how far they traveled. Certain he was in the company of demons, Gracio insisted they'd been led in a giant circle. No way to be certain, but Fagen's instincts told him the guides knew of the rendezvous and were doing their best. Just after dawn, the forest broke, and the party stopped at the edge of a wide ravine. A hundred feet across and two hundred deep, sheets of white water cascaded, boiled, foamed, and then pounded on black rocks below sending a cacophonous roar echoing up the vertical walls. They'd come to a dead end. Fagen's heart sank. The Igorrotes had made a mistake.

Atias motioned for everyone to sit. Then he removed his bow and quiver, walked to the edge of the ravine, sniffed, and then tasted the air. He cupped his hands and whistled into the forest on the other side. "He whistles to his gods for a miracle," Gracio complained. "Maybe we'll all get wings."

Slowly, almost imperceptibly, the leafy undergrowth on the other side of the ravine began to move. A moment later, two-dozen tiny men rose up and stepped forward, freshly cut vegetation tied across their backs, their faces and bodies painted green. Perfectly camouflaged, they'd been completely invisible. Their leader, naked except for an elaborate headdress and ankle-to-scalp tiger-stripe body dye, brandished a long staff on which were impaled six shrunken heads, the black, leathery skin sewn shut at the lips and eyes. Gracio trembled, and then groaned, "*Madre Mia.*"

Punctuated by wild gesticulations, bared teeth and rolling eyeballs, for five minutes Atias and the headhunter shouted at each other across the ravine. Their fantastic interchange reminded Fagen of the play he'd attended with Clarita in San Isidro. At the time, he thought the Filipino actors too melodramatic, too demonstrative. Watching the two native warriors shout and stamp their feet in the mud at either edge of a sheer precipice made Fagen wonder whether this too was some kind of act. Or could it be a greeting ritual or declaration of status? Impossible to tell.

In a moment it was over. The chief gave a signal, and eight more little men emerged from the forest, each carried long sticks festooned with shrunken heads. On the chief's order, the men lined up in two columns of four and faced each other six feet apart. Another man shot an arrow, a cord tied to its shaft, in a long arc that spanned the ravine and landed at Atias' feet. The Igorrote guide hauled hand-over-hand on the cord until he brought over a twisted skein of light rope and braided vines. Marthee helped, and soon they unraveled the little homemade bridge and made the ends fast to a nearby tree. When done, Atias stepped gingerly among the lines to the center of the ravine, looked once at the chief on the far side, and then turned and waved his party forward.

Gracio stared in astonished disbelief at Atias swaying precariously in the fragile web of knotted vines. "I do not know if I can do this, *Señor Capitán.*"

Clearly, the little courier was terrified. Fagen felt sorry for him. "Why did you agree to return with us, Gracio? You knew we had to go through these mountains to have any hope of getting there in time. You could have drawn me a map to Sampaloc."

"I had to come, *Señor*. My sister, Isabella, only fourteen, also goes to Culion. Your friend gave his word he'd watch over her if I delivered the letter. I have done this, and only God will know if he lives up to his promise, but just as you want to see your friend, I want to see my Isabella before they take her to the place where no man can follow."

Fagen tried to picture Gracio's young sister behind the walls of the San Lazaro leper colony. Was she portly like her brother? Was she also timid? Had her horrible disease so disfigured her that she'd abandoned all hope, or like her brother, was she still able to squeeze out yet one last ounce of courage when faced with another of life's many misfortunes? Fagen looked at the man standing before him, tremulous, fearful yet determined to see his sister again, to say goodbye one last time and felt his mission now had double purpose. "Hold on to me, Gracio. We'll go across together."

Atias waved again, and they moved out. The men tried to synchronize their steps as the bridge lurched under their feet and swayed through a wide arc. Gracio held tightly onto Fagen's belt and shut his eyes, would not look down at the white ribbon of water pounding over the rocks far below as they inched along the uncertain ropeway.

The warrior chief waited impatiently on the other side. The moment the travelers' feet touched solid ground, they were surrounded and searched for weapons. Atias and Marthee stood to one side while two little green men took Fagen's carbine and pistol, smashed them on the rocks, and then threw them over the cliff into the river below. Another man took Gracio's small bolo from its scabbard, tested the edge with his thumb, laughed derisively, and then jammed it back in place.

Satisfied they were unarmed and harmless, the chief stepped forward. A fierce, grim-faced man with a broad muscular chest, he ignored Gracio and walked in a circle around Fagen, looking him over head to toe. He gazed deep into the American's eyes for a long moment, then opened his mouth and yanked at his tongue. Fagen willed himself not to pull away or make a defensive move. He had no idea who or what they were up against and thought it best to follow Atias' lead and stand still. The headman finished by pinching the skin on both Fagen's arms, and then he turned his back on him.

Suddenly, the chief spun around, shouted and stomped the mud at his feet. In an instant, four men tackled Fagen and dragged him to the ground. At first startled, and then bewildered by their amazing strength,

Fagen put up no fight. The chief came forward, leaned over and brandished the hideous shrunken-head talisman in his face, and then drew a small bolo and pressed the edge deep into the American's throat. Fagen felt the blade cut flesh, knew he was to be killed then and there, and wondered whether the grim image of that wild man's countenance would pass with him into the next world. He looked up at the morning sun, saw it climb into the leafy branches overhead and tried to concentrate on the sound of water rushing through the ravine. The chief pressed harder, and Fagen felt a warm trickle of blood run down his neck and across his shoulder. He closed his eyes and waited for death.

"OWUOOO!" Atias cried, and then moved with lightning speed, locking his fingers around the chief's wrist and in a silent, face-to-face tug of war, lifted the knife away from the American's throat.

"OWUOOO!" He howled the war cry again, his jaws open wide, feet firmly planted, muscles straining in the contest to control the knife. The two men stood over Fagen, their battle of wills taking center stage over his execution. Fagen watched in horror, and it occurred to him that even if Atias overpowered the chief, won the struggle for dominance, respect or whatever they fought for, their lives were forfeit anyway. The headman's cadre of fearsome, camouflaged soldiers armed with spears, bolos and crossbows made that a virtual certainty.

Fagen couldn't understand. Unless they'd just wanted new ornaments to dangle from their hideous amulets, why'd they permit them to cross into their territory? Why had the chief picked him to die first and not the sheepish Gracio? Had Atias and Marthee been deceived too? Had their tribal cousins promised safe passage, and then double-crossed them? Whatever the situation, they were outnumbered, unarmed and at the mercy of headhunters, and Fagen saw no reason to expect any quarter.

"OWUOOO!" Atias screamed again into his opponent's face. Perspiration poured off the two men as they fought for the knife. Gradually, the chief's strength began to fail, and then fear crept into his eyes. Atias, his fingers locked around the man's wrist, forced the bolo up between them until its lethal blade was only inches from the headman's throat. The guide had won the silent contest of strength, and Fagen guessed it only a matter of seconds before the chief gave a signal and the arrows began to fly. Then Atias did the unfathomable. Still locked onto the chief's wrist, he pushed the warrior's arm high over his head and brought the bolo down in a sweeping arc until the point penetrated the skin over his own heart. Then he let go.

Silence reigned in the forest. Two-dozen men stood frozen in their places, unable, or unwilling, to move and watched while the chief, his knuckles white on the handle of the bolo, fought to regain his composure. Atias stood before him, his arms at his sides, smiling, as if to welcome the blade into his chest. The headman had only to apply the slightest pressure, the knife would slide between the ribs, and the guide would be dead before he hit the ground. Atias' smile grew broader, and he exposed the few brown teeth that remained in his mouth. "Owuooo," he whispered in the chief's face. "Owuooo."

The warrior leader gazed into Atias' eyes for a long moment, and then he too smiled and said, "Owuooo." Atias grinned and nodded his head. The chief turned to his men, said something, and then laughed out loud, his rough chortle like the clanking of steel on steel. All at once, his men laughed too, and then Atias and Marthee joined in. A moment earlier, that heavily armed band of fierce little men in headdresses and green paint had been ready to kill, and now they laughed hysterically. Lunacy to Fagen, madness, but suddenly, inexplicably, he felt the urge to laugh too.

The chief gave a signal, and the men released him and helped him up. Gracio leaned against a rock, his face drained of color. Hearing death's knell had been too much for him. The danger now past, his legs buckled, and he fainted. That set off a fresh round of laughter, and the chief waved his staff over Gracio, the grisly shrunken heads flopping wildly, inches from his face.

Fagen wondered what happened, what chance occurrence took place to turn those men from friend to foe and back again, but at that point, he didn't care. He wanted only to be on the trail. When all the merriment died down, Atias made a speech in a low, singsong monotone. He got his message across by pointing at the two lowlanders, and then back across the ravine several times. Fagen thought he heard his name, but saw no recognition in the chief's eyes and was mindful of how little the outside world intruded there. The chief barked a command, and a man stepped forward carrying one of the gruesome shrunken-head staffs, which he presented to Atias, its magic power a shield to ward off evil spirits for the duration of their journey. Atias accepted the ghastly, evil-savored gift with great humility, and without another word, the travelers set out on the path, Marthee no longer having to urge the reluctant Gracio forward.

For ten hours, Atias led them through jungle so thick they saw neither earth nor sky. Within a mile of the ravine, he'd tossed the shrunken-head staff into the undergrowth, spat a few words after it, but appeared otherwise unfazed by his confrontation with the tribal chieftain. By late afternoon, the forest thinned, and they came to a small hillock overlooking a wide valley. Gracio pointed to the low hills in the near distance. "On the other side of that ridge, is Sampaloc."

The valley was a patchwork of rice fields covered by dark, lowering monsoon clouds. Small groups of peasant farmers, their day's work done, walked wearily home, others talked among themselves, switched idly at their plodding *carabao*. These people were rebel sympathizers, and their casual, work-a-day demeanor indicated no Americans in the vicinity. Fagen motioned for Atias and Marthee to remain in the jungle, under the cover of the forest canopy. Marthee leaned back against a tree trunk and crossed his legs, but Atias stood up to follow. Gracio, eager to set foot on flat land, quickly set off down the hill. Fagen hurried to catch up, motioning again for Atias to stay put. The guide nodded and smiled, but then matched him step for step. Tribal peoples were never seen in the lowlands. Fagen worried the Igorrote's presence would attract undue attention from the locals, but Atias was determined, and having seen him function effectively in a most dangerous and unpredictable situation, Fagen reluctantly agreed.

Rain came down in thick, diagonal sheets, soaked their clothes and pounded a pizzicato against their faces. The peasant farmers, accustomed to the annual return of the monsoon, hunkered down in the relative dry of their nipa huts, while the travelers sloshed for an hour unnoticed over earthen dikes and through flooded fields. They reached the valley's edge and climbed the misty western foothills using the dense undergrowth for cover. Fagen had no idea what to expect when he reached Sampaloc, whether he'd even see Ellis, much less get the chance to talk to him. From the outset, the whole journey had been risky and with little chance of success, but when they crested the hill and moved down out of the overcast, he saw the situation, and it was much worse than he could have imagined.

Sampaloc was a tiny hamlet on the edge of a sand beach at the head of a crescent bay. A half-mile of narrow, winding road led from the village to a jetty protecting a long pier that extended a hundred yards into the South China Sea. At the end of the gangway, barely visible through the half light of the setting sun and partially obscured by scudding monsoon clouds, a white, two-masted schooner pitched and bucked against the waves.

This day, the road was packed with great, surging masses of humanity that had gathered on the wharf and covered it nearly to the end, so many people the pier itself seemed alive. Hundreds of hysterical Filipino men, women, old folks and children wrung their hands, tore their hair and moaned pitiable, heart-wrenching lamentations for God's mercy. Their woeful cries, their most perfect expressions of sorrow, rose up the hill and echoed off the clouds overhead. Awestruck, Fagen tried to shut his ears, but could not. Like the sea under their feet, the angry crowd surged and pressed farther onto the pier, desperate to get past the company of marines that held them at bay. Gracio sat in the underbrush, tears streamed down his face. "The people grieve because their loved ones go to Culion - to *hell*."

Fagen felt sorry for the timorous little courier who'd risked so much for the sake of his sister. "Gracio, surely you don't believe this superstition. Culion is an island, nothing more..."

"There she is!" Gracio jumped to his feet and pointed toward the schooner. "My Isabella!" Then he raced down the hill and disappeared into the teeming mass of humanity.

Fagen strained to see through the rolling fog at the end of the pier. A sudden gust of wind blew, the clouds lifted for a moment, and the sky lightened. Atias raised his arm, pointed, and then Fagen saw it too. Huddled together under the transport boat's gunwales, only twenty left to board, the lepers of San Lazaro marched like forsaken and insignificant children, single file up the gangplank.

Seeing the last of their stricken loved ones board the ship ignited the already frenzied Filipinos. A savage, collective roar arose from the crowd, and they pushed past the bayonets and raced to the end of the pier. Marines on the ship fired into the onrushing swarm. Several men and women fell, trampled by those that followed behind. Shrieks of terror and angry curses filled the air as the enraged throng advanced. Sailors scrambled to cut the dock lines and get the sails hoisted, and the captain fought to claw off the pier against the prevailing wind. That's when Fagen saw him. Bigger than the other lepers and twice as broad, Ellis reached out, swept up the child beside him and held on to the boarding plank with one giant hand while sailors hauled it on deck.

The wind swirled, the mizzen staysail went up, and the ship caught a puff of air and lifted her head. As the boat lurched away from the wharf, scores of overwrought men and women flung themselves into the sea in a desperate attempt to follow. They swam as hard as they could, struggled against the green foam, but then the captain tacked, eased the sails and picked up speed, his course south by southwest. Now completely drained of life's energy, the mournful, grieving Filipinos staggered about in little death-march circles, bawling and gnashing their teeth. Others dropped where they were, exhausted and defeated.

Darkness came quickly that stormy afternoon. The clouds thickened and gusts of cool, salt air washed over the mournful crowd. Fagen watched the schooner disappear into the mist. Maybe there was something to the Filipinos' superstition, he thought. Maybe those poor, lost souls were sailing down old Acheron, the river of woe, headed for the abode of the damned. Fact, fancy, it made no difference. For David Fagen, only one truth remained in the universe, one incontrovertible reality. At that moment, Fagen knew for certain he'd never lay eyes on Ellis Fairbanks again.

Grim faced, Atias turned in the gathering darkness, put a hand on Fagen's shoulder and spoke the only word of Spanish he knew. "*Malo.*" Bad.

CHAPTER 21 - COMMENCEMENT

The radioman on the gunboat, *Vicksburg*, entered Fredrick Funston's cabin and handed him a message from General MacArthur's headquarters. Routine, except for the last two lines, which he read twice.

...Major Baston captured in skirmish with insurrectos near San Isidro, presumed dead. Colonel William Russell assuming temporary command.

Damn, the general thought to himself. I told that idiot administrative duties only, nothing more in my absence. He ignored my orders, let his ambition rule, and now he's devoured by his own covetous desire. The last thing I need is Bill Russell snooping through my affairs for the next three weeks. Who knows what mess I'll be in when I get back!

Funston crumpled the message, opened a porthole and pitched it into the monsoon raging just outside. Damn this weather! Asia's a hellhole fit only for savages. Why couldn't things go as planned? Granted, the boat ride from Manila to Casigurian saved a two hundred mile march over impossible terrain, but how could he foresee the punishment they'd take in just a few days on an angry, wind-tossed sea?

At first, Newton and Mitchell had tried to ignore their mal-de-mer, but couldn't fight it and hadn't come out of their cabin in two days. The Macabebes lay scattered about on deck clutching to anything to keep from being swept overboard. The moment they'd sailed out of Manila Bay, Hilario Talplacido claimed he was near death and made the captain swear to transport his body to dry land for burial. Only Funston and the implacable Spaniard, Lazaro Segovia, were fit for duty. Too bad for the rest of them, Funston thought. They'd a rebel leader to capture, and he wasn't about to let a little storm at sea stop him.

Funston gripped the starboard rail en route to the bridge deck. Captain Barry, a bearded, classical figure of a mariner, stood behind the helmsman peering into the green water, his legs spread against the rolling of the boat. Just as the general entered the pilothouse, a wave broke over the bow and sent five gallons of cold sea spray rushing down his backside. The captain ignored Funston's curses, tried to keep from smiling. "The sea must like you, General. She's given you a kiss."

"Now I know why the ocean is referred to in the feminine. It's rancorous, churlish and contentious. As a mode of transportation I'll take a horse and saddle anytime."

"Pardon me for saying so, sir, but a sailor learns to sail the wind he's given, not the wind he wishes for, or the wind he thinks he deserves," Captain Barry glanced at the army general, "but some men never understand this."

Funston didn't like the tall, broad shouldered captain. Just a little too quick with his tongue, he may be God on this boat, Funston thought, but everywhere else I outrank him. He made a mental note to review inter-service protocol when he got back. "Are we still on schedule?"

"Dead on, sir. We'll lay off Casigurian by midnight, if these costal charts are accurate."

The general knew the gunboat skipper called it as close as he could. On several occasions, he'd conducted land operations with poorly drawn maps, a fact of life in Asia. "I know you'll do the best you can. Just remember to stay well away from shore. We can't risk being seen, and the slightest whiff of coal smoke will alert the enemy to our presence."

The cargo hold of the 2000-ton *Vicksburg* reeked of bilge grime and the acrid stench of body odor as eighty-five Macabebe scouts jammed in out of the weather to receive their mission briefing from Lazaro Segovia. When their journey began, Segovia had announced Guam their destination. The Spaniard knew rumor would spread among the men in minutes. Two days later, he suggested they might be headed for Singapore, maybe even San Francisco. Segovia theorized that during their boat trip, the Macs needed both something to fear and to wish for. He knew they feared going to Guam, but travel to America, or even Singapore was beyond their wildest dreams. These rumors provided the little Filipino fighters with something to occupy their minds during their rough journey up the coast.

Segovia believed General Funston's plan to capture Aguinaldo brilliantly conceived, but only half-baked. The devil was in the details. Success hinged upon the flawless execution of each step along the way. The counterfeit correspondence they'd written to *El Presidente* on rebel stationery had set the stage, but once on the ground, the actions of the sullen, disputatious Macabebes would be the deciding factor. Segovia knew the Macs had no use for Tagalogs, often treated their countrymen with disrespect, sometimes cruelty. Therefore, he began their instruction in that dialect.

"Soon, we will land near the costal village of Casigurian where we will obtain provisions, and then trek over the mountains to Palanan, the headquarters of General Emilio Aguinaldo. Our mission is to capture him, thereby forcing the rebel insurrection to an end." Oil lanterns swayed with the rolling of the ship. Segovia peered through the dim lamplight. No reaction, no expressions of surprise or dismay. The Macs didn't care where they went, Segovia thought, as long as they killed Tagalogs. "Colonel Talplacido is your commanding officer. From this moment on, you will obey his every word. The punishment for any breech of discipline, however slight, is death. Is that perfectly clear?" No response.

The Spaniard continued. "The success of our mission depends on an elaborate ruse. We will pose as one of General Urbano Lacuna's companies previously operating against the Americans in Nueva Ecija province. Two months ago, we were ordered to join Aguinaldo's forces at Palanan. Since then, we have journeyed northward to our destination. While crossing the mountains, we ambushed a small detachment of Americans doing survey work and took prisoners." Segovia paused for a moment to let the information sink in. But for the drumming of angry waves on the outer hull, silence in the cargo hold.

He turned his attention to the sweating, ashen-faced Hilario Talplacido wedged between bulkhead girders for support. A pathetic excuse for a man, he thought, but the general hadn't given him time to recruit someone more reliable. A hedonistic coward, at least Segovia knew he could control him. Disliked and distrusted by everyone, if things went awry, he'd make the perfect scapegoat. "Colonel Talplacido will now provide further instruction."

The chubby, reluctant conscript stood before his men trembling with fear and fatigue. He coughed twice and mumbled through dry, swollen lips. "Comrades, do you see how I clear my throat before speaking? If you want to be taken for a Tagalog you must do this. Also, when you meet another person in a village or on the trail, you must inquire about his health and the well being of his family. If the conversation continues, you must ask about the activities of the village headmen."

At that, one of the Macabebes snorted, said something in his native dialect. The men around him laughed. Talplacido stiffened and pointed at the man. "Tagalog only! Abandon now all Macabebe language and

237

mannerisms. It is exactly that kind of mistake that can compromise our mission. You must begin now thinking all Tagalogs are your brothers, and you must do more than just play a role. Until we reach our destination, everyone you meet is a friend. We are rebel soldiers now. Ask yourselves, how could we harm anyone sympathetic to the revolution?"

Hearing the sound of his own voice made Talplacido feel better, and he continued, his words gaining in pitch and tone. "On this mission, I am your commander. I do not think of you as Macabebe scouts, but loyal Americans with the opportunity to restore order and prosperity to our land. When I speak, when I give orders, my words are from General Funston directly, and his come from none other than his Excellency President McKinley himself!"

Madre Mia, Segovia murmured. This man is a bigger idiot than I thought. But then he glanced at the faces of the scouts and saw for the first time since the briefing had begun, someone had their full attention. He decided to let Talplacido continue.

"Therefore comrades, unless you wish to suffer the great and terrible wrath of the President of the United States, do not, by the most innocent slip of the tongue, the slightest wink or nod, betray our purpose. Your vigilance alone insures the successful completion of our mission." Finding himself inexplicably at a temporary loss for words, the portly colonel bowed slightly and surrendered the floor to Segovia.

The Spaniard stood, ready to speak, when the iron hinges on the cargo hold door groaned, and a member of the *Vicksburg's* crew stuck his head in. "The general wants all you indians on deck now!"

Funston paced, waited for his turn. He watched Harry Newton, Burton Mitchell and the last of the Macabebe scouts climb into the lifeboats going to shore. They'd made four round trips, some of their provisions had been washed overboard, but so far, everyone had been transported safely. He buttoned his coat and secured his hat strap under his chin, Teddy Roosevelt style. He reminded himself to be careful, the little open boats pitched, bucked and pounded against the hull of the gunboat, and he wasn't as young as he used to be.

"Good luck, General." Captain Barry leaned over the rail and shouted. "We'll be off Palanan in five days awaiting your signal. Give President Aguinaldo a warm how-do-you-do from the United States Navy."

Stinging rain pelted Funston's face as he looked up at the captain waving to him, and for an instant he wondered whether he'd live to make the rendezvous. Then he called out, "I'll bring the little monkey with me. You can give it to him yourself."

The landing party soaked through, but safely ashore, could do nothing but huddle shivering on the sand and wait for daylight. Funston ordered Captain Newton to inspect weapons and ammunition. Lieutenant Mitchell inventoried their remaining supplies. Segovia led a small reconnaissance party to determine whether anyone had seen them come ashore.

In an hour, the rain stopped, the clouds rose, thinned, and drifted east. Thousands of bright stars twinkled overhead, and the night turned cold. Funston felt he couldn't risk a fire. He wasn't sure how close they were to Casigurian and didn't want their presence known until morning. The Macs grumbled. One man got up to find dry wood, but the general sent Segovia to intercept him. The Spaniard carried in his pocket a small, flexible bludgeon wrapped in black leather. He had only to show it to the shivering, disheartened scout, and the search for firewood ended.

Morning brightened the eastern horizon and like blossoms, the men turned to face the warming rays of the sun. Segovia and their guide, Cecelio Segismundo, searched over the near horizon in an effort to pinpoint their exact location. "The news is not good, General," Segismundo reported to Funston. "I know this territory. Casigurian is still twenty miles away."

The information came as a shock. Funston had planned to land three miles from the village, far enough to remain unseen, yet close enough not to add too much distance to the hundred miles between Casigurian and Palanan. "Then we'd better get started."

They marched north for several hours on a wide sand beach that followed a line of sheer cliffs rising two hundred feet to a forested plateau. On the chance their party might be spotted by locals living in the jungle above them, Funston, Newton and Mitchell removed their insignia of rank and walked in the center of the column, playing early the role of prisoners of war. By mid-morning, the tide had risen, and they found themselves wading in waist-high water, searching for access to higher ground. Soon, the dense jungle above them broke, and Segismundo led them single-file up a steep embankment to a plain of huge, jagged boulders stretching as far as they could see in all directions. Under strict orders not to address the Americans until the mission over, Segismundo gave his report to Hilario Talplacido. "I am sorry, *Señor* Colonel, but we must cross this rock field. It is the only way to get to Casigurian."

Talplacido's heart sank. Certain he couldn't traverse the huge, black stones, he hoped Segovia would seek another route. He turned to the Spaniard. "What should we do, Lazaro?"

"Each man crosses on his own. Tell the scouts to separate. No one knows how these rocks will shift when men stand on them. We'll gather on the other side."

The landing party spent the rest of the afternoon scraping, climbing, descending and doubling-back among the rough boulders. Funston was reminded of a colony of beetles following a scent, or a magnetic field, or whatever compelled those tenacious little insects to surmount impossible obstacles.

The trek took its toll on the general, more so than he'd expected. Shortly after he'd started, the muscles in his legs ignited, and he was sure his chest would explode. He wiped sweat from his brow and cursed the bully beef, a staple of his diet in Asia. He'd have to remember to cut back on that greasy concoction, or at least, wash it down more thoroughly with quantities of wine. Thank heaven, Funston thought, for Burton Mitchell. A veritable mountain goat, he'd pushed and pulled the general over the rocks all afternoon with seeming ease. Without him, he'd be in that torturous field for days.

When they reached the other side, Hilario Talplacido waited for General Funston, and then pushed him roughly to the ground. "On your knees before this important personage, American dog!" Stunned and astonished, the general was about to react when he saw a Filipino peasant looking down at him from under a broad-brimmed straw hat. "See their ugly flat faces," Talplacido said, "and their pale skin? They do not look so invincible now, do they, *Señor*?"

The headman bent over and stared myopically first at Funston, then at Mitchell and Newton. Satisfied, he turned to Talplacido. "I have never seen an American this close. Soldiers came to our village once, but we ran into the jungle. We could not fight them as we had only three guns. Now you are here, we would not run away, but stand to our posts and show you how brave the people of Casigurian are."

Whole families stood outside their huts and stared in silence as the company of soldiers and their American prisoners entered their village. Afraid of making a blunder, his chest tight with fear, Talplacido was overjoyed when Segovia took the initiative and ordered the Macabebes to make camp a few hundred yards north of the village and the prisoners placed in a wooden chicken coop and the door locked.

Later, after sundown, Talplacido, Segovia and Cecelio Segismundo met with the headman and village council. Drinking homemade beer around a small fire, they listened while Talplacido told of their summons by Aguinaldo and their march over the mountains to Casigurian. The headman insisted Talplacido repeat the part about surprising the American survey party and the kills they made. When the chief had heard enough, Talplacido took a deep breath and sat back. Then it was the headman's turn to talk. He raised his glass to the courier. "*Señor* Segismundo visits us often in the course of his duties. He is a loyal servant of *El Presidente* and a friend to the people of Casigurian. I thank him for leading you brave soldiers to us." The men around the fire joined the chief's toast. Uncharacteristically, Talplacido only sipped his beer. He wanted to drink deeply, to anaesthetize his ragged nerves, but knew he had to keep his wits about him. The villagers were simple people, not stupid. He pictured his throat cut from ear to ear, his lifeless body food for buzzards among the rocks just south of the village and forced himself to concentrate.

The headman continued. "We know you have come a long way, and your journey is not yet over. The terrain between Casigurian and Palanan is very rugged. Worse by far than that which you've been through. We also know you need food. Of course, we will give you what we have. Unfortunately, it is not much. Aguinaldo sends soldiers here every month to collect our rice, sweet potatoes and chickens, but tomorrow we will go among the people, and again they will empty their cupboards in support of the revolution."

Lazaro Segovia thanked the chief, begged his pardon and asked to be excused to attend to his men and look in on the American prisoners. Talplacido explained the Spaniard was a most conscientious officer, always concerned about the well being of his men. The headman called Segovia, "*Capitán Considerado,*" and wished him goodnight.

The moon shone through the wooden slats and lit the general's face as Segovia pretended to check the lock on the door of the chicken coop. He told Funston of their success with the headman and their plans for the next day. The American listened without interruption. Segovia finished his report by asking for the general's instructions, and Funston responded in an urgent whisper. "We must be on the trail to Palanan in the morning. The headman will want to keep you here as long as he can. Each day we stay adds to his status among his people. Tell him you're under strict orders. Allow him to save a little face, but under no circumstances remain here past noon tomorrow. Collect whatever goods they're willing to give, then offer to buy anything else they have. We can't make it on the food we've got, and we're not likely to find much along the way."

Segovia nodded. "Anything else, *Señor?*"

"Compose a letter to Aguinaldo. Say we should arrive in Palanan in five or six days. Also, tell him about the American prisoners you have with you. Get Talplacido to sign it, and then ask the chief to have it delivered by his fastest runner."

Segovia rattled the lock one more time. "All these things I will do, *Señor.*"

"Lazaro, one more thing."

Si, Señor?" the Spaniard secretly delighted the general had called him by his Christian name.

"Post a guard on our cell tonight. These northern savages don't look trustworthy."

CHAPTER 22 - CONVERGENCE

In her dream, Clarita sat at a small table in a dark room, the only light a single candle flickering softly before her. Dark shadows prevented her from seeing the other people at the table, but from their familiar, familial essence, she knew she was in the presence of her mother, father and brother, Matco.

Clarita's heart filled with joy. She tried to speak, tell them how happy she was to see them. Her lips formed the words, but mute, no sound issued forth. She tried to reach out, touch them, feel her mother's warm, responsive embrace, but paralyzed, her limbs were frozen in place. She tried again to speak, to make her presence known, but she was powerless to overcome the force that held her back, and the more she tried, the more difficult for her to retain focus. The incorporeal beings faded with her efforts to hold them, and afraid of losing them altogether, she stopped trying and viewed them in silence.

"I see we've all agreed to be together again," Father said, and then reached out and pressed Mother's hand lovingly. "A most pleasant and fortuitous occasion. How long has it been? It's so difficult to keep track of time."

Young Matco chirped, "We see each other nearly every day, father, surely you remember. Just this morning, you taught me how to move a spider's web from one branch to another without breaking it. Last week, we read poetry together from one of your big books."

Clarita saw her father's lip curl and knew he smiled at Matco. "...And do you see Mother every day too, my son?"

"Of course," Matco replied. "She kisses me goodnight before I fall asleep, and on Saturday makes me berry cobbler."

"That is good. I also see Mother every day, but in different environs, and she visits us on terms of her own. Today, we've summoned each other at the same time under the same circumstances, and now we're all here together."

Matco leaned forward in his chair, his hands resting flat on the table. "I don't understand, Father."

Then Mother spoke, her voice music to Clarita's ears, "What Father is trying to say, Matco, is communication in this place is almost always one-way. You can summon me – or anyone else – any time you choose, and you can create whatever reality you wish, but the other person is not intruded upon. For example, I may wish for you to accompany me to the market Saturday. In my world, you spend the day with me, in your world, you spend the day eating cobbler. The reality I choose for myself does not encumber you. You create your own world and I mine, but obligations, responsibilities and accommodations come only from within. No outside interloper can intrude and make demands."

Clarita thought she understood her mother, but Matco seemed perplexed. "Can Father summon me too, for any activity, at any time?"

"Of course."

"Then can I be in two places at the same time? Is that possible?"

"Oh yes, my son. You can be in many places at the same time, but you are only aware of the present you yourself create. That is why we say communication is one-way. The exception is a time like now, when we've all created the same reality at the same time."

"One more question then, Mother. If I've summoned you to bake a cobbler, but you've summoned me to a day at the market, do I really get you, and you me? Is it really you that stirs the batter and sugars the berries, and is it really me who carries the shopping bag? Are these things reality or illusion?"

Mother took Matco's hand in her own. The sight of the woman's beautiful, bare arm reaching across the little table brought tears to Clarita's eyes, and longing for her mother's soft caress, she struggled again against the invisible power that held her back. The moment her concentration waned, the figures at the table began to fade. Bitter disappointment lingered as she forced herself to focus, discontent, but greedily taking nourishment in her role of unseen eavesdropper.

"Illusion is reality, Matco. Here, if someone chooses to fill his world with horror and pain and suffering, he is free to do so, but he cannot intrude upon another, the reality of his world is known only to him and is therefore illusion."

"I want to understand, Mother, but I have so many questions."

"Allow me to ask you a question, son," Father said. "What is the purpose of death?"

"Don't you mean the purpose of life, Father?"

"No, life has no purpose, Matco, except to define us – to show us who we are."

"Then please tell me, Father, about the purpose of death."

"Death is much more meaningful. In death, each person gets a fresh start, or to borrow a phrase from the classroom, a clean slate, on which he can write anything he chooses.

"Free from interference, exempt from responsibility to others, liberated from the hardships placed upon him by any world outside his own, acquitted of perfidy, relieved of unwanted strife, his true essence develops, naked, exposed, undistorted by outside influence, his quintessence, if you will. It is this extract – this decoction – that he presents upon entering the next plane of existence." Father leaned back in his chair, took a deep breath. To Clarita, his voice became suddenly thinner and more distant. She strained to listen. "Earlier, my darlings, I said this was a fortuitous meeting. I came here to tell you my slate is filled now, and it's time for me to present myself to the next plane. I must go."

No one else at the table reacted, but Clarita cried out, "No! You can't go. I've just found you. I have so much to say, so much to tell you!"

Father went on, "My departure from this place will not affect you. I'll still be in your world whenever you choose, and I will wait until you are in mine again."

"Are you leaving now, Father?" Matco asked.

"Yes, son, at this very moment. Goodbye, Mother. Goodbye, Matco."

Clarita tried again to cry out. "Father, don't go! Don't go!" she pleaded, but had no voice, and the image of her father faded into nothingness followed quickly by her mother and Matco.

"Clarita, it's time to go!"

She struggled to open her eyes, a dim figure hovered over her. "What time is it, Grandmother?"

"Past midnight."

"I had a dream, both wonderful and terrible at the same time."

"I know, dear. I let you sleep too long, but you were exhausted, you needed rest. Now, you'll have to hurry."

Clarita arose, slipped into her hooded goatskin raincoat and followed her grandmother down three flights of stairs to the cellar. "How many?"

The fortuneteller held the lantern higher as they descended. "Ten fighters for freedom."

"Ten! I expected thirty!"

"There were thirteen, but three changed their minds and left this evening."

"Ten… Grandmother, what's happening?"

The old woman stopped outside the cellar door, and Clarita saw concern on her face. "Things are changing, my darling. Recently, the Americans have garrisoned troops in every village and hamlet. Soldiers blanket the entire province. They call it 'Benevolent Assimilation,' supposedly for our protection, but now, two Filipinos can't have a conversation without an American looking over their shoulders. It's a hateful, insidious policy, and breaking the revolution. People are frightened to make a move. The flow of weapons and supplies from the barrios has been cut to a trickle. If the enemy suspects a villager sympathetic to the cause, he is immediately arrested, the trial short and the verdict predetermined. I'm afraid the tide is turning, my pet. I worry about our future."

"I too worry sometimes, Grandmother, but as long as *El Presidente* leads, we'll fight with what we have."

Grandmother tapped once, then twice more on the door, entered and ten Filipino peasants got to their feet. Shocked, Clarita signaled the men to sit as she walked among them in the dank cellar. Since she joined the revolution, she'd never seen such a wretched, miserable assortment of recruits. Barefoot, malnourished, sickly and without firearms or ammunition, they were the bottom of the barrel and clearly frightened out of their wits. Barely able to hide her dismay, Clarita smiled and approached one of the men. To make him feel more comfortable, she spoke in his native dialect. "What is your name, sir?"

The man jumped up and leaned on a wooden staff, his face animated. "Mauricio, *Señorita*."

"Have you no weapon, Mauricio?"

The man's eyes brightened, and he hopped on one foot for balance while he raised his crutch before him. "Oh, yes. I have this, my lady." Clarita glanced down at the man's foot, twisted at the ankle and dreadfully deformed.

"Here are *my* weapons, *Señorita*!" A boy of twelve sprang up and crossed the cellar floor, his outstretched hands proudly displaying two sharpened nipa sheaves and three rusty nails. "I can hide these in my hat and belt, and when the enemy comes close enough, I can stab him in the heart."

Clarita patted the boy's shoulder, and then moved among the recruits until she came to an old man sitting on a tattered blanket away from the others. Emaciated, thin white hair, deeply lined brow and sunken chest, he made no effort to rise. She knelt before him, and the man lifted his head. "I have no weapon, little face."

"Why did you come, Uncle? You should be home with your wife drinking tea, dispensing wisdom in your village."

"I have two sons, Meno and Pio, twins. They joined the revolution last year, and I have not seen them since. I had no choice, I had to come."

Clarita got the men up and gave them their orders for travel. When ready, the two women kissed good-bye and Clarita wiped the tears from her grandmother's leathery cheeks. "You'll have to hurry to get this bunch into the forest before daybreak," the old woman said. "Be careful, the Americans are everywhere. I know I'm a silly old fool, but I'm frightened I'll never see you again."

"General Aguinaldo will devise a way to outsmart the Americans, and the flow of recruits and supplies will resume. Soon, you'll have a cellar full of able-bodied patriots, and then as always, I'll be back to get them. Stay well, Grandmother."

Mid-afternoon, and H Company was on work detail two days from camp. Corporal Wheelwright looked up from his chores and spotted them first. "Sarge, somebody's coming!" All eyes turned up the road as a party of men approached followed by a supply wagon. "The lieutenant's back with third platoon, and there's another officer with them."

Rivers formed the men, and when the two officers rode into camp, called the company to attention and saluted. "Good afternoon, sir."

Smiling, Lieutenant Alstaetter touched his hat. "At ease, Sergeant." Then he lifted his head and spoke to the troops. "Men, I need volunteers to unload the wagon." Not an unusual request, soldiers heard it everyday, but the grin on their lieutenant's face unsettled them, and no one wanted to be first to raise his hand. An awkward silence ensued. In a moment, Alstaetter continued. "It's precious cargo boys - forty chickens, twenty pounds of mutton and twenty of beef, in addition to that, sweet potatoes, rice and hominy." He indicated the officer next to him. "And this gentleman, Lieutenant Bishop, reminded me to include fresh coffee, a ration of beer and a double ration of tobacco for each man." Speechless, the men didn't know how to respond until Alstaetter took off his hat, waved it in circles over his head and shouted, "Light the cook fires, boys, supper's on me tonight. We're having a party!"

Wheelwright trusted his eyes more than his ears. He turned to Minnefee standing next to him in formation. "What'd he say?"

"It's a jubilee, you fool!"

H Company's bivouac glittered with the candescence of thirty flickering campfires, the air thick with the pithy aroma of sizzling grease fat. Sergeant Rivers posted guards on thirty-minute rotations so no one was excluded from the festivities for too long. Delighted by the surprise, and rapturous with the unexpected bounty, the men feasted. After the meal, a full moon popped over the clouds on the eastern horizon making their camp bright as day. Satiated and happy, Corporal Moody took out his harmonica and blew an agreeable tune. Soon, Private Normal joined in on his Jew's harp, and Douglas and McMullen kept the beat with homemade tambourines. The music worked its magic, and in no time the men set aside their worries and surrendered to the mesmerizing influence of Negro spirituals sung to ancient African melodies.

Sergeant Rivers, elbows on his knees, sat in conference with the two officers, coffee simmered on the fire between them. "When did the orders come in, sir?"

"Day before yesterday. I've been reassigned to the Academy as associate professor. Of what, no one has yet said."

"You're going to be a teacher?"

"It seems so," the lieutenant smiled and lowered his eyes, "although I don't know why they picked me..."

"You'll be a fine teacher, sir."

Alstaetter reached for the pot and poured all around. "Lieutenant Bishop and I have had some time to get to know one another." He glanced over at the other officer. "I'm leaving you in good hands."

The young lieutenant straightened, cleared his throat. "May I say, Sergeant, how pleased I am to lead this fine company of men. Lieutenant Alstaetter has told me everything about you, and I'll consider myself lucky to receive half the help and support you've given him."

Rivers nodded. "Thank you, sir. Have you commanded Negro troopers before, sir?"

"Troopers? No, but my family is in the shoe manufacturing business in Ohio. We employ nearly a hundred colored men and women. You might say I've grown up among the races. I've always had an abiding respect for people of African descent." Bishop paused, peered into the darkness beyond their camp, and then fingered the buttons on his shirt. "I admit my inexperience in combat, Sergeant. Should we encounter difficult times, I'll need your strong hand to guide me. I've never before been responsible for men's lives, and I'm not sure how I'll bear up under fire. I pray that no matter what happens, we'll all get through this war safely."

"Yes, sir," Rivers said. "I do too."

Lieutenant Alstaetter stood up. "I guess I'd better tell the men."

H Company took the news of their commander's departure with equanimity. Reassignment and separation a constant in a soldier's life, the men had sometimes speculated what service under another officer would be like. However, status quo the queen of the fighting man's realm, no one wanted to see the company commander leave.

Ninety black faces looked back in silence while the young lieutenant walked among them, his thin blonde hair blowing in the breeze. "... This past year has been the most important, most momentous of my life. I stand here before you tonight humbled and truly grateful for the privilege of serving with you fine men. No officer - no man - has the right to expect, nor could any man fully deserve, the fidelity and the loyalty you have shown me. An unfortunate aspect of life is that all good things must come to an end. I want each of you to know the best part of my life has been the satisfaction and the honor I've experienced in serving with you."

No one spoke, the crackle of the campfires the only sound. In a moment, Minnefee, hesitant, hat in hand, stood up. "Sir?"

"Yes, Corporal?"

"Well, sir, I think I speak for all the men, sir, and we just want you to know we feel the same way."

"Thank you, Corporal. That's much appreciated."

"One more thing, sir. My uncle's a barber in Baltimore, Maryland, sir. He cuts the hair of Mr. Charles A. Tindley, the great Negro preacher and poet. Three months ago, my uncle collected one of Mr. Tindley's new songs, and he sent it to me. If the other men would help, I'd like to sing it for you now, sir."

Alstaetter smiled, bowed slightly. "I'd like that very much, Corporal Minnefee. Please proceed." Corporal Moody blew a note on the harmonica, Minnefee sang, and first one at a time, and then in pairs, the men arose and joined in:

Ye shall overcome...
Ye shall overcome...
Ye shall overcome someday.
If in thy heart, ye do not yield,
Ye shall overcome someday.

Soon, the entire company sang, their voices filling in behind Minnefee's.

Ye shall overcome...
Ye shall overcome...
Ye shall overcome someday.
And with His Word, a sword for thou,
Ye shall overcome someday.

Ye shall overcome...
Ye shall overcome...
Ye shall overcome someday.
If Jesus will thy leader be,
Ye shall overcome someday.

Ye shall overcome...
Ye shall overcome...
Ye shall overcome someday.
Deep in thy soul thy God speaks to thee,
Ye shall overcome someday.

When finished, the men stood in silence while the last of the harmonica's mournful notes faded softly into the night. Minnefee whispered, "There you have it, sir. I hope I got the words right."

Lieutenant Alstaetter bowed at the waist. "Thank you, Corporal. The words were beautiful. Thank you all."

Zing – splat! Zing – splat! Bullets rent the air and struck the trees around them. In unison, the men dove for cover. Sergeant Rivers scrambled for concealment in the darkness outside their perimeter, his eyes fixed on the sound of someone running towards him. As the man ran past, he hooked his arm and spun him into center of the camp. The man landed in a heap, Rivers over him in an instant. "Johnson, what the hell are you shooting at?"

Excited, the Negro private's words came in a rush. "Rebels, Sarge! I seen them. They walked right past me. I could have reached out and touched them!"

Rivers gripped the guard's shoulder and shook it. "Slow down, man. Tell me how many you saw."

"A dozen, but there could have been more. They was a sorry looking lot. One of them was lame. He's the one what carried the gun. They seen me and high-tailed it, but I got off two rounds before they ran away. I think I hit the one in front. I *know* I did! That's the right thing to do, ain't it, Sarge? Shoot for the leader? I *know* I hit him!"

"Yeah, that's right, Johnson. You did the right thing." Rivers stood and turned to Lieutenant Alstaetter. "You want to go after them, sir?"

Alstaetter scanned the blackness outside the perimeter. "You say they ran away, Private?"

"Yes, sir, they surely did, sir."

"Then tonight I'd rather stay here and sing another song."

CHAPTER 23 - CHARON WAITING

Fagen sat at the top of a little hill, his back against a fallen log and willed the leafy branches overhead to soothe his troubled mind. His body vibrated with fatigue. Exhausted, never enough sleep, his head was numb from the burdens of command. Two hundred yards below, Sergeant Canizares drilled the men. For several months, his troop had grown steadily and now numbered a hundred and eighty-five. The revolution wasn't going well, however. Officers were in short supply, and Colonel De Castro hadn't yet given him a replacement for Lieutenant Burgos. Until he was gone, Fagen hadn't fully understood or appreciated everything the lieutenant did. A million details; provisions, ammunition, spare parts for their weapons, couriers, codes, safe areas, facilities for the sick and wounded, there seemed no end to it.

Sergeant Canizares tried to take up the slack, did the best he could. Never a more courageous man on the battlefield, danger was mother's milk to him. Whatever the situation, however long the odds, fearlessly and without hesitation, he'd wade into the enemy and shoot them dead, cut throats, spill blood. He led men by hard example and force of will, but although the perfect man to take a beachhead, he was not suited to occupy the village. He had no love for the backside of combat, the logistical and administrative end, and so those duties fell to *Capitán* Fagen.

"Fagen! There you are! I've been looking for you. How are you?" No mistaking Colonel De Castro's high-pitched squeak. He'd climbed half way up the hill and stood waving. This day, he wore his dress uniform and Fagen thought of the pudgy little doorman outside the Regency Hotel in Nashville. "How are you? My star chart said this would be a day of surprises," the colonel shouted up the hill. "You have a visitor!"

When Fagen arrived at the command tent, Colonel De Castro had straightened papers, cleaned his spectacles and ordered more lemon water, his drink of choice. "You could have knocked me over with a feather when my aide announced this man's presence in our camp! I'd never met him before, but you only have to lay eyes on him to know his reputation is well deserved. I'll tell this story to my grandchildren!" Already tired, De Castro's flood of nervous energy made Fagen feel worse. He wished the colonel would sit down, keep his agitation to himself, and was about to say so when their visitor stepped in.

Over six feet, he was dressed completely in black save for a bright red sash above his waist. He wore a pistol on each hip, and two ammunition belts crisscrossed his huge chest. His head held high atop a thick, muscular neck, unsmiling, resolute mouth and dark, penetrating eyes, he paused a moment and surveyed the environment. Such an impressive man, Fagen felt compelled to stand. "*Capitán* Fagen," the district commander said proudly, "may I present Vicente Torres."

Silently, the man stepped forward and extended his hand, his iron grip crushing. His piercing, cold gaze mesmerized Fagen, and he uttered the first words that came to his mind, "Colonel Bloody Shirt."

A flicker of a smile, Fagen thought the man's face might crack. He'd amused him, no harm in that, but why did he feel like a mouse in the fangs of a tomcat? "*Capitán* Fagen, you're younger than I'd imagined. It is rare a man achieves infamy at such an early age."

"You're more gracious than I deserve, Colonel Torres. If my rude remark offended you, I beg your pardon."

Colonel Bloody Shirt scowled. "I took no offense. If I had, you would already be dead." Then he put a hand on Fagen's shoulder and smiled. "I ask you, *amigo*, should either of us be held accountable for the stories people tell?"

Colonel De Castro poured lemonade and offered some to the rebel leader. Torres looked at it as though a glassful of maggots, and then turned his attention back to the American *Capitán*. "General Sandico sends his regards. Since you've joined our cause, he scours Colonel De Castro's dispatches for news of the army's most – how shall I say it – extraordinary freedom fighter."

"I'm sure the General has better things to occupy his time, but when you next see him, please convey my good wishes."

"You are too modest, *Capitán*! Why wouldn't the professor-turned-general have time to study the activities of *El Presidente's* handpicked revolutionary? You're not just any other officer, *Señor*. You came into our midst bearing quite an influential pedigree. I myself have met *Presidente* Aguinaldo only once, and that was at an affair of state. My relationship with our supreme commander is purely professional. I've had no opportunity to make friends as you have. Perhaps someday, you and he will allow me to join you for tea and fellowship. We can exchange views on making war."

Fagen knew his innocent slip of the tongue had placed him on the wrong side of Colonel Vicente Torres. Unintentional, he was sorry for it and had apologized. No need for Torres to taunt him. His whole life Fagen had what was sometimes called a "long fuse." His native tendency to turn the other cheek had gotten him through some tight situations, but as Ellis Fairbanks once said, things change, and right then Fagen decided, bloody shirt or none, if that man wanted a fight, he'd not back away. Colonel De Castro had gone pale. Their visitor's capacity for violent rages was legendary. He sensed the danger and took a tentative step forward. "Please, gentlemen. Let's be seated."

Torres ignored him. The two men faced each other three feet apart, their eyes locked. Fagen lifted his chin. "I already know your view of making war, Colonel." Torres blinked, arched a brow. As forbidding as the man was, he expressed everything through his eyes, and Fagen found he could read him like a book. "I know it includes robbing and humiliating innocent American women." Fagen watched him try to recall, searching his memory, uncertainty momentarily on his face. He decided to help. "Merilee Shaw."

Fagen saw an array of emotion cross his brow, the man's entire thought process there to see if a person had the courage to look. Then Torres did the last thing Fagen expected. His feet shoulder width apart, fists balled on his hips just above his pistol belt, he took a deep breath, threw his head back and laughed. Not just a laugh, but an exultant, jubilant roar from the depths of his iron gut that filled the tent and sounded like barrels rolling around in a basement. Face to the ceiling, tears in his eyes, his entire frame convulsed with laughter. "Heaven be praised!"

Colonel De Castro, too afraid to join in and too afraid not to, cleaned his spectacles, smiled weakly and whispered, "Huzza!"

Still chortling, Torres finally said, "*Señor Capitán* David Fagen, You are a delight! Now I know the wellspring of your patriotic zeal! My journey here is rendered worthwhile. Tell me, what news of Miss Shaw? I trust she battles with us still from her comfortable apartment in Boston? Quite an imposing woman, she's possessed of many qualities and virtues I find admirable in a man."

Fagen couldn't keep up with the man. Too unpredictable, his thought patterns too capricious, mood swings too erratic. Right then, Fagen didn't care who summoned whom. He decided it time to end the interview and get away from Colonel Bloody Shirt before something popped out of him no one could control. "If you're through with me, Colonel Torres, I have my duties to attend to."

In an instant, the man's face turned hard, and the muscles in his neck rippled. "Not quite through, *Señor Capitán*. I've brought you a gift."

At that, he faced the tent opening and barked an order. Two soldiers entered dragging the body of a white man, which they dropped roughly at Fagen's feet. Naked, filthy, his emaciated body was covered head to toe with bruises and lacerations. His arms lay akimbo in the dirt, broken at the elbows, the joints black and distended. The fingers of both hands bloody and swollen, the nails were gone. Large patches of hair had been ripped from his scalp, and his front teeth were missing. Colonel De Castro felt for a pulse. "He's alive, but not by much."

Fagen turned him over. Deep bruises around his throat, rope burns. Numerous ugly penetration marks around the groin, he'd been tattooed. Fagen had never seen a man so horribly tortured. He pried open an eye, deep blue, like looking through a hole in the clouds. That's when he recognized him. He'd been so shocked by the man's pitiable condition, so horrified by the violence inflicted upon him, it hadn't occurred he might know him. When he peered into that cold, blue eye and realized who it was, the air went out of him, and a thousand memories flooded in. Captain Baston.

"He said he had information vital to our cause, but he'd only talk to you. My men did their best to persuade him to tell me. I wanted to – how shall I say it – spare you this nasty business, but even at this hour, he remains stubborn in his refusal to cooperate. I give him credit for *grit*, as the Americans say, but I wash my hands of him. He's yours now to do with what you wish."

Bloody Shirt gave another order to his men, and then followed them out. Pausing at the door, he turned and glowered down his nose. "One more thing, *Señor Capitán* David Fagen. I hear there's a price on your head. Remain vigilant. There's no end to what some people will do for money."

Fagen slept. Miguel awakened him at twilight. "*Capitán* Fagen, you must come to the infirmary."

"Is it the American prisoner?"

"No, sir. Please hurry, sir."

A throng of men ten deep hovered around the hospital tent murmuring among themselves, straining to get a look inside. The young medic shouted "*bumawi, bumawi,*" and the curious soldiers fell silent and let them through. Inside, a single lamp burned low, its feeble, flickering rays swallowed up by dark shadow. Miguel's assistant stood when they entered, but turned away, his face a mask. Frightened and consumed with foreboding, Fagen willed himself across the room to the operating table.

Nothing in his experience, nothing he'd seen in life, done, or even heard of could have prepared him for the shock of seeing Clarita lying wounded on that hospital bed. Fear and rage ravaged his consciousness, exploded in his brain, coursed painfully through his body. He wanted to cry out, summon curses vile enough to render God damned from Heaven for all eternity. He wanted to prostrate himself before Satan and sign a contract for revenge upon Him. Had he committed so many grave sins in his life that he deserved this? Had Clarita? He wanted to stand on top of the world, shake his fist and shout a never-ending stream of profane maledictions at the God who'd permitted this to happen, but he was in a daze, weakened, his brain had exploded and now only smoldered. Vituperation not then in his power, he sat down and asked Miguel, "How bad is she?"

"Bad, *Señor*."

"What can be done for her?"

"Not much. I've given her medication for the pain, but she's bleeding inside."

Fagen placed a hand on Clarita's flushed, feverish brow. She stirred, and then opened her eyes. In the dim light, he saw fear and confusion on her face so he kissed her and said, "You're safe now, my love."

She lifted her hand, the palm warm and moist. Fagen held it tight, rested his head next to hers on the pillow and tried to comfort her while she drifted in and out of consciousness. In a moment, he felt her hand move, the slightest pressure of one finger. He rose up and looked into her beautiful face. "Don't ever leave me," she said, and then closed her eyes.

Miguel hurriedly checked her pulse, listened to her heart. "She sleeps."

"How did this happen?"

The assistant left the tent and returned a few seconds later in the company of a shabbily dressed, shoeless, graybeard of a man. "This is Sofio, *Capitán*, one of the new recruits with Clarita when the attack occurred."

Hat in hand, the old man tentatively approached Clarita's sickbed, deep sadness in his eyes as he bowed his head in silent prayer. Fagen seized the old man's hands. "Sofio. Tell me."

"In the long valley south of here, *Señor*. We knew where the Americans camped. We heard their singing and thought we would pass well clear of their position. One of their guards saw us and shot his rifle. I don't know why he was out that far, *Señor*. It was dark, maybe he was lost."

Miguel thanked Sofio, and then dismissed him. As the old man turned to leave, he scanned the scalpels, clamps and bone saws on the hospital bench. He paused, hands trembling, knuckles white on the brim of his hat. "Excuse me, *manggagamot*, I would like to ask whether you know my sons, Meno and Pio." His eyes locked on the grisly tools of the doctor's trade, he added, "Whether they've been here to see you." David Fagen felt the old man's pain. He'd seen it in the faces of hundreds of Filipinos who'd suffered from the war. Under ordinary circumstances, he'd sympathize, but just then all he cared about was his own selfish grief, all he had room for, and he wanted that man to take his problems elsewhere.

More charitable, Miguel put his arm around the old man's shoulders and guided him to the door. "Return to your company, Uncle. I am busy now. Later, I will try to remember."

Time dragged. Each precious, agonizing hour Fagen spent at Clarita's bedside depleted his emotional and mental reserves. Lost in fog, sinking into madness, he knew he had to bear up even though every passing second took him closer to his own private hell on earth, life without the only woman he'd ever loved.

Fagen lay beside Clarita and held her in his arms. Before he left them, Miguel had propped the bed up to keep the fluid in her lungs from rising, but it was no use, each bubbly, rattling breath was more difficult than the last. Fagen didn't know whether she could hear, but felt an overpowering need to talk to her, to connect before it was too late. He rested his head on her pillow and whispered in her ear. He talked about their lives together, starting with the day they'd first met in San Isidro. He reminded her of the good times they'd shared and asked whether she remembered this incident or that. He told her a thousand times how much he loved her and promised he'd love her as long as he lived. He vowed that after this life they'd be together for eternity.

Later, Colonel De Castro tapped on the tent post, and then entered. Ashen-faced, eyes red and swollen, he stood at the opening and said, "Forgive me, *Capitán*. Some people wish to pay their respects."

Fagen didn't want any visitors. Nobody loved Clarita as much, and he wasn't about to share the few remaining hours. He started to object when the little colonel pushed the tent flap back and Fagen saw *Sargento*

257

Canizares standing in the shadows just outside with one hundred and eighty-five men, his entire company in single file behind him. Fagen's heart melted. Of course, those men loved her too, their grief no less genuine than his. They deserved the opportunity to unburden their troubled minds. He nodded consent, and one by one, the men stepped forward, identified themselves, and then said a few words to Clarita.

"This is Pablo. We want you back with us. Get well soon."

"Clarita, this is Ambrosio speaking. We all love you and wait for your return."

"The revolution needs you, Clarita. *We* need you."

Two hours passed before the last soldier took his turn at the entrance to the hospital tent. When finished, Canizares told the men there was nothing more to be done and ordered them back to the company area.

Miguel and another man entered the infirmary at dawn. "This is Father Diaz," Miguel said. "He is here to say the Viaticum." The priest was a little, grim faced man with deep-set eyes and a long, aquiline nose. Ignoring Miguel's introduction, he went directly to the table beside Clarita's bed, donned a silk scarf, and then spread the rest of his priestly paraphernalia. Fagen didn't like it. The man moved too fast, assumed too much authority, and besides, Clarita hadn't asked for a priest. Fagen stood up and blocked his way.

Diaz stopped in his tracks and let go an annoyed sigh, a dismissive look on his long face, as though he confronted a tiresome child. Miguel came between the two men. "*Capitán* Fagen, Father Diaz has traveled many miles to perform the Anointing of the Sick. It is the seed of eternal life. Clarita herself would have asked him if she were able." Fagen backed off. The medic was right, he thought. Just because he'd declared war on God was no reason to drag Clarita into it.

The priest mumbled over Clarita's bed for five minutes, made crosses in the air and periodically kissed his Bible. Then he passed a wafer under her nose and wet her lips with a few drops of wine. His service done, he glanced at Fagen down his long nose, and then said to Miguel, "The Church will provide what is lacking."

Another hour passed, and Clarita stirred. Fagen saw her chest heave in a desperate struggle for air, so he sat her up and rested her head on his shoulder. Her breath came in short strangulated puffs. She clutched Fagen's hand and murmured softly, "I love you, my darling."

Fagen gently lifted her head, and Clarita opened her eyes. No fear, only deep sorrow for a life that could have been. She held him in her gaze for as long as she could, but her lungs full, there was no more room for air. Pillows of pink foam formed at the corners of her mouth. She made one last, laborious attempt at breath, and then her heart stopped.

Fagen held her tighter, tried to shake life back into her. "Clarita, try again! Don't give up. I'll help, we'll breath together!" Finally, he realized it was no use. Clarita was dead and nothing anyone could do would change that. He laid her head back on the pillow, held her hands and cried while her warm, rosy color shifted to pale white.

"I wondered how long you'd keep me here tied up like a dog," he said when Fagen stepped into his tent. Miguel had splinted his fractured arms and they were useless, so the guards had chained his ankles and considered that good enough. He looked like hell, every part of his body bruised, broken or bleeding, infections from head to toe, but he'd been fed and watered, and quickly recovered his capacity for hatred. He looked up at Fagen and sneered. "I heard they put your little Filipina split-tail in the ground a couple of days ago. What a shame, my condolences."

"Careful, Captain. I snap my fingers and you're dead."

"For the record, it's Major Baston now, but why should you care? You possess the absolute power of life or death. Wonderful, isn't it? It's what makes the world go around, and you possess it now, just as I once did." The American glanced down at his naked, ravaged body, "but like a beautiful woman continually changing partners, you cannot own it!"

Fagen didn't need that monster to remind him of destiny's capricious nature. He'd been fate's whipping boy as long as he could remember. He was just glad the man hadn't spoken her name, probably didn't even know it, but even if he did, he had no right to utter the syllables. The memories were Fagen's, and he didn't have to share. The name his too, if the word "Clarita" had escaped the major's lips, he'd have finished him then and there.

Fagen didn't attend the funeral. When she died in his arms that morning, something inside let go, and when they finally got him under control, five men held him down while Miguel administered the sedative. He awoke two days later. The services over, he lay at her gravesite for hours, overwhelmed by the grief, anger and sorrow that percolated within him and at last burst forth and soaked into the blanket of flowers surrounding her grave. Fagen thought that would heal his tormented soul, but he was wrong. During the day, everything he looked at, touched, smelled and tasted told him Clarita was dead. At night, his every thought was prefaced and punctuated by an inner voice reminding him Clarita was dead. Slowly, he realized he'd never let her go, she'd always be with him, and the only peace he'd find was in his own death.

"Don't just stand there, man! Take these chains off so we can get out of here."

"What?"

Baston lifted his legs, "The fetters! Remove them immediately! You don't expect me to walk out of this god-forsaken jungle shackled like a circus elephant."

"I don't expect you to walk out at all."

"What are you saying, man? You bet I'm walking out, and you're going with me – as my prisoner, of course."

"*Your* prisoner? You must be insane."

The major sat up, rested his broken arms on his knees, a fire glowed in his eyes. Still an imposing man despite the weight he'd lost and his deplorable condition. "Look here, Fagen, we've got no bad blood between us. Think back. What'd I ever do to you? Nothing! Did you ever see me abuse a colored man? No!

"I realize an enlisted soldier doesn't love an officer. Hell, that's the army, but that only goes so far." Baston paused, thinking it over. "Truth be known, it's probably not natural for a colored to love a white, and vice versa. We all stick with our own kind, that's natural too. It's not my fault there's differences between us, it's the way God made us, but after everything's said and done, aren't we Americans first?"

Fagen turned his back and faced the wall, too drained of feeling to respond. Baston continued, seemingly drawing strength from Fagen's weakness, a vampire as well as a demon of destruction. "Consider this. We go back together, and I'll work to get the charges against you reduced. I'll tell them you saved my life. We'll say you were a prisoner too, forced on pain of death to serve the rebel cause. We were both captives, but together we pooled our resources and managed to outwit the enemy. You'll be reinstated. I can get you a promotion, maybe even a medal. Do you hear me, man? A commendation! Picture yourself walking down Main Street in your home town wearing a shiny medal."

There had been a time when Fagen feared Major Baston, paid attention to everything he said, if for no other reason than to avoid crossing his path. Now no longer the case, now the white man was shit-scared, dodging the inevitable, prattling on about the glorious future he could engineer. Fagen wasn't buying. He walked over and leaned in close. "Do you think that's what I want, a copper disk on my chest? A trinket on a ribbon to show the world I was a good little soldier-boy? If that's what you believe, then you're even more ignorant and insensitive than I'd thought."

Baston realized he was on the wrong tack and looked away, his turn to face the wall. Finally, he said, "I could order you to release me, Private. Technically, you're still the property of the United States Army, and I outrank you by a mile. To refuse is a hanging offense."

"Give all the orders you want, Major. You can only hang a man once, and as I recall, you've already made those arrangements."

"God damn you and your impertinence! You villainous bastard! By all that's sacred, I'll live to see you before a firing squad."

"You're going to have to try very hard just to live until sunrise. In fact, the only reason you're still breathing now is because Colonel Torres said you had information important to the revolution. Let's have it."

Baston reached out and pulled a corner of his blanket over his legs. He needed to cover his shriveled manhood to regain his composure, if not his dignity. Importunity and intimidation having failed, it was time for negotiation. "Supposing I do have certain information," he tried to smile, but swollen lips and broken teeth turned it into a hideous grimace, "what do I get in return?"

"Why should I give you anything?"

"Come on, Fagen. You know how the world works. *Quid pro quo.* I scratch your back, you scratch mine."

"The question still applies. Why should I give you something in exchange for information I can just take?"

"So that's how it is." Baston glared, unfazed by the threat. "I assure you, you traitorous whoreson, if that murdering savage Torres couldn't get me to talk, you won't either. Besides, you haven't got the stomach for his method of interrogation."

Fagen walked to the front of the tent and opened the flap. Sargento Canizares and a platoon of riflemen snapped to attention. He looked back at his prisoner and said, "I don't know Colonel Torres' methods of interrogation, Major Baston, but I know yours. *Sargento* Canizares, prepare the water cure!"

Canizares gave an order and the Filipino riflemen scattered. Gleeful shouts of "Prepare the water cure!" and *"Prepare el tormento de agua!"* echoed throughout the camp.

Baston flushed, and then turned pale and his whole body trembled. Suddenly unconcerned with his injuries, he let out a savage cry and lunged for the opening, but the heavy leg chains pulled him violently to the ground.

"FAGEN, NO!" he screamed, his voice as barbed and serrated as a rusty bolo. "Please! I beg you to have mercy!" Tears welled up, and then rolled out the corners of his swollen eyes, little muddy pools formed on the dirt floor beneath his cheeks. Wave after wave of convulsive sobs racked his body. His bladder and bowels let go simultaneously, fouling the air in the tent. Weeping turned to wailing when he heard the men outside repeat, "*Prepare el tormento de agua!*" "Prepare the water cure!"

When he hit the floor, he'd shattered the splint on his left arm and the bone snapped again, this time puncturing the skin just below his left biceps, but he didn't seem to notice. Fagen knelt over his prostrate body, gripped a handful of hair and whispered in his ear. "I don't make deals with men who try to murder me, Baston. If you've got something to say, you'd better start talking fast."

"For God's sake, man, have mercy on me!"

Sargento Canizares entered with three men. "We're ready, *Capitán.*"

"Take him."

Canizares unlocked the leg irons, and the Filipino soldiers got the major to his feet and dragged him outside.

"Fagen, make them stop!"

Fagen stood outside the tent and watched the Filipinos dance around the notorious American, finding hideous joy in their opportunity for revenge... "*Prepare el tormento de agua!*"

Just as they reached the dark jungle that bordered their camp, Baston looked back and wailed. "It's General Funston. He's gone after Aguinaldo."

Fagen held up his hand and called for the company sergeant to wait. Fagen knew a desperate Major Baston would say anything to avoid the water cure, but Funston after Aguinaldo? That wasn't news. Fighting Freddie had been after *El Presidente* for two years. There had to be more to it than that. "Bring him back."

Fagen asked *Sargento* Canizares to witness and a company clerk to take notes while Baston said his piece, and glad he did because the story was almost too fantastic to believe. Impressed with the detail he provided, Fagen paid close attention to what the man said because it was a tall tale, an unlikely yarn to spin on the spur of the moment and too easily verified to be of use if false.

After the major told his story, Fagen summoned Atias and Marthee, his Igorrote bodyguards who'd hardly been out of his field of vision since that terrible afternoon at Sampaloc. When they entered, Baston shrunk back into a corner and blubbered. "You're turning me over to those savages? After everything I've told you? I've lived up to my end of the bargain. I've given you information that can end this war! Fagen, think about it. Capture General Frederick Funston and negotiations for peace begin the same day!"

Fagen issued instructions to the Igorrotes in the pidgin-sign they'd worked out, and then Marthee stepped forward. Fagen turned to the major. "This man will get you safely through the jungle. When you reach a large crevasse, a ravine, you'll find a native suspension bridge. Cross it, and you're on your own from there." Fagen nodded to Marthee.

The little scout stood on one foot and leaned on his bow. He smiled, helped the major to his feet and murmured under his breath, "Owuooo!"

As the two men left the tent, Fagen ordered Baston to stop. "Now you see, Major, there's a fine line between patriot and traitor. Sometimes it disappears altogether. Which are you today?"

Atias gave Fagen an inquiring look, his eyes asking the question for him, *what will we do next, Capitán?*

"Atias, do you know the way to Palanan?"

CHAPTER 24 - PALANAN

Segovia circulated among the men and made mental notes of the problems that lay before them. General Funston had ordered him to leave Casigurian that morning, and he intended to obey. Just after dawn, the village headman roused the entire population to see them off, and as an added display of his support for the revolution, detailed a party of three tribesmen to accompany them on the march to Palanan.

The Spaniard had been only moderately successful in acquiring provisions for their journey. Aguinaldo regularly sent men to collect food from the surrounding hamlets, and to impress *El Presidente*, the loyal people of Casigurian barely kept enough to feed themselves. However, Cecelio Segismundo, taking advantage of his friendship with the village chief, arranged for yet another donation from the population. Pleading with the peasants to consider a higher purpose, together they collected two-dozen bags of rice, onions, sweet potatoes and cracked corn. Also, pursuant to the general's instructions, Segovia had purchased a hundred pounds of salted *carabao*. Not much for ninety-one men on a strenuous five-day march, and every moment they delayed put the successful completion of their mission in greater peril.

Leaving Casigurian behind, the party struggled through miles of leathery, waist-high scrub, interrupted now and then by muddy rice paddies. As they traveled north into the foothills, the terrain rose under their feet, and they soon found themselves in a dense forest. Huge trees, their gigantic trunks covered in moss, grew ramrod straight, and then disappeared in the triple canopy high overhead. No trail to follow, the men hacked for hours through a seemingly impenetrable tangle of clinging vines and thick, gristly leafstalk.

Segovia had thought Talplacido unwise to accept the three scouts offered by the Casigurian headman. During their march, the Spaniard assumed they'd be observed from behind every rock and tree, and his orders had been for every man to stay in "character." Indigenous personnel in their midst only increased the odds someone among them would make a mistake. Their imposter status revealed, the fastest runners would get word to Aguinaldo, and their entire party would end up in the same mass grave.

Nearly as upsetting was that he couldn't communicate with General Funston as frequently as he wished. He'd wanted the general's permission to keep marching, to not stop until out of that God-forsaken jungle. Segovia understood the perilous nature of their situation. The terrain punished the men, took too much out of them. The Macabebes carrying the food and provisions were already strung out a half-mile and struggled to keep up. Hilario Talplacido whined constantly, mopped his brow and swore he was dying with every step. The Americans seemed to fare better, but the general's face had turned an unpleasant shade of gray, and Segovia worried about him. The tribal guides said they'd be through the worst of the jungle by nightfall, and Segovia wasn't about to stop until he saw blue sky overhead.

By late afternoon, the forest thinned, and the party descended a gentle slope into a wide glade crisscrossed by a narrow, meandering stream. Segovia signaled, and Talplacido ordered the column to set up camp for the night. A steady rain fell, so the Macabebes split into groups, gathered palm fronds and forest leaves to build shelters. The Casigurian men set up their own camp some distance away.

Watched over by a Macabebe corporal, General Funston and the other Americans took shelter under a massive hardwood tree by the creek's edge. Segovia joined them, relieved the guard of his Mauser and whispered, "I need to speak with the general, go have your supper, but return when you see my signal."

"How goes the battle, Lazaro?" Funston asked, a faint smile on his lips. The general saw the strain of command in the Spaniard's eyes and derived sadistic pleasure in observing it in someone else.

"The men are well, General, except for that cow Talplacido. He blubbers like a baby with every step."

"You can't worry about him now. We've got to get those village guides away from our Macs. It's not possible to keep up this ruse around the clock. One slip of the tongue by anyone and our goose is cooked."

"I agree, sir. Shall I kill them tonight while they sleep?"

"I see no way around it. We're into this thing now, on dangerous ground, and failure is not an option. Segismundo can get us to Palanan."

Segovia ordered plates of food taken to the Americans. He hadn't eaten since the night before in Casigurian, but the Macabebes weren't finished, and as officers eat last in the field, he went looking for Talplacido to fill him in on the latest plan. He found the counterfeit colonel snoring under a makeshift shelter, the greasy remains of his supper still on his chin. Too odious to bother with, the Spaniard decided to conduct a final check of the camp, and then eat and retire.

As he walked the perimeter, he heard the Macabebes squabbling among themselves around the cook fire. Soon, they started pushing and shoving, the situation spinning rapidly out of control. Segovia pushed into their midst. "What's going on here? What are you men doing?"

What he saw in the firelight stopped him in his tracks. Talplacido had failed to put guards on the provisions, and the Macs had helped themselves. Every bag had been opened and raided. A twenty-pound slab of partially cooked *carabao* had been knocked off the spit during the ruckus and lay sizzling in the hot ashes. "You idiots!" the Spaniard screamed, "we have a four day march in front of us! We'll starve!"

Impossible to tell then how much they'd devoured, but even as Segovia drew his pistol and threatened to kill anyone that moved, men still grabbed for more, and then stole away into the darkness. Later, when he'd taken inventory, he found only six bags of rice remained and less than ten pounds of meat. Eighty per cent of their provisions for the entire journey had been consumed in one night. He'd been worried about their minimal food supply when they departed Casigurian, wondered whether they'd collected enough from the villagers. Now, no need for worry. The ignorant, undisciplined Macs had rendered starvation a certainty.

Segovia lay on the hard ground, exhausted but unable to sleep. Having had their glutinous fill, he was fairly confident none of the Macabebes would risk any more theft. Notwithstanding, he placed guards on one-hour rotation with orders to shoot anyone who came near their meager cache of supplies.

The rain had stopped, but gray monsoon clouds ghosted across the sky above. Segovia had one more job that night, but waited until the moon's silver light chilled the northeastern horizon before he made his move. Segismundo met him at the edge of camp accompanied by four handpicked Macs armed with daggers and bolos. In three teams of two, the men crawled on their bellies into the camp of the Casigurian guides.

Segovia had no real compunction about killing the tribesmen, they were pro-revolution and therefore anti-American, but they'd seemed like decent, inoffensive young men, so he'd resolved to make their deaths as quick and painless as possible. One chop to the neck from a Macabebe bolo, and it would be over. The men crept into the camp, weapons at the ready, only to find it empty. The food gone, the Casigurian guides had deserted. Disappointed at not finding someone to kill, the Macabebes cursed, kicked at the dying campfire and sent embers flying into the night.

At dawn, Segovia briefed General Funston on the events of the previous night. "I'd like your permission to execute that fat, lazy Filipino, sir. It is his fault this has happened."

"No it's not, it's yours," the general snapped. "Talplacido's your man. You selected him for this mission."

The Spaniard stammered, "But, sir, I had so little time…"

"Never mind! No more excuses. We play the hand we're dealt. I'd kill the gook bastard myself if we didn't need him."

"I agree, sir."

"Let's get this band of cutthroats moving."

David Fagen followed Atias into the steep mountains and narrow valleys of northeastern Luzon for two days and nights, but remembered little. A lost, silent, disembodied spirit, without substance or form, his very existence depended upon the unquestioning, unfailing loyalty of his Igorrote friend. Atias, both father and son to the tormented Fagen, fed him, kept him moving until time to stop, and then helped him sleep. The little warrior had no need for words. With gentle, knowing hands, he guided his Negrito Americano cousin over slippery mountain trails, across rivers, beneath the thick canopies of ancient forests and through underbrush so thick the smallest rodents couldn't penetrate. During the day, an angry, vengeful God sent hot rays from the sun to burn their skin and boil their brains. At night, stinging rain fell and brought a numbing, wet cold. Through it all, Atias remained a steadfast, constant custodian, Fagen's welfare his only concern.

Insensible to the outside world, like a mechanical man, Fagen put one foot in front of the other and kept Atias in sight. Life, death, good and evil had joined forces to shock his system, deliver blow after crippling blow and finally render him benumbed, stupefied. The moment a conscious thought worked through the blackness in his brain, a haunting, persistent voice came with it that said *Clarita is dead, Clarita is dead, Clarita is dead,* and he willed himself back into the safety of his oblivion.

What Fagen experienced then wasn't only grief. He'd grieved at Clarita's gravesite, held nothing back, left most of his anguish there. He'd weep for her until his last breath. More than just deep sadness, Fagen's conscious mind had retreated from the consuming moral and ethical chaos, the madness, he saw around him. In his world Pandemonium ruled, anarchy the High Sheriff. Nothing as it should be. No answers, because not even the questions made sense.

Atias' internal compass kept them headed in the right direction, skirting native villages along the way. They fed on edible tubers while marching and rubbed on garlic to keep the insects away. Once, in the deepest jungle, a snarling panther dropped from a tree and blocked the trail. Instantly and without concern for his own safety, Atias charged the animal, screamed at the top of his lungs and clapped his hands until the frightened and confused cat retreated.

On the afternoon of the third day, the men arrived at a little clearing in the forest next to a rushing mountain stream, and Atias made camp. Helpless, Fagen sat while his trusted friend constructed two small shelters next to the fire, and then prepared supper. Atias took a small quantity of rice from a woven bag and several thin strips of salted monkey meat. When the fire had burned down, he cut a trapdoor in a length of green bamboo, poured in the rice and an equal amount of water, then put the door back and placed the bamboo in the coals. He threaded the meat on a long stick and while it roasted, filled their canteens and gathered firewood. The two men ate in silence. Only the night sounds of jungle creatures intruded.

Later, Fagen lay quietly under the leafy roof of his shelter. No moon or stars overhead, the night was perfect blackness. Atias made a lamp with a chunk of gutta percha sap from a nearby tree wrapped in a huge green leaf. He lit it and placed it carefully on a log above Fagen's head. Its yellow light warmed the shelter and cast an ethereal glow that reflected dully in the stricken man's eyes. Then the Igorrote squatted by the fire, threw in a few sticks and spoke for the first time in three days.

Atias believed deeply in the power of magic, and he knew from experience a man troubled in the head could only be cured if the gods interceded. No chanting, agitated medicine man with greasy salves and irritating balms could help his friend. He'd have to call the gods forth, entertain them, and then beg for their help.

In his strange, singsong dialect, Atias recited an ancient, mystical legend of the mountains, *Why The Dead Come Back No More*. Hour after hour, he spoke into the fire invoking the names of all the great spirits that lived in the clouds above the highest peaks. He told the story over and over, repeating certain lines and passages for emphasis, until he was sure every god had been equally catered to.

A very long time ago, when the hills and rivers and trees were new, a woman lived with her three children. She was a good woman, and she loved her children very much. She loved them so much that each day she went into the valley fields to work until sundown just to be able to feed them. One day, the woman fell ill, and in a short time, she died. Her spirit went to Kadungayan, of course, because she had lived a good and virtuous life. But she was not happy in paradise. Her only thoughts were of her children whom she'd left on earth, and she worried that no one cared for them, and they might be hungry and cold. As she could find no peace, she decided to go back to earth.

When she reached her home, she called out to her children to open the door. Recognizing their mother's voice, the children immediately obeyed. The woman entered and spoke to her loved ones, but she could not see them because their fire had gone out and the room was so very dark and cold. The children had not built a fire since their mother had died. They were too young and did not know how.

The woman sent her eldest child to beg for fire from the neighbors. The shivering child went to the first house, but when he told them his mother had returned and wanted the fire, the people just laughed and would not give it to him. He then went to the next house, but the same thing happened. Thus, he went from house to house, but no one would believe his mother had come back from the dead. They thought the poor child had gone out of his mind. So the boy went home without the fire. The woman was very angry with all the unkind people. She asked herself, "Are my children to die a miserable death just because men are so selfish? Come, my children, let us all go to that better place where I have been – Kadungayan. There are no selfish people there."

The woman filled a jar with water and took it outside in the yard. She shouted into the blackness of night to all the people who were her neighbors. "Listen you selfish people! From this time on all people will follow my example. No man will ever return back to earth after death." With those words, she smashed the jar on a big stone making a frightful sound. All the people heard this and became silent in fear.

The next morning, the people came out to see what had caused the great voice. They saw bits of broken pottery, but the three children were nowhere to be found. They now knew the woman really had come to earth that night, and in her anger at their selfishness, returned to Kadungayan with her three children. The people were very sorry for refusing to help the child, but since that time no dead person has ever come back to earth.

All night long, a parade of god-spirits appeared in their little camp, found amusement, and then departed. Atias felt their presence all around him, but as no mortal could actually look upon a god and live, he kept his eyes tightly shut and moved only when necessary to tap the carbon ash from the lamp by David Fagen's head. First came the god of fire, then wind, then water and so on. Atias paused in his narrative to welcome each spirit by name, thank him for appearing and beg him to return his friend to health. A true believer, the Igorrote's powerful incantations and most humble supplications worked to fill the little clearing by the creek with ghostly manifestations.

At dawn, David Fagen awoke to see his faithful friend squatting next to him smiling. Fagen felt as though someone had lifted a black curtain from before his eyes. "Where are we?"

Atias grinned and made a sign. "Look around you. We're in the jungle."

Sudden dark thoughts of Clarita shot through Fagen's mind, the muscles in his chest constricted, and he found himself gasping for breath. But this time no voice attended, his conscious mind did not flee, and at that moment, he realized for the first time he could live with the crushing sadness of Clarita's death. He sat up, looked around, and then turned to Atias. "Is there time? Can we still make it?"

Atias made a sign. "There is always hope."

On the fourth day, General Funston and his mock insurrectos came out of the forest and marched until midday along several miles of ocean beach. A clear day, the burning sun shone high overhead, and the white-hot sand soon blistered the Macabebes' bare feet. Funston called the column to a halt to permit the tortured stragglers, starved, exhausted and in pain, to catch up. The Casigurian guides gone, the American again took command of the landing force, keeping to his disguise of submissive prisoner in appearance only.

Following the general's instructions, Lazaro Segovia issued that day's nourishment, a single cupful of rice boiled with the bones of two chickens left over from their first day on the march. While the men gobbled their meager repast, the Spaniard berated them for their gluttony, shortsightedness and careless disregard for the success of the mission and announced thenceforth everyone would be placed on quarter rations. The Macabebes sat in silent, sullen compliance while the Spaniard talked of the hardships that lay before them and threatened the most severe punishment for the slightest transgression.

Funston's gaze fell upon the two American officers beside him picking unenthusiastically at their rice stew. Harry Newton appeared to be holding up, but Burton Mitchell, seemingly invincible at the onset of the journey, looked ill and complained of stomach problems and loss of strength. Perhaps he should have selected a more seasoned man, the general thought to himself and made a promise to keep an eye on the boy.

In point of fact, little more than half way through their march, the general wrestled constantly with second thoughts and creeping doubts. He'd been a fool to rely on the narcissistic Segovia. Funston told himself he should have retained more control. Even under the watchful, suspicious scrutiny of the Casigurian guides, he should have found a way to do the Spaniard's thinking for him. Now, without food, alone in enemy territory, the general recalled MacArthur's words the day he'd briefed him on his plan, "Nothing you come up with surprises me anymore, Freddie." Music to his ears then, Funston wondered now whether MacArthur's then flattering comment had meant something else entirely.

Funston lamented the missed opportunities. They'd only been one day out of Casigurian when those ignorant Macs raided their food supply. Perhaps they should have gone back and re-provisioned. No doubt they'd have needed force, perhaps even to raze the village. The local peasants had precious little for themselves, they'd have fought to the death. Better them than us, the general thought. Now, the whole mission was in jeopardy, compromised because of hunger and fatigue. Funston saw no remedy but to go on, but how? Travel slower, conserve strength and starve, or move faster, become enfeebled and collapse with exhaustion? The mission all that mattered, he cared little about the cost. If their adventure was star-crossed, it was the fault of idiots and savages. He'd not let their incompetence deprive him of what was rightfully his. He'd capture Aguinaldo single handedly if he had to. Segovia's shrill, lisping shouts brought Funston out of his reverie.

He looked down the beach and saw the Spanish turncoat lean into Hilario Talplacido's red, sweating face. "Get up you pig! Have you no shame?"

The portly Filipino narcotics dealer and make-believe colonel lay prostrate in the sand, blubbering and exhausted from the march. "Lazaro, have mercy! I can't go another step. Leave me on the trail to die. I beg you to have pity. Segismundo tells me a difficult mountain lies in our path just ahead. I'll never make it."

Disdainful of the miserable creature at his feet, Segovia snarled, "If we didn't need you, you'd already be dead."

An idea suddenly struck Talplacido, and he rose up on one elbow. "I'll pay. I have money!" He reached into his shirt and pulled out a fistful of bills. "Surely you can't object if I pay."

Segovia spat in the dirt, and then feigned a kick to the fat man's belly. Talplacido gasped, opened both hands to protect his flabby midsection, and peso notes fluttered in a circle around him. "Ask these men to carry you like some Roman emperor? You're supposed to be their commander. What will they think?"

The Filipino waved generally in the direction of the imitation insurrectos. "My men love me. It pains them to see me in distress. Besides, when has a Macabebe refused the opportunity to pocket a little silver?"

"Your men! Love you? If they knew you carried that much currency, they'd have killed you themselves and saved me the trouble." The Spaniard turned his back and walked away, sending a final warning over his shoulder. "This column marches in ten minutes with or without you."

General Funston gave the order to get underway, and the invaders dragged themselves to their feet, four of the strongest transporting the suffering Hilario Talplacido on a makeshift litter.

In two hours, they came to it. A huge fortress wall of black granite, one hundred feet high, extended into the sea and completely blocked their path. Talplacido groaned. Not even the strongest men could carry him up the sheer cliff. He dropped to the ground and begged for death.

Funston ordered the stronger men to climb first, find the most favorable route to the top, and then assist the weaker men following. Five hours remained before sundown. A difficult, dangerous climb under the best of circumstances, in their weakened condition a nighttime ascent meant certain death. As the column began the slow trek up the rock face, the courier, Segismundo, gave the general more bad news. "We must reach the top and descend to the beach on the other side or we will lose a day to the ocean tides."

All afternoon, the men struggled to reach the summit. Once there, they briefly rested, and then marshaled the strength to hazard the treacherous descent in the darkness just after sunset under a heavy monsoon cloudburst. Later, on the beach, a few of the men made palm leaf shelters to protect against the rain. Others, beyond exhaustion, fell paralyzed to the sand and slept exposed to the elements.

Dawn broke cold and wet. Segovia detailed several men to gather driftwood for cook fires, while others searched the beach for clams, mussels and crayfish – anything edible to go into the stew pots. The soldiers moved like zombies, their joints stiff, minds benumbed. When boiled, the small quantities of shellfish they found did little but turn their heated water into brackish, gray slime. Just the smell of it sent Burton Mitchell into a paroxysm of violent stomach spasms.

Only one day's food supply remained, but Funston knew his men had to have nourishment to get them to their final camp that night, and he ordered half the remaining rations distributed. Barely two thimblefuls of rice, but each soldier clutched his portion in greedy, protective fingers and savored each flyspeck morsel as it went down.

In two hours, the tide rose and forced the column into a huge Mangrove swamp bordered on all sides by a dense, impenetrable jungle. Tormented by clouds of angry, voracious mosquitoes and stinging black flies, the men waded for miles through brown snake-infested water. All day long Lazaro Segovia shadowed the weary soldiers, reminded them of their mission, entreated them to keep moving and resist the temptation to eat the leeches they pulled from their bodies.

By mid-afternoon, the party broke clear of the swamp and saw in the distance a tiny native village built on a rocky outcropping at the edge of the sea. "Dinudungan, sir," Segismundo said. "Aguinaldo maintains an outpost of soldiers there. Palanan lies just beyond those low hills."

They'd done it, the general said to himself. A hundred miles through hostile terrain with no food, and they hadn't lost a man. One for the history books, but he had no time to reflect on that pleasant notion. The most dangerous part of their mission lay before them.

Movement in the village. Funston raised his field glasses and counted twenty heavily armed insurrectos dressed in clean, white uniforms heading their way. "Get Talplacido up here fast."

Palanan, in the province of Isabela, was a little village of nipa-thatched houses situated on the banks of the river bearing the same name and one of the most isolated places in northern Luzon. The only means of communication with the outside world was by rough trails and footpaths over the mountains west to Ilagan, or south to Casigurian.

Having narrowly escaped capture by advancing American forces in the south, Emilio Aguinaldo chose Palanan as his headquarters because of its seclusion and the generous hospitality of his countrymen. He'd remained there several months, directing the revolution by sending coded messages to his commanders through a sophisticated network of couriers and runners.

In his headquarters, Aguinaldo gazed fondly across the conference table at his old friend and Chief of Staff, Colonel Simon Villa. When the general and his cadre fled from the Americans, Villa had made *El Presidente's* safety his personal responsibility and on numerous occasions placed himself in harm's way to shield his commander from danger. Fearless in battle, no one was more dedicated to the struggle, and Aguinaldo knew the months of inactivity in Palanan away from the fighting weighed heavily on his friend's heart. "Besides my staff, how many able-bodied men in camp now, Simon?" the general asked casually.

"Major Alhambra commands forty-five, Emilio. At this time, two are down with fever."

"Add to that the reinforcements sent by General Lacuna, and we have nearly half a battalion."

"That is correct, sir."

"Recently, I've considered a campaign of interdiction in the hills south and east of here, something to keep the Americans off balance and divert their attention away from this lonely outpost. I calculate a hundred men more than enough for this duty, but they'll need an exceptional commander. I wondered whether you could recommend one."

A smile broke out on the colonel's strong, dark face. He leaned quickly forward in his chair, squared his shoulders, but then sat back and studied his hands. "Major Alhambra is an excellent officer, sir."

Aguinaldo stood up, put his hand on his friend's shoulder and smiled. "Simon, I want you to lead these men."

"But, sir, my duty is here with you."

"I love you for your loyalty, my friend, but your talents are squandered in the role of bodyguard. I think we will both be happier with you in the field protecting this headquarters from sneak attack."

A tap on the door, and Dr. Santiago Barcelona entered. A quiet, sophisticated man, the doctor had served in the *Katipunan* with Aguinaldo in the early days of the revolution. The general handed him a cup of tea. "What news of the replacements, doctor?"

"Just a few minutes behind me, *Presidente*. Tired from the journey, half starved, but otherwise none the worse for wear. It seems they had problems rationing their provisions and have been without food for several days. Asked to render a medical opinion, I'd say their officer, Colonel Talplacido, carried it all inside himself."

"What of the American prisoners?"

"Three, sir. Surveyors I'm told. They're to remain under guard on the far side of the river awaiting your instructions."

Aguinaldo turned back to his friend. "Well, Simon. It appears your new men could benefit from discipline training when they recover from their march. You'll be a busy man."

"I can't wait to get started, *Presidente*."

Dr. Barcelona walked to a window, opened a jalousie shutter and pointed. "You won't have to. Here they come now."

The new recruits stood at attention in the plaza in front of *El Presidente's* headquarters. An honor guard consisting of twenty of Major Alhambra's troops there to receive them, when Aguinaldo stepped out, they fired a salute welcoming the reinforcements to Palanan.

Talplacido, looking considerably better after a full night's sleep and three hot meals, gave the command, "Present arms! Colonel Hilario Talplacido reporting for duty, sir!"

Aguinaldo returned the salute. "Your men may stand at ease, Colonel. I would be honored if you and Captain Segovia will join me inside." The officers left the assembled soldiers, Funston's Macabebes, and Aguinaldo's guard, facing each other, fifteen feet apart.

Aguinaldo made the introductions, and Colonel Villa and the doctor warmly greeted the new arrivals. An aide brought cigarettes and tea. "Please, gentlemen, be seated." The general pulled a chair up to face the two men. "You've had a difficult journey. How long were you on the march?"

"Twenty four days, *Presidente*."

"A long march indeed. How fares my friend General Lacuna? Is he well? He speaks highly of you both in his letters."

Taking his cue from Segovia, Talplacido kept his answers brief. "The general sends his regards, sir, and prays we find you in good health."

Simon Villa spoke up. "*Capitán* Segovia, what arms do the men carry?"

"Mausers, sir, Remingtons and a few Krags."

"Ammunition?"

"More than ten thousand rounds." Pleased, Villa lit a cigarette and sat back, already planning his campaign in the south.

Doctor Barcelona opened his mouth to speak, but paused when Segovia stood up. "If you will permit me, *Presidente*, I must attend to the men. They are also in need of rest."

"Of course, *Capitán*, how thoughtless of me." Aguinaldo accompanied the Spaniard to the front porch. "Major Alhambra will show you where the men will be billeted. Rest now. Later, when rations are prepared, you will be notified."

David Fagen heard three volleys of rifle fire, cursed himself for being too late, and then scrambled the last two hundred feet up loose shale to the crest of the hill overlooking Palanan. Two companies of soldiers stood in formation in front of a large house on which flew the flag of the Independent Filipino Republic, Aguinaldo's headquarters. Still too far away to see clearly what was happening, Fagen made a sign, and Atias pointed to a trail leading to the village.

Worried they'd encounter a Filipino patrol and be fired upon as intruders, Fagen covered the last half-mile carefully, keeping to the underbrush. In fifteen minutes, they reached the village, and in another ten, moved unseen to the edge of the central plaza. Fagen counted the soldiers standing at parade rest in the hot sun. One hundred and twenty. Major Baston had said "around ninety" Macabebes in Funston's raiding party. Some of those men must be Aguinaldo's, but which ones?

Not knowing what he'd find when he arrived in Palanan, Fagen had not formulated a plan. He'd hoped to arrive in time to warn Aguinaldo of the plot and see him to safety, but now, peering from behind a native hut with ninety of the enemy within a stone's throw, he realized it didn't matter that he had no plan. The situation was hopeless.

Fagen watched the imposter army before him and tried to decide what to do. Atias hissed, and then pointed to the headquarters building. The door opened and General Aguinaldo stepped out onto the porch. Soldiers snapped to attention. Smiling warmly, El Presidente shook hands with a captain. Fagen didn't know the man. Tall, broad shouldered with sandy, brown hair, certainly no Filipino, it could only be the Spanish turncoat Major Baston had spoken of. Fagen couldn't believe his eyes. Had the ruse worked so well? Had General Emilio Aguinaldo been so utterly deceived? Fagen couldn't permit this to happen. Whatever the cost, he had to warn his commander in chief of the treachery. He was just about to call out when the Spaniard drew his gun and shouted, "Now Macabebes! Give them all you've got!"

In less than a heartbeat, the stillness of the little plaza was shattered by volley after volley of rifle fire, and then punctuated by the screams of panicked and bewildered guerilla soldiers as the bloodthirsty Macabebes decimated their ranks. In seconds, three-dozen Filipino soldiers and civilian villagers lay dead or wounded in the dust.

Hearing the outbreak of gunfire from the other side of the river, General Funston and his men jumped up and raced across. Not to be denied their share of the killing, their Macabebe guards ran through the village shooting at fleeing soldiers and civilians alike.

Aguinaldo stood frozen on the porch, too overcome with bewilderment to move. Through white billowing clouds of gun smoke, Fagen watched the Spaniard turn his pistol on the rebel leader and shout, "Hands up, General! We are not replacements for your insurgent army. We are Americans, surrender or be killed!"

At that moment Simon Villa burst through the door, pistol in his hand. Segovia fired two quick shots, and the brave colonel slumped to the floor. Aguinaldo knelt over his wounded friend, shielding him from further harm and cried out, "Stop! Stop this killing!"

Then, Doctor Barcelona rushed onto the porch waving a white handkerchief. "We surrender, *Capitán*! This is the flag of peace!"

No soldiers left to kill, the Macabebes ended their slaughter, and save for the terrified barking of village dogs, quiet returned to the little plaza. Fagen, stunned by the earth-shaking event he'd just witnessed, was gripped by a deep, gut wrenching sense of loss. He'd raced a hundred miles to save the revolution and failed. His heart fluttered in his chest as he wrestled with thoughts of what would happen next. He'd never even considered a Filipino struggle for independence without Emilio Aguinaldo. It didn't seem possible they could carry on without him. What other man had the intellect, the vision, the iron will? What man was so beloved, so revered? Who else could inspire an ignorant, peasant population armed with little more than bolo knives and nipa sheaves to wage a death struggle against a nation as powerful as the United States?

On seeing General Funston's approach through a window, Hilario Talplacido, who'd thrown himself to the floor when the shooting started, now rushed outside and grasped Aguinaldo's arm. "I have captured the villain, sir!"

Ignoring him, Funston bounded up the porch steps, faced the Filipino President and declared, "You are a prisoner of the army of the United States. I am Brigadier General Fredrick Funston, commander of this expedition. You've been ordered to surrender. I suggest you order your men to do the same. Unless I have your full and immediate cooperation, my soldiers will finish what they've started here."

Aguinaldo lifted his chin and returned the American's gaze. "So be it, General." Then he pushed past him and walked to the center of the plaza, the bloody bodies of his countrymen scattered around him. Fagen watched in silent dismay while the man who'd promised him a future stood at attention in the dust with tears in his eyes and cried out, "I,

Presidente Emilio Aguinaldo, commander of all national forces, now entreat every Filipino patriot to lay down his arms. Enough of killing! Enough of blood! Enough of tears and desolation! Henceforth, let every man seek peace."

General Funston and the other Americans escorted Aguinaldo into the headquarters building. The Spaniard gave an order, and the Macabebes began a house-to-house search of the village. Seeing nothing more to be done, and concerned for their safety, Atias tugged at Fagen's sleeve and made a sign.

He was right, there was nothing more to be done. The revolution was over. Millions of Filipinos prayed every day for the killing to stop, for the struggle to end. Now, that day had arrived. Fagen remembered the afternoon Colonel Urbano De Castro drank lemon water and told him he was a wanted man. He knew then someday, no matter which side won, he'd have to face the fact he was a man without a country.

Atias tugged at his sleeve again, and David Fagen followed him out of Palanan. Navigating on instinct, the little Igorrote led his *Negrito Americano* comrade north and west deep into the remote jungle mountains until he reached the place of his people, the place no outsider had ever seen. The place he called home.

CHAPTER 25 - LUZON, PHILIPPINES
JUNE 1945

The moon dipped behind the western horizon, and the morning stars followed quickly in its silent wake turning the night sky into a featureless, impenetrable black curtain over their heads. Captain Nygaard and Sergeant Rosa stared into the thick bed of smoldering embers glowing in the bottom of the Dakota hole. David Fagen tapped ashes from his pipe, took a deep breath, and then stood up. "It's time, Captain."

Rosa moved among the men, checked their gear, and then signaled the patrol ready to move out. Four Igorrote tribesmen took the lead, the Americans in single file behind them. They traveled south and east along a twisting, narrow path that took them through two miles of dense underbrush into the Mariquina River valley.

After a while, the captain gave up trying to figure out the direction they marched. Too dark to read a compass and no visuals in the undergrowth, he could only hope the old Negro was trustworthy and knew what he was doing. Nygaard still didn't know what to make of the stranger or the story he told that night. Almost too fantastic to believe, the patrol leader decided if Rosa hadn't been there to hear it with him, he'd have already chalked it up as a dream, a stress induced delusion.

He asked himself whether it was possible for someone to live so long in the jungle mountains with savages. The man had to be in his seventies, yet looked twenty years younger and appeared in excellent health. Had he really been on this island fifty years, Nygaard wondered, or was he just a crazy old ex-patriot booted off some tramp steamer sometime during the Japanese occupation, and then adopted by superstitious natives?

Nygaard knew Sergeant Rosa had knowledge of Filipino history and America's war with Spain, and he hadn't seemed troubled by the old man's story. But how was it possible the United States conducted itself so despicably for so long in the Philippines? The tale too far-fetched, the captain decided the old man was mad and pitied him, but if he really could get them past the Japs and back to their own lines, he resolved to help him if he could.

The first rays of sunlight touched the riverbank as the men broke out of the underbrush and entered the little clearing. The Igorrotes spread out, and then disappeared into the jungle around them. The old private knelt and with a stick drew a map in the mud. "We're here now. The Japs are here, a mile behind us." He looked up at Rosa. "You recognize this wide bend here? It's where the rapids are."

Rosa nodded. "We crossed there a few days ago."

"It's just a half-mile downstream. You know your way home from there?"

"Yes, sir. No problem."

"Then I'll say goodbye." The old, gray haired Negro shook hands with Rosa and saluted the captain. "Good luck to you, sir."

Nygaard returned the salute, and then watched the man who'd just saved their lives turn and walk away. "Private, wait a minute. Where are you going?" The patrol leader caught up, put his hand on the old man's arm.

"I'm going home, sir"

"I feel we owe you something. After all, you just got us out of a pretty tight spot."

Fagen smiled at the young officer. "You don't owe me, Captain."

"Isn't there anything you want or need?"

"No. Thank you, sir."

"Nothing at all I can do for you?"

Fagen sighed. "Captain, if you've got something to say, why don't you just come out with it? I'm too old a dog to play games."

Nygaard hesitated, looked the old man in the eye and said, "I don't know whether that story you told last night was true, but it doesn't matter. Come back with us now. You don't have to stay out here in this wilderness. The war will be over soon, and then we can all go home."

Fagen walked slowly to the riverbank and sat down on a huge fallen hardwood tree. "You want me to go back to the States with you?"

"Sure! You're an American aren't you?"

"Yes, sir, I am, but I'm also a colored man, and in America that's a deeper brand." Nygaard started to protest, but Fagen interrupted. "Let me ask you something, Captain. You're in the army. How many Negroes in your company? How many colored officers? Back in the States, how many black children go to school with your kids? How many live in your neighborhood? Name some of the Negro business leaders in your city, the coloreds you've elected to public office." Fagen picked up a flat rock and skittered it across the river. "No, Captain, my home is here."

Not ready to give up on the crazy old man, Nygaard said, "Fagen, I admit it's not a perfect world back home. I don't think there is such a place, but things are getting better between the races, and it's still the best damned country on earth."

"Is it?" Fagen smiled at the naïve young officer. He wondered whether a white man could ever understand how tightly the doors to opportunity remained closed to millions of men and women only because of the color of their skin. Fagen had realized long ago, for most Americans racism was a crime they didn't know they committed. Bigotry and prejudice were built into American society, even into the language. A man perceived unworthy was blackballed or blacklisted. A blackguard was a scoundrel with a black heart, and you might find him at the black market. They called the bubonic plague the Black Death, but when something ugly needed covering, it was said to be whitewashed, usually by little white lies.

Fagen recalled his own youthful, optimistic outlook on life so many years ago. At the time, he'd not been so different from the young captain who stood before him now. Educated, intelligent, physically strong, he had much to offer, but unlike the patrol leader, he had black skin and therefore little chance in a world where exclusion and intolerance were practiced every day in a million subtle ways.

"Let me tell you about the place I live," Fagen said softly. "My home is among people I love and who love me. I'm part of a society where a man is judged by what he does, not what he looks like. We don't have automobiles or big houses, but we have everything we need to live.

"You say America is the greatest country on earth. Maybe it is. I think it could be, but not until you learn to live with one another without fear of your differences. A friend once told me all she wanted, all she ever wanted was to live in a society where children can grow up free from hatred and bigotry. I ask you now, sir, is that asking too much? Isn't that what we all fight for?"

David Fagen turned away from the patrol leader and walked slowly to the edge of the clearing. Nygaard spotted the Igorrote headman standing just inside the tree line waiting for him. When he reached the jungle shadow the old man stopped, then looked back and smiled. "By the way, Captain, if you want to know whether my story is true, you can look it up."

EPILOGUE

While much has been speculated, little is known of the "real" David Fagen. Historical records show he enlisted in the army on June 4, 1898 at age twenty-three and after a brief break in service, was sent to the Philippines one year later to participate in the suppression of what the United States termed a "rebel insurrection."

For the Americans, The Philippine campaign was an extension of the Spanish-American War, for the Filipinos, a continuation of their struggle for independence. However viewed, it was certainly America's first experiment in imperialism, the first time African-American soldiers had been engaged in a major overseas war of conquest and occupation and the first convergence of the three cultures involved.

No doubt, Fagen, like many of his comrades, felt caught "between the devil and the deep sea" on the war. In order to further their military careers and advance the cause of blacks in the States, African-American soldiers faced imposing upon another colored people the same kind of racist system they were victims of back home. For them, this dilemma made the white man's burden a heavy load to bear.

Shortly after arriving in the Philippines, Fagen participated in a two-month campaign against guerilla forces in the hills around Mt. Arayat. Reports suggest that later, when he began having difficulties with his superiors, his actions on the battlefield were all that saved him from court martial. Rather, he was issued in-company punishment instead. Several of his fellow soldiers claimed Fagen was "picked on and made to do all sorts of dirty jobs." According to others, Fagen had difficulty getting along with his sergeants, and on at least one occasion, asked for a transfer. So much of the testimony concerning David Fagen conflicts, it may be impossible to know his true motives, but certainly his tenuous position within his own ranks contributed to his actions on the night of November 17, 1899 when he slipped past the guards, and in the company of a Filipino guerilla officer, rode away into the night.

Military censorship practiced at the time obscures Fagen's activities as an officer in the army of the Philippine Republic. It is known he was promoted to Captain and participated in at least eight battles against American forces. Fagen quickly gained a reputation for being a "bold and audacious leader of men." African-American soldiers temporarily held captive by the insurrectos, upon their release reported he was "loved" by his men and referred to by them as "General."

Inevitably, despite the army's efforts to downplay the defection, Fagen's activities began to be reported in the press back home. The *New York Times* and the *San Francisco Chronicle* portrayed him as "a cunning and highly skilled guerilla officer." The *Manila Times* described him as "daring as he is unscrupulous."

Twice, Fagen's insurrecto forces clashed with General Funston's Kansas volunteers. As America's most celebrated guerilla fighter and commander of the district, it fell to "Fighting Freddy" to capture the defector, David Fagen. More than a little concerned about "Negro turncoats," in his ranks, Funston declared that if Fagen were captured, he would not receive prisoner-of-war status, and "if he surrendered, it would be with the understanding he would be tried by a court-martial in which his execution would be a practical certainty." For more than a year the army hunted Fagen as a "bandit pure and simple and entitled to the same treatment as a mad dog." Wanted posters in both Tagalog and English went up in every town and village in the province offering $600.00 for "Fagen, dead or alive."

The army closed the book on David Fagen when a Filipino hunter and scout named Anastacio Bartolome arrived at the American outpost at Bongabong and presented evidence of Fagen's death. To prove his claim of having killed the American outlaw, Bartolome produced a canvas bag in which were weapons, clothing and a "decomposed head of a Negro." Although no record exists of the army having paid the reward, General Funston was only too happy to accept Bartolome's slender proof and pronounce the matter of David Fagen ended.

Was that how Fagen met his death? Researchers agree at least two other possibilities exist consistent with the evidence. Bartolome could easily have stumbled upon one of Fagen's camps in which some of his personal possessions had been abandoned, seized the items and concocted a story; or if an actual meeting took place, the two men could have conspired to fabricate evidence, thereby providing Fagen freedom from pursuit while at the same time enabling Bartolome to collect the reward. In either case, all that would have been needed was a decomposed "Negro" head – not too difficult to find in a nation at war.

Did David Fagen live to a ripe old age in the northern mountains among his Igorrote cousins of color? No one knows. What is certain is that Fagen's struggle for freedom was more than just a contest of black versus white, American verses Filipino. Fagen's actions demonstrated that if pushed and left with no options, a man will seek alternatives outside the boundaries of his society.

Upon Aguinaldo's capture, newspapers around the country put out special editions with headlines that read: *The Thrilling Story of Funston's exploits* and *The Captor of Aguinaldo Has Been the Hero of Scores of Thrilling Incidents*. Fredrick Funston's feat was welcome news to a war-weary nation, and as a result he was branded a hero. His fellow Kansans immediately proposed a governorship, and later talked of a Roosevelt/Funston ticket in the Presidential election of 1904. Americans needed a man they could admire to rise out of the dirt that was the Philippine Campaign, and for a while at least, Fighting Freddy was it.

Some months after Aguinaldo's capture, Funston suffered complications from an operation for appendicitis. Requiring additional care, he was transferred back to San Francisco where subsequent operations and reoccurring bouts of malaria made his recovery slow. Funston used this downtime from his military duties to achieve celebrity status, riding the wave of patriotic fervor over his exploits. He willingly accepted invitations for lectures, guest appearances and dinner speeches. His public appearances took him to dozens of cities across the U.S. where, as was his wont, he freely gave his opinions on every aspect of the Philippine campaign. Apparently carried away with himself, and showing particularly poor judgment, Funston got himself in real trouble when he outraged anti-imperialists at a dinner speech in New York by suggesting their protests at home had prolonged the war.

About that time, a junior officer in Funston's command came forward with accusations of atrocities against Filipinos in connection with Funston's ordering of the water cure and other inhumane acts toward prisoners of war. Newspapers began calling for his court martial. Funston's star was falling fast. Roosevelt, thinking Funston a loose cannon and a political liability, ordered him not make any more public speeches, and a letter of censure was placed in his permanent file.

Funston finished his military service with a series of undistinguished duty assignments in Cuba, Hawaii, Mexico and Fort Leavenworth, Kansas. On February 19, 1917 Fredrick Funston died suddenly from a heart attack at the age of fifty-one.

Within a week of his capture, Emilio Aguinaldo was returned to Manila where he took an oath of allegiance to the United States government and renounced his connections with the revolution. Two weeks later, while the Taft Commission made final preparations to take control in the Philippines, Aguinaldo issued his peace manifesto, in which he called for all Filipinos to lay down their arms and for "the complete termination of hostilities." With the exception of occasional uprisings by Moro tribesmen of the southern islands, these acts brought a swift end to the Filipino struggle for independence.

Aguinaldo spent the next three decades away from public life on his farm in Cavite. Active in postwar rural restoration projects, he organized and ran a veteran's administration for revolutionary soldiers. In 1934 the Tydings-McDuffie Act passed in the U.S. Congress declaring the Philippines an independent commonwealth, and Aguinaldo was encouraged by his supporters to run for its first Presidency. Not the political type, the former general lost badly to the powerful and savvy, Manuel Quezon.

In January 1942, the Japanese occupied Manila without resistance, declaring themselves there to rid the people of the "American yoke of oppression, and enable the Filipinos to establish a free and peaceful nation." Aguinaldo, along with several other prominent Filipinos, accepted appointment to the Japanese-organized Council of State, charged with administering Japanese controlled Filipino territory. Members of the Council, Aguinaldo included, made radio broadcasts appealing to American and Filipino troops fighting in Bataan to surrender to the Japanese. Some students of this period claim Aguinaldo, in his seventies, had been taken in by Japanese propaganda, others suggest his actions were motivated by his aversion to witnessing another Filipino bloodbath in his lifetime. Either way, the general's conduct during the Japanese occupation was certainly the low point in an otherwise long and distinguished life.

On July 4, 1946, at the Independence Day parade in Manila, Aguinaldo carried the 1898 revolutionary flag of the Philippine Republic that never was. On that day, he finally removed the black bow tie he had worn for nearly fifty years as a symbol of grief and mourning for his fallen countrymen. Emilio Aguinaldo died February 6, 1964 at age 94.

The Filipino nationals, Lazaro Segovia, Hilario Talplacido and Cecelio Segismundo were awarded cash payments for their participation in the capture of Aguinaldo. Of the three, only Segovia's fate is known. Army officials reported the Spaniard died a violent death in 1910, ostensibly at the hands of one of his many enemies.

Aguinaldo confidants and advisors, Simon Villa and Santiago Barcelona returned to civilian life in Manila. Dr. Barcelona died in 1947 and Colonel Simon Villa in 1945.

The Americans, Harry Newton and Burton Mitchell returned to the United States, prospered, lived long and died peacefully among their loved ones.

Ellis Fairbanks, Clarita Socorro, Sergeant Warren Rivers, Major Lawrence Baston and Lieutenant Matthew Alstaetter are fictitious, products of my imagination and therefore cannot be held accountable.

OTHER BOOKS AVAILABLE FROM TWENTY FIRST CENTURY PUBLISHERS

RAMONA

How did a little girl come to be abandoned in the orange scented square of the Andalusian City of Seville? Find out, when the course of her life is resumed at age seventeen.

Ramona catches the mood of Europe in transition, as Ramona, brought up in a quiet village in southern Spain, moves into the cosmopolitan world. Her strange background holds a mystery, revealed as the novel develops, but then events take on a different hue as a new perspective emerges. But that is not all, and reality seems to bend further, but does it?

From a novel within a novel, we move on to ... well, let's not say. Read it, and the author challenges you to predict each step of the unfolding plot, and just when it defies belief, read on – you will believe.

Ramona by Johnny John Heinz
ISBN: 1-904433-01-4

MEANS TO AN END

Enter the world of money laundering, financial manipulation and greed, where a shadowy Middle Eastern organisation takes on a major corporation in the US. As the action shifts through exotic locations, who wins out in the end? Certainly, the author's first hand experience of international finance lends a chilling credibility to the plot.

As well as being a compelling work of fiction this book offers, in a style accessible to the layman, a financial insider's insight into the financial and moral crisis, which broke in the early millennium, in the top echelons of corporate America.

Means to an End by Johnny John Heinz
ISBN: 1-84375-008-2

THE SIGNATURE OF A VOICE

The Signature of a Voice is a cat-and-mouse-game between a violent trio, led by a psychopathic killer, and a police officer on suspension. Move and countermove in this chess game is planned and enacted. The reader, in the position of god, knows who is guilty and who plans what, but just as in chess, the opponents' plans thwart one another. The outcomes twist and turn to the final curtain fall.

There is a sense of suspense but also anger as the system seems to be working against those who are fighting on the side of right, while the perpetrators of vicious crimes seem able to operate freely and choose to do what they wish. They choose the route of ultra-violence to stay ahead of the law in an otherwise tranquil community: they plan and execute, in all senses of the word. Is it possible to triumph over this ruthlessness?

The Signature of a Voice by Johnny John Heinz
ISBN: 1-904433-00-6

TARNISHED COPPER

Tarnished Copper takes us into the arcane world of commodity trading. Against this murky background, no deal is what it seems, no agreement what it appears to be. The characters cheat and deceive each other, all in the name of grabbing their own advantage. Hiro Yamagazi, from his base in Tokyo, is the biggest trader of them all. But does he run his own destiny, or is he just jumping when Phil Harris pulls the strings? Can Jamie Edwards keep his addictions under control? And what will be the outcome of the duel between the hedge fund manager Jason Serck, and brash, devious, high-spending Mack McKee? And then one of them goes too far: life and death enters the traders' world........

Geoff Sambrook is ideally placed to take the reader into this world. He's been at the heart of the world's copper trading for over twenty years, and has seen the games - and the traders - come and go. With his ability to draw characters, and his knack of making the reader understand this strange world, he's created an explosive best-selling financial thriller. Read it and learn how this part of the City really works..

Tarnished Copper by Geoffrey Sambrook
ISBN 1-904433-02-2

OVER A BARREL

From the moment you land at Heathrow on page one the plot grips you. Ed Burke, an American oil tycoon, jets through the world's financial centres and the Middle East to set up deals, but where does this lead him? Are his premonitions on the safety of his daughter Louise in Saudi Arabia well founded? Who are his hidden opponents? Is his corporate lawyer Nicole with him or against him?

As the plot unfolds his company is put into play in the tangle of events surrounding the 1990 invasion of Kuwait. Even his private life is drawn into the morass.

In this novel Peter depicts the grim machinations of political and commercial life, but the human spirit shines through. This is a thriller that will hold you to the last page.

Over a Barrel by Peter Driver
ISBN 1-904433-03-0

THE BLOWS OF FATE

It is a crisp clear day in Sofia and three young friends are starting out in life, buoyant with their hopes, aspirations, loves. But this is not to be, as post war Eastern Europe comes under the grip of its brutal communist regime. Driven from their homes and deprived of their basic rights, the three friends determine to escape ... but one of them cannot seize that moment. It may seem that life cannot become worse for the families who are ostracised and trapped in their own country, but the path of hopelessness descends to the concentration camps and unimaginable brutality.

For those who escape there is the struggle to survive, tempered by the kindness they encounter along their way. We see how talent and determination can win through. Yet, though they may have escaped those terrible years in Bulgaria, they can never escape their personal loss of family, homeland, friends and love that may have been.

While life is very difficult for the three friends, they do not forget each other. After forty years of separation, they meet. For each one fate has prepared a surprise....

Can beauty, art and love eclipse the manmade horrors of this world? You will think they can, as Antoinette Clair brings out the beautiful things in life, so that the poignancy of her novel reaches into the toughest of us, and moves to tears.

This is a tale of beauty, music and a grand love, but it is also expressive of the sad recurring tale of Europe's recent history.

The Blows of Fate by Antoinette Clair
ISBN 1-904433-04-9

THE GORE EXPERIMENT

William Gore is not a mad scientist: he is a dedicated medical researcher working on G.L.X.-14, an AIDS serum. He is on the brink of a major breakthrough and seeks to force the pace, spurred on by his knowledge of the suffering to be spared, if he is right, and the millions of lives of AIDS victims to be saved. But as things begin to go askew, how far dare he go? What level of risk is warranted? What, and who, is he prepared to sacrifice? The answers become worse than you can imagine as William Gore treads a path to horror.

The Gore Experiment may be fiction, but it addresses real issues in the world of experimental vaccines, disease-busting drugs and genetic engineering. Is science unknowingly exposing us to risk through overconfidence in ever narrowing fields of expertise, ignorant of ramifications? Or is the red tape of bureaucracy signing the death warrants of the terminally sick? Well, William Gore at least is confident. He is convinced of what he must do. Should he do it?

This is not a book for the faint-hearted. H.Jay Scheuermann adds a new high-tech dimension to the traditions of vampires, Jekylls and Hydes as William Gore paves his own road to hell. But there is a twist....

The Gore Experiment by H. Jay Scheuermann
ISBN 1-904433-05-7

CASEY'S REVENGE

Is this the best of all possible worlds? Well, almost, or so Casey Forbes thinks. She is a college professor with bbb successful career and good friends; boyfriend trouble in the past, perhaps, but who hasn't? And her prospects are excellent.

But no woman can expect to descend into the real life nightmare, that envelopes Casey ... out of nowhere.

Mary Charles's heroine is forced to confront the darkest side of human nature and the most bestial of acts committed by man. Yet it is the strength of will, the trauma inflicted on Casey's personality and the resourcefulness of the female psyche that Mary Charles explores in this novel. What does it take to survive overwhelming adversity and does Casey have it?

Many dream of revenge but wonder if they have within themselves the capacity to carry it out. Can Casey? And is the price going to be too high?

Read this thriller and one thing is certain: don't ever let this happen to you.

Casey's Revenge by Mary Charles
ISBN 1-90443-06-5

SABRA'S SOUL

From the heart of the California rock music scene comes this story of much more than just love and betrayal.

Does Sabra know who she is? She thinks she is a loving mother and a trusting wife, but her husband Logan, a powerful figure in rock music, seems consumed by commitments to his latest band, 23 Mystique. Sabra begins to feel that something is missing, to feel a yearning for something more. Is she too trusting and too slow to spot Logan's lapses in behaviour?

When Sabra meets the pop idol of her sub-teen daughters, things begin to change. She can't believe the attraction growing in her for this youthful figure, her junior by several years.

Lisa Reed paints a picture of virtue and vice in this tale of love, lust, betrayal and drug-induced psychosis, set amidst the glitter of the rock scene. It is not fate that leads these people on but their own actions. Can they help it and where does it lead?

Who better than Lisa Reed, with her access to the centre of rock, to weave this tense plot as it descends from the social whirl into the deadly serious. If you are a successful rock star, this is a book for you, and if not ... well, read on and dream.

Health warning: this book contains salacious sex scenes demanded by its setting.

Sabra's Soul by Lisa Reed
ISBN 1-90443307-3

FACE BLIND

From the pen of Raymond Benson, author of the acclaimed original James Bond continuation novels (Zero Minus Ten, The Facts of Death, High Time to Kill, DoubleShot, Never Dream of Dying, and The Man With the Red Tattoo) and the novel Evil Hours, comes a new and edgy noir thriller.

Imagine a world where you don't recognize the human face. That's Hannah's condition - prosopagnosia, or "face blindness" - when the brain center that recognizes faces is inoperable. The onset of the condition occurred when she was attacked and nearly raped by an unknown assailant in the inner lobby of her New York City apartment building. And now she thinks he's back, and not just in her dreams.

When she also attracts the attention of a psychopathic predator and becomes the unwitting target of a Mafia drug ring, the scene is set for a thrill ride of mistaken identity, cat-and-mouse pursuit, and murder.

Face Blind is a twisting, turning tale of suspense in which every character has a dark side. The novel will keep the reader surprised and intrigued until the final violent catharsis.

Face Blind by Raymond Benson
ISBN 1-904433-10-3

CUPID AND THE SILENT GODDESS

The painting Allegory with Venus and Cupid has long fascinated visitors to London's National Gallery, as well as the millions more who have seen it reproduced in books. It is one of the most beautiful paintings of the nude ever made.

In 1544, Duke Cosimo de' Medici of Florence commissioned the artist Bronzino to create the painting to be sent as a diplomatic gift to King François I of France.

As well as the academic mystery of what the strange figures in the painting represent, there is the human mystery: who were the models in the Florence of 1544 who posed for the gods and strange figures?

Alan Fisk's Cupid and the Silent Goddess imagines how the creation of this painting might have touched the lives of everyone who was involved with it: Bronzino's apprentice Giuseppe, the mute and mysterious Angelina who is forced to model for Venus, the brutal sculptor Baccio Bandinelli and his son, and the good-hearted nun Sister Benedicta and her friend the old English priest Father Fleccia, both secret practitioners of alchemy.

As the painting takes shape, it causes episodes of fear and cruelty, but the ending lies perhaps in the gift of Venus.

'A witty and entertaining romp set in the seedy world of Italian Renaissance artists.' Award-winning historical novelist Elizabeth Chadwick. (*The Falcons of Montabard, The Winter Mantle*).

'Alan Fisk, in his book Cupid and the Silent Goddess, captures the atmosphere of sixteenth-century Florence and the world of the artists excellently. This is a fascinating imaginative reconstruction of the events during the painting of Allegory with Venus and Cupid.' Marina Oliver, author of many historical novels and of Writing Historical Fiction.

Cupid and the Silent Goddess by Alan Fisk
ISBN 1-904433-08-4

TALES FROM THE LONG BAR

Nostalgia may not be what it used be, but do you ever get the feeling that the future's not worth holding your breath for either?

Do you remember the double-edged sword that was 'having a proper job' and struggling within the coils of the multiheaded monster that was 'the organisation'?

Are you fed up with forever having to hit the ground running, working dafter not smarter - and always being in a rush trying to dress down on Fridays?

Do you miss not having a career, a pension plan or even the occasional long lunch with colleagues and friends?

For anyone who knows what's what (but can't do much about it), Tales from the Long Bar should prove entebrtaining. If it doesn't, it will at least reassure you that you are not alone.

Londoner Saif Rahman spent half his life working in the City before going on to pursue opportunities elsewhere. A linguist by training, Saif is a historian by inclination.

Tale from the Long Bar by Saif Rahman
ISBN 1-904433-10-X

EVIL HOURS

"My mother was murdered when I was six years old." Shannon has become used to giving this explanation when getting to know new arrivals in the small West Texas town of Limite. She has never hidden the truth about her mother, but she is haunted by the unresolved circumstances surrounding her mother's murder and the deaths of a series of other women around the same time. It is when she sets about uncovering the truth, with the help of an investigator, that the true depravity of Limite's underbelly begins to emerge.

The very ordinariness of the small town lends a chill to *Evil Hours*, as revelations from a murky past begin to form a pattern; but much worse they begin to cast their shadow over the present.

As Shannon delves behind the curtain of silence raised by the prominent citizens of Limite, she finds herself caught up in a sequence of events that mirror those of the previous generation…and the past and the present merge into a chilling web of evil.

In *Evil Hours* Raymond Benson revisits his roots and brings to life the intrigue of a small West Texas Town. Benson is the author of the original James Bond continuation novels: *The Man With the Red Tattoo*; *Never Dream of Dying*; *DoubleShot*; *High Time to Kill*; *The Facts of Death*; and *Zero Minus Ten*. He has recently released a thriller set in New York, *Face Blind.*

Evil Hours by Raymond Benson
ISBN 1-904433-12-X

PAINT ME AS I AM

What unique attribute dwells within the creative individual? Is it a flaw in the unconscious psyche that gives rise to talent, influencing artists to fashion the product of their imagination into tangible form, just as the grain of sand gives rise to the precious pearl? Or is it more?

To the world around him, Jerrod Young appears to be a typical, mature art student. He certainly has talent as a painter, but hidden within the darkest corners of his mind are unsavory secrets, and a different man that nobody knows.

H. Jay Scheuermann, author of The Gore Experiment, gives us another great psychological thriller, delivering a chilling look inside the psyche of a man whose deepest thoughts begin to assume control over his actions. The needs of the darkness within him seem to grow with each atrocity, his ever-increasing confidence fueling an inexorable force for evil.

Hell is not a place, but a state of mind, a state of being: it exists within each of us. We like to believe we can control it, but the cruel alternative is that our choices have already been made for us. Jerrod has accepted his truth, and is resolved to serve his inner demon.

Special Agent Jackie Jonas has been given her first assignment, a case that may mark the beginning and the end of her FBI career, as it leads her into a web of violence and deception, with each new clue ensnaring the lives of the ones she loves....

This gripping story brings to life the awful truth that the Jerrod Young's of this world do, in fact, exist. It could be one of your co-workers, the person behind you in the supermarket checkout line, or even the person next door. Can you tell? Are you willing to stake your life on it?

Paint Me As I Am by H. Jay Scheuermann
ISBN 1-904433-14-6

EMBER'S FLAME

"He could focus on her intelligent conversations and the way her aqua blue eyes lit up when they were amused and turned almost gray when they were sad. It was easier to admire the strength she carried in her soul and the light she carried in her walk. Now, seeing her in five inch heels and hot pants..."

Ember Ty is majoring in journalism. Graced with stunning looks, she finances her studies by dancing in a strip club. She has a hot boyfriend in a rock band, a future writing about the music world, and yes, she's working hard to achieve it.

But it all starts to go wrong. There is a predator on the loose, and Ember is sucked into a nightmare that none of us would care to dream, let alone live.

Vulnerable and threatened, Ember is drawn into a love triangle that might never have been, with the man she is to marry and the man she knows she can never have.

Ember's Flame by Lisa Reed
ISBN 1-904433-15-4

THE RELUCTANT CORPSE

"Stewart Douglas could not, under any circumstances, be considered your average human being. He'd always been a fan of agony as long, of course, as it wasn't his own." Well, Stewart is the local mortician, and maybe he has a less than healthy interest in the job. Every community has its secrets, and Savannah, Georgia, is no exception. The questions are: exactly what are those secrets, and who do they belong to?

Mary Charles introduces us to a community of characters, and although we do see the mortician at work, everything is comfortably tranquil, or so it seems. But strange things are afoot. Who can you trust?

It may be best to let things rest, but events have their own momentum.

There is a foray into the antique art market, which gives the plot a subtle twist, and as the sinister undertone begins to take on real menace, you will be unable to put down this exciting suspense novel.

"Set within the confines of Savannah and Southeast Georgia, The Reluctant Corpse confronts the reader with frightening images lurking just behind closed doors and stately homes. Well written and enjoyable." William C. Harris Jr. (Savannah best-selling author of Delirium of the Brave and No Enemy But Time).

The Reluctant Corpse by Mary Charles
ISBN 1-904433-16-2

THE AFFAIRS OF STATE

A philandering president. Rumors about The First Lady. Public lies about private lives. Talk about impeachment. Unstable world events that could lead to war. Sound familiar?

It should. It was all possible in 1940.

Immediately after Franklin Roosevelt won an unprecedented third term and World War 2 was heating up, a brand new radio network aired information about the First Family that was true but had never been made public.

Michael Audray, the network's high-profile host of the most listened-to radio program in the country, asked *the* question that set off a chain of events that changed modern history before and after Pearl Harbor.

The Affairs of State is about power politics, broadcasting, private lives and the public's right to know. It's fiction, but it meshes with the historical record and asks questions that challenge us to face the moral ambiguity that emerges.

The Affairs of State by Tim Steele
ISBN 1-904433-17-0

SINCERE MALE SEEKS LOVE AND SOMEONE TO WASH HIS UNDERPANTS

Colin Fisher is long-divorced with two grown-up children and an ageing mother in care. He is not getting any younger. Perhaps it is time to get married again. There are hordes of mature, nubile, attractive, solvent (hopefully) women out there, and marriage would provide regular sex and companionship, and someone to take care of the tedious domestic details that can make a man late for his golf and tennis matches. All Colin needs to do is smarten up a bit, get out more and select the lucky woman from amongst the numerous postulants. What could be easier?

Christopher Wood had adapted various personae to write over fifty books, ranging from high adventure to saucy picaresque. He has also written the screenplays for fourteen movies, including two of the most successful James Bond films ever: The Spy Who Loved Me and Moonraker. When not writing, he makes wine at his home in France.

Sincere male seeks love and somone to wash his underpants
by Christopher Wood
ISBN 1-904433-18-9

GUY DE CARNAC: DESCENT

The character from the Dr Who New Adventure, Sanctuary, and the audio drama, The Quality Of Mercy, returns in a full-length novel.

Set in 1303, young Templar Knight Guy de Carnac begins a long and life-changing journey when everything he holds dear is torn apart into mayhem and intrigue between the French crown and the Papacy.

Guy de Carnac: Descent by David McIntee
ISBN 1-904433-19-7

To hear about new publications or to give us feedback on Cousins of Color, please visit our website:
www.twentyfirstcenturypublishers.com